C000148916

STRAIT

Also by Kit Craig

Gone
Twice Burned

STRAIT

Kit Craig

HEADLINE
FEATURE

Copyright © 1995 Kit Reed

The right of Kit Reed to be identified as the Author of
the Work has been asserted by her in accordance with
the Copyright, Designs and Patents Act 1988.

First published in 1995 by
HEADLINE BOOK PUBLISHING

A HEADLINE FEATURE hardback

10 9 8 7 6 5 4 3 2 1

All rights reserved. No part of this publication may be
reproduced, stored in a retrieval system, or transmitted,
in any form or by any means without the prior written
permission of the publisher, nor be otherwise circulated
in any form of binding or cover other than that in which
it is published and without a similar condition being
imposed on the subsequent purchaser.

All characters in this publication are fictitious and any
resemblance to real persons, living or dead, is purely coincidental.

British Library Cataloguing in Publication Data

Craig, Kit
Strait
I.Title
813.54 [F]

ISBN 0 7472 1379 8

Typeset by Avon Dataset Ltd, Bidford-on-Avon, B50 4JH

Printed and bound in Great Britain by
Mackays of Chatham PLC, Chatham, Kent

HEADLINE BOOK PUBLISHING
A division of Hodder Headline PLC
338 Euston Road,
London NW1 3BH

For Peter S. Prescott
excelsior

1

Change is like death, inevitable and just as certain. Unlike death it is subtle. It can creep up on you and slit your throat while you are smiling and looking at something else.

You're going along one way, happy, secure. Not paying attention because you think what you have is really yours. Like a trip wire, change yanks you off your feet. What! You weren't distracted for that long, you only looked away for a second, and now . . .

Everything is slipping. What you assumed is not necessarily the case. The life you thought was forever has been yanked out from under you in a wild, celestial magic trick. Health and fortunes fail. Worse. Relationships that you took to be certain, like friendships. Marriages. Not just theirs. Yours. The people you love best have turned against you. The house you've built on trust is built on sand.

First you will deny it. Even though something awful is happening we're OK. It's OK. Then why is finishing the day still standing up so much harder than you thought it was?

You are in the process of losing everything you've been given.

If this kind of thing happened overnight Clair Sailor would know what to do: pull up the drawbridge and arm the perimeter. Prepare to repel all boarders. Maintain perpetual vigilance. Clair stays in shape; she's good at taking care of herself, smarter than most and quicker than most to sense impending disturbances, but there are some things you can't guard against.

1

Change is insidious, rolling in so gradually that at first even she will not mark it.

Right now she's too happy – high on snow and sunlight and the fumes of rum and chocolate – so caught up in the exigencies of Ethan Frome Day that she's lost her imagination of disaster. If she's too happy, she has reasons. The central given in her life, Nick Sailor is back at her side, flushed and laughing in the glittering snow; he is strong and grinning, fine, she tells herself. *Fine*, back from the jaws of . . . Went to work in spite of the flu, defied walking pneumonia to do a Boston TV show, kept teaching until his body betrayed him and his lungs filled up. It almost leveled him. She slept in the hall outside the ICU, terrified because there is nothing without him; he came so *close*, and in the folly of women who love too much she tells herself they've made it back safe from the brink – paid our dues, she thinks. All paid up, for now.

The sky is clear here at the lip of Kingman's Gorge; the air is like ice water. Intense! In a minute George Atkinson will fire the starter's pistol that launches the mass psychic explosion that some inspired unknown hero has named Ethan Frome Day.

Everybody Clair Sailor cares about is out in the snow today: Nick and their two children, their best friends and favorite students and assorted townies all lined up at the edge like astronauts waiting for the blastoff. All Evard College and half of Evarton has turned out for the event – young-old faculty and students alike in layered vests and ski jackets and legwarmers and mufflers, rock in place in lug-soled boots, flattening the snow for a faster takeoff. Squinting in the unaccustomed sunlight like freed prisoners, they stand with bobsleds, outgrown Flexible Flyers, saucers, cafeteria trays, anything that will slide. At the college president's signal they'll throw themselves down and go hurtling downhill at tremendous speeds in a giddy replay of the climactic scene in the Edith Wharton novel.

Unlike Ethan and Matty, who smashed into a tree and lived to suffer, the revelers will glide to the bottom and throw a champagne party.

The sky is flawless; the sun on the ice-glazed trees is almost warm. Reinforced by the people she loves best, Clair is sick of winter and laughing too hard to think about anything but the bright day and the celebration. What a rush: cutting loose at the exact moment when you think you're going to die of compression.

They are all poised in the moment before the plunge.

2

Interesting, being up this high and knowing you're going to rush into that deep chasm. It's like a fun ride – scary, looks dangerous, but the park is safe so you can count on a safe landing. The drop into Kingman's Gorge is steep but there's fresh snow to slow the sleds and cushion the fall if you wipe out rounding one of those naked trees. It does not feel like a precarious situation.

At the moment, the atmosphere is madly festive.

It won't occur to Clair Sailor to mark this as the Last Good Time, but it is. This bright afternoon before Will Strait is even imagined.

Right now it seems like a time of extreme silliness.

In this enclosed community with its deep, murderous winters, frivolity is essential to survival. The timing is as spontaneous as it is mysterious. Somebody looked outside at dawn today and declared this the deepest day of deep winter, at the end of the flu season but weeks before the thaw, when the air inside is irretrievably stale and pets and kids and even the most committed lovers are fighting out of sheer boredom. It's the day when the snow mounts to the point where people give up shoveling and nobody, not faculty nor townies nor the pent-up young men at Evard can stand the sensory deprivation – loss of light and color, loss of blue skies, loss of sensation in those thermal-layered bodies and those gloved fingers – nobody can stand things the way they are a minute longer.

It's the day the sun comes out. Time to go a little crazy.

Phones began to ring. At eight the college bells and Evarton factory whistles sounded for ten minutes. Now everybody's here. Some old star said it first but it was Teddy Hart who laid it out for Clair when she was new. 'You've got to make your own fun around here.'

Wedged into a sheltered gap in the rocks near the Canadian border, Evard College is like a feudal city, effectively insulated from time and change as the rest of the world knows it. A little fiefdom that tends its own fires and enforces its own rules, Evard seems to exist in a time warp, a fact that appeals to the parents who send their sons here. It is a gorgeous anachronism – an all-male college. The place looked too good to be true to Clair, coming in: Gothic buildings in a neat row on top of the hill, colonial and Victorian houses clustered on the orderly, tree-lined streets leading downhill into a Grandma Moses town center, but now she is part of the picture.

The tiny college is fixed in time and space, like an ice castle in a paperweight. Turn it upside down; shake hard to make the snow fly; throw it across the room if you want to. When the globe clears the castle is exactly where you left it, perfect, changeless. It's so remote from everything Clair knows of real life that it's like living in a story somebody else is telling.

A gust catches her and she looks up. The air is filled with crystal: sun glittering in flying frozen flakes.

Safe in the globe, laughing in the snow with her family and colleagues, friends-for-life and students romping like big children, she feels protected. Safe. Evard takes care of its own. If there is a drum beating somewhere just out of sight, she can't hear it.

The college band is playing courtesy of good old Walt Ettinger's yellow plastic boom box and the fresh snow is already stained black and blue by crepe paper streamers in the college colors. Ginny Arnold put flowers in ink for Betsy Atkinson's mad bouquet of black and blue carnations and she and her friends have pinned colored carnations to their ski jackets, a touch lifted straight out of a high school movie, and if it's all a little over the top, that's part of it.

Today's fad is lurid Ecuadorean knit caps and scarves in psychedelic patterns. Even Teddy, whose hobby is being *next* in fashion, has added an Ecuadorean muffler. Last year, as if a uniform of the day had been ordered by E-mail, almost everybody turned out in real and fake variations of the Russian fur hat with scarves in earth tones. Today the icy slope is like a field of anemones, blooming in primary colors.

Everybody who matters is stamping at the lip of the gorge today, buzzed on rum toddies and warmed by fires set in oil drums, massed K-mart barbecues, hibachis. The picnic tables are piled with hampers filled by the college's inspired cooks, who spend more time reading *Gourmet* magazine than they do on research because in this this tiny arena their egos are tied up in these performances. Strings of black and blue pennants hang from barren trees and, brilliantly different in their ground-dragging black coats and black mufflers, Teddy's Kafka students set candles in wax paper bags and plant enormous torches, proof against encroaching twilight.

Nick has eight-year-old Davy and his little sister perched on the big sled between his legs, clamping them in place. At the starting gun he'll take the kids down so Clair can flop on her belly on the Flexible Flyer, knifing down solo.

To her right is her best friend Teddy Hart, looking like the Abominable Snowman in his agglomeration of scarves and furs and his wraparound

4

RayBans, while beyond him their oldest and dearest friends Gabe and Jane Stevenson have paired up on a toboggan with rock 'em sock 'em Pete and Ginny Arnold, who make a big show of being happily married and are always fighting. With a conspirator's grin at the Stevensons, Teddy whirls and gets off a snowball that silences Pete Arnold in mid-reproach.

And Nick – God he was sick; God he looks better – the ex-convalescent released from house arrest, the man Clair loves best, grins like the returned Lazarus as friends stop to tell him how glad they are.

So maybe what is about to happen is her fault – her mistake for noting her own happiness. 'Teddy!'

'Happily ever after,' he says with an eloquent shrug.

But Nick mutters, 'The natives are getting restless.'

They are. Bulky in layered clothes, the students trample the snow, breathing steam like impatient buffalo. They're hung up on the starting gun, which George Atkinson is too preoccupied to fire.

Standing in front of the band, the college president has turned his best profile and is working the visiting US senator while the photographer he begged Clair to assign shoots the pair eight ways to Sunday. Tall, rockbound George Atkinson is a good man, solid, irreproachable and absolutely humorless. It's a little like having Abraham Lincoln for college president. He is also ambitious. At the moment he's so intent on his career in Washington that he's forgotten the opening day speech. As they wait, George pulls Evarton's mayor and his entourage people into the power grouping and smiles and smiles while the starting gun droops, forgotten, from indifferent fingers.

Poised, they are stalled until he remembers.

Nick says under his breath, 'When do you think George the Great is going to get around to it?'

Clair takes a shrewd look at their leader. 'When Delbert's shot the whole roll. I should have told him Delbert wasn't available.'

He grins. 'At least you told him I wasn't available. I'm sick of being his favorite photo op.'

'Your fault for looking like Sting instead of the Big Professor,' Teddy says.

'Shut up,' Clair says. 'He's cuter than Sting.'

'Just younger. Or I used to be.'

'Don't, Nick.'

Laughing, Nick's acknowledging how sick he was. 'Until I checked into the local roach motel.' He means the Evarton Hospital.

'Mo-m.' The kids are jabbering. Last year Nelly was too young to go down on the big sled. Now she can't wait. 'Is it time yet?'

Teddy growls, 'Not until our leader quits working on his ticket to Washington.'

'Soon, OK?'

Davy tugs at Nick, 'Now, Dad?'

But it is Clair who answers, 'Not yet, OK?'

Nick's distracted. Pinned to his sled at the top of the slope, he's a captive audience. First an earnest jock pounces, then a would-be poet pressing Nick to conduct a front-lines student-teacher conference while his children nag in counterpoint: 'Are we starting?' 'Is it fun yet?' Hugging them absently, Nick says something that makes the student laugh and sends him away, satisfied.

'Now, Dad?' 'Can we go now?' 'When can we go?'

But Nick's dealing with a series of – not suppliants, exactly, Clair thinks – admirers? Bill Rossiter from History mumbles his secrets and Nick says something that makes Bill nod, relieved. He's the third – suppliant, psychiatric patient, penitent, what? – in the last five minutes. It's not Nick's fault that everything flew apart while he was sick but it may be his fault that too many people depend on him for advice and counsel, to settle disputes, to do everything that needs doing and run anything that needs running – the department, the division if Ad Bishop steps down – perhaps by this time next year, the college.

Looking less like a colleague than a great, sad rabbit in her white fur anorak, plump Mary Roeg slips in to take Bill's place. The resident Victorianist is excited today. She leans close to murmur in Nick's ear and then giggles and turns pink. Nick knows how to make her smile in spite of Mary's well-rehearsed loneliness.

Mary's urgency makes Clair murmur, 'What was *that* about?' but Ad Bishop has moved in to crouch next to Nick. The dean has failed badly; in the bright sunlight Clair is struck by it. It makes her shudder; she does not want Nick to get old here.

The kids are getting shrill. 'Why isn't it starting?'

'Soon,' Clair answers for Nick. 'At least I hope so.'

Until it does they're stuck on the brink, sitting ducks. Clair gets her share of drive-by requests: cover this in your magazine, photograph that. Friends stop to gossip, but Nick is the center of attention here. Handsome

6

guy, big grin, teaches English but gets on TV because he has a second line in the pop horror novel and delivers perfect sound bytes; wonderful guy, do anything for you, and if this leaves Clair a little jealous of his time, never mind.

('They'll use you up,' she warns. 'They'll use you to death.')

'It's the least I can do.' *Oh, Nick!* 'I just need to give back a little of what I've been given.' This is Nick, the idealist.)

Wherever they go in Evarton, people contrive to bump into him. It's a little like hanging out with the Godfather. Or a country doctor who can come up with a prescription for any problem, no matter how rank. Like the Godfather, Nick hears their complaints – confessions? – with that bright, unwavering grin that marks his success here. No matter what people lay on him, Nick knows how to leave them smiling and dismisses his clients so gently that they don't realize it's over until they're out on the street. 'I'll see to it,' he promises Ad, who looks too frail to be outside.

Getting to his feet the dean says, 'I don't know what we'd do without you.'

Clair thinks uneasily, they are already treating him like the president.

Nick catches her watching. 'Clair!'

She sticks her thumbs in her ears and wiggles gloved fingers. 'Nicky!'

Long and spare, handsome, he laughs like a boy. 'Ready?'

Teddy says, 'We've been ready for days.'

Clair hears a giggle rising in her throat. Nick looks like a big kid in the stocking cap and the muffler she made him wrap around his throat – his one concession. He sees her laughing and flings out his hand, but there's no telling whether that's the peace symbol or if he's giving her the finger because in the rush to Kingman's Gorge today he jammed on Davy's Tony the Tiger mittens. 'More than ready.'

Davy is getting shrill. 'Then why don't we go?'

Nick says with that maddening Boy Scout rectitude, 'Because we have to wait for orders.'

'Orders!' It's the thing about him that exasperates Clair the most. 'Who cares about orders?'

'Fuck orders.' Teddy won't march to your usual drummers; it's the best thing about him. 'I'm off!' Raising his sled he hurls it down, sending up ice spray as he roars toward the bottom.

Clair thinks she hears him yelling, 'Geronimo!' and in the second after Teddy starts down, part of her goes after him and is afraid for him.

It never occurs to her to be afraid for all of them.

'Kids,' Nick says in solemn TV commercial tones, 'don't try this at home.' And goes to remind George of his duties here.

Like runners frustrated by a false start, Clair and the others mill dutifully. At the fringes a few students let go as somewhere below Teddy coasts to a safe stop with a joyous shout. Her heart goes after him, while at the distant bottom Teddy rips off his hat and his scarf and with that great careless laugh of his waves them on like the starter in a chicken race.

Clair hears a woman, *sotto voce*: 'What a waste.'

'What?'

Jane Stevenson has shed the Arnolds and drifted over. 'You know.'

She does. But although in her heart she thinks so too, Clair has to say loyally, 'I don't think he sees it that way.'

After which she has no choice but to hurl herself on her sled and go rocketing after Teddy. Nick yells 'Wait for me!'

Within seconds everybody's on the steep, icy course, bombing downhill with shrieks streaming behind them like banners, and like a traveler on a distant planet, good George Atkinson says through a megaphone, 'I declare Ethan Frome Day officially open,' and belatedly fires the starting gun.

Clair meant to wear goggles so she could see where she was going; she meant to start coming out here after the first November snow to get in shape for this; she meant to come early today and go down a couple of times to scope out hazards, but it's too late now. Snow raised by the front runners fragments into icy particles that hang in sheets and then, as she tears through them, vaporize, knifing into her lungs so she gasps for breath, giddy and blinded as speed tears the wind out of her and her sled skids over bare patches of frozen ground and gathers momentum, skimming across ice patches and into territory she cannot see. Then when she is blind and vulnerable, a long sled materializes on her left at a sharp diagonal, almost of a piece with its tall rider, knifing into her path. Screaming, she swerves to to avoid it.

'*Who?*'

But the air is ripped out of her. Hurtling into a new trajectory with the life torn out of her chest, with her eyes slitted against the ice spray and her concentration shattered by the screams and hysterical laughter of unseen others, Clair is jolted by a huge shout that she will decipher only later: 'Watch out!' She hears Teddy screaming: 'Ditch!'

'What? What!'

God! There is no telling what; she rolls off her sled, terrified because she can't know who or what may be barreling downhill behind her, roaring like a juggernaut into a space she had thought of as safe. She's going too fast to roll out safely and even in layered jackets, wrapped as she is in scarves like a piece of bric-a-brac ready for shipping, she'll land hard. Crazed and blinded, she lets go. Thudding into the snow, she rolls, gasping as the Stevensons and Arnolds go roaring past on her right, steering their bobsled in a wide arc to avoid the huge, craggy shape that rises out of the snow right in front of her.

It is quick and terrifying.

Sick, Clair sits up just in time to see her sled rise in the air and fragment like a car exploding in a movie. She hears shouting, 'What! What?' in a voice she does not immediately recognize as her own.

'Boulder!' Dodging sleds like a broken field runner, Teddy is the first to reach her. 'See?' He pulls Clair to her feet, turning her so she can see how close it was.

A rock shelf sticks out of the snow like the back of a huge, waking animal. 'My God!'

At Teddy's back there are others approaching; she is too shaken to see who, but at the bottom of the run a man gets off the long sled and stands, baring his light hair and looking uphill at them: tall, taller, tallest.

She hears Nick shouting, 'Clair!'

And can't find the breath to answer. Her voice is too thin for anyone but Clair to hear. Only two words come. 'My God.' For a second Teddy has to support her, which he does with one arm while with the other he waves his muffler, warning off the last of the sledders as Nick comes pounding through the snow with his mouth wide and his face torn apart by worry. Two words, over and over.

Clair's fine; she is. Really. There's nothing the matter with her except she can't stop saying, 'My God.'

'Shh. Be cool. Shh. Here's Nick.' Teddy understands that she's just about to lose it. With a hard squeeze he hands Clair over to Nick and calls the kids. 'Nelly, Dave, come over here a minute and let your Uncle Teddy explain the meaning of the world to you.'

Nick's breath warms her. 'Are you all right?'

Clair wants to answer but she can't, quite. She's fine, just fine, OK? It's just that her arms and legs aren't taking messages right now. Nick is her

9

shelter. She buries her face in his front as he clamps her close. She needs to be alone for a minute, but when she looks up everybody in the world is heading this way.

Although only a few were near enough to see the near disaster, everybody's heard. They're all talking; like crowd noises in a movie, a steady budda-budda-budda builds with one word knifing up like a leaping fish, swift and alarming: lucky, they say. So lucky.

Half the world is abandoning sleds and saucers and crunching uphill through the snow like St Bernards, friendly and solicitous. The Arnolds are coming over. The Stevensons are coming over. Shaken and titillated, students come running, shedding ski caps and mufflers as if that will help them see better.

The rich Garsons and their house guests are coming over, a couple of their regulars led by a stranger, who is tall, taller, tallest, he's . . . She won't look up and see exactly what he is.

Even plump, sixtyish Betsy Atkinson has turned her back on the senator to come their way, pink and puffing with good intentions; in the absence of a day job she is a professional mother: 'Poor, poor . . . Oh God, you are lucky.' *Don't.* As Nick lifts Clair off her feet she hears somebody – Betsy? – say, 'A charmed life.'

'Don't!' she cries.

Nick says from somewhere deep, 'What's the matter?'

She can't tell him. It's more frightening than the accident. Surrounded, uneasily marking the solicitous murmurs and the touch of loving hands and the overblown bouquet of pink, earnest faces under fuzzy headgear, she hears her own small, sour inner voice saying automatically, *Not a charmed life, OK? Nothing special about it.* It's not that she isn't grateful. It's just that if you accidentally note how well things are going, you'd better act fast to counteract it. *Not lucky here, OK?* You have to disarm the fates before God doubles back and gets you.

Her freshman intern Fred Keller armed her for this moment: 'There's a Yiddish word for that. For when you forget and say out loud that things are good for you? Watch out or things won't be good for long. You have to say *koena horra*. Even my Bubby doesn't know how to spell it, but she knows how it works. It's a charm against the evil eye.'

If some fool accidentally curses you by saying, 'Charmed life,' act fast: *Koena horra.* Like Betsy, burbling, 'Best loved couple in Evarton.' *Koena horra.* Or the Garsons's handsome house guest, who is oddly out of context here. *Tall, taller* . . . See him throw his hands wide, shouting as if you are good friends, 'So lucky!' and protect yourself.

('If Job had known the right word,' Fred told her, 'everything would have come out differently.')

Like Job in the good times you need to guard your house and fill the air with noise so God won't get wind of your good fortune and take it away from you.

Koena horra.

2

Jammed into the Evard field house and jumping to music that won't let them stop, Clair and Nick are surrounded. Everybody's dancing: the mayor and the town council; the gringo-stiff and the limber, get-down faculty alike doing steps they learned in high school; funky and preppie Evard students vying for space, so deep into the event that they've forgotten which are which. The frenetic young of the college are like sailors on shore leave, spinning with cute townies in heavy makeup and scrawny, voracious high school girls with Dayglo hair, while Teddy's gay students dance with each other and leap a little higher to make certain everybody sees. Clair's student intern Fred is dancing with redheaded Sally LeFleur – dream on, Fred – and with supreme kindness her intern Sam Jones is dancing with blowsy Mary Roeg who is his English prof.

Everybody brings their own baggage to these things: brassy, overripe Mary who gets so drunk at parties that she's always left over after everybody else has left, crying in somebody's living room because she doesn't have a man; pretty, hopeful Sally who'd do anything to get out of this town; and dumpy, aging Betsy Atkinson who's afraid if George goes to Washington he'll leave her behind. Betsy flushes, giggling, as in a fit of generosity Teddy takes her for a drive around the floor, heroically matching her late Forties Lindy. God, she loves these people – Teddy, the Stevensons, the Gellmans, even Pete and Ginny Arnold who fight and then sob out their stories as if this completes the act.

13

The room where they're dancing is extraordinary. Built at the turn of the century by some major donor, the field house is a neo-Victorian monument to foolishness, a single huge space almost as tall as it is square. Glass skylights designed in a more generous era let in pure moonlight and, above them on the mezzanine, dogged runners thump in circles on the indoor track. In a feat of exalted vision, Clair sees the field house as a giant jewelbox with strobes pulsing and the floodlights' glare crashing out the glassy peak of the roof as if to take the Ethan Frome night party into the sky.

The music stops. The student rock band, Fetal Alcohol Syndrome, manufactures a fanfare for George Atkinson who hoists himself onto the platform for the annual Ethan and Matty tribute. Fans form a half-circle around the bandstand. It's the same speech; the jokes won't be any funnier this year. Clair lets her attention wander. Skimming the group like a speed reader, she studies faces – old friends. Students, who are always new and never new. It's as if there are predetermined units in colleges – grade grubbers and jocks, computer nerds, rebels, acid heads. When a unit graduates there is an identical unit waiting to take his place. New name but same person, really, so commencements are never sad.

The Evard community is of a piece, she thinks, looking around the room as George drones on. Except for the Garsons who were born rich and try too hard to fit in with a faculty that they could buy and sell. The academics envy the outsiders their money and don't see that the Garsons are over-impressed by their intellectual blather and advanced degrees, the fact that they hold regular jobs. Gail and Vance Garson court Evard with lavish parties baited with new faces: fresh blood. Their tall house guest has collected the Arnolds and the Gellmans and made them laugh. Clair is drawn; she'd like to see the stranger up close, find out what draws her friends, but his handsome face blurs as he bends to speak to Mary Roeg who has touched his elbow with a drenched, hopeful smile.

But a change in George's tone distracts the stranger and he turns to the platform, rigid and intent. 'Given in our founder's honor once in a decade . . .' Startled, Clair looks up. Nick's leaving her side. ' . . . and I'd like him to come up here right now. Senator Cobb, Mayor Stangle, faculty, friends, I present our most outstanding friend and colleague Nicholas Sailor, winner of the Ralph G. Evard Distinguished Teaching Award. Congratulations, Nick.'

14

So Nick's on the platform looking embarrassed and tickled and when George puts the medal around his neck and calls on him for a speech, he opens his arms to the room with that beautiful grin and signals the kids in the rafters just before he says, 'Thank you all.'

At Nick's wave a flight of balloons explodes into the room like champagne bubbles, liberating the audience so the party can go on. Then he escapes the platform and she raises her arms to him and they join with an almost audible *click* of, what, rightness. They fit. But over Nick's shoulder she sees: the Garsons' house guest dancing with Mary Roeg; his back's to them but earnest Mary leans out with her face pink and a mouth like a crushed rose, dancing hard and trailing her silk scarf with a look of triumph so precarious that it makes Clair cry: 'God!'

'What?' Nick looks down at her, surprised. 'What?'

So that here in the middle of the frivolity Clair is found looking into herself and examining what she finds at lightspeed: heart, doubts. Past and present. 'I'm glad you're you,' she says. And to her surprise she finishes, 'I'm glad we're here.'

Nick says with a joyful little lift, 'Me too.'

Bemused, she murmurs, 'Who knew we'd like it here?'

Not what she thought when they first came. After the welcoming reception she was ready to pack and go. Ten years ago this place was a closed community. The insiders George and Betsy invited to meet the Sailors in the presidential front hall were all older, circling the new couple with wise smiles that made Clair feel twelve years old. Perhaps out of kindness, perhaps out of prurience, each made it a point to ask at least one polite question, but nobody wanted an answer. With protocol observed, the studiously chic and the militantly unstylish and the earth-toned hand-woven types alike turned away. Clustering, they took up the never-ending story they'd been spinning for years. If they weren't laughing at the Sailors, they were laughing at things Clair and Nick weren't privileged to know about.

The subtext was, she wasn't part of the text. It was like walking in on the prisoners with the joke book – together for so long that they have it by heart. All their exchanges are encoded. Say the right page number and you still couldn't make them laugh. *It isn't the joke, it's the way you told it.* Right. Flickering behind the polite smiles Clair caught the savage glint of the insider: *So. You don't know the numbers? Tough.*

15

Who was it – Ginny Arnold started a story, 'Well, you know Betsy. But of course, you don't know Betsy,' and grinned and wouldn't finish. One of a dozen false starts. They were cast adrift in a room full of turned backs.

'They don't need us. They don't care if we ever know what they're talking about,' Clair said as they fled the house.

'I guess you had to be there,' Nick said.

Forgive her, she said, 'I don't even know if I want to be here. It's so . . .' Trying to sum it up she blurted, 'Not *real*.'

It looked impossible: heartless insiders on an unbreakable loop. What she understood only later was that, rather, she and Nick had walked into the middle of the endless novel the community was writing. No. The endless comic book. Everything stylized. Fixed.

Sewed into this enclave like early settlers into winter underwear, the lifers turned to narrative; it was a lifeline, seeing them through the icebound winters. Instead of eating each other, they fed on the never-ending story. When the long nights are cold and gossip savage, it's safer inside. In time, Clair would catch up on backstory and pick up the narrative. To her horror and guilty pleasure she would spin new installments with the best of them, but that night she was overwhelmed by the close air inside the paperweight, the changeless place where nobody comes and nobody goes.

She wanted to be tough; she did all right until they got back to the house. Standing out front on the idyllic smalltown street, she cracked. Digging in her heels, she pointed to the shutters, window boxes – pretty, stultifying. Bleak. 'Geraniums!' She was trying not to cry. 'This isn't real life.'

She was ready to pack up and go until Teddy dropped into their lives. Nick brought him home for a drink after the first faculty meeting – parked his new friend on the porch while he came in to apologize for not warning Clair. 'I brought home this guy Teddy Hart, from Classics?' He dropped his voice. 'It's OK, he isn't staying for dinner.'

'It's OK,' Teddy said, popping into place next to Nick before she could say anything. 'He isn't staying for dinner.'

Like a genial host their first friend at Evard pulled the Sailors into their own living room and put them at ease. Kindly, he let them ply him with bourbon and in return began. 'Let me put you into the picture. Evarton may look like a nice, Grandma Moses kind of place to you, but in the winter it's a lot more like Francis Bacon. Bleak. It's so bad even Grandma

Moses would hang herself in the root cellar or slit her throat with the ice off the dog dish.' It was as if he saw Clair's heart dropping like the ball in Times Square. Flashing a chipped front tooth, he gave her the winning, irregular Teddy Hart grin. 'Be cool, we have ways of handling it.'

'We know it gets really cold.'

'Cold.' Teddy laughed. 'Cold is no problem. The problem is, when it gets cold it also gets very bored out.'

'Bored!'

Nick cut in. 'That's the last thing she needs to know.'

'Let me guess. You have enough problems with small.'

Clair's voice was low and tight. 'Try claustrophobic.'

'No problem,' Teddy said. 'This place finds endless ways to entertain itself.'

'You kill and eat each other. Oops.' Clair covered her mouth.

He laughed. 'Close. We feed on gossip. And whatever's out there. Things everybody gets into when they get into things.'

'Sex and drugs and—'

He shook his head with that grin. 'More like affairs. Fighting and making up. This place is very provincial. That's why we need all these parties. Look, it's after six. I'd better be—'

'Not yet,' Clair said before Nick could. 'Have another drink.'

'Well, maybe one more.'

'I'll get nibblies.' Clair produced peanuts and brie and crackers – anything to keep him in place. With Teddy in her living room she felt connected.

'Don't mind everybody,' he said as if she'd already told him everything. 'They're just twitchy because you're new.'

'*They're* twitchy.'

'Good-looking couple, come from outside, look like a threat. They hate anybody that might turn out to dance better than they do.' He turned to Nick. 'Like you. Some kind of standout.'

Nick turned it aside with a self-deprecating shrug. 'Sure.'

'It's OK, you'll handle it. You could end up running the show. But look, there are a few simple songs you need to know.' He raised his hand as if for a downbeat and began. 'This is the year of dancing and petty flirtation. Count your blessings, one year it was *t'ai chi*, talk about your orthopod's wet dream. Watch out for the Arnolds' big parties, there's no room you can walk into without finding somebody mashed up against somebody unexpected, doing something unsightly.'

'Sex and drugs and—'

'Rock and roll. Not really. Sort of. It's hard to explain what happens. You won't understand until you see it happening.' He leaned back in their favorite chair with such ease that for the first time since she hit town Clair felt easy here. 'Is that a little Kandinsky?'

She blushed. 'My mother's second husband was a collector.'

'You have some good things.'

Nick grinned. 'We stalk junk shops on Saturdays.'

'A good eye,' Teddy said. 'And there's some good hunting here. Two years ago everybody was ravaging the local antiques barn, but that was before they got into Persian rugs. Just as well, half of them don't know a Bedemeier from a Barcalounger.' He didn't wait for the laugh. 'I followed your husband home because I wanted to meet you guys. We need people like you around here. You have style. Which hardly anybody does.'

Clair said quickly, 'Except you.'

He grinned. 'Except me and the Garsons. Benzes and Balenciagas, Issy Miyake, a little too chic for poor Betsy Atkinson. All they want is to convince us they're intellectuals when all we want is to be rich. House guests from real places. Manhattan and Brentwood. Anyplace where it's happening.'

She caught the tune and did a riff. 'I didn't see anything like *that* at the Atkinsons'.'

'Certainly not. The Garsons don't belong to the college.'

'Well, neither do we.'

Without missing a beat Teddy said, 'You will. They won't. They're much too hung up on what we think of them.'

Evard might turn out to be OK, Clair decided, if this Teddy Hart would only hang out in her living room and keep on entertaining her. 'If year before last was the year of antiques and this is the year of dancing and petty flirtation, what was last year?'

Teddy laughed. 'The year of Oriental rugs. Lucky you missed it! Some Iraqi in Chemistry made a fortune selling his castoffs, bilked everybody and split. Gabe Stevenson, for instance. Mr-Always-has-to-be-first. Got stuck with a fabulous fake. Ginny Arnold, whose taste would fit under her left hind toenail, dropped a fortune.' He was like a standup comic, testing the room. 'Four years ago we had the year of getting drunk and atoning for excesses. People got boiled Saturday night and threw themselves in the snow on Sundays, rolling around and beating themselves with birch twigs at this swamp Yankee's sauna and fitness club.'

His recital set Clair rummaging through her inventory, sorting and discarding instant meals she could make out of whatever, pizza, cake, anything to keep him talking.

Teddy had just lifted the edge of the rug the community had thrown over George Atkinson's single infidelity when he stood up. 'Preview of coming attractions. Now I really have to go.'

She and Nick both said, 'You can't.' It was Clair who pressed. 'The year of antiques and the year of Oriental rugs and the year of dancing and petty flirtation. What's next year going to be?'

'We'll save that for another time.'

'Stay for dinner.'

'I can't.'

'Please. It's just spaghetti. Come talk in the kitchen so I won't miss anything.'

('Teddy sings for his supper,' Jane Stevenson said when she got to know Clair and they began telling each other everything.

'But he sings very well.'

'I love Teddy, but you can't count on him. He'll tell you he's coming for dinner and then beg off if something better comes up.'

Clair said, 'He doesn't come around because he's hungry.'

Jane said wryly, 'It must be hard work, being consistently charming.'

Clair knew more than she was telling but all she said was, 'Nobody likes going home to an empty place.')

Leaving that first night, Teddy said, 'Hang in. Stay tuned. You'll feel differently about this place in another year.'

Another year! Clair thought. I don't know if I'm going to make it through the winter.

It's been ten. Her life and Nick's are so deeply woven into the never-ending story that she's surprised by the memory of her old misery. Somebody told her she'd forget the pain of childbirth; it was a filthy lie. What she's forgotten is the pain of being excluded in a society that has since embraced her.

Until Evard, Clair had never lived anywhere for more than four years. A foreign service brat, she moved too often to belong anywhere. She knows about life on the move; you'll never belong and nothing's for keeps. When things are bad the misery is only temporary because sooner or later every tour of duty ends. Make friends fast and don't get too attached because you'll only have to leave them behind.

At Evard, this all changed. For the first time in her life she belongs. She can plant a tree and see it grow big enough to shade the house. Watch her friendships maturing, like wines. She can paint a room knowing that she'll live here long enough to get tired of the color. The pharmacist asks how Nick's doing; the owner of the local fruitery sends a fruit basket to the hospital. Kids from Arbor Street or Evarton Hollow bring the Sailors' runaway Airedale back to Clair no matter how far he wanders because everybody in town knows Bugs is their dog. She's rooted in this place, settled in her house and surrounded by friends whose kids came up with hers, playing at each other's houses from infancy, when they were put down in each other's cribs while their parents ate together by candlelight. In a pinch Clair can count on the Stevensons or Josh and Lauren Gellman to pick up Davy and Nell after school or keep them overnight. Neighbors and close colleagues, friends, they loan coffee urns and stepladders, take in each other's newspapers and water the plants; they tell their secrets in each other's kitchens, give Clair a cup of sugar, let her use their laptop, anything. They keep keys to each other's houses, in case. The Sailors and the Gellmans have provisions in their wills: if either couple gets wiped out in an accident, the other will bring up their children as their own, and because the Stevensons don't have anybody they trust as much as Nick and Clair, the Sailors have also agreed to take the Stevenson children if ever. In case.

She has a job she loves. Her title is University Editor and fresh wind from the real world blows in by phone and by fax; Evard graduates land in high places and her alumni magazine is read in the corridors of power – thus her connection to the senator.

Nick rose even faster: early tenure when he published his first scholarly book on American writers of the Twenties and early promotion to full professor when his trade book on the horror novel came out. *Horrors* gave his career that extra flip that gets him job offers, invitations to write for national magazines. Now, a mixed blessing, he's department chair. Next fall he'll probably take over for Ad Bishop as Dean of Humanities, unless George Atkinson gets that job in Washington. And, Clair thinks with mixed feelings, there's the possibility that George wants to take Nick along.

This is her home.

In a lifetime of never belonging, Clair finally belongs. At Evard, at this party with Nick. They move together like accustomed lovers, and if his hand on her back is not as firm as it should be and his chin feels hot against her face she will only dance faster because they're dancing together again and she can't imagine it any other way. As people fall back to watch Clair hears Gail Garson saying in mixed admiration and resentment: 'Look at them. They were nothing when they came here, and now they're the best-loved couple in Evarton.' *Koena horra. Koena horra* and thanks, I guess.

Then something goes wrong: a stir at the periphery – the sound of a scuffle? Does she hear a low cry?

Mary Roeg has lost her dancing partner – the Garsons' house guest, Clair thinks. What happened? Why is she so upset? What did he murmur into Mary's frizzed hair, how exactly did he touch her just before he stepped away? Is Clair wrong about this, was it somebody else?

Overblown but pretty in a mad way, flushed and frantic in her brocaded Russian shirt and gold glass beads some man gave her in Europe last fall, Mary plows across the floor with her head down, zeroing in on Teddy Hart. Crazy, Mary. Upset, Clair tells herself. No. Crazy as a bat.

'Oh, Teddy.' Gathering momentum, Mary is avid, intent. What has she lost? What kind of substitution is she trying to make? She advances with her arms wide and those red lips parted as if she's rushing into the arms of a lover, fixing Teddy with a tragic, hopeful smile that makes Clair think: *Oh don't.* There's something about the spiky eyelashes and the moussed blonde hair on this plump, klunky academic that is sweetly touching. *Don't be so sad. Oh Mary, what were you hoping for when you got all dressed up tonight?*

It's not Teddy's fault that he doesn't see Mary coming or feel her touch on his shoulder, and not his fault that he doesn't hear her little cry for attention. He's busy with Sally LeFleur and at that exact second he turns away, pulling Sally onto the floor.

It's like watching a near miss at an intersection.

Mary waits with her arms out and her mouth open as Teddy and his partner wheel, showing her their backs. Everything changes. Only Clair sees the raw, hurt look. The rage.

Mary is turning into something else.

Just then George Atkinson calls Nick over to the president's table and Clair finds herself marooned on the floor with Mary, breathless and dancing alone. Mary's mouth is a red smear; her face is charged with blood. To spare them both embarrassment, Clair goes on dancing, expecting Mary to pick up the step so they can bop in place, pretending they're both waiting for partners to come back.

Clair asks: 'Are you OK?' *Has something happened to you?*

Mary doesn't hear. She glares. 'What's the matter with me? What the fuck is the matter with me?' People are watching.

'Shh, Mary, don't. What is it? Oh, please.'

Her voice is ugly, harsh. 'Something, goddammit, but what the fuck is it? What's the matter with me, everybody? Answer me!'

'Oh Mary, what's the matter? What's happened to you?'

Whatever it is, Mary is stewing in it, twisting her gold beads as if she wants to knot them round Clair's neck and strangle her. 'What is my problem that nobody wants to dance with me?'

'Of course people want to dance with you. Pete and Gabe, I saw them. The Garsons' friend.'

'*Never mind the Garsons' friend.*' Mary's voice is on a little roller coaster going up. 'What's the matter with me?'

'And Nick. Nick would love to dance with you.'

'No he wouldn't. He belongs to you.' Up. 'Well, nobody belongs to me.' And up. 'I shop in all the right places. I keep in shape. Look at my fucking figure. It's better than most people's.'

Clair makes shushing motions. 'It is, Mary. Really. You look terrific.' She'd like to turn and flee but she can't, not really. She can't leave poor Mary out here on the front lines, unprotected.

'And sexy.' Mary is spiraling. 'I may be fifty-two years old but I am still very good at sex, you guys.'

'Shh. It's OK, of course you are.'

'I'm good in bed. You can bet your ass I am.'

Around them, dancers stop cold and stare.

'Shh shh,' Clair says, trying desperately to get Mary off the floor before something worse happens. 'I know you are.'

'No you don't know, but there are plenty of men around here that do. I could name names. You, OK?' She points randomly. 'And you. And you.' Mary's so wired that she can't stop herself, any more than she can stop with the beads, sawing them back and forth savagely, scraping her pale neck raw. 'I'm still a very attractive woman. There are men standing in line to get in bed with me.'

This woman Clair pities but does not particularly like is close to the edge, but why? Is she drunk? Something more? Or worse?

What has befallen her while they were partying here?

She shouts, 'And I give them a damn good time!'

Flying apart, Clair thinks. Mary Roeg is flying apart right here on Ethan Frome night. 'Shh. Shh. I know you do.'

'No you don't. You don't know shit, you with your cute children and your perfect, perfect man. What do you know about going to bed alone night after night after miserable night?'

'You'll be all right, Mary.'

'In hell! You wake up one morning and there are no men left.'

'Of course there are. There's . . .'

As this is a sentence she can't finish, Clair's almost grateful when Mary says in a voice that fills the room, 'No men anywhere! You sons of bitches. I'm all alone.'

'No you're not. People love you. You have plenty of friends.'

'In hell. You're all jealous.' It's Mary's misfortune that she thinks of herself as much smaller. Angry as she is, she's enormous, twisting the gold beads in her big-knuckled hands. 'The women are all scared to death I'll swoop down and eat up their precious man when half of these guys, I wouldn't have them on a stick.'

'No they aren't. I mean . . .'

As the band strikes the last chord, Mary shouts. Each word separates and drops into the room as if into its own specially prepared silence. 'Pricks! *I wouldn't have you on a stick!* And you . . .'

People who used to be her friends stir uneasily and back away. Guilty. Disturbed.

'Bitches! You're all scared shit I'll take your man!'

Typical Evard, they chatter with their backs half-turned so they can watch while they pretend not to.

The students are less cool. They're staring. Tomorrow morning a hundred of them will sit in Mary's Victorian novels class and remember this. Even if she's too far gone to remember, Mary will see it replayed in their faces when she begins to lecture. She'll see it every time she meets a class. *Got to get Mary out of here.* But Mary has raised her voice as if she's already in the lecture hall. 'Well I don't want your fucking men, so you can rest easy.'

'Oh, Mary. I trust you,' Clair pleads. 'Now let's go wash our hands or something, OK?'

By this time Nick is heading in to help effect a rescue before the mayor and the senator see that Mary's yanked her beads to one side so she can open the collar of her Russian shirt, the first move in a mad attempt to get naked.

'I never wanted anybody but who I wanted,' Mary begins and her final twist pops the string. Beads fly out in a golden spray. Trying to catch them all with both hands and watching as they spring away from her, she finishes with a beginning sob. 'The only one I've ever wanted is heartless, fucking Teddy over there.'

Clair touches her arm gently, murmuring, 'Teddy isn't.' And notes that, as he always does in crises, Teddy's disappeared.

Mary shows all her teeth. 'Don't you try and tell me what Teddy is. I'm still sexy, he's ready.' Oh God, if she'd just stop yelling. 'Big bang theory of conversion, my invention. I'll show you!' By this time Nick is at Mary's elbow along with a couple of people from Security who are dressed for dancing but look ready to cope with anything because police are not welcome on campus; this is an enclave that takes care of its own. 'Leave me alone, OK?'

Clair extends her hands to Mary. 'We're trying to help.'

'Well big deal.' Mary is huge in her gold brocade with those lilac-stained eyelids rimmed in runless mascara, huge, funny and tragic as she cries, 'You've got what you want.'

Astounded, Clair gasps. 'I do.' Then she grips Mary's arm, weeping. 'Now let's get out of here.'

Mary's face crumples like pink tissue paper. 'So what's the matter with me?' she shouts just before the words all run together and stop being words but instead convert to pure sound that won't quit until Al LaMar comes on the run with his black bag and seeing that this problem is too big to contain and too severe to treat in the privacy of the college infirmary, calls the paramedics.

'What the fuck is the matter with me?'

What's happened to Mary is disturbing.

Worse. It leaves everybody vulnerable. One of their own being taken away like that when like children they expect the college to protect them inside the gates and keep their scandals locked inside. Instead of waiting it out in the infirmary, Mary is at the hospital downtown. She's being transferred to the state hospital today. Clair feels as if she's been rubbed raw and kicked downstairs. She's afraid to see Mary and she knows she ought to visit. What can she say to poor Mary, who knows Clair saw her hit bottom? How can she pretend everything's OK?

Meanwhile Nick worries about continuity – what to tell the students and who's going to take over Mary's classes. Nick, whose doctor thinks he's taking it easy until he's back to full strength.

By noon the local medical team has evaluated Mary. When Clair calls the office, Al LaMar keeps pointing out he's an internist, not a psychiatrist. 'I gave her a sedative, Clair. That's all I could do for her.'

'Al, the state hospital! You could have kept her here.'

'Not the way she was. It got worse, believe me.'

'You could have kept her in the infirmary. We're supposed to take care of our own. We solve our own problems,' she reminds him. 'We always have.'

'I know you're pissed at me, Clair, but some problems are too big for us. Mary's being committed to the state hospital for her own protection, OK?'

'Protection!'

So much for professional confidentiality; the college doctor says, 'It's not the first time she's tried to put herself out.'

'Al!' Too much. They're transferring her today. If all goes well, she'll need a year to come back from this psychic earthquake and the aftershocks. She may even return to what passes for normal, but at the moment the psychiatric resident at Evarton Hospital doesn't know whether she'll ever be well enough to teach again.

Mary will have to be replaced, and fast.

It's too much to hope that Nick can turn up a qualified Victorianist who's up to the mark and also free to drop everything to come to Evard. He's more likely to get stuck with a third-year graduate student who'll commute. Distracted by orals, dissertation, whatever, Mary's replacement will fly in and out of the Evarton airport, weather permitting, and leave most of the bases uncovered.

But the academic grapevine is so tightly strung that by Monday Nick has a phone call from his friend Jack Nelson, a Victorianist at Columbia, who seems to have heard about Mary's collapse in grim detail and in living color. 'Don't ask,' he says. 'Word travels fast,' he says, and Nick's too grateful to ask how he found out. Jack happens to know this amazing scholar who's more than qualified to step into Mary's job, probably better than she is. A fine, magnetic, extraordinary person.

Nick grins. 'Who cares about magnetic? He's available.'

What is it about this effusive praise that makes her so uneasy? Why does it sound rehearsed? 'Don't make up your mind until you get a look at him.'

It is the good offices of well-meaning friends, then, that bring Will Strait to Evarton.

3

After Mary's collapse the women at Evard examine themselves with a certain uneasiness. Nobody will admit it; Clair and her friends are as furtive as doctors thumping their own bodies, secretly listening for that hollow sound, the spongy *thunk* that signifies incipient illness, an expanded area of vulnerability. Will one of them be the next to crack? To cry when she can least afford to be discovered in a weakened condition, or begin a class and find when she opens her mouth that no sound comes out? Or accidentally blunder into an enclosed space with one of Evard's randy nineteen-year-olds and for the first time in a lifetime start coming onto this *boy* because she's so terrified of losing it that she has to prove she hasn't already lost it?

The place is so enclosed, the society stretched so taut over such a small surface that when one strand snaps, the others fray and jangle. It will be months before the jagged tear this has made in the fabric of their lives begins to mend. Unless their surfaces melt like polyester under a hot iron – fused, perhaps, but ugly, never quite the same.

In a way it's a relief that Mary can't have visitors. With Mary incommunicado, safe in her private room, surrounded by their burnt offerings and baskets of fruit and flowers with falsely optimistic get-well cards, Clair can pretend that misery isn't catching and everything's fine. She doesn't have to confront Mary's bewildered stare, those fringed eyes blinking like a cow's at the thud of the knacker's mallet.

Mary hasn't self-destructed because of them; she's doing it *for* them.

27

This brutal season demands a sacrifice.

Everybody feels it, here in the dark belly of winter.

The women are still shaken, days later.

'Could have been you,' Clair says.

'No it couldn't,' Jane says.

'Could have been me.' She's out on the hill with her oldest friend. Jane is steady, reassuring, with her good, square face and her solid, comfortable flesh. They cross the campus in the gray light, skating over glassy sidewalks in foul weather because anything's better than being stuck inside where worries collect and layer, like dust. The air is pure as crystal; the naked trees are shrouded with ice, glazed and beautiful. Lights break through the leaded windows on Administration Row, patterns fragmenting on the snow as if laid out especially for them, and students who might have been chosen for good looks go by, hailing them by name. It is a benign atmosphere, carefully tended, controlled.

The college belongs to them. Under the sky like this, Clair can pretend it's staying light a little later today, even though the polar night is already crunching down on them.

'Wade, Davy, cut it out!' Jane yells at their boys as if her Jake and Clair's Davy are both her children; the Stevensons and the Sailors have been friends for so long that it's almost true. With the Gellmans and even the Arnolds, these friends form a communal unit, tight as a kibbutz. 'Stop throwing your boots and I mean it.' Without missing a beat she gives Clair a serious answer. 'No it couldn't. We have built-in support groups. Nick. Gabe. Kids.'

'We do.' Clair examines her own guilt like a poker hand. 'At least until something creeps up on us and we lose it too.'

'Don't talk like that.'

'Poor Mary.' When she comes back Mary will see the details of her breakdown written in two hundred faces. Clair's face. 'Everybody knows. This place is just so *small* sometimes.'

It's true. Evard is too small for comfort. The stone buildings fit neatly on this hilltop, with the Gothic tower visible from the main street of Evarton, tidy as a tableau on a postcard. A screen of hemlocks disguises the yellow brick Humanities tower. College planners have stashed the other modern buildings on the far side of the hill to keep from disrupting the picture. Nobody wants you to know the new gym is huge and hideous or that the back of quaint-looking Administration Hill gives on developments and strip malls.

Outside the gates the married faculty, kids and dogs are set in colonials and pocket Victorians like so many china ornaments while the unmarrieds and live-togethers skulk off to developments on the far side of Administration Hill or hide out in condos in the nearest big town or small city, anyplace big enough to give the illusion that their private lives are actually private. The streets leading down to the kitschy town center are lined with relentlessly maintained houses. Christmas wreaths stay wired to front doors until spring, when straw hats and artificial flowers fill the gap until it's warm enough for the hopeful to set out rosemary and geraniums.

Follow Arbor Street down to the town green with its diagonal walks and a Civil War memorial attributed to St Gaudens. Brick and frame buildings line the green like hotels on a Monopoly board. One is in fact a hotel, the Evarton Inn, where the college puts up distinguished visitors. Note the evergreen garlands, the polished brass, the mobcaps on the chambermaids. Everything orderly, unreal.

It's like walking into a Christmas card, except you can put cards away as soon as the season is over. Clair's life is here.

In the world outside, nations suffer; cities fester. Outside, people fight and kill each other, but they are protected here.

Evarton is both confining and sheltered. Clair and Nick live their lives in this jewel of a town far from the exigencies. Life marches in order, along with the seasons; students come every fall and leave the first week in June; people like Nick live the life of the mind, write their books and get promoted – everything predictable in this regular society where hard work and virtue are rewarded, and if Clair wonders how she'd fare in the real world after all this time, no matter.

Somewhere on the other side of the campus Nick is interviewing the last candidate for poor Mary's position; he might as well be on the other side of the world. He's already seen three graduate students from New Haven. Today it's this friend of a friend, the man Jack Nelson sent with such heavy recommendations that it made Clair ask, 'Why is he giving you such a hard sell?' And Nick? Exhaustion has cut into his good humor; he snapped, 'Just let me do this, OK?'

Never mind. When they get home tonight Nick and Clair and their kids will join in the funny miracle of closeness that's wrought every time the family sits down at the dinner table and draws the blinds against the world.

'Poor Mary.' Clair touches her freezing face. 'It's so sad.'

Jane stops on the walk and rewinds Clair's mohair muffler so that it covers her mouth. 'I know. Single is single, most people have their solutions, but at her age it's kind of pathetic.'

'Was pathetic. Now it's terrible.' Clair skates a piece of ice along the glazed sidewalk for Bugs to chase. Her breath freezes on the hairy mohair. 'It wasn't her fault, it was her expectations.'

'She only wanted what we all want.'

'Jane!'

But her good friend says in a sexy rasp, 'Everybody's got to get it somewhere. Like it or not, it's the *zeitgeist*.'

'Sex.'

'Sex. The have-nots think about it all the time.'

All that flailing and the women's movement has started eating its own tail; the world is going two by two by two again. Clair says meditatively, 'Whatever happened to being happily unmarried?'

'Fine, as long as you have a significant other.'

'I had aunts who lived whole lives all by themselves, and you know something? They liked it that way.'

'It's the times,' Jane says. 'Plus media hype. Everybody's supposed to get it somewhere. And if you aren't, you're set up to feel guilty.'

'Margit Collier manages on her own. So does Stephanie.'

'They're both younger.' Unconsciously, Jane touches the loose skin under her chin.

'Any number of people,' Clair says.

'In the real world, maybe. This is Evard.'

'And I've got to get back to the office.' She'd like nothing better than to go home right now and hang with the kids, make something elaborately comforting for dinner and crash into a welter of quilts, but at the main gate she has to kiss them goodbye. Jane will drop Nell and Davy at Lauren Gellman's. Clair takes the Gellmans' three girls twice a week while Lauren commutes to the state university – she's getting a master's at Clair's urging and is happy to return the favor any way she can.

Clair is on deadline. The alumni magazine is going to press with an article on most favored nation policies that the senator pressed into her hand at the last minute – 'A special favor, OK?' Clair said, 'Anything for you.' *The Alumnus* is more than a collection of class notes. Small as Evard is, the magazine is surprisingly influential. Where the faculty stays behind, students go out and make careers in government and finance; many rise to high places, fierce and articulate men who communicate through Clair's pages. She and her student interns Sam Jones and Fred Keller worked into the night yesterday, remaking the book to make room for the senator's piece. Typical kids, Sam and Fred overslept today, leaving Clair to pick up the pieces and modem the copy to the printer. She can't go home until she's checked on the Ethan Frome Day photos Sam and Fred are supposed to crop and modem to the printer.

The publications office occupies the top floor in the Gothic tower of the administration building, one big, cluttered room. It's like its own kingdom. Even when they're off duty, Clair's kid assistants like to hang out there, listening as she fields calls from federal judges, bankers, every alumnus who has a message to get out, or views on how Evard should be run, faculty begging for coverage so their programs will look good. It makes the interns feel in touch. They've brought in a boom box, CDs, posters. She puts up with coffee rings and crumpled candy papers, wall to wall rock music and crumbs in the keyboards because the kids are smart and they'll do anything for her.

The Frome photos have already gone and with a grin Clair doesn't at first understand, her friend Sally is getting ready to Fedex the dummies. With a jerk of her head, she indicates Sam and Fred. This is Sally's fourth year in the office. She's good enough to be running the magazine, Clair thinks, but when she first started she was just a pretty townie who'd never been to college and didn't know how smart she was. In the bizzare way of women who've outgrown their home towns, she's priced herself out of the market here. The louts she went to high school with are intimidated and the junior faculty are too busy chasing other PhDs. Now at Clair's urging Sally's in her second year at junior college; she's applied to the state university for next fall. Clair's pulled a few strings because Sally grew up here and she deserves better than a life sentence to this town. At state, she'll come into her own.

The sooner the better, Clair thinks, because this year's student helpers hang around Sally with ragged, edgy grins. Every year new students come in, big, raw-looking – handsome, some of them, almost men – amalgams of hair and bone and flesh and pressing needs, just growing into their bodies and vibrating with expectation. They are caught on the verge, a mixture of confusion and desire.

The new pair are square-jawed, handsome Fred, with his oh-please look, and black Irish Sam Jones with his blue eyes and freckles standing out on transparent skin. Fortunately for the rhythm of the publications office, Sally's made it clear to them that she's too old for undergraduates. Cracking her gum, she fends them off with a tough grin. 'Think of me as Uncle Sally.'

In spite of which the atmosphere in the room is charged today. Sally's working with more concentration than usual, as if it's her business not to notice what's going on. At the far counter where they enter and dummy the college paper on the oldest Mac, Sam and Fred and their wifty friend Gig Jamison are hunched over the color monitor, snickering. Fred's pushing an image around on the screen and Sam and their shy, anxious little protege are so deep in the process that until Clair speaks, they don't even know she's there.

'I suppose you're doing something gross on that computer.'

Gig chokes and goes pink; his face contorts in embarrassment.

'Who, us?' Caught, the other two laugh and quickly store so she won't see what they've brought up on the screen. Last time she caught them Fred was morphing poor Betsy Atkinson's photo; the president's wife was up to the hem of her boiled wool jacket in some federal reflecting pond. 'Evardian stuff, OK?'

'Sure. Tell me you weren't making President Atkinson naked.'

Fred laughs. 'Rather die. We aren't even growing fur on him.'

But Sam mutters, 'We've got better things to grow fur on.'

Penthouse lies open on the counter by the scanner – split beaver centerfold. 'Don't tell me, let me guess.'

But Fred's busy erasing the file and all backups. 'You don't want to know.'

Clair says, 'Are you sure you don't want to print that?'

Sam blushes. 'You don't want to see that.'

When she looks back at the screen the display is a publicity photo Mary Roeg had taken when she was promoted. With sweet, sad formality, she's staring directly into the camera. In a flash, Clair sees what they were doing: Mary with that split beaver for a mouth.

'I think you guys need to go roll in the snow and chill.'

Sam says, too fast, 'Or something.'

'Oh man,' Fred says. 'I'd like some of that *something*.'

'Get out of here.' All-male college, Clair thinks. Snowed in. What did his parents think they were doing? ''Bye, guys.'

Sally puts on her coat. 'Don't mind them. They're just sex-starved computer geeks.'

Clair's throat tastes sour. 'It isn't healthy.' Starved, she thinks. Healthy eighteen- and twenty-year-olds trapped in this closed environment in a stupendous feat of compression. It's too intense. No wonder everything that happens around here gets huge. No wonder we get anomalies, like Mary's eruption. Gossip and reproaches. Hysteria.

'Be cool,' Sally says. 'They'll grow up.'

'I suppose.' Clair would like to get these kids a scholarship to some all-co-ed city like Boston, pack them off for an expense-paid sojourn at some party school. In deep winter George Atkinson's Boys' Town turns into a pressure cooker, but the president defends the all-male policy with an outrageous quote from the founder. 'Education is serious. We don't need girls fluttering around to distract our men.' Surprisingly, alumni back him up. 'If it was good enough for us, it's good enough for them,' the letters say. 'If Evard goes co-ed I cancel my gift of a new auditorium.'

Time to launch an editorial campaign to co-educate and civilize this place, Clair thinks, right before the full weight of winter settles on her. As soon as it stops getting dark at 4 p.m.

Then: something cracks.

All the air rushes out. It's as if the room is hermetically sealed. Clair puts her hand to her throat. 'God!'

Sally stops buttoning her coat. 'What!'

'I don't know.' The stillness is profound, palpable as a barometric shift. Disturbed, she begins shoving papers around, slipping the skin mag with its raw centerfold into the recycling bin. *What?* Heart? What's the matter here? 'It's nothing,' she replies. 'I'm cool.'

'Are you sure?'

No. Everything is suspended.

They are in the split second before the next thing rushes in.

Just as Clair identifies the phenomenon as causeless, nonspecific dread she feels as exactly that. Dread. Shaking, she covers. 'Really. It's no big deal.'

But Sally lingers. 'Do you want me to stay and help clean up?'

'That's the kids' job,' Clair says, pushing their notes and printouts to the back of the *Evardian* table. 'We're done until the blues come in.' Blues: offset proofs. Blues: this other, way down feelbad thing. Why is she so tired? Was Mary tired? Mary, did it start this way? She says unsteadily, 'It's just winter; I'm cool.'

Like Mary. Don't! Can't wait to get home.

Tonight she'll pull the family around her and keep the monster at bay with junk food – call Domino's, give them Dove Bars for dessert; the kids will be thrilled. Nick won't complain; he's running too hard – no margin. It takes everything he has just to make it through the day. She'll have supper waiting when he comes home from the last interview. She sees them rolled up in quilts by eight.

Surprise. Nick already *is* home, picking up newspapers and sending the kids and their junk on a forced march to the toybox. He's fending with the electric broom. 'Hey, what kept you?' For the first time since Mary cracked and he began this last-ditch scramble to fill the gap, Nick looks relieved. His color is better. He's lost that shaky look he's been getting at the end of the day.

'What are you doing home so soon?'

'We made our hire.'

'So soon? I thought you were widening the search.'

'No need. There wasn't any question.'

'This Anne Eldridge was that good?'

'Not the woman from Yale,' he says. 'She's smart, but she's only a graduate student. We've got an established Victorianist. Oxford is publishing his book.'

'You're talking about the old guy. Jack's friend.'

'He's our age, Clair. Maybe a year younger.'

'So you bought Jack's hard sell.'

Nick is grinning. 'He sold himself.'

Weird, she thinks, Jack's insistence, but no weirder than Nick's enthusiasm tonight. *I don't know why I'm digging in like this, I'm just tired.* 'You hired him on the spot?'

'I did.'

'But so fast!'

'I can't go on teaching Mary's courses.'

Right; it was killing him. She tries to think of something nice to say. 'He must have terrific letters.'

'Oh, we didn't have time to solicit letters. The résumé was enough.' He hands her the laptop she keeps on the coffee table and goes on sprucing up the room like a kid for his girl friend's folks. 'You'll understand as soon as he comes in. It's immediate. Gabe and Josh liked him because he's smart. George liked him because he's well-connected. Even Ad Bishop liked him. The department liked him. It's going to the committee tomorrow, but that's only a formality.'

34

When she puts down the laptop and begins struggling with her damp, hairy scarf he adds unhelpfully, 'He's an amazing guy.'

'If he's so terrific, how come he's available?'

'What's the matter with you?'

'Don't mind me, I'm just tired.'

'Wife's rich. He took time off to write a book.' Nick doesn't give Clair a chance to ask time off from what? 'Fantastic project, relating fiction to painting. Mann. You know. He's been in Venice.'

'I thought you said he was a Victorianist.'

'That too. Not everybody gets stuck in one area.' Nick sees her rushing to the next question too late to forestall it.

'He wants to leave Venice for *this*?'

He beams. 'He's here. That's why I'm home early. Ah.' She knows that look. 'I know it's crunch time for you and all but, ah. Guess who's coming to dinner?'

'You didn't.'

'I did. Night flight from Europe, first night in Evarton, would you make him eat downtown alone?'

Clair manages not to give any of the obvious answers. 'Nuke some chicken, OK? I'll think of something clever while I change.'

'I love you. Thanks.' As she heads upstairs he says, 'You'll like him. Everybody does. As soon as you meet him you'll see.' He's too intent on making this match. 'He's an amazing guy.'

This makes her turn on the stairs. 'Wait a minute. Did he put something in your coffee?'

Nick goes on as if he hasn't heard. 'I'll feed the kids.'

'Give you funny cigarettes? Uppers? Poppers?'

'It's hard to explain.' Nick's willing her to see what he sees. 'It's . . .' He probably wishes she'd just go on up and leave him alone to write his answer but Clair waits with her thumbs hooked in the belt loops of her jeans. 'What can I say?' he says finally. Nick, who thinks the best of everyone. 'When he talks, you listen.'

The doorbell rings.

'Forget changing.' His voice lifts in relief. 'He's here.'

Then Will Strait walks in and Clair— She doesn't know. A flicker of . . . *tall, taller* . . . recognition.

But he is upon her. 'I'm Will Strait.' Handsome, graceful, smiling, the unexpected guest advances as though her welcome is a foregone conclusion, as if he has won her without firing a shot. 'I've heard a lot about you. You're . . .'

She will not say, 'Clair.' It's strange. Even though Will Strait stands with his hand out, graciously waiting for her to supply her name, he already knows. She knows him. That figure at the bottom of Kingman's Gorge: *tall, taller. Tallest.* He has fair hair, like Nick, the same fair hair as . . . Wait. 'Didn't I meet you at the—'

'Dance,' he supplies with a smile that lights the room. 'I'm an old friend of Vance and Gail's.'

'Oh.' Blinking, she replays Ethan Frome night, Mary Roeg's dancing partner, this smooth, fair head floating in the dimness as friends clustered around poor Mary, the outsider at the periphery. 'Nick thought you were here for the—'

'First time,' he says, anticipating her, smiling until he makes her smile, and then Strait says as if he understands the intricacy of insiders and outsiders and knows better than Clair how peripheral the Garsons are, 'First time in the college, yes.'

4

Clair can't get comfortable. She's deep in her favorite chair with dinner cooking and the dog asleep at her feet; her kids are playing upstairs and the man she loves best is opposite her on the sofa, laughing over the faculty face book with the perfect guest, and the edges of her teeth don't quite match. Strait is appealing, with that brilliant smile and shadowed eyes that defy a quick reading, and he's easy with Nick who's more relaxed than he's been since Mary's collapse, yet Clair can't quite manage to smile when he smiles. Nothing you could put your finger on but here he is in her living room saying all the right things and somehow it seems all wrong and she can't know if there's something the matter with her that makes her feel bad, or if it's something about him. She sits back, thoughtful and silent, while Nick leans forward on the sofa, smiling like a stage mother anxious to make the match.

So far he's done everything right. Fresh from Venice, or is it midtown Manhattan, he took one look at the grey Bokhara, at the carefully chosen color of the east wall, at the objects the Sailors have selected to surround themselves – paintings, artifacts – and said, '*This* isn't Evarton.'

Then he apologized for landing in their laps. Admired the art, the jade ax, admired for God's sake the bean dip Nick threw together while Clair was changing, admired Clair when she came back downstairs looking only marginally better collected. Offered to take them out to dinner instead and when they refused thanked her in advance for the extra effort. He's brought dessert to sweeten his arrival. The wine he chose is perfect; carnations are her favorites and the children are tickled by the presents – nothing compromising, just K-Mart gliders and some Bubble Stuff to let them know he thinks they matter. 'Just wait,' he told them before Nick sent them upstairs, 'wait till my kids come to town. They're just about your age. You'll be great together.' Then he gave Nick that look, *between us dads*, and added, '*If* you go upstairs and do your homework the way your father said.' He even played tug with Bugs until Clair took mercy and hid the rubber bone, and still . . .

She wants to pull Nick out of the room and tell him – what? She doesn't know. Figure it out, lady; think before you speak.

At the moment she hasn't had much chance to speak. Will Strait has read everything Nick ever wrote, all that wonderful stuff on Fitzgerald and the long dead golden days, what made you turn to horror novels?

'The flip side of the American psyche,' Nick says. 'The beast within that we're afraid of turning into.'

'Unless it's the beast we're in love with.'

'Nobody wants to be that.' Nick is laughing. 'No. You're right. I'm out to prove that, secretly, most of us do.'

This time it is Strait who says, 'Nobody wants to be that. You ought to do a spot on my friend's TV magazine. I'll make some calls. But you need to tell me what you think flipped the American psyche,' he says, bringing Nick on as if they are the only two people in the room, modestly turning aside questions about his own work as, flushed with pleasure, Nick talks on. Clair nudges the dog off her foot and slips into the kitchen. Bugs, at least, notices and comes padding after her to help cook while, absorbed, Nick and Strait talk on and on. With increasing carelessness as to whether the noise disturbs them, she crashes the colander into the sink and starts washing lettuce.

Then just as she's bashing the lid of a locked olive jar with a knife handle, not caring whether she opens the thing or breaks it, Will Strait comes into the kitchen. 'You shouldn't have to do dinner all by yourself.'

She turns away, banging the jar on the counter. 'It's in my job description.'

'You know better. You're that terrific writer who happens to cook.' He says out of nowhere. 'Those short stories. Where do they come from?'

For Clair, this is extremely personal. She's so new to fiction that comments about her work come in like questions about her sex life. She tries to create a diversion. 'You mean *The Alumnus.* I try to get the best writer for the subject. People who write books, not people who teach them.'

'You know I'm not talking about the magazine.'

Instead of turning to answer she goes back to whacking the jar with the knife handle. The lid won't yield in spite of her battering. When she doesn't respond he waits, content to let the silence get bigger. Even with her back turned, Clair is acutely conscious of the physical presence. She comprehends the way Will Strait fills the space: the long, strong body moving easily in the blue Oxford shirt, the artfully aged jeans worn to silver and the cashmere jacket; the body is finely tuned and aggressively fit. Powerful. There is nothing stale or winterbound about the man. The only smell he gives off is the soap he scrubbed with just before coming here for dinner. She's aware of the glow of the winter suntan, the lights in that smooth, fair hair.

'I mean your fiction. Your story in the *Paris Review*.' He takes the jar from her. With one twist he opens it and shakes the olives into a colander and with unnerving certainty tells her what she thinks but has not told anybody because she isn't sure. 'It looks like the opening of a novel.'

It's not his fault she is sharp with him. 'It's too soon!'

'Nick says you've had a hard day.'

'Every day is hard,' she says, willing him back to the living room. But if Strait gets the message, he won't act on it. He rinses his hands and wipes them on a paper towel, smiling.

Upstairs Nick is getting the kids ready for bed; Davy is thumping back and forth and Nelly's squealing in the tub but all Clair can hear is her mother's voice: '*A man in my bed.* I got married and when I woke up the next day there was a man in my bed. Do you know what that's like after twenty-two years of privacy?'

Like this, Clair thinks. Intimate. Weird. With Will Strait in the narrow space where she spends much of her time on Arbor Street, holds her most important conversations with her children, makes crucial phone calls, tells Nick things she's never told anyone, Clair is struck by how personal a kitchen is, how private. How like a bed. Comfortable when you are in it with the right person. She looks past him at the open door, as if that will hurry Nick.

'He said to tell you he's washing Nelly's hair.' He shrugs apologetically. 'I hope I'm not in the way.'

'Oh no.' The power that keeps us from killing and eating each other at Evard is manners, she thinks. Unless it is the trap. 'Not at all.' To her surprise she manages to hit the right tone – friendly, light. 'If you don't mind watching me cut up vegetables.'

'Let me help.'

'You don't want to get anything on that jacket.'

Instead of insisting, he lounges against the counter, tossing this compliment into play. 'Your stories. I've read them all.'

She is surprised. 'Some of them are hard to find.'

'They were worth looking for.' He gives her that four-alarm smile. Then he says something exactly right. 'I'm not sure I go along with what you're doing, but I sure as hell admire the way you're doing it.'

Laid back. Perfect. 'To each—'

'His or her own.' Will Strait's picked up so fast that she almost smiles.

Then she does smile. Nell and Davy thud into the kitchen in their Mighty Morphin Power Rangers pajamas with the grippers on the feet and she is surrounded, reinforced by her own. Hearts of our hearts. Bodies of our bodies. Our genes, our blood and bones, here to hug her good night. Looking at the newcomer over the warm, familiar heads of her personal support group, she squeezes them so tight that Nelly squeaks. *I thought you'd never come.*

'I thought you'd never come,' Strait says to them.

The coincidence makes her laugh.

Even though he's assembled the balsawood glider Will Strait brought him and long since crashed and broken it, Davy asks, 'Who are you?'

'Will Strait.' The stranger in Clair's kitchen adds disarmingly, 'Don't be scared. I'm just another professor.'

'This is Professor Strait, Dave. He's new on the faculty.'

'Oh, right. You're the emergency guy.'

'Davy!'

Strait is momentarily nonplussed. 'Emergency . . .'

'You know.' Davy's wise look reminds her that the curse of faculty life is that nobody in a college town talks baby talk because everybody knows kids are just small, not stupid. They all talk to their children like grownups. Or talk like grownups around them. Her eight-year-old is explaining to Will Strait in a whisper so intense that it's filled with spit, 'Because Ms Roeg went crazy.' Then he turns to Clair. 'Dad says she's a nympho-*what*?'

'Shut up, Davy.'

'At least they think that's what it is.'

'That's enough.'

'She went bats right in front of everybody.' Davy hits the hoarse tone of a Scoutmaster telling ghost stories in front of a campfire. Then as Strait bends politely to listen, Davy says conversationally, 'Did you ever see anybody go crazy?'

'I said, that's enough!'

But Davy won't be stopped. 'I bet you don't know what she did.'

To Strait's credit he does not say, no, what? Instead, like a good father, he creates a diversion. 'How old did you say you are?'

'Eight.'

'I would have thought you were at least ten. You're the exact same age as my boy. His name is Chase.' He laughs. 'Like, "cut to the chase". Get it?'

Davy giggles.

By that time Strait is on his knees, careless of what Clair may have spilled on the kitchen floor because he's intent on addressing Nelly at her level. 'How old are you?'

'Six.'

'You're not.'

'I am too.' She looks so pleased!

'Six years old. My little girl is just exactly six years old. Her name is Maddy.' He's still on his knees. 'Do you like Barney?'

Nelly's torn; she knows the family position and she doesn't know what to say. She is watching Clair's face.

Strait is watching Clair too. A careful reader, he says, 'Maddy doesn't like Barney.'

'Me too!' Nelly beams like the faculty brat she is. Too smart for smarmy mind candy, says Clair. No Barney in this house.

Davy says confidentially, 'Everybody hates Barney.'

'Everybody around here, at least.' Clair laughs.

Strait makes a face that makes the children laugh. 'Me too.'

'Beat it. Daddy's waiting for you.'

They milk the last good night and go back upstairs. Clair and Will Strait are alone again, almost nose to nose in these remarkably close quarters, enclosed by the pressure of the winter night on this fragile house, by the world of snow and ice held at bay by this bright, illusory circle of warmth and light, by the strange intimacy of the kitchen. With the newcomer standing opposite, Clair is strongly aware of the area she identifies as personal space. It seems essential to maintain it. Will Strait is not encroaching, he's waiting at the periphery.

Nothing has happened.

Then, although nothing's happened it is as if something has happened.

She is strongly aware of his body: physical presence. The way he *is* in the space.

He hasn't moved; he isn't coming on to her and yet the man has made her comprehend his body – the way his clothes feel against it, the way a woman's touch would feel. The way his flesh would feel under Clair's fingers, and he has done this without moving and without speaking. He has simply called it into the air between them. The room is filled with possibilities.

It is as if he is waiting for a signal.

In her early days here Clair made an enemy of Nick's first department chair without knowing how it had happened. Jane Stevenson explained when she got to know Clair better, 'Eric's mad at you because you won't flirt with him.' So *that's* what that was. Is this what Strait is doing? She thinks not. Tall, assured, the outsider stands easily in this enclosure. He's content to be silent for as long as she is silent. He isn't coming on to her; he isn't, what is it, flirting. If he is assessing the situation, he is too practiced to let her know it. He isn't doing anything.

He's waiting for her to do something.

The silence just goes on being a silence.

Upstairs Nicky is hearing prayers and inventing tonight's bedtime knock-knock joke, while here in the kitchen Will Strait whom Nick has invited into their lives considers her.

The air in the steamy little kitchen is charged with something Clair is ready to identify as sexual tension when Strait exhales in a long sigh. Holding his breath? It is a surprise. So that's what he was doing. It's not what she expected.

When he speaks, it's not what she expects either. Will Strait says, out of what appears to be not desire but exquisite pain imperfectly held in check, 'Pretty picture.'

'What?'

'Beautiful kids, close family, good food, cheerful kitchen. Nice life.' She can't know what frays his voice at the edges; he sounds immeasurably sad. 'It's perfect. It's . . .'

'It's no big deal,' she says hastily. 'Your average family on a good day.'

'No. It's . . .' The furnace kicks in. The chimney vent creaks open. Life hums on yet he lets the rest hang in the air; it is as if he is considering some secret grief that he can show but can't afford to tell.

It is an odd moment.

'It's very sweet.' He tries. 'It's just so . . .'

But Clair can't bear to hear him name it, what she has, that he may not have, for fear God will hear and say, that's enough of that. Turning to the stove in a klunky movement she says, too loud, 'I need your help after all. This damn dish is too heavy for me.'

He reaches out as if to touch her arm. 'I'm sorry if I—'

'Oh no,' she says; yes, she is maundering. 'It's perfectly all right, it's just this damn casserole is about to bubble over and wreck the stove.' With a clatter she opens the oven door and hands him the quilted mitts. 'Here. I'll hold it open and you grab.'

But Strait stands back as if waiting for Clair to acknowledge what he has just tried to tell her. They exchange a look.

When he does speak it is not about anything that's just happened. Instead he moves forward and puts on the oven gloves, saying, 'You're going to love my wife. Her name is Mara and she's a pianist.' His smile softens. 'Her mother was a Garson. No relation, but we've known the Garsons practically for ever.' He looks at her. 'Vance Garson is a friend of mine.'

'Everybody's a friend of yours.'

He picks up the oven dish and turns to face her. 'I know. Nick too, I think. More than just a teacher. On the rise. We have a lot in common.' He makes a pause to underscore the question. 'And you?'

'Let me get the dining room door for you.'

He doesn't move. 'Clair?' The newcomer inclines his head with a smile that is so open and so openly appealing that Clair knows she ought to step outside herself and study this: motives. Intent.

Instead she hears herself responding gratefully. 'Of course.'

Safe at last at the dinner table. They are in their places, one, two, three: Clair on one side, at the head Nick, her partner, lover, protector, and at the foot Will Strait. They are not yet antagonists, not early settler and his wife, happy pioneer couple and sinister marauder, but just new friends sitting down with their heads bent over the pretty table, eating an unexpectedly good meal. Will Strait is intelligent, amusing, grateful to be sitting here at their table, glad to be settling into this nice community life after the elegance and confusion of Venice. And Mara, he says, Mara can't wait to get here. My wife thinks smalltown life will be really good for the children. She's

43

like me, she loves learning new colleges. I told Mara you had two wonderful children and she can't wait for Chase and Maddy to meet them.

He is a splendid audience, the kind who says Oh, no! at just the right time and always cheers for the good guys. He wants to hear all their material about Early America, which is the way the Sailors think of Evard in the Eighties, when they first arrived. He knows just what to ask to start them digging into the fossilized layers of gossip that fuel their winters and amuse them in the long summer twilights. Strait loves the vintage setpieces and he's quick to pick up on the longer continuing stories whose outcome is not yet certain, and if Clair and Nick talk too much it's because gossip is a lot like liquor: one shot leads to another until caution flows into intemperance.

Clair and Nick telling everything, bla bla bla. Giving away the store.

He makes their best stories sparkle and they expand, telling more than they should about things only insiders can tell. Unlike the Garsons, the only other couple Strait knows in Evarton, Clair and Nick have the insider's power over the details – what the Atkinsons are really like, that Betsy used to beg George for a baby and he bought her cocker spaniels until it was too late – 'Now he won't even let her have a dog.' They tell him about Gabe Stevenson's secret ambitions and the gross symptoms of George's political ambition; they can tell him what it is with Pete and Ginny Arnold, who love each other even though they're always fighting; that the Gellmans and the Stevensons are the world's best people.

Within minutes he's absorbed their material and taken it as his own; he makes a joke about Betsy having puppies. Clair swivels to look at him. She feels traduced, faintly soiled, as if in the heat of conversation she's given away things that aren't hers.

Then Nick gets up for more wine.

Strait asks, 'What did happen to this poor Roeg woman I'm replacing?'

'I thought you knew Mary.' It bothers her that he finds it necessary to ask.

'I never had the pleasure.'

But on Ethan Frome night . . . She says softly, 'I think she thinks she knows you.'

He doesn't respond. Then Nick sits down again and Strait changes the subject, asking with boyish openness, 'OK, am I really going to like it here?'

By dessert she's laughing again. Warmed by the talk, Clair goes to the kitchen for coffee. When she comes back, everything is brand new. She stops in a weird double take. It is as if she's seeing the two men for the first time. At this hour, in this light, at first glance her husband and the newcomer look alike; it is so strange! Nick and Strait turn to her with their heads inclined at almost the same angle, smiling the same smile. They're both fair-haired, with strong, regular profiles, and if there are differences the immediately obvious one is that Will Strait is taller than Nick, heavier. Bigger. More polished, like an upscale model car.

There is another difference. Nick sits lightly in the room, like a bird in the air or a fish in the ocean, an easy man at home in his element, whereas the newcomer's head looks as if it's been carved somewhere else and set down here like an alabaster bust. Where Nick's face is all light and mobility, Strait's is as smooth, as carefully wrought and as carefully expressionless – as dense – as Greek sculpture.

It is as if Will Strait has found it necessary to compose this face to keep people from seeing whatever lies underneath.

No wonder I can't get easy with him.

He catches her looking and smiles. 'Wonderful dinner.'

'I'm glad you came.'

He shifts in his chair. 'Now I've got classes to prepare.'

'Right,' Nick says gratefully. It's been good for him to have Strait here but the post-pneumonic fatigue has caught up with him; to Clair's distress it still does at this time of night. It's about to knock him flat and roll over him. 'And I've got three less to prepare.'

Right, Clair thinks; this is transactional. He's doing something for Nick that I can't do. She smiles. 'Let me get your coat.'

'You were terrific to take me in like this.'

'You're terrific to take over for Mary on such short notice.'

'My pleasure. It came at the right time for me.' Strait shrugs into his raincoat – too lightweight for winters here – and Clair wonders if she ought to offer him a scarf. 'And now I'd better get myself down to the Evarton Inn before they lock the doors on me. The sheets are yellow and the rooms are cold, but the management turns back the beds and leaves mints on the pillows.'

Is this a hint? 'I thought the Garsons . . .'

The face he turns to her is bright and disingenuous. 'Oh, they don't know I'm here.' He sighs. 'For my sins, I'm at the Evarton.'

'I thought they were your best friends.'

45

'They're not like us,' he says and waits for her to offer him the guest room.

If Nick wishes she'd give Strait what he wants, he's not about to do it for her. Family life is such a tightly wound mechanism that in busy times, privacy is essential to maintaining it.

'You know how Vance and Gail are,' Strait says, as if prompting her. 'Unreal. Of course I love them,' he says, and as if he and the Sailors are bonded tonight, unaccountably kindred, he adds confidentially, 'But they're not like us.'

This is true. They're too rich to belong. Vance pretends to work at managing his portfolio and cataloging their collection of works by lesser painters and sculpture of no known pedigree, but he's never had a day job. Gail talks about auditing classes at Evard but doesn't follow through. She's never had to follow through on anything. For all the care the Garsons take with appearances, for all the money they spend, they're nothing more than overdressed, wistful hangers-on at university functions, perpetual outsiders pretending to dance the dance when they can't even guess the tune. They're like polished sightseers in a foreign country, speaking phrase-book English and thinking they fit in because when the natives see them they smile. They're temporarily captivated by this feudal town which is everything to the inhabitants but not to them; to them it's just another stop on a whirlwind trip around the world. Stay a while, scoop the cream off the top of the village – best jeweler, best potter, best painter; whatever you pay in these primitive countries, your purchases are a steal; enchant the natives, spoil them for everyday life, cut your losses and move on.

And Strait? How does he figure here?

But he's through waiting her out. He's shaking Nick's hand. After a moment in which he considers hugging her and decides correctly that it's too soon, he shakes her hand. And now Clair is studying: Strait, with those clear eyes and that wonderful smile.

Herself. Her unaccountable reluctance to accept the man for what he wants to be when he wants more than anything is to be accepted.

Which, she supposes, is what sends her upstairs in the dark the minute the front door slams. She needs to kneel on the window seat and see Will Strait leaving. She has to see him down the front walk. She will watch him out of sight without knowing why. What she does know is that he's come into their house, into their lives, unbidden and she needs to see him go.

Now Clair sees the newcomer stop at the end of their front walk. Strait stands with his back to the house, fixed in the glow from the street light with his head bent, as if he is considering. He is tall, monolithic in the topcoat. As she watches, he straightens his shoulders and lifts his head. And turns to look back at the house.

Cold as it is, Will Strait is hatless, so the overhead light carves shadows in his face. It is the same face he showed them at dinner, exemplary but in this light inscrutable, smooth as an obsidian mask. In the next second something – the angle, the light – changes. Clair could be studying one of the paired masks carved into the proscenium arch of the college theater: comedy, tragedy. Mysteriously, she can't tell which.

Downstairs Nick calls, 'Honey?'

The guest has said good night. Bugs has gone out and come back in and the back door is locked. This is the time in the evening when she and Nick sit down for the instant replay. They do it even when they're exhausted but here is Clair on her knees on the upstairs window seat with her nose stuck to the window by ice made by her own breath, watching him. A trick of the light, she tells herself. It's only a trick of the light.

While downstairs Nick calls again. 'Clair.'

Her shoulders twitch as if somebody's run a knife handle down her back. *Something.* She can't know whether it comes in an intuitive flash or if she reaches this point deliberately, crossing on stepping stones of deduction. What matters is that she knows. *Something's the matter with him.*

Surprise makes her teeth grate. What she feels is as sudden as it is visceral. Chemistry? What? It is dislike.

'Are you OK up there?'

On the walk outside, Strait turns and goes.

'I'm fine.' Released, she turns away; in the spot where she's separated from the frozen window, her nose burns. 'Be right down.'

Nick's cleared the table; he's in his favorite chair with his shoes off, waiting for the instant replay. What can she tell him? That she doesn't have the heart for it? Not Nick. Not tonight. It's been a hard month. She kisses him. 'You look beat.'

Standing, Nick hugs her and rocks, resting his chin in her hair. 'What did you think of him?'

'I think we'd better go to bed.'

'Clair?'

He's waiting. She says the best thing she can think of. 'I'm just so glad you have somebody to teach Mary's classes.'

47

'Me too.'

He's still waiting but all she says is, 'It was killing you.'

'I knew you'd like him,' he says quickly, as if he can override her reservations. 'He loved the Evard backstory. He took hold right away.'

'He did.' Whether it was the wine or excitement or her need to fill the silence in which her doubts raised their heads, stirring like nightcrawlers, she's told him too much. The Arnolds' fights and the Atkinsons' secrets are as much Will Strait's now as they are hers. 'He's a quick study,' she says.

'Is that all you're going to say?'

'For now.'

'Well,' Nick says finally, 'I'm really glad he came. How about you?'

It's clear he's exhausted; she's exhausted. Maybe he really is fine, she tells herself. Maybe it's just winter, getting to me.

Nick is waiting and she says for his sake, 'I think he's going to be fine.'

5

Ben Messinger

Every time the sun comes up and his mother comes in his room again, his mouth dries out. Fog builds in his head. Everything in him is toxic. Foul. When she smiles at him Ben has to turn away and cover his mouth so he won't let it out; he could poison a toad.

Is it in his blood or was it something he did that brought him to this? Cracked in two and laid open, like a ruined skull.

He can't even be sure how it came down. You don't expect it, God knows you don't know you were asking for it, but one day something cracks you wide open. It makes you look inside. What you see is revolting. Boiling with corruption. How could you go around like this and not even know what you are?

The guilt: *I brought it on myself.* Find out the truth and your life is over. Know what you are and you want to die.

The hell is that the worst things that can happen to you are not necessarily the ones that kill you. They are the ones you have to live with.

You plan to die. Wait until she's out. Lock the door to your room and gulp the pills. Take all the pills in her medicine chest, fuck the directions. Write a note if you have to, some lie to protect the survivors. Correction. Survivor. Delia. Poor Mom. Lie down and compose yourself, consider it over. Say goodbye and you may still wake up in the morning in a bed fouled with your own vomit because, as with the monstrous thing that drove you to this in the first place, you are ignorant, stupid. Failed.

All you want to do is die and you live.

You lived in spite of *that*. Now you have to live with this. *I can't even fucking kill myself.*

Ben's mother found him and did not dial 911.

Instead she dragged me to my feet and walked me into the shower. Ben Messinger with his frayed fingernails and cuticles gnawed to shreds, with his clean brown hair and his eerie white body not altogether clean because he can no longer bear to see himself naked, not even to scrub.

His mind rushes ahead to an alternate future in which he does the job. He sees himself dying. His mother finding the body. At least it would be over. No. He sees the undertaker, or is it the coroner, stripping the body. He sees their horror at the discovery. The moment in which . . . Delia's face when she finds out the truth.

The possibility makes him shudder.

No. Got to do it right. Blow myself up, go down at sea and get eaten up by fishes. Anything to destroy the evidence. Nothing left, so she'll never have to know. Jump off something big. Fall hard and splatter in so many pieces they'll never know.

He'll do it, right? As soon as he can make it to the top of the insurance tower. Except at the moment Ben has a hard time getting out of bed, much less outside. There's no way he can make it to the bus that runs to the business district so he can do the deed.

He's too weird to leave the block right now.

He just can't let anybody see him. Not the neighbors, not the bus driver, no pedestrians, for God's sake no little kids. He can't understand how Delia can look at him and not know how vile he is. Disgusting? One look would corrupt you. Turn you to stone.

After the pills he was so sick that for a minute he got lucky and forgot. Dry heaves. Aches. Miseries. When she found him, Delia hauled him into the shower. He could feel his mother's body jittering as she sobbed. Ben didn't cry at all. What he feels is too deep and dreadful for expression.

When he could stand without support, Delia propped him against the sink. She peered into his eyes. 'I'll get the doctor.'

No! Terrified, he flew apart, shouting, *'No doctors!'*

Another mother would have called the police, the paramedics. Stuck him in the nearest institution and called down the suicide watch. Another mother would have begged the shrinks to make her son quit killing himself, but Delia only touched Ben's cheek with a sweet, mournful look. 'You're right. Psychiatrists. Hospital. You don't need that. What would I do without

50

you?' Delia was divorced before Ben was born. He is all she has. Her sigh shook them both. 'We can handle this.'

No we can't. Ben put his face in her hands and willed her to see inside. What it's like in there. He made her look and she just smiled. Is she blind or stupid or is it a special gift mothers have that they can look at hideosity head on and still think you're beautiful? He groaned. 'Yes, Mother. We can handle this.'

Delia faced her only child in sweet collusion. 'You'll be fine here at home.'

Our secret. Ben, in his willful rush toward death.

'Our secret.' Right. She handed him dry pajamas and pretended nothing had happened. Patted him, *there there*. 'All this has been hard on you.' Poor Delia. One woman alone. She doesn't even know what *all this* is. 'All you need is a little rest,' she said and put him back to bed again.

If he can't be dead he is the next best thing. He is lying here. Bed is about all he can handle right now. He holed up in bed right after they shipped him home from Europe last December, and except for the night he blew his suicide, he's spent most of his time in bed. If she'd just leave him alone he could starve to death and get it over with. But every morning before work Delia brings a tray and stands over him until he eats. Reads tidbits from the paper, trying to interest him in something. Anything. He eats to get rid of her. Then as she takes the empty tray she always says, 'Better today?'

He never answers. He hasn't talked much Since.

'Poor Ben. It can't possibly be that bad.'

Yes it can.

She says, 'Tomorrow you'll feel more like doing things.'

There is absolutely nothing Ben can say to this.

Today, instead of leaving, she puts the tray on the window seat. 'If you'd only *talk* about it.'

Not too close. Holding his breath, he waits for her to give up and go away before the poison gets out and kills her dead.

'Ben?' She sits down on the edge of the bed. 'You were such a good student. If you'd just talk to me . . .'

All he has to do to get rid of her is construct one cheery sentence but he can't think of one. He's just too tired. If that's what it is. *I should have died over there.*

'Ben?'

Go away.

But even though it's past time for her to leave for work, Delia Messinger won't leave. Her weight on the bed is disproportionately heavy. She touches his shoulder. 'This has gone on too long.'

Alarmed, he sits up.

'I'm calling a doctor.'

He knocks the tray off his lap. *No!*

'What's the matter, Ben? What's the *matter* with you?'

Can't even fucking kill myself. At the moment, he can't even find the right thing to say to get his mother out of the room. He forces it: 'Nothing.'

'I think we ought to get someone to look at you.' She says quickly, 'No hospitals. We'll get a doctor to the house.'

'No!' He leaps away. He's standing in the middle of the rug before he even realizes he's out of bed.

Forever Delia. God! No matter what he does the woman rebounds like a pop-up clown, grinning and hopeful. 'You're up!'

'Leave me alone!'

'Look at you,' she says brightly. 'At least you're up.' It seems to be enough right now.

Ben creates a desperate grin for her, holding it until she leaves the room with that sweet mother's smile that makes him want to weep. Standing in the middle of the room he listens. She isn't leaving. He can hear her rustling out there, folding linen, rearranging the hall closet, pretending to brush her teeth again.

She calls through the door with that irritating, persistent cheer, 'Now that you're up, maybe you can get in touch with your friends.'

I don't have any friends.

It is a threat. 'Unless you want me to call them.'

'I'll take care of it.' With a groan he rummages for some clothes: sweatshirt, jeans, Nikes. Accidentally sees himself in the mirror. What! He looks almost like a person. Tall, slight, with straight brown hair and skin creepy and white from too many weeks inside, he regards himself. At first sight he shows no signs of the corruption. But he knows that like the smell of decaying flesh it will not leave him. Anybody but a mother would smell it coming off him.

Damn Delia. 'Are you coming out now?'

He shows himself just to make her go away. Her smile at the sight of him is enough to put him back to bed again. Even though it's been weeks,

Ben feints as if to start downstairs, glowering until she precedes him. It's late. She's late for work. Lingering at the bottom, she reaches for her coat. Just now she seems to be having almost as hard a time leaving the house as Ben does.

What's the movie where they're all trapped in the house for no apparent reason? *Exterminating Angel.* Stuck in there even after they kill and eat the sheep. Staying on without knowing why.

Will you please just leave, please?

But Delia hangs on the front door, looking up with that indefatigable smile. Her look of hope shames him. Therefore Ben clears his throat and starts downstairs. He grabs his jacket from the coat rack, hefting it as if he's about to go out and do something. Then with that tremulous smile Mother tells him to have a nice day and runs for the car at last, knowing that the half-hour she's missed will come off the top of her paycheck.

She leaves the front door open for him.

Ben will speak if he has to. He'll dress and come downstairs. Anything to maintain his isolation. He'll go outside even though it costs him dearly. Let Delia look in her rearview mirror and see her only son striking out boldly for the corner. Anything to keep her from calling a doctor. An MD would see it at once. The damage. A psychiatrist would know even sooner.

Her Toyota stops at the corner. Even though he's weak from so much down time, Ben starts walking. To his relief, she waves and drives away. Brave little Delia.

It's not his mother's fault that the grey winter light is so strong that it almost blinds him. After months indoors, even soft daylight is much too bright for him. Like bats and ugly things that live in dark places, Ben feels raw, exposed out here. The long shadows on the snow make sharp, brutal outlines. The shadows the crags and contours in his face make in the morning light must be hideous: blade of a nose, blackness pooling in eye sockets as black as the holes in a skull. *Oh God.* Poor Mother, bopping downtown in her little blue Toyota with her mind on Ben, who couldn't even survive four months in Europe without getting shipped home wrecked. Poor Delia, pretending that all he needs is a little rest when he is being eaten alive from the inside out, pretending because in her worst dreams she can't conceive of the misery that devours him.

'Time off,' she tells the girls at work in that sweet, uncertain voice of hers. She speaks in his tones. 'He's taking a little time off to get his head together.'

How can she know what the inside of his head is like?

'In the fall he's going away to Wesleyan.'

Sure. Like I'm going to be around by then.

She'll tell her boss, 'Why, he got up and went out for a long walk today. I was tempted to take a comp day and go with him.'

She doesn't have to know that he'll only go as far as he can without being seen. He needs a bell like a leper's, a sign to keep people away. For their protection he'll have to turn and run back to the house: the monster slouching back in, trying to get unborn. He can't let the neighbors see him, much less the neighbors' kids. Not the way he is, OK? Ben won't do that to anyone. Even though to look at him you might not know it, he is vile.

Never mind what you think. Ben knows.

He's scared to death that whatever he is, it may be contagious. The eyes, yes, the eyes that corrupt, unless they are the eyes that turn you to stone. He is a pestilence. Yes, he is crazy. No, he isn't crazy. He is simply changed. No. Removed from life as most people know it.

He knows what he is now. Hideous. Hideous and powerless. Ben Messinger, who will go to elaborate lengths to spare the outside world. Who'll do anything to keep you from having to see.

Who's a little surprised today because he's been out in the air for at least ten minutes and his face hasn't begun to rot – at least he doesn't think it has. The palms Ben turns to the sky are pale and smooth, not scored with lines and covered with greasy, matted hair, as he imagines them. *If I can make it this far . . .*

The open sky is thunderous.

Terrified, he is out of breath and already tottering. *If I can make it this far maybe I can make it to . . .*

Then a car rounds the far corner. Like a scorpion scuttling back under its rock, Ben darts for the house and after a moment of panic in which he fumbles with the unyielding lock, shuts himself inside again.

6

It's Wednesday; Clair goes in early because she hasn't been to the gym since Nick came home from the hospital. Only the access road is plowed; the alleys and paths are deep in snow and ice, the history of this year's storms encrusted in layers. This is the side of Administration Hill that outsiders never see.

Getting out of the car, she is arrested by movement on the glassy incline leading to the crest. The sun is in her eyes so that what she sees presents itself in silhouette. A little chain of people is marching to the top of the ridge. Stiff, deliberate, they move as a unit, as if some distant drummer is tapping out a beat. Students. Anybody who can get students out at this hour . . . It is an odd exercise for kids in college in the Nineties, struggling up the slippery incline single file. They look archaic, stylized, like figures marching across the pediment of a primitive temple. The little procession goes cautiously over treacherous ice, each marching with his right hand on the right shoulder of the marcher in front. The commanding figure at the head of the line is taller than the rest; he takes large steps while the kids in his wake slip and falter but keep climbing, kept in place by the continuity of energy: hands clamped on shoulders, link on link, the mysterious chain drawn by its leader.

Then the man in charge stops. The marchers stop. They are at the top. He shouts. They raise their hands to their heads and for a minute Clair thinks it is their faces they're tugging at, pulling them off like so many rubber masks. Then she understands that they've made this climb blindfolded. At a word from their leader the students turn and look back at the distance they've come. Even from here Clair hears them shouting with joy as they cluster around the man who has brought them to this point. With the passage completed, he swivels to survey the hillside. She knows that laugh.

Still shading her eyes, Clair squints to see who.

Of course it is Will Strait.

There is something about this moment that seems private, arcane. Is she supposed to be seeing? Not seeing? She forgets that without the sun in his eyes, he can see her clearly. 'Clair!' he shouts with a sweeping, grandstand wave. Not his fault she doesn't respond; she turns and goes into the gym.

When she gets to her office at eight the door's already open; little Gig Jamison is riffling through the papers on her desk.

'What's going on? How did you get in?'

He chokes and can't answer.

'What are you doing here?'

Withdrawn, scrawny Gig, who's never said two words to her, lifts his head with a visionary smile. 'Looking for something for Professor Strait.'

This makes her angry. 'Well you won't find it here!'

He flinches as if she's hit him; she can see the blood rushing under that thin skin. The outlines of his head blur – he's shaking with embarrassment. Unlike her freshman interns, this student is closer to child than man; it's as if all his nerves are too close to the surface, raw and exposed, quivering and vulnerable. The hurt look makes her want to send him home to his mother until he's big enough to take care of himself. Her voice softens. 'I'm sorry, Gig. I can't have students rummaging in here.'

'Yes, ma'am.' His voice is so low she can hardly hear.

Poor kid, this wasn't his idea. He looks so whipped that she tries to make a little conversation to ease him on his way. 'You're in Professor Roeg's class?'

He looks a little less like he's about to cry. 'It's Professor Strait's class now.'

'Was that you guys out there on the hill today?'

He nods.

Clair tilts her head. 'What was that?'

'An exercise in trust,' he says, and with that same visionary look he gave her when she came in, Gig blurts, 'It's a really good class,' and escapes before she can make him talk any more.

Later that morning George Atkinson calls. The pretext is his commencement speech, which she usually writes. He says, 'It's never too soon to start.'

Clair takes notes with the sense that he's writing his valedictory and says, 'Are you planning to leave us, George?'

'Anything I say would be premature.'

'This is premature. Commencement's months away.'

He clears his throat and in the tone of a busy man, moves on. 'Another thing. Free up about ten pages; something's come up.'

'You've got to be kidding. The issue's closed.'

'Not the winter issue. Your next one. Spring.'

'It's tight but I'm keeping your column open, George. I've got something major coming in and I can't spare an inch.'

'This isn't for me,' he says. 'It's for you. Something you're really lucky to have. He's bringing it over after his ten o'clock.'

'George, what are you talking about?'

'He took some convincing, but Will's agreed to let you use his chapter on Peggy Guggenheim's collection.'

'George!'

'This is a major coup. He's giving us a chance to publish before his book comes out. Don't worry, my office is paying for the color separations on the art. Out of the discretionary fund.' When she doesn't leap at this he adds, 'I'm counting on you to find a way. He's a real addition, Clair. We're anxious to keep him here.'

This leaves her in an ambiguous position. The entire April issue is committed to a discovery in genetics made by a medical team who are next in line for a Nobel; loyal alumni, the doctors are releasing an article to her to run at the same time that the technical paper appears in the *New England Journal of Medicine.* It can't wait, but here's George pushing her to bump it for a faculty member, the kind of academic logrolling she won't do. Say no and it makes her look mean. Say yes and the *Alumnus* turns into the kind of provincial promotional slick she hates.

'Tell him I'll look at it.'

'I'll be expecting advance proofs,' the president says.

'I *said,* I'll look at it.'

Strait is in her office within minutes. He finds her alone.

The man walks in like a star, grinning and confident of his welcome. It's remarkable, how thoroughly he fills the space, smiling even though she hasn't looked up, pretending to be reluctant to bother her, impatient but holding back in a little miracle of control, like an actor pretending to hold back. He is impeccably scrubbed, trimmed, brushed and buffed to a high polish like a cherished piece of art. She doesn't recognize the aftershave.

'Is this a bad time? Geo said you were ready and waiting.'

'*Geo?*' This makes Clair look up. 'Oh, you mean George.'

'He said you'd be honored.'

Hey, the man is new here. Don't blame him for unleashing George. Then because it's a nice smile, easy and disingenuous, she says, 'Oh, George. Don't pay any attention to George. He's always promising favors he can't deliver.'

He chooses not to hear what she's telling him. 'I hear your magazine reaches everybody that matters. Just what I need.'

'Look, we're full up. I'm committed into next year.'

'Unless you tear up an issue and make it over for something major.' He weights the next words. 'Like the senator's piece.'

'Who told you I did that?'

'Oh, Geo and I got talking. He says when it's important, you'll make room. What your leader wants, your leader gets, right?'

'I don't know what he told you, but . . .'

He brings a manila folder out from behind his back with an expansive grin. 'I'm looking forward to working with you.'

'I'm sorry, George spoke too fast. I really am locked in.'

'Don't say that until you see what I have.'

He's getting too big for the room. He's getting so big that she says, 'Tell you what. Leave it. I'll look at it and get back.'

'I'll wait.' He pulls a chair over and sits down. 'I don't mind, I've got nothing but time. Nick's class isn't till one.'

'I have a lot of other stuff to . . . Nick's class?'

'Joint meeting with my Vic. Poets. Poor guy looked like he needed a break.'

'If you'll just leave it, I'll get to it as soon as I can.'

'No.' His voice is getting bigger too. 'I'd rather wait.'

Clair doesn't usually end up doing things she doesn't want to do, but this is what she's doing now. Alone with him, she is surprised by how much space Strait occupies; it's like having a glossy show horse or a bronze of a war hero planted by her desk. Where he has been flattering, complaisant, now the outsider is fixed in concentration, bearing down as if he can will her to do what he says. While Clair skims his article the silence is intense. She can't even hear him breathe. The thing isn't badly written, he's a graceful writer, but it's thin, like something turned out by a publicist hired to promote Will Strait; she starts flipping the pages.

He shifts impatiently in his chair.

If he thinks she's reading too fast, too bad. He goes to the layout table and spreads his glossies, printed on that special Japanese paper that hypes colors and makes them sing. When she puts the piece back in the folder he summons her with a jerk of the head. Pointing out the paintings, he first-names the artists like best friends. 'Peggy had fabulous taste. You know we were close.'

'Will, I'm sorry but I can't run this.' She tries to hand him the folder and when he smiles but won't take it, drops it on the table. 'I'm overcommitted and it's not our kind of thing.'

'Your April issue will be fine.' His expression zigzags; it won't stay in one place. 'If I have to, I can rewrite.'

'I'm sorry. It's fine, but it's wrong for us. George made a mistake. We don't do scholarly articles. Policy.'

'But you made the policy. You can change it whenever you want. For something important.' He is not used to being refused. He taps the folder. 'Like this.'

It's a perfectly civilized exchange but Clair finds herself putting the table between them; relentlessly charming as he is, she finds herself gauging the distance between herself and the door, herself and this Will Strait. Chill, Clair. He isn't going to hurt you. The worst he can do is try and charm you to death.

'I told you, it's not the kind of thing we do.'

'Yes it is.' He moves so quickly that she jumps. Oh. He's only picking up the folder. He circles the table and thrusts it at her. 'Keep it. Keep it and count yourself lucky,' he says.

Then Ginny Arnold asks them to dinner. 'Nothing special, just a little party for Mary's replacement. He's wonderful,' Ginny says with a proprietary air. Pretty, directionless Ginny is possessive now. 'He's so lonely.' Confidential. 'He loves you and Nick.'

'You've had him over?'

'Twice. We like him a lot,' Ginny says. Ordinarily Clair loves parties, get-down talk in their friends' cosy, cluttered living rooms, but something about finding Strait at the center of her and Nick's inner circle makes her hesitate. Surprise? Ginny's color is brighter today; she could be offering house seats to a Broadway premiere. 'Saturday night.' Ginny's – what? Hustling her. 'We're expecting you.' Like George, who hustled her to run that piece. As if somebody is pulling the strings.

It makes her say, 'We can't.' There's no room for a polite lie. Everybody in this tight enclave knows what everybody else is doing on any given Saturday, who's stuck in town, who's free, who isn't and why. Whose car is parked in front of whose house. They feed on each other, fueling their lives with these parties, tending the never-ending story with pieces of their lives.

The fun is as manufactured as it is frenetic: festivity for its own sake. In spite of fiascoes, every party is built on hope. The air in these winter rooms is heavy with the freight of expectations. Unspoken wishes blossom like hothouse flowers. We've been together for too long; we'd give anything to make one of these nights come out differently. They never do. Still we dress up for each other and meet: men whose wishes are encoded in their costumes, Shepler's or Armani or J. Press; women surprised by the shock of cold legs in sheer stockings pick their way over the ice in unaccustomed high heels or sit in each other's hallways and grapple with snow boots so we can make a star's entrance in shoes we'd rather carry than spoil. Festivity turns us into tremulous kids who exchange makeup samples and shop the catalogs and study each other's jewelry in the hope that each entrance we make may turn out to be *the* entrance, and whatever comes next will be a surprise. In this enclosure a new face is a magnet. Introduce an outsider and old patterns shift. We dance harder, act better because he's watching us; the old equation is altered by the addition of the unknown, the mathematical possibility of a different outcome, intimations of life in a larger world.

'It's for Will. He especially asked for you.' Ginny is, wait, like a public relations hack, she's *working* Clair. 'You're his favorite couple in all Evarton.'

'I'm afraid we have to say no.' This makes Clair feel small.

'After everything he's done for Nick it's the least you can do.'

She should be grateful to the man for taking up the slack; Nick doesn't have to meet Mary's classes or do Mary's job. Mary's orphaned students have quit coming around to Nick for extra help. What's more, even though pneumonia left him drowning in departmental paperwork, he's surfacing, thanks to Strait. Still Clair will not be manipulated. 'I'm sorry, we can't.'

'I think you'd better, Clair.' Ginny's voice drops to an intimate rasp. 'If you want to know the truth, Clair, the poor guy's afraid you and he got off on the wrong foot.'

'I don't know what gave him that idea.'

'Is it something he said?'

'Nick's in over his head right now, OK? We'd better pass.'

'Oh, if it's Nick you're worried about, he's already accepted,' Ginny says. *Gotcha*. 'Didn't he tell you? He promised Will.'

It is like the first pebble in an avalanche. Mary's misery dislodged certain portions of the community's inner life; everything in their frozen world shook loose and moved a fraction of an inch so that the details in the picture are the same but slightly off center, a fault that can't be rectified in overheated rooms in subzero cold. Health, or is it wholeness, will have to wait for spring. 'We'll be there,' Clair says through gritted teeth.

There is a moment when Wanda arrives to babysit in which Clair and Nick exchange looks. 'We don't have to do this.'

He gives her that Eagle Scout look. 'Yes we do.' Honorable Nick has promised. He won't be turned. The man would go to a roach parade in west hell if somebody expected him to show the flag. For him, life marches in order; sometimes Clair thinks he soldiers on as if the thing that matters most is soldiering on.

Clair leaves instructions and they go. It's sleeting. Their eyeballs freeze before she and Nick navigate the half-block to the Arnolds' house with their filled ice bucket and Clair's mushroom pâté. Their friends are marshaled: Lauren and Josh Gellman, who got married in college and are so close that they finish each other's sentences; her best friend Jane and rumpled Gabe Stevenson with his Smokey the Bear hug; Clair and Nick. It's the same dinner party that moves from house to house most weekends of their life. Ginny's put an extra blonde rinse on her hair. Her eyes are still pink from crying and her eyelashes stand in spikes but her smile and the flush at her throat suggest that whatever it was she and Pete were wrangling over before the guests came, they've already made up. Pete holds Nick off, gauging his recovery. 'Man, you almost died.'

'No he didn't!'

Sometimes you have to go out to hear the truth. They've both been deep in denial. Clair overhears him admitting, 'I guess I got totaled. Al says it takes weeks to get back up to speed.'

Pete mutters to Clair, 'I just want you to know, Ginny and I have never been closer. Ask her to show you the ring.'

She doesn't have to; Ginny's in the kitchen with her hand spread under the Tiffany shade while Jane tends the stove and Lauren touches the sapphire band and says all the right things.

Clair peers over Jane's shoulder. 'Eleven *filets*. Who else is coming?'

'Vance and Gail Garson, if you'll excuse it. Will's dying to get to know them better.'

Like a gyroscope, Clair remembers what he said and automatically corrects. 'Maybe he meant get them to know us.'

'We already know them,' Ginny says. 'But the *Garsons*, in our own little living room. Do you think I ought to warm the plates?'

'I think you ought to give them skim milk and soda crackers; one pound of us is worth a ton of them.'

It is Jane who grins. 'There's already a ton of me.'

'You're not heavy, you're just . . .'

'Substantial. Ooop. I hear the bell.'

'It's them.' Ginny slips into overdrive. 'Unless it's him.'

It is him, Will Strait, new in English, so very like us.

The arrogance that surfaced in her office last week has disappeared. He's engaging, boyish and apologetic, so sorry to be late but Vance and Gail. Well, you know Vance and Gail. Thus Will Strait sets the parameters for the evening, moving into the knot of insiders so easily that when the Garsons arrive, late and studiously underdressed for what is, after all, a Saturday night party, Clair understands that in the rhetoric of the distinction *us* and *them*, Strait is allied with the *us*. After all, he's faculty: PhD with a heavy teaching load; like us he'll have to steal time to write his books. Never mind the cashmere coat and the Oxford cloth shirt that's custom cut; he's just a working stiff, like us.

At dinner he brings Nick on. 'Clive Barker. I'll meet you and raise you Stephen King.'

Nick laughs. 'Child's play. Ramsey Campbell to you,' doing counterpoint in a way that makes them both shine.

'Who knows what evil lurks in the heart of man?'

'That's a different story.'

Gabe says, 'You two are so good you ought to go on the road.'

'A team,' Nick says. 'We may collaborate on a book,' and Strait gives Clair a targeted smile, while at his side beautiful Gail Garson tilts her head as if she's trying hard to keep up with the class but can't find her place in the text.

It all seems easy and natural, listening to Will discussing departmental business with Nick's measure of earnestness. Laughing, he segues into a three-minute impression of his stint in Venice, doing all the voices and acting all the parts: explaining Tiepolo to kids who think Leonardo is a rock group, playing tour guide, clinical psychologist, campus cop, coping with a disparate bunch of post-teens intent on losing passports, getting puking drunk and trampling public monuments and falling into the Grand Canal. The tone is light, self-deprecating. Right. Surrounded by her friends, with the Garsons yearning at the periphery to underscore her own wealth in friendship, Clair thinks she must have read him wrong.

Give him a break, she thinks as the men laugh and Ginny leans forward with that smile. Still, deep in the Arnolds' sofa after dinner, warmed by her friends' good food, surrounded by her own and riding along on the evening, she watches him. He's too perfect. The part of her that stands back and judges can't stop waiting for him to say something wrong.

No. Not wrong. She's waiting for Will Strait to say anything she can pull out and identify, listening for the first false note without even being sure what it will sound like when it comes.

But Strait has pulled the Garsons into the circle and in a feat of diplomacy, or rhetoric, has made them characters in his story about a party at River House in Manhattan, which he follows with a story about skiing in Gstaad, high-roller stories told with the ease that suggests old money. Pete and Gabe and the others lean forward slightly, pulling with him as if Strait has just cut the ribbon at the opening of the bridge between the two cultures – the shabby academic and the glitzy circles they only read about in the style section of *The Times* and *Vanity Fair*.

He's just about to turn the two worlds into one where they will all be welcome; it is a little miracle.

Gabe sighs. 'Bellagio. I'd love to go to Bellagio.'

'Well, there's no reason you shouldn't,' Strait says. 'I'll write a couple of letters.'

Pete says, 'I wouldn't mind being invited to that conference in Prague,' and Ginny's eyes glitter like Czech crystal when Strait says he'll start the machinery. Even Nick develops wanderlust. Why shouldn't they summer in London? Will's English friends would be happy to loan their flat. Strait knows how to make people see what he sees. It is like a curtain lifting, and the icebound group fades out of yet another smalltown evening and into the best of the best of all possible worlds, a parallel universe in which escape from Evarton is easy and return is sweet. Strait makes them believe they can go out and conquer and get home safe for Sunday night TV.

He gets up to refresh his drink and, no surprise, Ginny gets up to refresh her drink, following him out to the sun porch where Pete keeps the bar. Her green eyes are too bright; her lipstick is orange against her translucent skin. Bending to hear what she's trying to tell him, Strait murmurs something that makes her smile.

Pete lifts his head like a deer at the beginning of hunting season, fixed by the sound of the first shot.

Strait handles it gracefully, showing open palms. Keeping Pete's restless wife talking, he draws her back into the living room as his host relaxes and looks into his big hands with an unexpected smile. Then as smoothly Strait moves to the sofa, sitting down next to Clair.

'That was nice with Ginny.'

'Trouble, waiting. I recognize that look.' Modestly, he changes the subject. 'Nick is everything around here, isn't he?'

'Close. He has a lot of irons in the fire.'

'Everything to everybody,' Strait says. 'Phenomenal. He never misses a beat.'

Clair looks over at Nick. The lines along his mouth are drawn thin. 'It's taking a lot out of him.'

'Don't worry. I've got the extra classes covered. I'll take up all the slack I can. Your man is too good to have to worry with logistics.' He pauses to let her absorb this. Then, as if this, too, is transactional, he says, 'I'm so glad you reconsidered.'

'What?'

'My piece. Between us, I need it to sell Rizzoli on my book.'

'George said your book was about to be published.'

'I never said that. If you want to know the truth, it all hinges on this.'

She stiffens. 'I told you, it isn't right for us. Look, if it will help, I'll get my friend at the local paper to let me do an interview.' Why is she trying so hard to appease? 'My stories get picked up by AP; most of them go out on the national wire.'

'No,' he says too quickly. 'No interviews.' It takes the man a second to recover that worldly, confidential tone that has pulled her friends into his orbit, making them shine like little moons. *Between us.* 'I'm much too elusive.' When he smiles at her like that it is as if they are alone in the room.

But it's too late for Clair, whose curiosity has snagged on a rough place and won't let go. 'What was it with you and Mary?'

'Who?'

'Mary Roeg.'

'Oh. Poor lady. Terrible story. I never met her,' he says.

'I saw you with her on Ethan Frome night.'

'No you didn't.'

'Right before she snapped.'

'You must have seen somebody else.'

'How did you get to Evard anyway? How did you hear about Mary and this job?'

His face darkens; it's like watching an eclipse. 'I said, no interviews.' He raises his hand so abruptly that she flinches. Then even though she sets her jaw so firmly that her teeth grate he curves his index finger and runs his knuckle down her cheek, saying in that tone she recognizes but cannot identify, 'You know, you're a very pretty girl.'

'I'm not a girl.'

'Yes you are. A lovely, lovely girl.' Strait's tone is still easy, light. He just leans forward slightly. Making her aware of his power. It is immediate, physical. Sexual. 'I'm so glad we're going to be friends.' Then he leans back.

Something new has come into the space between them.

Then it's nothing.

'Look. Here's our host.'

Grinning, Pete circles the room with fresh glasses and a bottle of port. Strait touches Clair's arm as if nothing has happened between them. 'Excuse me.' He gets to his feet with that smile and instead of giving the flowery toast she half-expects says, 'You're all wonderful.' He drinks. 'Thank you all.'

There is an awkward little silence. Nick lifts his glass: 'Thank *you*.'

But Strait ducks as if dodging compliments. 'When Mara gets here I'll pay you all back. I want to celebrate this place. Lobster. Champagne. The best rock band we can get.' Embroidering as if the air in the room hasn't already quickened, he lifts their hearts. 'Dancing party. I hope you'll all come.'

Not knowing the name of the game but anxious to be first, Gail Garson flows to her feet. 'But not before you come to ours.'

As if they see the door to the big world opening, the people of Evard flush with excitement and accept on the spot.

Then at the end of the evening they cluster in the hall behind the Garsons in their raccoon coats, lining up in pairs to say good night like couples leaving the ark.

Under the front porch light, Strait is standing alone.

Sad, she tries to tell herself. No, lonely, here without his wife. No. What? What disturbs her most is what she does not know. Something's the matter, she thinks, and in the circularity of self-examination is delivered back to the point where she started this evening, at odds because something is wrong and without knowing what it is, without being able to name it, she can't make Nick understand.

It's late. They're both tired. She tries anyway. 'There's something about him.'

Nick sighs. The efforts of the week are written on his face. 'Did he do something? Say anything?'

'No. I don't think so. That's the trouble, I don't know.' She doesn't. Her mind keeps sawing back and forth over the rough places, edges that don't quite match. On the short walk home she took apart the evening's conversation and replayed it line for line and she still doesn't know.

'You don't like him because you don't like him because you don't like him.'

'Something like that.'

Nick's jawline is too sharp; he's lost weight. He brushes back that fair hair with an impatient gesture. 'This isn't about him,' he says. 'It's you. It's all or nothing with you.'

He's right. She is an absolutist. In his own way, so is Nick. At the moment they are absolutely on opposite sides. She steps up to the mark. 'Well what if it is?'

Nick surprises her. He doesn't argue; he doesn't fire a shot; he only says, 'For me. Just leave it be for now.'

He has his arms out. And because they've been married for so long that they can fight and kill each other and still love each other absolutely, she moves into them. They can fight and kill each other and then go to bed and forget in love, but this does not prevent Clair from saying, 'If you promise to watch your back.'

7

God I miss Teddy.

The first, best friend Clair ever made at Evard is off in Miami giving a paper; dear Teddy, who will love you for ever, comes equipped with an exquisite self-protective mechanism that kicks in just when you need him most. Love him, enjoy him, but maybe Jane's right when she says, 'When there's trouble, color him gone.'

But what exactly is the trouble here?

It's too dark to see. The winter sits on her shoulders like a great shaggy beast, holding her down. Nick's coughing again; the kids have winter rashes and her skin's so dry that her face feels like a mummy's face. The world is obscured; there is nothing outside but ice. She gets up in the dark and comes home from work in the dark. It's too dark to think. It's too dark to make phone calls, too dark to begin anything and too dark to take Nick's face in her hands and try to make him see.

The season is a tunnel that allows no turnoffs, constricting, dim. Nick slogs along with his shoulders hunched and his head down, intent on making it through. His close call took more out of him then he'll admit; there's no margin for questions or argument. Today Clair begged him to stay home but he shook her off like a soldier leaving for the front. George has asked him to pick up the pieces for Ad Bishop; the dean's gone in for a biopsy, could be bad. George is running hard to get to Washington; in the order of merit and distinction – no, in the order of deserving it, Nick is in line for his job. How could he refuse an administrative request? Without wanting to want it, Nick wants George's job, one more particle among too many particles in this tunnel with no visible end.

What else is George asking for? Strait's Venice piece. Today Clair snapped. 'If you think it's that important, get it printed separately and we can piggyback on the next *Alumnus* mailing.' No. He wants it *in* the *Alumnus*, not inserted like those smelly cards that fall out of Betsy's fashion magazines.

'You know your budget's under scrutiny?'

Why so much pressure over such a small thing?

The women she depends on are distracted, as if packing for a trip to a distant planet. Decisions consume them: which hair would be right for the big event? What shoes? They are girding themselves for the Garsons' party as if only clothes credential them and death of the soul comes when you're turned away at the door.

These parties are fabled events, tales brought back by sailors, of Dom Perignon and Top 40 bands, lobsters you crack in the driveway with the heel of your shoe. People go to these things, but not people you know. The guests are imported – like wines, according to the Atkinsons, who've been to the Hedges exactly once. This is the first chance for ordinary civilians to see the inside of that expansive neo-Victorian with its east and west wings and turrets that beggar Camelot. The Garsons live like the early Scott Fitzgeralds, showing themselves to the people in designer clothes so low-keyed that we'd blanch if we could see which labels or guess how much, and then stomp into the deli for the Sunday papers playing *just folks*, except for their wraparound shades and parkas that fall open just far enough to give us a glimpse of the linings, chinchilla, we think, suggesting that the most elegant things are the ones people like us don't see. And look, our new professor is definitely special, because instead of enduring the usual do at the Atkinsons', hearing old George run on while we swirl tepid Freihoffers, we get to dress up and go dancing in the brownstone citadel.

Just imagine. Us going up the hill to that splendid place with its paintings and antiques, a far cry from our tacky stomping grounds on this side of Kingman's Gorge. Imagine. Us meeting chic people from circles we don't usually travel in. Listen, maybe we'll get to be friends. The great and the near great will beg us to call next time we're in the Big Apple or on the coast. Imagine, us. Stuck in this hick town, when there's a whole world out there.

70

Imagine us hanging out with these trendy people who come to us fresh from *The Times* Style section and the pages of *Vanity Fair*. This stylish new guy is opening doors for us.

The Garsons – No. Our new friends Gail and Vance. Good old Gail and Vance – are presiding at the marriage of the community to Will Strait.

Could be the Garsons are – could they be – *stooping*? They have better things to do than entertain the likes of us. They act impressed by the plethora of PhDs, but there's an edge to their praise because Gail and Vance hate what they envy and in a complex act of insecurity console themselves with that superior look that says: We could buy and sell you. We could buy and sell all of you.

At least Clair thinks so. In ordinary circumstances she'd refuse, but circumstances haven't been ordinary since Mary's collapse. George expects her to assign a photographer for the *Evardian* and write a few lines for the *Dispatch*. Under the circumstances, which are sliding around so fast that she can't figure out exactly what they are, it would look bad if she said no.

The pressure is intense. Her friends turn to her with slitted eyes, shiftily asking, 'What are you wearing?' as if there's a prize for the right answer and the wrong one's going to send her down a chute into the snow.

In the presence of other women, even the ones she's close to, Clair's always been slightly off balance, like a gawky kid or a sparrow in a pigeon coop. *Not like them.* Maybe when she moved through puberty to adulthood her outsides grew up but her insides stayed young: awkward, curious and irreverent. Different from the rest of the flock. If they find out, they'll peck her to death.

God, I miss Teddy, she thinks morosely, and retreats to the office with a sense of relief.

When she skates through a welter of comics to reach her desk, when she finds computer games loaded on the office system or has to sift through candy wrappers for her phone slips; when she walks into the middle of a joke and gives the punch line an extra flip that makes everybody laugh she thinks: These are my people, yes. And this is my place. The students she works with are more like her than she is like her adult friends. Playful and flexible, still at the brink, they're aggressively in flux. Like me. Like Teddy. Looking at her friend she can't imagine him old.

Sam and Fred are in the publications office all right, along with Gig Jamison with his stammer and his funny walk, but instead of entering alumni class notes for the next issue, typing information off the forms that come in with class dues, her interns are opening windows on something else. The screen is a gorgeous color.

'Hi guys.'

They're surprised to see her. Blinking, Fred runs fingers down his stubbly face. 'Wuow, Clair. Is it that late?'

'It's this early.'

He grins. 'Outta sight. All-nighter.'

Sam pushes aside the Dunkin' Donuts cartons. 'Sure flies when you're having fun.' The rubble on the floor is ankle deep: pizza boxes, crumpled printouts, a pyramid of coffee-stained styrofoam cups. Her kid friends are sprouting day-old beards.

Weedy Gig touches his bare chin with a proud little smile. He is different today; his eyes have that hacker's glaze. 'Come see.'

She wades through paper to look over their shoulders. What she sees on the screen is intricate and amazing. 'I thought you guys were keyboarding class notes.'

Sam says quickly, 'We did everything that's come in so far, it's just, we have this other thing?'

Fred says, 'It's major. Major!'

Shy Gig is so caught up in the convolutions of the design that he forgets himself and answers. 'Everything depends on it.'

She looks over his shoulder. The device is intricate, confusing. Multiple windows open and close on the screen like anemones. 'What's this?'

'Special project. Gig needed more memory than we've got in our PCs. Like, mega, megabytes.'

Fred says, 'It's for class.'

'Mary's class?'

Sam grins. 'Not any more.'

Gig's face burns with pride. 'It's for Will. I mean Professor Strait.' It's as if he and the others have spent the academic year – no, their entire lives – preparing for this moment, and every minute with poor Mary was dead time.

For her scuzzy nineteen-year-olds, Strait has pulled the Victorians into the computer age. Using Adobe Photo Shop and a series of pictures of formal gardens combined with text, Sam and Fred and their withdrawn, brilliant little friend have conceived the Victorian novel as a boxwood maze.

72

Click.

Here are the doomed lovers. Here the antagonists.

And there at the remote, apparently inaccessible center, the menace that will not speak its name until the very end.

Stammering, Gig explains the parts he's still working out. Click the mouse to get into your favorite novel. Click and you're at the top of the Rochester house. Click again and you are in the presence of Mrs Rochester, who is crouched and ready to spring. Behold and be afraid. Then go back to the main menu because you may have the specifics but you haven't comprehended the maze. Flushed and driven, he's trying to tell her something more but words elude him and he runs his fingers through ropy tan dreadlocks, willing her to understand. The words explode. 'It's the key to everything.'

Sam says, 'Don't mind him, Professor Strait is his god.'

'Don't say that!' The kids don't see Gig's hand swirl in a swift, mysterious pattern, almost as if he's crossing himself; it is a little shock.

Fred grins. 'What d'you think?'

The program is intricate, seductive. Brilliant. 'Wild!'

'There's lots more, that you don't see.'

'It's all our professor. He's . . .' Filled with passion, Gig – Eugene, she thinks it is – stammers, grimacing. Anything to make her see what he sees. 'It's . . .' He can't finish. It's too much.

She says evenly, 'I see.'

'All good things are constructed around a secret,' Fred says as if this is a given, and concealment and delayed discovery are a matter of course. 'The whole thing is finding it. At least that's what Will says.'

Fred demonstrates. Open a window. That isn't the secret. Open another. This isn't it either. Open a third. This may look like it, but it isn't. You won't find the secret until the novel wants you to, in that terrifying confrontation just before the end. In its own way the complex construction is quite wonderful – seductive, elegant, drawing you in to the discovery.

At the center lies the secret blooming red, spreading like a poison flower.

The design makes Clair shiver.

But Gig is restless and muttering, intent on events to come.

'We've got to go,' Sam explains. 'Will's giving a double demonstration for two sections. His class plus your husband's class.'

'Why would he show it to Nick's class?'

'Special favor,' Sam says. 'You know.'

In seconds, they've packed floppies, printouts and gone. Fred waves. 'Later. Need some time with Will before it starts.'

These compelled scholars are the same scruffy intransigents who used to come in after Mary's classes doing Mary Roeg impressions so accurate that to keep from weeping, she had to laugh.

Fire, she thinks. For the first time since they started college, these students have caught fire. If Strait is this good with students, she tells herself, maybe I'm wrong about him and everybody else is right. *Koena horra?* I'd love to be wrong. It would be a relief not to roam around sniffing like an overzealous sheepdog – the only living thing on the mountain that smells the wolf.

'You pick the worst times to go away.'

Teddy's just back from the Queer Studies conference at the Fontainbleau. He and Clair have run the length of the post office with their arms spread; they feint three times, then meet in a hug – one of their running gags, but more than a gag. So glad to *see* him. Teddy laughs. 'Let go. People will talk.'

'Fuck people.' Clair stands back but won't let go. She's just so glad to see him with his fresh winter tan, and his hair wet from the shower, same dear Teddy Hart with his same rumpled, good-looking face, that same comic grin. 'I'm sick of people.'

Then he isn't grinning. 'Are you OK?'

'Not really.'

'You don't look so good.' Teddy pulls her outside. They can see their breath but nobody can hear. 'Is there something going on that I don't know about?'

'Yes. No. I don't know. This guy Nick hired.'

'Jack Nelson's friend.'

'You've met him, right?'

'Only at the interview. Big. Smooth. The Victorian flash.'

'If that's what he is. I don't know what he is.' She doesn't mean to make it sound urgent, but it is. 'What do you think of him?'

'The buzz is good. He looks OK.'

Clair's voice sinks. 'I think maybe he isn't.' This is as far out as she's come with anyone.

'Then what's the matter?'

'That's the trouble. I don't know.'

'Any outward and visible signs?'

'Not really.' Sighing, she waits.

Teddy wants to please her but he can't right now. Or won't. Like the friendly doctor with the repulsive medicine, he means well enough: *for your own good.* 'Look at it this way. He's picked up a lot of the pieces for Nick. Maybe you should give him a chance.'

She groans. 'Not you too. It's like the pod people around here. Everybody thinks he's wonderful except me.'

'Lay back,' Teddy says. 'Be cool. Right now he's hot because he's a novelty, but that never lasts. They'll get bored. They always do.'

'I'm not so sure.' She wants to sort it out but she can see ice forming in Teddy's freshly washed dark hair. At his back, students are going by with their heads down, burrowing through the ugly cold, but Teddy stands bareheaded in the frozen slush as if this is still Miami and it won't matter that his coat is open and ice is forming on his hair. 'We'd better get inside. You're going to catch your death.'

'Coffee.'

'I need you on this, Teddy. Your place or mine?'

So they feed the machine and take their paper cups into Teddy's cluttered, comfortable office at the top of the Humanities tower. It's like an overgrown kid's room with its stuffed Gila monster and twin porcelain dolls and alligator skull and ivory chess set and posters and family photographs and antique Star Wars mugs and three-D glasses and an upscale replica of the Batmobile and Persian rugs and exquisite prints all demanding equal space.

When she has him alone with the door shut, Clair thinks in spite of past experience, *the one person I can count on.* She tries to begin. 'I need to know what you really think of him.'

'You want the truth? I haven't thought about it at all. Been busy.' He smiles that crumpled smile. 'I've been kind of in love.'

'Oh Teddy!'

'In Miami.' He coughs apologetically. 'It took longer than I thought.'

'You were gone forever.' She's one of the few people Teddy trusts enough to talk about his love life; she asks, 'Who is he?'

He makes a face. 'It doesn't matter now.'

'I thought you were in love.'

'I was but now I'm not. You know how that is.'

She doesn't, really, but she loves him too much to let him know it's hard for her. 'That's so sad.'

'It's never sad at the beginning.' Teddy has that rueful look he shows only to her. Then he says something that makes more sense to him than it ever will to Clair. 'It's the nature of the game.'

'I wish . . .'

Teddy knows what she wishes. 'Don't wish.'

'I just wish you could be happy.'

'That isn't all you wish, so don't. You want me to be happy,' Teddy says; in some pain he spells out what is understood between them. 'But you don't want the details.'

'I'm sorry.' She looks down at her hands.

'People are who they are.' Teddy's tone is sweet and grave. This is the lesson he's tried all their lives together to teach her. 'It's your job to be OK with it.'

Then with that characteristic comic flip, Teddy releases her into laughter. 'Don't worry, I'm cool. Men are like street cars. If you miss one there's always another one coming along.'

Now it is her job to fill him in on the business of the last two weeks. 'Something is creepy and I can't tell Nick, at least not now. Even if I could it would only make him miserable.'

Teddy says, 'He tries so hard to do everything right that the last thing he needs to hear is that he's done something wrong.'

'And George is jerking us around. Phones at odd hours and no matter what, Nick's supposed to drop everything and go.' She sighs. 'Like he won't be our next president if he doesn't run over and hold George's hand while he waits for the senator's call.'

'Heir apparent, right?' Teddy is only half kidding.

'I hate it. You really think he'll get that government job?'

'That or something else. George has lots of feelers out. Dean of that, presidency of this. Boca Raton. If this falls through he's up for something in Boca Raton.'

'Boca Raton! But it's so *not enough.*'

'At this point he'll take anything.' Teddy shrugs. 'He's out of here so the big job's up for grabs. And Nick's first in line.'

'I don't know, Ted.' She sees herself standing by the curving stair in Betsy Atkinson's bottle green party dress, making nice at all those presidential receptions, memorizing Betsy's bright little speeches, having that hair. 'I like our lives the way they are.'

'Listen, Nick deserves it. He's given his life to this place. Cheer up, it could be fun. Could be a step up to being president of someplace warm. Or real.'

'I'd settle for bigger.' Clair says what she and Teddy say to each other around this time every year, locked in this ring of ice. 'We're so closed *in*.'

'Bigger would be good.' Teddy grins. 'So would different.'

'I wish.' Does she really? After a childhood spent in transit, she's rooted here. Turned into an agoraphobe, furnishing a place she loves and defending it like her cave. If anything pulled Clair out of this town, essential parts of her would rip.

But Teddy is trying to do her a favor here. 'It could happen. Look at it this way. Handsome. Responsible. Organized. Everybody knows Nick is right for this. Who else is right for the job?'

She looks at him: handsome, responsible, smart. Funny, but if pressed, Teddy can hide the funny part. 'You. You are.'

He nods; it's true. 'But Nick has a smart, good-looking wife.'

At some level she thinks if Teddy moves in a society where not much is permanent . . . Look at it this way, if he's given up hope for true love in his life, at least he can have power. 'You run all the faculty meetings for George. And the writers' program. Publish all the time. You've got just as much going for you.'

'Nick's personable. What you want to meet the public.'

'So are you.'

Teddy says pointedly, 'Family man.'

She still doesn't get it. 'You'd be terrific.'

'Not in this life.'

'Why not?'

'I said, *family man*.' Now Teddy looks at her dead on: how could you be so stupid? 'Have you ever seen a gay president? Of the US? Of anything? A president that's all the way out, I mean?'

'Sure I have. There's . . .' She rummages; it's embarrassing. She can't come up with one.

'They don't look at people like us when they're deciding things like that.' Teddy puffs his chest like a candidate. 'Got to please the constituency.' Then he goes on in conversational tones. 'Have you noticed how many guys stay in the closet until after they get tenurized?'

'Don't ask, don't tell?'

'More like: if somebody asks, lie.'

77

'But after they get tenure . . .'

His grin slides out of shape. 'Don't tell if you want to be famous for anything besides being gay.'

'It shouldn't matter!'

'It's a tradeoff, Clair. What we are for anything else we think we want.'

'It shouldn't make any difference.'

'It does.' Now Teddy is facing Clair directly and he is as serious as he has ever been about anything. He says carefully, so she won't mistake him, 'It's one of the choices you make when you come out. To forget about ever having certain things.'

'You'd be a terrific president. You would! Look,' she says in a new context, 'Don't ask, don't tell.'

He says gravely, 'That would be a lie.'

'That's terrible.'

His eyes look pale in his tanned face – pale and clear. He keeps his voice light. 'That's how it is.' Gently, he turns the conversation. 'But you came in bent out of shape over this guy Strait. What do you think is the problem?'

'The problem. Yes.' *Somebody's going to get hurt.* She recoils; where did that come from? But Teddy is waiting. This isn't the right answer but it's one of the answers. She says, 'Did you ever see *All About Eve*?'

Teddy looks at her sharply, waiting. They're almost there.

Then three things happen: in the hall somebody knocks and a man calls Teddy's name. She recognizes the voice, Will Strait's, as the phone rings – Teddy's Kafka class, wondering where he is. Ignoring the knocking (how long has Strait been out there, has he been listening?) Teddy picks up the phone and, pretending to respond to the babble at the other end, he puts his hand over the mouthpiece so he can address Clair's fears, and this is the third thing. His look is designed to make her feel easier when all it does is leave her feeling bereft.

'This isn't a movie,' Teddy says.

8

Out on the hill with Jane and the kids on yet another brutal afternoon, Clair thinks, I can't stand one more day of this. It's still February. The month that never ends.

Suspicion boils up and fills her; all this damn compression, no wonder she can't concentrate. So what is to come will be Clair's fault; tunnel vision leaves even the most vigilant so focused on survival that they don't see where the real danger is.

Heaped snow funnels the women into one of the few paths that has been plowed. Terrorizing their sisters, Davy and his pal Jake Stevenson cross-hatch the narrow path with their heads down and their arms spread, zooming like killer bats brought out by the encroaching gloom. Students sweating inside layers of wool crunch along the margins on desperate winter errands, heading uphill in the failing light while in the pit of shadow at the foot of the administration building, dark shapes stir.

The beginning of something the women will have to deal with later, but are too preoccupied to see.

It's the first time she's seen Jane in days. Her best woman friend has been tied up with realtors, driving Strait here, there. She's cut back on research time, just until Will finds a place. Jane and Ginny and even Lauren take turns driving him to malls and local antiqueries on the search for the perfect object for the new house. The man is spending thousands, ordering everything held for delivery until he has an address. The women attend this as if taking lessons: 'He has fabulous taste.' Rapt, they watch him prepare a setting for his wife Mara, who comes from old money and is used to the best. Her friends say exactly this to Clair, explaining why they can't drive Thursday or fill in for her at Meals on Wheels or take Nell and Davy on the usual afternoons: 'You know, Will's wife comes from old money. She's used to the best.' But all these conversations circle back on themselves, returning to Topic A. Her friends touch their faces uncertainly. 'The party. What do you think Mara Strait's going to wear?'

It's so dark Clair can't make out what the kids are doing. They are moving black blobs against the snow. She hears the boys making bat screeches; the little girls squeal. 'Mo-oom!'

Clair raises her voice: 'Knock it off, you guys.'

'I'm thinking about sequins,' Jane says anyway.

The women lurch and slide over a mixture of sand and ice that's thawed and refrozen in a cobbled mess of deformed footprints. Late afternoon and it's too dark to be out, too dark to do anything but stick to the path and keep her eyes on the ground, going along with her head bent and her shoulders hunched because this tunnel never seems to end.

Jane says, louder, as if there is nothing going on, 'I *said*, what are you wearing to the Garsons' party?'

'What? Oh.'

'Earth to Sailor, Earth to Sailor. What planet are you on?' Somewhere outside Clair's head her friend has been burbling in that light, amused way of hers. Party, bla-bla. Wardrobe, bla-bla. Jade earrings, bla-bla. Sequined shoes. It is Jane's pleasure to pretend that she dreams the dreams of an everyday housewife, not a mathematician who weighs problems so abstruse that even Gabe is left behind.

'Oh, the party. When is it?'

'Saturday week.' Jane's voice lifts as if it's actually sunny out. 'So what do you think? High drag or laid back? They're so *rich* it's hard to know.'

'Beats me,' Clair says, thinking, Jane. Maybe I can talk about this with Jane. 'Whatever you put on, you'll think it's wrong.'

'Clair, what's the matter with you?'

Her stomach aches. She can't get warm. The dismal sky is an exact match for the inside of her head. 'Don't worry, you'll look fine.'

Intelligent Jane wants the impossible. 'Glamorous would be good.'

'OK, glamorous,' says Clair, who wants it for her. 'Your silk with my sapphires.' If they just keep talking maybe she can talk about her suspicions with her best friend, who's been out in the car with him. Has Jane caught a false note in the music? Does she have questions of her own? Look, she and Jane even shop for each other, *I knew this would be perfect for you*; they wear each other's jewelry. Their kids sleep in the same beds. If she can count on anybody for a reality check, it's Jane.

'Your sapphires. Oh, Clair!'

'It's no big deal,' Clair says absently, trying to find some way to broach it. She can't figure out what makes her feel so guilty and furtive. Mean. A part of her is out reconnoitering. Both Nick and Will Strait are safely tied up in class. The kids are trying to make snow angels in the unyielding crust of ice that tops the snow. The beginning disruption on the steps of the administration building is too remote to factor. Even with college trucks strewing sand and students crunching past on urgent errands, she and Jane are essentially alone here. The day is on the wane. And this? It's like confession. Some things are easier said in the dark. She says carefully, 'Jane. About Strait.'

'Oh, you mean Will.'

'He's so smooth.' Clair lets her voice get maybe a little too heavy with significance. 'What do you really think of him?'

Her good friend responds with a question. Jane's voice has a hollow, actorish tone as if it comes from somewhere high in her skull: the tone that can rivet audiences, even in the back row. 'I don't know,' she says deliberately, 'what do you think?'

Yes, she should beware but Clair is deep in the tunnel. 'That's what I'm trying to tell you,' she says without telling her.

'What, Clair? What are you trying to say?'

How can she explain when she doesn't understand herself? As with Teddy, she can only start with part of it, but it is a different part. 'I don't know if he always says the same things.'

Jane's voice takes on an edge. 'What do you mean?'

'I don't know. I can't . . . I just, I just wonder what you really think of him.' She is riveted by – what, a distant cry? Something getting bigger – whatever's going on up there in the shadows at the top of Administration Hill. It sounds like a struggle to Clair in her exaggerated state, quick and savage, frightening: wolves bringing down a student, maybe. Cossacks attacking, a gang fight, a child or woman crying for help or only her imagination? It's too dark to tell. She looks to Jane. That old Karloff movie. *Do you hear it too?*

But Jane's back is to the disturbance; she stands blocking the path in her bulky coat so Clair can't see around her and she can't make out what terrible encounter is going on up there, any more than she can know why the disruption leaves her so unsettled, shaky and distracted. Back, idiot. Down, Clair.

Then Jane says something that changes everything. 'I really don't get you, Clair.'

Up on the hill, somebody screams. Wild, Clair cries, 'What *is* that? What's going on?'

Jane won't even look. 'Nothing. Students, probably.'

'It sounds like something else.'

The trouble with Strait, the thud of blows in the boiling shadows, sounds of a struggle Clair can't see get all mixed up with each other in the dark; as a result her concentration is split when Jane comes in low and hard. 'It's just so odd.'

Poor Clair; she's like a motorist stalled on a railroad track, so busy trying to start the car that she can't hear the oncoming train. This jerks her to attention. 'What is?'

While her best friend Jane condemns her in somebody else's words. 'You know. You. He just can't figure it out. Especially when he's doing so much for Nick.'

Clair's voice is heavy with pain. 'Who can't?'

Then when it's clear she won't take the bait, Jane, whose tone is innocent of everything but loving worry over a best friend who's at odds with another, lays the words out for Clair one by one like so many glossy prints: scan, enter, E-mail to the entire world. This is the text with which Strait is damning her.

'He just can't figure out why you don't like him when he admires you so much.'

'Oh!' Without even being present, Will Strait has scored a direct hit. A noise comes out that Clair doesn't recognize.

Jane says, 'Are you OK?'

'I'm fine.' Her groan gets lost in the shouts coming from the top of the hill.

'Then relax,' Jane says. 'It's nice out here.'

'Getting late.' Gasping, she punches the words out. 'We'd better head back.'

'Soon,' Jane says absently. She goes on as if nothing has happened between them. 'By the way, I'm going to need your recipe for olive bread. Will's cooking tonight.'

But Clair is increasingly distracted by the sound of battle up there at the top of the hill: trouble in the shadows. Something is happening, something beyond her control.

'He's making his famous Market Street crab. Poor guy, stuck at the Evarton Inn like that, no family, sick of hotel meals, you knew he was lonely and you just let it go by, not like you, Clair, so we're cooking together and I thought of your olive bread.' Her eyes narrow possessively; she hits a tone Clair remembers from high school, *my boy friend now.* 'He's promised to teach the kids figure skating on the Garsons' pond.' Mine now. My friend. *Fait accompli.*

But there are worse things going on; up there on the stone steps there is a confusion of bodies, a violent tangle of arms and legs, the collision of metal and flesh. Clair can hear the thud of fists against leather and the *hoo* of escaping breath. Alarmed, she cries, 'He's *staying* with you?'

'As of tonight.'

Oh Jane, why are you so pleased. 'I see.'

She hears an ugly scream. What's happening up there? Somebody hurt? She doesn't know. The violence spills off the steps and onto the icy cement at the head of the path where the women stand, entangled, struggling bodies rolling down on them over rutted ice, a living knot gathering speed as it rushes downhill on a collision course while sweet Jane stands with her back to the jumble as if nothing has happened between them and nothing is happening up there, and smiles and smiles.

But the seething clot of people is closing on them, grappling with such fury that, disproportionately afraid, Clair cries 'Jane!'

'For God's sake what's the matter with you, Clair?'

'Up there!' With an effort she sorts out and identifies the figures as nineteen-year-olds zipped up in leather and caught in what looks like mortal combat, indifferent to the women standing in their way. Hurtling over the lumpy ice, the students are choking and pounding on each other, half wrestling, half punching with guttural shouts as on either side the little boys circle with wild bat screeches and in the distance, Nell begins to cry drearily.

It is not the end of the world, but it will do for today.

'I don't care what you think of him,' Jane goes on as if nothing has fallen between them and all hell isn't coming down, 'I think he's terrific. So does Gabe. Dammit, so does Nick. Get real!'

'Look out!' The fighting machine is almost upon them. Thwack. *Hoo!* Clair's mind races for the exits and finds them all closed. 'Jane, we've got to stop this!'

And her good friend says, 'Stop what?'

Just then the kids, because that's all they are, really, big kids, come crashing down on the women and as suddenly part and with tremendous absorption re-engage immediately below them on the path. Clair points. 'That! People are getting hurt!'

'Oh, that,' Jane says. 'Don't mind that.'

'The call box! The cops.'

'They'll just tell you to call Security. It's nothing.'

'Nothing! They're killing each other!'

'No they're not.' Jane smiles complacently. 'That's just Will's guerrilla theater group.'

'Will!' Clair studies the knot of bodies that almost overturned her before it split and flowed around the women and reassembled on the hard ice below. Like a statue of *Laocoon*, the fighting machine topples and breaks apart. Now the antagonists tangle in pairs, writhing like snakes on the glassy surface of the snow; one pair spills onto the margin close to Clair; she sees the one on top pounding the blood out of the other with his fists, unless he's just pounding the ice or doing push-ups over his partner – unless this is humping, an armored parody of sex so violent that she understands that even in the insulated world of Evard, these things are always close, so close that even at this range you can mistake one for the other and not really know.

Screaming, the others fall on their partners or antagonists and drag them off across the frozen snow.

Clair cries, 'Nelly. Dave!' She needs to have them close.

As she and Jane turn on the path and lead their children back downhill, they pass the spot. Happy and possessive, Jane is murmuring on about dinner, bla-bla salmon, raspberries and asparagus specially flown in, bla-bla hollandaise, but Clair isn't listening.

She's looking for the place. When she finds it she stops, studying the broken crust where this so-called guerrilla theater exercise fell apart. There is blood on the snow.

'What were they *doing*?'

'It's only an exercise.' Her friend turns, smiling. 'What else could it be?'

'It looked real to me.'

'Oh, you,' Jane says with love. And this is how her best friend dismisses Clair and all her anxieties. 'You know what your problem is? You worry too much.' Jane is talking about more than one thing here and they both know it. 'You get all hung up on things that don't mean anything.'

Then she is invited to Betsy Atkinson's for lunch. 'Just us two.' They have sandwiches in the little conservatory where dumpy, ageing Betsy with her girlish smile likes to spend her winters feasting her eyes on green plants. It's steamy, pleasant, close. Clair understands that although she doesn't want to leave Evard, this dutiful Fifties wife will do anything to hold the ladder for her man. She is scoping Clair out. Will she do as a president's wife? Clair supposes she ought to sit up straighter, arrange her napkin correctly, not cross her legs, think nice. Fuck this shit, Clair thinks, and is simply herself. If it's right, fine. If it isn't right, that's fine. She doesn't belong where she doesn't belong. She breathes too fast in the steamy air, watching the condensation freeze on the glass overhead where, as they talk, the noontime sky brightens as the sun gets high and the ice begins to melt.

'Washington! For a while it looked doubtful but, you know.' Betsy leans forward. 'George has made a very influential friend.'

'That's wonderful.'

'We've both learned something very important.' Betsy lowers her voice. 'In the circles those people move in, *who you know* is even more important than what you do.' She's full of it; Mayor this, Senator that, flossy hotel H.E.W. put George in when he went for the interview. As the little woman on the verge of becoming an old lady talks on, Clair understands what Betsy doesn't. George may be going to Washington but Betsy is too plain – too old – to make the transition; she just could be left behind when George moves to the capital on his first foray into the corridors of power.

It's sad. Clair wants to warn her; she wants to say something comforting but instead she listens politely as Betsy segues into Evard's petty official business, detailing the ritual duties of the president's wife – sherry at the opening reception, cocktail party for the freshman parents, homey gatherings for lonely frosh who come in groups until every boy – she calls them boys – has had the thrill of drinking Betsy's hand-pressed cider and eating Betsy's doughnut holes and her triangular sandwiches with tinted cream cheese. And of course the plants. Mesmerized by the pattern of frozen moisture and fresh droplets on the glass, Clair tunes out, nodding, Yes, Yes, until Betsy puts her hand on Clair's knee. And says in that sweet, motherly voice, 'But there is one thing.'

Clair jumps. *What*?

'You know the poor man can't figure it out . . .'

It's like an echo picked up on sonar. *Ping*. 'Don't!'

Too late. Sweet, dreary Betsy leans forward like a wrinkled college girl in her sweater and pleats; Betsy Atkinson, who always gets things wrong, sounds the attack and rings a change on it, to new effect. 'He can't understand why Nick doesn't like him.'

'Betsy!'

'Especially when he admires *Nick* so much.'

Take that! Clair blurts, 'Nick doesn't. I mean he isn't.'

'Everybody sees it,' Betsy says.

'It isn't Nick.' No! *It's me*. 'We aren't . . . It's *not* . . .' Alarmed by the power of the lie, Clair blunders on even as she realizes how bad this looks. How bad it makes Nick look. 'Nick *loves* Will Strait. He thinks Will is terrific.'

'I'm sure he does, dear,' Betsy says.

She thinks bitterly, nobody asks what's the matter with Strait that makes us so suspicious.

But the people she trusted don't trust her. Friends she's known all her life in this place are asking what's the matter with Clair?

Now she sees how Strait will destroy them: '*What's the matter with Nick?*'

'And another thing,' Betsy says. 'George asked me to speak to you about this article you refused. Poor Will—'

'Excuse me!' Clair lurches out of the conservatory before Betsy can ask her what's the matter. Her suspicions are everybody's business now, poor Will, so new to Evard and so bewildered by that lovely Clair's hostility that he's confided here, confided there, hates to say anything *but*, smiling as he lets the Sailors' good friends drag it out of him.

So it won't matter what Clair says or does. Strait's been there ahead of her.

Betsy's sweet voice drifts out after her. 'See you at the Garsons' dance?'

Clair runs for the parking lot without caring how often she slips and falls on the ice. All her disparate parts are in collision, alarms all going off at once. By the time she gets home she's jangling like the robot on *Lost in Space*, rolling into the house honking WARNING, WARNING, all flailing arms and flashing lights.

'Nicky. Urgent! We've got to talk!'

Clair crashes through the kitchen door still calling, 'Nick!' Then as she skids into the sunlit room panting, sweaty and flushed, she realizes there is a second person here in the kitchen with Nick and that for the first time in her life in this house, Clair has blundered into a private space.

Here is her husband Nick turning away from the stove with a surprised look. In the breakfast nook beyond, Clair can see her two children scowling at the interruption – *why aren't they at art class* – her two children playing with two beautiful blond children as her Nick brews coffee for the woman he has brought into her house. Whatever Clair has to say to him – whatever warnings or pledges of support – it's out of the question now.

WARNING, WARNING. There's so much she needs to tell. Be cool, be *careful*. All four children are laughing delightedly and the woman in her kitchen is tall, beautiful, composed, the simple fact of her presence making it impossible for Clair to do anything but apologize for blundering in.

Anything she has to say would look ugly here. She is silenced as completely as if she'd been pushed out of the room.

The lean, blonde visitor is so graceful that it makes Clair want to run out and wash her hair and put on silk and come back in and start all over again. Instead she stands there sweating in her woolly coat, panting and awkward in the presence of all this grace. She's like the robot when it goes haywire, standing at attention, going klunk. Klunk. Klunk.

The thin winter sunlight strikes golden bars across the faces of the visiting children, two towheads of different sizes with broad mouths and big grins, well-built and politely turned faces so sunny that it makes her own two look crabbed and withdrawn, while in the foreground the woman smiles at her unwitting hostess with that same pleasant, direct look. She is a bright presence here in the shaggy belly of winter, all delicacy and light, and distraught and sweating as she is, Clair thinks: How pretty they are.

But Nick is turning to her with a courtly little grin. 'Honey, this is Mara.' He looks so *pleased*. 'And this one's Chase and that one's Maddy. They're exactly the same age as ours.'

Even Mara's voice is beautiful. Modulated. Right. 'And they've really hit it off.'

Nick grins. 'They have. It's gangbusters.'

Clair wants to be polite; she does, but she feels so ugly standing here that all she can do is gasp, 'How . . .'

'They're just in from Venice. The Garsons drove them up from Logan last night.'

Clair tries to put her hand out. 'How do you . . .'

Tall, expensively dressed and beautifully assembled, the stranger in her kitchen is already advancing with that nice smile of hers; this graceful woman turns aside the formalities with an easy hug, embracing sweaty Clair and greeting her in that low, gentle voice that makes her feel awkward and shrill.

'I've heard so much about you. I've been dying to meet you. I'm Will's wife,' she says.

9

Ben

Wrecked as he is and rotting inside, jittering and miserable, Ben Messinger is secretly getting better.

It's the last thing he wants.

Every morning he scours his heart in the hope that some nameless pestilence has hold of him and he is already dying.

Instead, he is getting stronger.

Something's terribly wrong. He came home expecting to die. Nobody feels this way and lives. But he's still living. A terrible waste, after he's spent all these weeks waiting. Lying in bed with his eyes closed in anticipation of his own death. Every day he wakes up and taps his chest, listening for a rattle; he runs his fingers over the furry surface of his tongue and feels for buboes in the armpits: signs of black plague, maybe, or the red death. Suppurating flesh. Fresh pustules. Anything. If he neglects this cut on his hand, can he catch the strep that devours your body in a single weekend?

Inside, Ben Messinger is a charnel house – parts hanging in decaying strips, other parts pooling underneath, slippery and foul.

You'd think it would show in your face.

But when he takes his mother's hand-mirror and checks for signs, his face looks just the way it always did, only thinner. He will not look at the rest because he already knows what it is like down there. Unspeakable. God! All he wants is one gross symptom of disease. One encouraging sign. The mark of invading cancer, or buboes, the sign of some gross pestilence that will grab him and carry him off. Any symptom. Any sign that he's started the long downhill slide to the appropriate place for him, which is somewhere north of death.

Instead his face is filling out. He's restless all the time now. He can't stop twitching.

It's getting hard to keep this a secret. The minute his mother puts down the tray and shuts the bedroom door, Ben springs out of bed and does sit-ups. He knows this won't help him die; it might even improve him, but he can't stop himself. Energy builds in him until he can't stand the pressure. He will do anything to relieve it. When Delia's away at work he crashes out of his room and roves the house, stalking in circles like a trapped wolf.

His mother is going to walk in on him one day and find him doing frenetic push-ups. She'll catch him running in place.

He can't afford it. Delia would read it wrong. She'd tell herself stronger means better, when all Ben is trying to do is figure out how to do what he came home to do in the first place, which is eradicate himself. Let Delia catch him out of bed and she'd have him downstairs and out the front door before he could resist. 'A nice ride will do you good,' she'd say, frogmarching him to the car, talking nonstop to drown out his protests because she can't afford to hear what Ben has to say right now, or recognize the depression that crouches on his chest, waiting to smother him.

She probably thinks all he needs is a trip to a nice mall to put things into perspective. Her hopes chill his blood.

'Oh look, they have a Ruby Tuesday's.' No matter what he said or did Delia would drag him out of the car and make him go into the mall with her, keeping up that patter that is half threat, half desperate cheer.

Cheerful, *cheerful*, she'd drag him along. Foul Ben Messinger, terrified and gasping. Out in the open with his naked face showing. Show myself in a public place like that, no way, all those horrified shoppers gagging and staggering backward in their haste to get away from me. Delia's used to me, but they . . . He can hear them screaming. Throw my coat over my face for their protection. Nobody needs to see this, he thinks. Nobody needs to know what I am.

And all the time his mom would nudge him along with her sweet, blind smile as if life's a celebration and none of this was happening. 'Aren't we having fun, dear?'

With the mother's gift for oblivion, poor Delia treats him like an ordinary person. The truth of it would bury her.

When they peeled him off the walls of that European hotel and overloaded him with tranquilizers and stuffed him into the plane for Newark, all Ben wanted was to find the nearest hole. He wanted to dive in and pull the dirt in on top of him. Delia was at the airport to meet him. The people who ran the program had pronounced him defective merchandise and shipped him back to her but you'd think he'd come back from World War Two. Her hero. Her eyes filled from the bottom up and her mouth trembled. She clamped her arms around him. Sobbing, he tried to tell her, but no words came out.

There might not be any words for this.

Never mind. Delia didn't want to hear. She pulled him close so she wouldn't have to see. At the house she had to help him out of the car. Ben grabbed the banister. Hand over hand, he hauled himself upstairs, staggering toward his deathbed. He went to earth in his old room in the house where he grew up.

He pulled up the covers. Composed himself and waited to die.

His mother came into the bedroom and pulled down the shades. She tried to put her hand on his forehead. 'Poor darling,' Delia murmured while his belly shrank and his lips glued themselves tight shut.

Don't touch me. Don't look! He jerked away.

'Don't, dear. Things will look better in the morning.' She thought he'd come home to get well. She told herself this was the end of some strange illness he'd caught from drinking the water in that dirty foreign country. She couldn't know it was only the beginning of something much worse. She leaned closer. He turned his face to the wall. He just didn't want her to die of the poison.

'You need time,' she told them both.

All I need is to quit breathing out.

'All you need is time,' his mother said without question and, closing the door gently, she left him.

He fully expected to die. If half of hell is knowing what you want and not having it, the other half is trying desperately to do a thing and not being able to do it.

Now he has worse problems. He can't keep still. When Delia's at home he clamps himself to the bed like a monkey on a life raft so she won't find out the truth. He tries to keep still but even when she's in the room he can't keep from jiggling his legs under the covers, flexing his biceps. He can't stop drumming his fingers or flipping his hands on the covers, back to front, front to back, making fists so tight that tendons in his jaw twitch.

If his mother notes this, she hasn't said so. He's afraid she doesn't altogether mind him coming back in this condition. In a funny way, she has him where she wants him. When he left home for Europe last September her life as a mother was as good as over and what else is she anyway? She goes to the office to make money to live on, but motherhood is something else. She's put her whole life into this job. A single parent for years, uncertain and fearful, Delia sobbed all the way to the airport. When he came back in pieces in December she was upset, all right, but at the back of her eyes Ben saw flickering the savage glint of the single mother, surprised to get her job back, but secretly glad.

She has him to herself again. They've slipped into their old roles: lonely mom on a bad day, put the only son to bed and call in sick so you can stay home with him. *Sore throat? Let me take care of you.* A solitary in school, withdrawn and timid, Ben used to play to this. A cough would get him out of baseball tryouts or the math test or talking to savage sixth graders when being eleven was all they had in common. He could escape the exigencies. Confrontations.

But he isn't in sixth grade any more. All the worst parts of his life have surfaced here. They fill his bedroom, crouching in corners and crowding the bed, building up until they drive him out.

Delia laughs. 'You're up!'

Caught in the act, he wheels and lunges for the bed.

It's Saturday again. Her face shines. 'Feeling better?'

He turns his face to the wall so he won't have to see.

'Well you look better.'

But not well enough to kill myself.

10

Nick ought to be all better but he isn't. He's coughing again, won't go to the doctor; that would be admitting something. So would staying home from the Garsons' party for Will Strait.

'We don't have to go to this.'

'Yes we do.' She knows better than to argue when he gets that look. 'I know you don't love him, but Will's counting on me.'

'You'll catch your death.'

'I already had my death.' Nick throws a white scarf round his neck with that dashing grin she loves and says with that dogged Nick gallantry, 'I'm all better now.'

He looks some better; his color's back and his eyes are bright. Buzzed on pre-party cocktails at the Stevensons', crunching up the walk to the Garsons' house, Clair wants to believe.

Like a poppy in the snow, the Garson place is brilliant. Evarton is dismal in winter but this is not Evarton. The Garsons have touched old Anson Evard's house with money like a magic wand and turned it into something else. Lights bloom everywhere, gaudy in the night. Topiary animals lurch through the snow.

Clair comes through the carved Jacobean doors with the sense that for tonight, at least, the rules of winter are suspended.

The big house is like another country, rich with paintings and exotic, glossy interiors that beg to be photographed for shelter magazines. This place will never be published. The stylish Garsons are snobs. They don't want design students scratching at the double doors or art historians milling in the private rooms any more than they want potential thieves to know what they have assembled here. They don't even want tonight's guests picking up their *objets* or setting drinks on inlaid wood surfaces. The bar is in the marble foyer so the people of Evard College can be channeled into the ballroom in the east wing without broaching any of the rooms. *It's good enough for them.* They can peek into parlors along the way, but anyone who tries to go in is intercepted by the Garsons' help – the junior staff of the Evarton Inn, buttoned into chocolate velvet uniforms for this event. It is their job to round up strays, cutting them off with laden silver trays so deftly that guests say, 'Oh, thank you,' and take two of whatever is offered. Two pretty junior college students are pouring champagne in the ballroom, and this week's house guests have begun circulating with an air of *noblesse oblige* while the Garsons dance as if somebody else is giving the party and they've just happened by.

Their hosts circle the dance floor like the king and queen of the world. Temporarily delivered from winter, Clair and Nick are dancing too. They move with the lightness and ease of accustomed lovers, forgetting everything as the music pulls them in, and if Nick's color is high and his skin hot to the touch, so is Clair's. It's just excitement, she thinks. This is good for us.

Tonight the theme is medieval; Vance has dressed the long ballroom with crossed banners and hung it with starbursts of swords and shields with strange devices. Sunflowers nod in tall vases and the only thing missing from the fieldstone fireplace with its brass firedogs is the spit with the crackling suckling pig. Green velvet draw draperies cover the long front windows that overlook the icy hillside and on the tapestry above the bandstand, paired wolfhounds course across a field of matching green.

The band has orders to play without a break but in spite of the beat only a few guests move out. As guests Ad and Mandy Bishop are A students, doing their earnest foxtrot in front of the bandstand even though Ad's stitches have just come out, while in a corner Teddy does an updated shag with Sally LeFleur so blithely that it's clear the Garsons' approval means nothing to him. And Sally? Secure in Teddy's arms, she blooms. The Serbian house guests are dancing; the Sailors are dancing and the Garsons are dancing.

That's all. The others mill at the fringes, slipping back to the bar in the foyer as if one more drink will help them crash the sound barrier and achieve entry. In the presence of all this wealth, nice people Clair *thinks she knows* have turned into something else. Next to the Garsons in their low-keyed black velvet tuxes and five-hundred-dollar boots, next to the Garsons' house guests clothed in the ease that comes with old money, Evard's academics look overdone and uncertain in whatever they may have chosen to put on. Even women with taste – Lauren, Jane – look all wrong in layers of sequins and silk, too much makeup, clunky jewelry, too much everything. Posturing like extras in a costume movie, the women of Evard look anxious with their spiky eyelashes and red-rimmed, carnivorous smiles, teetering at the brink of something new.

What do they want? Clair wonders, secure in Nick's arms. What do they expect to come away with, that they don't already have?

For her just now, dancing is enough. *Torchères* and the flashy rock band, house guests flocking like exotic tropical birds on the glistening parquet, the almost incidental splendor of the Garsons' great hall, the easy synchronicity with Nick so lift Clair out of herself that the Straits' arrival will come as a shock: *I almost forgot.*

The guests of honor are late.

Mara called as Clair and Nick were leaving the house. The Straits' sitter never showed; Will was tied up, could she bring her two over along with ice cream and Happy Meals for all the kids and an extra twenty for the Sailors' sitter? In another world Clair might be able to forget about the Straits, but in claustrophobic Evarton, everything's too close. Houses. People. Lives. The Straits have moved in two blocks away. The kids play together all the time now, eat in each other's kitchens and go home together after school. Mara's request was perfectly logical. Sure, Clair said but she thought: As long as you're the one who brings them, not him.

It defies logic but she likes Mara Strait. She has wonderful children, and in the strange, necessary ambiguity that lets her accept the kids even as she rejects their father, Clair's happy to have them in her house. Chase plays better with Davy than Jake Stevenson, who is a bully; the little girls run like a matched pair. What does it matter who their father is? Clair can't blame a six-year-old and an eight-year-old for their father's – what? How can she fault them when she doesn't even know?

Mara's lovely, intelligent. Genuine.

'*Here they come.*' Someone murmurs, 'Look at her!'

Standing at the entrance to the Garsons' great hall with her big, handsome, ambitious husband, Mara Strait is something else.

Clair doesn't want to acknowledge this, but she does. Impeccable in her floor-length canvas shift and a pre-Columbian gold medallion, her friend Mara is less her friend than she is Strait's partner. She is his ornament, his asset, his ally in whatever game he intends to play, leaning her blonde head against her husband's to demonstrate that they are together in all things. The tall, perfectly matched Straits are working George Atkinson so smoothly that the flattered college president won't even know what they're doing, alternating lines and smiling matching smiles.

They are no longer Mara, whom she likes, and Mara's husband, whom she mistrusts. They're a unit.

Mara's eyes sweep the room, meet Clair's and quickly move on.

She's not herself, Clair thinks, and Mara? Clair has the unsubstantiated suspicion that Mara may be ashamed. Maybe she doesn't want Clair to see her like this: attached, an ornament. Unless she is his instrument.

Weird, she thinks. Like catching a friend in the middle of doing something she may not want you to know about.

Nobody can see inside a marriage.

Leading Nick so subtly that he won't know it, Clair steers him toward a safe corner where she won't have to see and Mara won't have to see. At her back she hears George Atkinson still greeting the Straits like the minister at the altar welcoming the groom. Then, like the minister summoning the reluctant bride, the earnest, bungling pastor intent on making the marriage, George lifts his voice in that phony, actorish way of his, projecting manufactured good cheer. 'Oh, Nick. Nick Sailor.'

Not Nick's fault he doesn't hear; they're close to the music. She leans into him, nudging him into the shadow of the bandstand where they can dance on without complications and be happy, for now.

Not Nick's fault either that the beat picks up. Grinning, he lifts her hand and as if he's never been sick he spins her out, so that just when she most wants the party to go on without her, Clair is caught facing the trio in the door.

Strait sees. He murmurs something to Evard's president. George nods and hails them again, louder. 'Nick. Clair. Oh, Clair.' If she yields, George will join their hands and the Straits' with ministerial authority and make them promise – what?

Instead she spins back in, hitting Nick's chest with a little thump; as long as they keep dancing they won't have to deal.

George calls louder. 'Clair . . .'

We've met, George. Don't you know how many times we've met?

Nick murmurs into her hair. 'Mmm?'

'Nothing,' she says. Words drift in from some old fairy tale. 'It's only the wind.'

Folly, trying to cling to the moment. George whispers to Will Strait; both heads swivel. The two men smile knowingly. Clair doesn't know what Strait is saying but she knows the subtext. *Take that.* Damn you. His smile broadens. Then with a careless wave that makes it clear that unlike the other guests he and Mara are at home with all this opulence, Will Strait abandons George the Great and moves his tall wife out onto the Garsons' waxed parquet.

On the dance floor Mara follows every move. Stark, almost shroud-like as it is, her canvas shift is slit to the bikini line: perfect. The priceless necklace is perfect too. Whatever they are together when nobody's around to admire them, the Straits are good together tonight. As he dances toward Clair, Strait dips, bending Mara back so far that her shining hair flows and her drooping, graceful hands almost brush the floor. Then he hesitates with his wife draped over his arm, holding her in place until he sees that he has Clair's attention: *she'd let me drop her if I wanted to.*

The grin is brilliant, charming. 'Oh, *there* you are.'

'Caught. In the act.' Nick laughs but Clair can feel his arm tighten against her back, holding her in place. *Do this for me.*

Strait's voice is bright. 'Change partners?' Languid, half mesmerized, Mara leans back with her eyes fixed on the ornamented ceiling and her fingertips grazing the floor.

Nick murmurs into her hair, 'D'you mind?'

She stiffens. 'Yes.'

'Would you please just do this for me?'

She keeps her voice low. 'What is it, Nick? What are you trying to make me do?'

He sounds so confused. 'I just thought we could . . .' Swap partners. Be friends.

Miserable, she stumbles; she can't catch herself. For an hour there, Clair had almost forgotten what the last few weeks have been like. In the magic hour before Strait arrived she almost got back to happy. Now he's here. The contrast leaves her breathless. *I knew it was bad, but I didn't know it was this bad.* 'I can't.'

Naturally everybody sees Clair pull Nick away from the attractive new man, who is only trying to be nice.

Look at her, acting that way when all the Straits want is to make friends. Those *nice* people are so handsome and stylish, so obviously at home in these opulent surroundings that speak of world-class society. Clair's just jealous, that's why she's acting that way. Clair Sailor, jealous. Terrible. It looks bad.

And with a triumphant look Strait rights the graceful, pliant Mara and dances away as if Clair's refusal fits right into a larger figure he's been designing.

Now the new couple moves in increasingly grand circles, synchronized like trained athletes or accomplished dancers who spend hours rehearsing. Strait's steps are bigger than Nick's, slick and so showy that on the sidelines the locals – *their friends* – begin to applaud and the music stops for Clair.

'Oh shit.'

Nick tugs at Clair. She is frozen like a piece of junk sculpture, rusted in place. Won't move. Exasperated, he cries, 'What?'

She gestures. 'Them.'

'What's the matter with you?'

'It's too hard to explain. I'm sorry, Nicky.' How to explain Strait's just ruined dancing? She won't be out on the same floor with that accomplished, showy dancer and his pliant partner, smiling and going through the motions. She won't be part of this. *What will he take over next?*

'What's the matter with you?'

'Tell you when we get home.' *Don't want to do anything he does, OK? Or be what he is.* And thinks, *Whatever that is.* She can't tell Nick this in the middle of the dance floor any more than she can tell him how dirty her suspicions make her feel. 'I just don't want to be here, OK?' She drags her fingertips down his arms and lets go. So this is how she separates from her partner for the evening – Clair, who is usually so carefully attuned. Careless, Clair. She bolts without caring who sees.

Her first instinct is to head for the end of the east wing, where a Gothic arch gives onto stone stairs. She'd like to wait out the party in some upstairs room, escape the exigencies.

But she is intercepted by a pretty girl in the Garsons' brown velvet and a starched apron, whose job it is to keep guests on the approved paths because in rich people's houses the private rooms are private and guests who aren't quite up to their standards are relegated to public rooms. Sighing,

Clair lets herself be directed to the approved powder room. She needs time to get her head together but the room's already occupied. The sink in front of the mirror is filled with soapy water. Brave in the white apron and brown velvet that are the uniform of the night, one of the chambermaids from the Evarton has laid out mascara and eye liner and blush on the marble counter, lining them up like a soldier field-stripping his weapon. Intent on the mirror, the girl is repairing eyes wrecked from crying so she can pick up her silver tray and go out and fight again.

'Whatever it is, I'm sorry,' Clair says and goes into the little room with the mauve toilet and matching bidet and closes the door so she too can cry a little.

By the time she emerges, the guests are being herded into the foyer for the toasts. When the last few have gone by she comes out, slipping behind a column as the mayor begins to speak. The guests are marshaled around the main staircase while the stars of the party wait to address them from the marble steps. Here come the tributes: the senator to the next deputy at Health, Education and Welfare, our own George Atkinson; George to their hosts the Garsons but first and foremost to Senator Cabot, who came in by helicopter just in time to make this toast; Vance Garson to George and the senator and most of all to their wonderful friend Will Strait and his lovely wife Mara Cabot Strait, whom they are welcoming into the community, to be followed, by popular demand, by a few words from the distinguished guest of honor. Disguised as toasts, these stand-up routines are really speeches. Overblown, boring. Long.

Clair hates speeches. In her time at Evard she's heard too many. She knows how the next hour will go. Typical academics, the faculty guests are already making hasty notes on the backs of their invitations, which they brought under the impression that they needed to show them to get in, scribbling madly in the rush to show off. Excited as they were to be included, hopeful as they were when they knocked at the great front doors tonight, these earnest teachers and their chosen partners are aware that in metropolitan centers they don't even visit, the chic life has left without them, like a missed plane.

They are out of place here. Never mind how much they looked forward to the party or how hard they shopped or how drop-dead fine they thought they looked when they checked their bedroom mirrors before stepping out, this trip into another world has been hard on them. Dancing well is hard. Wardrobe is hard, if not impossible; they're all standing here wearing the wrong thing. Speaking may be the one thing these academics are good at, and the little company in the foyer is going to be leaning against columns, shifting on sore feet and weeping with boredom before the last toast is done.

Teddy isn't anywhere. He's slipped away just the way he told her he would, after he'd been seen and marked present.

(Typical Teddy tactic. 'Charm the hosts and get away before anybody notices you're gone.'

'I'll be lost without you.'

He shrugged apologetically. 'Late date.' But he was beaming, told her it would jinx it if he named names.

When she said, 'Right when I need you,' Teddy was good enough to ask why.

'You know.' Strait: Clair needs just one person she trusts to agree that this isn't just paranoia. 'Reality check.'

'Late date,' Teddy said again, closing off the conversation in that circular Teddy way, but to make her feel better he added, 'I'll put my best people on it.' Dear Teddy, gone again.)

Will Strait is mounting the marble stairs. She won't get close enough to hear what he's saying, but even at this distance Clair can catch the tune – smooth, hypnotic, assured. She hears applause. She even hears laughter. Sooner or later Nick will have to get up there and respond. Probably she ought to go in and stand by him, but she can't be part of that. More. She's afraid to gauge his relative success, Nick's worth as registered on the applause meter measured against Strait's score.

In the foyer Strait's voice lifts. There's more laughter. Wild applause. Clair retreats before Nick can catch her slouching in the doorway like some shaggy outsider and beg her to join him in the circle. It's a big house. It's a big party. Nobody will miss her.

If she could beat the winter, Clair would make her escape through the ice-shrouded gardens; she might even slide down the great hill and walk home, but on these nights after ten minutes outside your eyeballs glaze and the surfaces begin to crack; skiers develop frostbite in minutes and even seasoned hikers can freeze to death. She could go back to the ballroom and wait out the speeches behind the long green velvet curtains; she could hide with her nose pressed against the floor-length leaded casements, studying the icy hill below the balcony, but when Clair turns she discovers that the staff has evaporated. They're in the kitchen readying the midnight supper. For the moment the place is effectively deserted.

She can go anywhere she wants in the house.

All those unexplored rooms and corridors sprawl like the great houses in her dreams – seductive and apparently endless, filled with treasures waiting to be discovered. In dreams you can go anywhere in perfect safety.

Clair moves quietly, noting the sculpture sprouting in niches and the small works by great artists that hang in the halls and fill every room she passes. Cross-hatching, Clair works her way down the main hall to the west wing of the building, where she finds the library. She is drawn by the ornate painted ceiling. It's either a fabulous fake or else it has been lifted whole and transported at great expense from an eighteenth-century French country house. Part of the confusion here in the Garsons' house – no, part of the seduction – is not knowing what is real and what is not. Wondering whether those are genuine or fake bindings on the books that line the second tier, she sits down.

Clair is tempted, not to open the virgin editions of English novels in their gold-stamped slip cases, but to find a pad and pen and sit at the Regency table and see what words will come to her.

By this time she's been pulled so deep into the splendid house that she won't know that Strait, too, has tired of the speeches and slipped away from the foyer.

You can pretend and pretend and not make a story. When too much time passes and words still won't come, Clair pushes back from the table and goes from object to object in the richly furnished room, getting her first close look at the Garsons' fabled art collection. She is surprised by the odd mixture of the real and careless fakes: maquette of a Henry Moore, Permastone reproduction of a tiny Greek satyr, sweet little Matisse that looks real, a baroque frame on a Hogarth that at this distance she can see is only a giant Polaroid. It's as if these people are interested only in *effect*. Either the Garsons have been bilked or else they don't care what's real and what isn't, only about the way their objects sit together here. Either way, the discovery cheers her. The place is grand enough, but it's not as grand as anybody thought it was, and the owners? Not as grand as she thought either. Vance, Gail. Colored hair. Teeth veneered. Probably had that extra rib removed, to enhance the languid bodies.

Only a pack of cards, she thinks, somehow liberated by the presence of all these fakes. I can do anything I want here.

Then at the end of the east wing, in the Gothic arch leading to the stairs, she finds a Venus standing on a pedestal, centered in front of the leaded window. She runs her hand over the draped haunch. It is a bad reproduction. Lovely at first sight, the thing is made out of cheap marble so soapy that it might as well be polyvinyl resin. Bad fake, she thinks, grinning like a savage.

Pretend what you want, she says in her head, preparing speeches for anybody who discovers her. I'm a real person.

Therefore she goes upstairs without hesitation, amused to see that the Garsons have not yet found the perfect objects for the Gothic alcove on the second floor. The vacant pedestal in front of the window looks naked and forlorn. She goes along without even wondering what her hosts would say if they found out she's discovered all their fakes and broached their private chambers: bedrooms, dressing rooms. Curious, she begins the long passage from the west wing to the main body of the house and across to the east wing. If the house is as symmetrical as she thinks it is, she'll find another Gothic arch and a matching staircase. With any luck, she'll come down in the corridor outside the ballroom; she can pretend she's been there the whole time.

Who, me? Come out from behind the velvet draperies. Smile and yawn like Alice, waking up. *I must have fallen asleep behind the curtains.*

If she hoped to find the second floor in disarray, a revealing shambles like the picture of Dorian Gray after decades in the attic, Clair is disappointed. Oh Clair, stop looking for secrets.

You can pretend and pretend and not make a story.

The place is as dull as good George Atkinson. Open doors give on high-tech exercise rooms in all their banality, brightly lighted twentieth-century bedrooms, pretty, dull rooms without any apparent function. She's tempted to look through the Garsons' closets. She has her hand on a doorknob when she hears somebody cough.

She doesn't even want to think about who. She runs. Heading for the stairs at the end of the dimly lit corridor, she's too rushed to notice that there are moving shadows framed in the Gothic arch until she is almost upon them.

Surprise stops her.

The scene is brutal, shocking. Two figures grapple in the stone archway that frames the window, a girl in brown velvet with her starched bandeau ruined and sliding out of her disordered hair as the man presses her against the stone wall at her back. Sounds come out of the girl. Clair sees the man in the frame smashing against her body like a figure in a movie, although at this moment in this light she can't make out whether it's a vampire picture she's watching or a graphic rape or a willing seduction like Sonny Corleone's as he and Connie's bridesmaid take their pleasure against a door at the reception –

– sees the two either grappling or fucking and then over the girl's messy hair sees the man lift his head and, God, recognize her. Acknowledge her with that smile, and this is the hell of it: *she's not sure what she is seeing.*

Whatever it is, it is over. His hands have dropped. He separates from the girl. With a gasp, she slides until her feet touch the floor.

Then he turns the girl lightly, as if they've only been dancing, and looks at Clair over her shoulder. Strait does not speak.

Clair does not speak.

She has no idea what there is to be said here.

For a second they just hang there. Strait. Clair. The girl.

Then Strait releases her and she turns. Clair sees it is the Evarton Inn chambermaid she found at the marble sink in the guest bathroom, the girl who'd been crying and didn't want anybody to know. She faces Clair with her smirched mouth, beginning tears, but in a weird mismatch of intention and act, the girl is smiling. She smiles at Clair with those smeared eyes and that smashed, trembling mouth as, with a prodigiously insolent look, Strait turns and heads downstairs as if nothing has happened here.

Clair takes her arm. 'What's happening? What's going on?'

Instead of thanking her the girl cries, 'Look what you did! Just when we were about to . . .' She yearns after him, crying, 'Don't go. Wait!'

'Are you all right?'

She turns on Clair. 'Leave me alone!'

'Did he hurt you?'

'Of course not,' she says, but she won't look at Clair.

'That's not what it looked like to me.' Clair's voice is low, charged with urgency. 'I know I saw something. Just tell me what I saw.'

'Nothing. You didn't see anything.'

'Yes I did. Did he hurt you?'

'No! We weren't . . .' She sobs. 'We were just . . . Don't tell my boss. Oh please, I'm so in love.'

'Then why are you crying?' Clair won't let go. 'If you're hurt, you have to tell somebody.'

Outraged, she cries, 'Why would I be hurt?' She still won't look at Clair. Fixed on some point inside herself, the girl says, 'He wouldn't hurt me, he's in love with me.'

'I thought I saw—'

'Well, you didn't see anything. Now go away.'

Clair's voice trails off. 'I don't know what I saw.'

'Nothing. You didn't see anything.'

'I promise, I won't let him hurt you. If he's done something to you, you have to tell the police.'

'No way!' The look she gives Clair as she backs away makes it clear that she's gone too far. 'I would never do that,' she cries, still backing, and this is how the girl separates herself from Clair and all her ugly suspicions. Weeping, anxious and miserable, she turns at the head of the stairs, stopping just long enough to let the words mark the distance between them, closing this particular door for ever. 'I told you, you don't get it. People like you never do! I told you, we're in love.'

In the ballroom where her friends in their uncertainty besiege the buffet table, Clair darts here and there, looking for Nick. Desperate, she blunders from one group of old friends to another, discovering that in these clothes on this night, they are all strangers. 'Who, Nick?' They turn to her with their mouths blurred and their eyes emptied out by the evening. 'I don't know.' Smile vacantly. 'I don't know where he is.' It's as if the waters have closed over him. Then Clair feels fingers close on her bicep, clamping so tight that the nails bite through her sleeve. Before she can cry out or jerk away, Will Strait has pulled her close and begun moving her backward, clamping her so tightly that she can feel the strong body moving against hers and know he is powerful in love. She feels his chin digging into her scalp. She can smell the clean, spicy perfume of the soap he showered with tonight.

It is sudden, terrifying, swift.

He smiles, he *smiles*.

It is as if they are dancing.

Before anybody sees, Strait has propelled her the length of the ballroom, backing her into the green velvet draperies that cover the long windows. They part as if he has always known how to find this opening. Before Clair can resist, he pushes her through swiftly and the heavy green velvet falls back in place without a ripple. They are in the stone alcove. At her back the leaded bay windows are open. Outside, the cold night glitters. The lined velvet is so dense that she can barely hear the dinner music playing. She can cry out; she can fight; she can do anything she wants. It won't make any difference. They are as good as alone here.

She is as cut off from the Garsons and their tipsy, earnest guests – as far from Nick! – as if they'd found their way to the face of the moon just for this confrontation.

'Don't.'

'Don't what?' Strait smiles. 'I haven't seen enough of you.' They are so close that she can feel his breath on her face: distinctly his, like no other's. It is like having him in her bed.

Clair is beyond words. Drawn, no, repelled . . . Repelled, she pushes him away. Then in a fluid movement as carefully designed as any of his dance steps, Will Strait moves her in a half-turn that puts her off balance, backed against the sharp leaded frame of the deep casement window.

'If you think you know something,' he says through his teeth, 'you don't know anything.'

Clair is strongly aware of the open casement at her back and the low balcony rail beyond, and below, the steep, glassy surface of the hill. Without having to see them she acknowledges the great stones that stud the frozen garden. *Is that what he's trying to . . .* He could, she knows. He could push her out and say she fell. Worse. He could say she jumped. He could say anything and have them believe him, but that is not what Will Strait is about here.

He has one big hand on her front: chest, breasts, it's all the same to him in this particular passage. Like a marauder who has sacked her house and is ready to crush her too, Will Strait is holding her in place with the flat of his hand as with the blade of his left forearm he cuts into her neck and pushes down hard. If she wants to breathe, Clair has to turn the way he wants her to, twisting her head to ease the pressure on her windpipe.

She can't escape the man any more than she can escape his breath, which is redolent of brandy, sweet. Will Strait bears down hard. The ridge of the lead casement cuts into her neck just below the ear. *My God! What is he trying to do to me?*

The frame is sharp; the pain is disproportionate. In the part of Clair's brain where things remain clear she thinks: *If this makes a mark, I'll have something I can show them.* She can barely speak. She rasps, 'What do you want? What do you want from me?'

'It won't matter what you say about me,' he says, now that he has her attention. His tone is light, conversational. 'Nobody's going to believe you.' Then, with that assured, insolent look that she will know by heart before this is over, he releases her.

She touches her neck. No blood. There will be nothing to mark this moment except in her memory. She grunts; she can't find speech. Nothing she says will factor here.

He is already dismissing her with a smile so bright that they could be at the beach in broad daylight. 'But remember,' he says, propelling her toward the opening in the draperies. 'If you say anything, I can make it very hard for Nick.'

He parts the heavy velvet and they emerge, Strait holding the draperies aside for her in a graceful gesture, ushering her into a ballroom where none of this has taken place. Clair moves from terror into anger as the couples nearest them turn bland pink faces, *so glad to see you two getting along at last, yaas, yaas, lovely evening,* smiling so complacently that she understands that Strait is right. He's poisoned the earth so completely that there's nothing she can tell these people that they will believe. He grips her elbow and twists until her breath catches. Then he releases her.

Sickened, stunned and shuddering, she pushes through the dancing couples, flushed faces nodding like overblown hollyhocks. 'Where's Nick? Have you seen Nick?' *I need Nick.* She'll push him down and kneel on his chest and make him listen. She won't let him up until she's told him everything. Then, by God, he can – what? She doesn't know. All she knows is that she never should have left him there on the dance floor at the beginning of this terrible evening, she never should have . . . Somebody jerks her arm. 'Al!'

'It's OK,' the college infirmarian says incomprehensibly. 'I've got him lying down.'

She pushes past absently, intent on her search; she has no idea what the doctor is telling her. 'I'm looking for Nick.'

Al LaMar doesn't respond directly. He just goes on in that good gray doctor tone. 'The paramedics are on their way.'

'What? Oh, somebody's . . .' Never mind. 'Have you seen Nick?'

'I don't think it's serious but I'd like to get him on monitors for a couple of days.'

She keeps trying to get past him and find Nick and Al LaMar keeps getting in the way; as they come into the foyer he stands aside and the little circle of people parts so she can see.

Al is saying comfortably, 'Probably just a sudden drop in blood pressure, but we need to be sure. You'll get him back Monday, I guarantee.'

And Nick looks up at her from the bed made of coats on the hard marble and grins. 'Sorry about that. It's nothing. I'm fine.'

11

Ben

Look, he's well enough to give it a try.

Ben is in Delia's forbidding basement, made even more treacherous because he's blundered down in the dark on the off chance that he'll trip on the stairs and smash his head open on the stone floor. He ends up crouched by the furnace with his knees drawn up, shivering. What is he, trying to die in the crawl space like Sylvia Plath? Does he really think he can stay here until he phases into a trance state, pure alpha waves? Is he trying to tell himself a person can suck in his breath and go comatose and starve to death? That by the time Delia finds him there won't be anything left of him but a skeleton?

Right. She'll find you as soon as the body starts to smell.

Grief and frustration drive him to his feet. He charges the stone wall with his head down. Ghah! Again. *Ghah!* Again and again until blood runs down his forehead and into his eyes and he has to go upstairs and find some way to stop the bleeding and wash his hair and dry it and wash it and dry it again so Delia won't come home and see the gore and blow the whistle on him.

The last thing he needs is to get sent to a hospital.

The next day Delia's car comes into the drive just as he reaches the attic. Ben has skinned up through the trap door in the hall ceiling. The rafters creak; the house is laughing at him. He's going to throw a rope over the rooftree and try to hang himself. If he hurries he can still do it before his mother gets out of the car. He's brought a rope to the attic and a plastic bag to hurry things along. A chair. As the car door slams in the driveway below, he crawls toward the midpoint. Kick the chair out from under me and throttle.

By this time Ben is desperate. He hates himself too much to go on like this. He doesn't care any more who knows what happened to him and who doesn't, he just wants it over with. He doesn't want to be this person.

He doesn't want to *be* at all.

But the part of him that still wants to keep Delia from having to find out what he's turned into is already running along ahead. Maybe she won't find me. Let her think I've gone out for a beer, skipped the country. The trap door is shut. The attic's cold and so dry that the air will dehydrate what's left of me. It won't stink; what remains at the end of the winter will mummify in summer heat and Delia may never have to see this. This, on me.

The house below shakes as the front door slams. Scrambling, he tries to find a place where he can stand. The attic ceiling is too low. Even at the highest point Ben has to hunch his shoulders to stand upright. Where in hell is he going to put the chair? He hears her calling downstairs. Despairing, he lets himself down and closes the trap door behind him, scuttling to his room so she'll find him in bed.

Another day. He has to think of another way.

Ben has studied it. Pills don't work. She cleaned out the medicine chest after he blew it last time.

With his history he'd never get a gun permit even if he could make it to a gun shop.

This leaves him with the first solution, which he knows is the final solution. A terminal jump. The insurance tower.

The trouble is, he still can't exactly go out. How's he going to get downtown when he can't make it to the corner? Every time he gets to the front door his hands freeze on the knob and his heart fails. He just can't. To his credit, he tries. Every day he tries. He tries at just about this time every afternoon, when the sun is low and the street fills with shadows. And fails.

Now he is trying again. He lunges for the closed door. *Now.* Maybe today. Dammit. Hung up again.

Ben is stuck to the handle. Shaking with frustration and self-loathing, he hangs.

But today there is a difference. To his astonishment this time he gets the door open. Cold air blows in. Suspended midway, Ben Messinger is caught between inside and outside.

The combination of cold air and intense concentration has recalibrated his breathing, altering his metabolic rate. His joints lock. Entranced, he clings. Thoughts and fears escape him. For the first time all his old patterns are damped down to pure alpha waves. Ben enters a state of intense concentration in which he is no longer himself. Time moves on without his knowing it. Twilight slides into night. By the time Delia's car comes down their street the street lights are on.

Fixed in the doorway, arrested in this exaggerated state, Ben has been hanging here for a very long time.

Caught. This is how Delia finds him. Gently, she pries her son's fingers off and leads him back inside. She won't recognize the self-disgust that makes him resist. 'Now that you're up and around,' she says briskly, 'it's time to talk.'

The part of Ben that he wishes would go away forever returns. Like it or not, he has come back to himself. He's back in the house with his mother. His miseries have come back inside with him. Everything inside him groans.

'We need to make some changes.' Delia's had this line prepared for weeks, for just this occasion. She is all business now. Pushing him into the living room, she backs him into a chair. 'Sit down.'

He is trembling with rage at his own helplessness.

Delia is angry too. Her thin hair has gone flat; it falls in strips across her greasy forehead but she is not aware of the effect any more than she knows what exhaustion has done to her color or that all the skin has let go of her skull, hanging off her face in slack wrinkles. 'I thought you were too sick to get up.'

Ben can hardly look at her.

'I said, sit.' She pushes; he resists. When Ben was in bed she was all solicitude, the single mother taking care of her sick child, but now that he's standing unsteadily in her living room everything abut Delia changes. It may be catching him at the door looking like a normal person; it may be standing toe to toe like this and finding out that he isn't really sick; some discovery goads Delia and instead of asking how he is, she starts.

'What happened to you in Venice, Benjy?' Her fists hit his shoulders: thump. 'What happened to you?'

'Nothing!' He staggers and the chair grabs him. *Whump.*

'Don't give me that.' Questions erupt. They come boiling out of her. 'What did this to you, Benjy? What did it anyway?'

Somewhere between the office and home tonight her lipstick wore off and the mouth Delia turns to him is chapped and bitten, wrenched out of shape by emotion. Glaring, she is a little furnace; anger and suspicion glow red behind her eyes.

'What changed you from an ordinary student into a . . .' She can't find the word. Choking on it, she rubs her eyes, which are red-rimmed and filling again. Then she leans over the chair and grabs Ben by the shoulders. She just starts shaking. Anger makes her hideous. He wants to stand up and push her away, knock her down if he has to, anything to get away from her with her ugly questions coming out of that unaccountably ugly face. But he can't. She shakes him and shakes him; his head bangs against the back of the wing chair; she can't stop shaking him.

'What was it, Ben?'

He says mildly, 'I don't know.'

She's so close that Ben can smell her breath: apples, the canned vegetable soup she had for lunch today. Deep in the chair, he has no place to retreat. She is inexorable. 'Oh yes you do.'

'No I don't!'

It is astounding. His mother is nose to nose with him but Ben can't see her any more. He blinks and blinks and he still can't see her. Almost absent-mindedly he breaks her hold on him and pushes her away so he can stand.

'The hell you don't . . . you have to know what turned you from a *nice guy* into this – basket case! You didn't just accidentally *get* this way . . . You . . . It . . . Whatever . . .' Delia is still talking but all Ben hears now is white sound, a terrible, unremitting buzz. ' . . . something happened. Didn't it?' She grabs him again. She is sobbing. 'Didn't it?'

He doesn't see or hear his mother but he can smell her breath and feel the pressure of her hands. Words fall out of him. 'Don't. Stop. Let go.' Now he is crying too. 'Oh please, this is terrible.'

She grinds hard knuckles into his shoulders. 'What is it? Who did this to you?'

'Oh don't, this is so awful.' Blind to her, deafened by the buzz in his ears, Ben knows that she isn't going to stop, this is going to keep happening until he figures out how to make it stop. He finds some words to buy her off. It's the best he can do. 'Nothing,' he says, too loud. 'Nobody!'

She just breathes and waits for an answer; he can hear the air going in and out of her face.

'I don't remember!' he says at last.

Unexpectedly, his mother lets him go. 'You don't remember!' It is too much for her. 'All this and YOU DON'T REMEMBER.'

Oh my God I've got to get out of here.

Like a hostile army, the woman is marching toward a place in him that he can't bear to name. She has brought him up and loved him and found the strength to let him go and then, my God, when they shipped the wreckage back to her she just met the plane with that deathless mother's smile and welcomed him as if nothing bad had happened. All these months Delia has carried trays and denied the grief that immobilizes him and all this time she's been lying in wait. Under cover of all that niceness all her inner forces have been marshaled and marching toward this confrontation.

He is trembling. 'No.'

'Oh yes you do.'

There is a terrible pause.

When Delia speaks again it is in a new voice. Mother, phoenix, ready to rise again. 'Now that you're up and around, it's time for the next step. Therapist, hypnopsychiatrist, detective, brain surgeon, anybody who can find out what's the matter with you.'

'There's nothing the matter with me.'

She slaps his face. '*Then what's the matter with you!*' She is inexorable now: the embattled mother cornering her only child. Her treasure and her failure. With the terrifying tenderness of a woman who has invested her entire life in this enterprise and intends to see it through, Delia touches the spot she hit with gentle fingers, *there, there.* 'Whatever it is, it can't be that terrible.'

'I don't remember.' He does remember. It is.

Damn her. Damn her to death. Delia says cannily, 'You can't be the only one this has happened to.'

'I told you, *nothing happened.*'

So this is how she nails her only son into place and stabs him in the heart. Delia Messinger, who withdraws to a safe distance and looks right into him – *Oh my God don't let her see* – and shouts in a loud voice, 'Oh yes it did,' as desperation fills him like vomit, rising until it threatens to explode out of him in words he is afraid to say.

Delia goes on, deliberately widening the crack in his life and threatening

113

to break him beyond any repairing. Her hair shakes loose in her rage, falling in flat strings over the flaking skin of her angry face. Her nose is pink; the loose skin under her eyes is hanging off her face. 'You didn't just *get* this way.'

She has never been so ugly.

'It's OK, son. You can tell me.'

I'd rather die.

He can't stand seeing her this way. So this is what breaks Ben out finally and drives him into the street – revulsion. It is overpowering. He hates himself. He hates her. He hates what he has made of her, what she has turned into because of him. He can't be in this house with her. With what he is. He can't be on this block or even in this neighborhood. He can't stand to be in the same county. He can't bear to see how hideous she is in her grief, and it is guilt that propels him out the front door, perhaps forever, while behind him his mother screams in a voice so big that it will follow him no matter where he goes.

As he wheels and plunges into the dark at the end of the street Delia Messinger shouts after him, 'WHO DID THIS TO YOU?'

Everything in him lets go. 'Nobody,' he screams, flashing on it: *if you say one word* . . . He starts to run.

She is running after him. 'Benjamin!'

'No!' Everything rushes out in a tremendous sob. He's running so hard that words stream behind him like a banner – pure sound, indistinguishable. Incomprehensible. Desperate to escape, Ben Messinger is sobbing, 'You don't want to know what it is, Mom. I . . .'

Her voice comes from somewhere far behind. 'Oh, son!'

'It was me, Mom.' His heels hit the ground like piledrivers; as he escapes her, every footstep jars another word out of him. 'I did it, OK? I did it. It was. Me.'

He doesn't hear her any more; he is alone out here in an agony of understanding. *Oh my God I can't do this any more!*

No.

I can't be this any more.

12

Like so many things about his life here, Nick took the use of the posh Hickson Lounge for granted, but while he was out sick, Will Strait moved in on the penthouse lounge and claimed it for the Victorian Studies Room.

Donated by a rich man whose son was killed in a skiing accident on Frontz Peak, the elaborately paneled lounge at the top of the Humanities tower is the best place in the college, with mahogany bookshelves and brass lamps, rich rugs and overstuffed leather chairs. Lesser works by great painters glow under painting lights. This could just as easily be a private room in a posh men's club – rich, secluded, redolent of privilege. Isolated as it is from the office cubicles and classrooms with their strip lighting on the lower floors, equipped with its own kitchen and bath, it is beautifully self-contained. Take a class into the Hickson Lounge for any occasion and the rich surroundings do the work.

In this opulent setting students feel special, chosen. Privileged to learn whatever Nick or any other professor may choose to teach.

Clair knows Nick isn't necessarily pleased that the lounge is no longer available for his senior seminar, but he is too honorable to complain. It's the thing about Nick that infuriates her most. Once the man takes a position he defends it to the death, never mind that Will Strait's moved in on the lounge as if possession is his natural right. Nick Sailor's place every spring? No more.

'Oh, really?' Strait said when somebody called it to his attention. 'I'm new. I didn't know.' Smiling, the big man directed the movers who had

115

unaccountably arrived with a hundred cartons of books pulled out of storage somewhere and delivered to Evard where, as far as Clair knows, Will Strait is employed only to complete the term.

'Fiction and theory go next to my desk. We'll shelve my art books and gallery catalogs over there.'

For days his students have been going in and out, bringing extra chairs, velvet hangings from Theater to cloak the long windows, Art Nouveau lamps with beaded shades, pillows made of prayer rugs, treasures Will Strait has found in college attics or wheedled out of Betsy Atkinson's storehouse of cherished items or charmed out of the college archivist: Queen Anne side tables, a caged stuffed bird with a music box in its base, a portrait that looks like Dorian Gray Before. He has the college electrician wiring the reading alcove for his computer and has disposed of the Hickson family cabinet to accommodate a strange, intricately carved mahogany desk that materialized along with certain other personal possessions he's installing in what used to be a communal lounge.

The strong, assured operator from the outside world has been here only a few weeks to their ten years and already Will Strait has expanded into the space to the point where Clair wonders how much longer there will be room for her and Nick.

Nick's relapse has put her in an ambiguous position. It is Strait who covered for Nick while Al LaMar had him in for observation and Strait who covers late meetings when Nick's pact with his doctor sends him home. For which Clair is grateful. Whether or not she likes it, his persistent presence protects Nick from himself. Nick is the kind of man who goes through sleet and snow if he has to, to meet his obligations. It's what laid him out in the first place, and if Strait can keep him out of the hospital, fine.

There is also the converse. Strait, that night: 'I can make it very hard for Nick.' Passing in the hall he turns with that polished, bionic smile.

Still the encounter at the Garsons' sits on her shoulders like an ugly brute that she can't shake off and she can't forget. Scarred by clashes with Ginny ('Everybody knows you're jealous of them') and even Lauren ('If you're having a problem with this, Clair, maybe you need help') she understands that Strait's whispering campaign is insidious and complete. There's nobody she can turn to now. She needs Nick but the relapse has put him out of reach.

It isn't illness that's distanced him; it's something more profound. He

116

passed out at the Garsons' and ended up in hospital for observation; nothing serious, Al LaMar says, nothing life-threatening. 'If Nick does what I say. If he doesn't lay back and let himself mend, I'll be trying to figure out how to reinflate his lung.' Ever since he came home he has been fixed in concentration, driven. The eagle intent on touching all the bases, dotting all the Is and crossing all the Ts.

Women understand physical weakness; anyone who's had a baby does, but healthy men in their forties don't have a clue. For the first time in his life Nick comprehends the shadow that falls between the will and the strength to do what he wants. The first time he landed in the hospital it looked like an accident: surprise, man. You can't walk around with the flu. Now his body's failed him twice. What seemed like a freak occurrence may be a pattern; coming home he said, 'I don't want to be the kind of guy who gets sick!'

He carries himself differently, as if this episode has opened the door on last things. He's still in shock. He has acknowledged the possibility of his own death. It's odd, watching him forge through the days like the Faulkner character who wouldn't sleep because he thought death could not get him unless it caught him lying down.

While the great creature on Clair's shoulders stirs, weighing her down. A dozen times a day she thinks she'll tell Nick what happened; then she looks at him and knows she can't. Nick is fixed on what he sees through that open door, that she can't see. Like a specter it stands between them every time they talk. He burns like a flame, concentrated on proving the strength of its own light. Nothing else figures in the larger scheme of death and survival. If she told him, the knowledge wouldn't kill him, but anger could: what he might do.

Still she has to tell him something. 'I think you ought to do something about the Hickson Lounge.' When he shakes his head impatiently she says, 'If you're not careful he's going to walk away with the store.'

Preoccupied, he says, 'I'll mention it to him at the party.'

'Party!'

'Will and Mara's party tonight. Did you forget?'

'I thought we were staying home. You can't go, you've been—'

Pride flashes. 'Why, do you want them to think I'm sick?'

'Al told you to—'

'Take care of myself. Well, I'm sick of taking care of myself.' He lifts his head. 'I can't afford to be sick, Clair. If I let down here, people are going to start acting like I'm already dead.'

Before she knows what she's going to say, it just comes out. 'Well, I'm not going.' It is a relief.

'They're counting on us.'

'I can't. It wouldn't be right.'

'Will especially. He says he wants to get to know you—'

She cuts him off. 'Better. Well I'm not going, OK?'

'You sound like one of the kids. What's the matter, Clair?'

'Nothing's the matter. Really.' Her throat constricts. Her chest is tight. Interesting. The more you don't tell a person something, the more you don't tell them. It is either a discipline or a trap. 'I just don't want to go.'

At least part of Nick comes back from wherever he's been traveling. 'Has something happened that I don't know about?'

Again she weighs it: Nick in all his vulnerability against the thing that sits on her shoulders, breathing in her ear. In any other winter she would tell him everything but this winter has cost him dearly. The gray eyes he turns on her are really fixed on something else. Oh God, she thinks, leveled by a sense of loss. I've got to take care of him or I'll never get him back. 'Really, no.'

But he's on his feet, pulling her close so he can look at her. No, look into her. 'Clair.'

'OK,' she says. It takes her a minute to find and frame the right words: minimal, accurate, true. 'I can't be around the guy. I don't like him.'

'Is that it? Is that all?'

'I'm sorry,' she says. In a funny way, she is. If she liked Will Strait none of this would have happened. She and Strait never would have clashed. She and the man she loves best would not be standing here at this odd little impasse with Nick not knowing what questions to ask and Clair poisoned by answers that she can never give, secrets boiling up and destroying her from the inside. Say too little and Nick will never let her get away with it; he'll join her hand and Strait's and beg them to be friends. Say too much and Nick will— She doesn't know what Nick will do.

'If there's something you're not telling me, I just wish you'd tell me.' The head tremor, the drained face tell her how much this is costing him – being in the world right now, getting through the days.

He thinks he wants to know but he doesn't really want to know. She shows him as much as she can afford to. 'I think he's after your job.'

'Oh, that,' Nick says, relieved. 'I can handle that. Is that all?'

She struggles with it. Is she supposed to warn him, paint it over, what? Angry because she has to protect Nick when she most needs him, she is sharp: 'I think you should watch your back.'

'He's only doing what I brought him in to do.' Strait was his choice and changed as he is by his time in the hospital, Nick is before everything an absolutist. He defends his choices to the death. He sighs. 'What do you want me to tell them?'

'Tell them I'm sick.'

'That would be a lie.'

'Tell Mara I'm sorry.' Diminished by the loss, pressed by the necessity of protecting him and pushing against it, she snaps, 'Tell them I died.'

God, he looks tired. Distressed, Nick holds her in place. With love, he misreads her. 'If you feel that way about him, you don't need to see him.' Rashly he promises, 'You'll never have to see him again.'

'I wish *you* never had to see him again.' Shut up, Clair. Nick can't help you. Wait for a dark night and catch the bastard red-handed at whatever. Shoot him through the heart.

Forgetting the exigencies of the Evard calendar, forgetting the promises the Sailor children made to the Strait children when they said goodbye only this afternoon he says, 'I promise. You never have to see him again, but I do. I'm the department chair. I got him to leave a terrific setup in Venice and take this job in west hell so you're going to have to forgive me, I have to do work with him and I have to do right by him.'

Make a bad decision, Clair thinks, and you force yourself into an untenable position. You end up denying everything – even your own best instincts – because you're so hung up on proving you're right.

'I have to go to his party and enjoy it, I have to read his manuscripts and have lunch with him because he came on short notice and walked into a bad situation and as far as I know, he's doing a good job. I hired him and he's my colleague and my responsibility.'

'Let me go, Nicky, I'm tired.'

'No.' He pulls her close. His voice is even, gentle, loving. Nick, Nicholas Caton Sailor, fantastic partner and loving father, gifted critic and all-American professor who was, and don't you forget it, an Eagle Scout which at some level he still is, honest and faithful, clean, brave and reverent, is acting true to form. Never backs down and never lies.

'You never have to see him again but you have to understand, Clair. I do.'

He holds her close so he won't have to see her face and this is how he lays it out for her, perhaps only explaining but perhaps begging for her blessing because joined as they are in flesh and in love, they are at odds over this. 'I love you more than anything and I have to work with this guy. I have to let him teach his classes and I have to thank him. You don't have to see him, but I'm his boss and I have to live with him. I live with him every day.'

Her kid friends are raiding the publications office. She comes in at night to pick up some folders and finds them walking out with one of her Macs. 'What the hell are you doing?'

'We're in a hurry, it's important.' Caught, Fred blushes. 'So, if you could hold the door for us?'

Instead of holding the door Clair stands in front of it, trying to look big enough to fill the space. Never mind the work he and Sam are supposed to do and haven't; they're moving on her equipment, taking it away. 'Wait a minute. What's going on?'

'It's been approved.' Behind Fred, Sam staggers with one of the office printers.

Behind him is little Gig Jamison, carrying the color monitor under one arm. His wispy dreadlocks have been erased by a buzz cut, revealing an irregular, gnomish skull. It is oddly shocking, like catching him naked. 'Gig! What happened to you?'

'Special project.' It's the first time she's seen him smile. When she doesn't move out of the way Gig says with new authority, 'If you'll excuse me.' He brushes his free hand across the back of the naked skull. The weedy, withdrawn computer genius is trying to get past her and let her admire him all at the same time.

'I said, what's going on? The haircut. That suit!'

As happens with stammerers under extreme pressure, he speaks with great clarity. 'Professor Strait says if I'm going to be a major player I have to look like I belong in the game. Now if you'll just let us by?'

'Hold on. Where did this come from? Did Sam and Fred give you the idea that this was OK with me?'

The look he gives her is almost condescending. 'Will said it would be OK with you.'

Will? 'Well, it's not.' She wants to take Gig by the arm and hold him in place until he tells her what's happening to him.

He turns to Sam and says in that new, cold voice, 'Explain.'

'It's OK, Clair.' Good Sam gives her that broad Irish grin. 'Electronics said we could have this.'

'They said you could have one of my computers?'

'Will got it authorized,' Gig says.

'But the stuff on my hard disk.' She turns to Fred. 'The class notes. You guys were supposed to—'

'I'm sorry. Something came up. Something big. I promise I'll get back to it as soon as . . .'

She says coldly, 'As soon as what?'

'As soon as we get up and running,' Fred says in that authoritative male way that Clair finds both irritating and appealing in these boyish, not-quite men. 'Don't worry about your Mac, it's only a loan. It's only until the new equipment comes in.'

'New equipment!'

'The 486es,' Gig says. 'Color monitors, color printers, the whole setup. It's all on order.'

They're taking turns working her. Fred says, 'Should be here next week. Will got his own budget line.'

Sam finishes. 'The Garsons are putting up the money. You know, those rich people from town?'

'I know who they are.'

'Key players,' Gig says. 'Will is *like that* with them.'

Fred feints with the corner of the computer, trying to move her out of the way. 'They're funding the Garson Victorian Novel project.'

Sam tries to move her with his Irish charm. 'Thanks to you.'

'Me!'

'Really.' Unlike poor Gig, Fred is a handsome kid but in his own way he too is a chronic A student in spite of that sleepy, mussed look and earnest, love-me grin. 'This is so major and it all started here. With you. Like, you let us pull that all-nighter on this old clunker.'

Gig says, 'It was a major breakthrough thing for us.'

'You mean the maze you designed?'

'Will's going to sit down with us and make it work.' He's filled with it, plum-colored and going pink to the top of that naked skull. 'He says it isn't much yet, but it's a start.'

'A start! I saw your program. It's fabulous. How is he supposed to improve on what you've already done?'

121

'Mrs Sailor, he's a professor!' Reproving her, Gig says, 'Will knows a lot of things we don't know.' He doesn't have to say: *he knows a lot you don't know.* 'We're getting written up in *Wired.*'

Sure.

'He says when we get it in shape he'll get it published. *The Victorian Novel Conceived as a Maze.*'

'He's giving us credit in his piece.'

'His piece! You think he'd put your names in his piece?'

'Isn't that terrific?'

'Three students?'

Gig's belligerence surprises her. 'Why not?' He pushes past and goes through the door. 'Are you guys coming?'

'Wait a minute,' Clair says.

'Can't,' Sam says and even though she hasn't budged he leads with the computer, closing on the space between her and the door.

'Wait.'

'Hurry up! He's expecting us, Mrs Sailor. We have to hurry.' While the other two linger in the office, Gig stands in the hallway; it may be a trick of the light but she thinks his eyes are glittering. 'If we're late we don't meet his expectations.'

'And he doesn't let us into his special session tonight.'

She says, 'Fred, I thought you were working for me tonight. The notes are due. So you can just tell Professor Strait—'

'You won't need the notes this issue. His piece is going to take up a lot of room.'

'He says it's a whole issue piece.'

'So if you don't mind, Clair, we have to go before Gig freaks.'

'We do.' Sam appeals to her. 'This is major, OK? Will's planned this private meeting. It's a really big deal.'

'It's not for just everybody.'

Fred says, 'It's for his particular students.'

'What?'

'You know. The best of the best. Sam. Me. Gig. A couple of people you don't know.'

'Sally?'

'I don't think so. Not tonight.' One of the chosen, Fred has a positively evangelical look. 'Tonight he shows us where Poe fits in the larger context of Victorian—'

'I thought Poe was—'

'I guess you had to be there.' Sam's tone is too close to condescending: poor Clair, you just don't get it. You couldn't possibly. 'Will says Edgar's a Victorian at heart.'

'That's great, I guess.' She knows there's no stopping them. 'You're meeting in his office?'

'Oh no. The Hickson Lounge. He says it's time we got treated like grownups.'

Angry, Clair says, 'Brandy, cigars.'

Sam doesn't exactly meet her eyes. 'Sort of.'

'That's great.'

Now there's an edge to Fred's voice. Something in his usually pleasing grin makes her step aside. 'You bet it is.'

Clair doesn't know how, but in a subtle choreography she's been too distracted to mark, these two students she thought she knew have moved her out of their way and are standing in the hall. 'Have fun,' she says as they close the door, wondering why this leaves her feeling so lonely and betrayed.

Sally LeFleur comes in an hour later.

'Sally! What are you doing here?'

'I just came to pick up a couple of things.' Sally is seeing somebody; Clair doesn't know who. Whoever it is has put a new bounce in her step; most mornings she comes in grinning with the smug grin of a woman with a secret. Clair remembers this game: half the pleasure is in having a secret, the other half in keeping to herself exactly what the secret is. She looks up from the phone; she's already checking her voice mail. 'What are you doing here?'

'Picking up the pieces after the kids.'

'The kids.' Sally's expression is a puzzle. 'The kids.'

'Did you know they were boosting one of our computers?'

'Oh, that. You might as well know, they didn't ask me.'

Her voice is so muddy that Clair asks, 'Are you OK?'

Sally does not answer right away; she's busy with her mirror, smoothing her lipstick with her little finger and trying to make sense of her crinkly red hair, back-combing, sliding in a silver clip. Absorbed, she says, 'Why wouldn't I be OK?' Then her salty friend Sally, who's auditing Mary's survey because Clair's plotting her transfer to the state university next fall, strong, self-sufficient Sally turns to her and says in a little girl voice, 'Have there been any calls for me?'

'Nothing that isn't on your voice mail.'

'I mean tonight.'

'Not since I've been here.'

'Then nobody called?'

'Not tonight. Why?'

Sally stands. Her arms float up from her sides. Her voice floats. 'Oh. I thought they might be looking for me.'

Then Sally is gone. Fred and Sam are gone and one of her computers is gone; it's as if her substance is being boxed and carried away.

That night she dreams that while she and Nick are sleeping the front door crashes open and faceless workmen come stamping in. There are intruders downstairs, raising their voices as if they don't care whether the householders hear them or not. When in her dream she finally disentangles herself from the covers and runs to the upstairs front window she sees men in hoods carrying rugs, lamps, her paintings out of their house, stealing everything they care about while glued to the upstairs window, powerless and unable to produce sound, Clair watches and cries and cries and cries.

13

Oh my God, this is so strange. Even though it's high noon on a work day, even though she knows he isn't in there, Will Strait overshadows the house. It's like standing unarmed in front of a locked fortress or trembling at the mouth of a cave. She has the sense of forces gathering to march out but she can't even guess at the size or shape of the enemy stirring within.

In the silence she can almost hear its breath.

Oh stop it, Clair.

That's easy for you to say. All this *subtext* and you and she let your children play together just like any other kids.

It takes her ten minutes to get out of the car. She prepares a smile for Mara Strait and when she has it right she goes up to the front door and knocks. Waiting, she peers through the beveled glass panel as if she half expects to see all her grotesque fears made flesh and slouching across the front hall to rip the door open and confront her, when all she sees is a festive patch of sunlight falling across the bare, shiny blond hardwood floor.

Revulsion makes her tremble. Oh God, this is folly.

It is also an anomaly.

Her children are inside with the Strait kids, four nice children sitting at the kitchen table for one of the irreproachable Mara's careful lunches – sandwiches on wheat bread, carrot curls or fruit, and to prove she knows what kids really want, Devil Dogs for dessert. If Clair feels guilty because she's bad at kid lunches and her kids are sick of their own toys and their

Legos are irretrievably scattered, if she apologizes because her two would rather play here, Mara says, 'Please, you're doing me a favor. They keep each other entertained.' They get along so well with the Strait kids that Clair can leave them for hours and not have to worry.

Her children are inside eating lunch with the Strait children and in the ambiguity that has brought things to this pass Clair knows that she hates this even as she knows they're perfectly safe.

This isn't even a loaded moment. Mara doesn't have to know how she feels and she doesn't need to know what Clair knows. What if she does have unformed suspicions? What if she did catch Mara's big, handsome, oddly voracious husband tangling with a hotel chambermaid? He's not the only man at Evard who fools around.

What she knows is no big deal.

What she doesn't know is the issue that freezes her here on the Straits' front porch with her jaw clamped tight and her joints threatening to let go when all she's doing is what ordinary moms do all the time – picking up her kids.

Mara opens the door. Her voice lifts. 'Clair! You're early.'

'Am I? Oh God, I'll come back.'

'No, really, this is great.' The woman looks so *nice* standing there in her fisherman's sweater with sunlight catching in her smooth blonde hair. 'I'm so sorry you missed our party. It was . . .'

She hasn't seen Mara since the Straits' party: light and music spilling out of the outsider's windows, a lot of people she cares about inside, what was it Lauren said, *people think* . . . She doesn't care what they think as long as she doesn't hurt this nice lady who likes her so much, means so well. Guilty Clair coughs. 'I was so . . .' This is a sentence she'd better not finish. 'I'm sorry too.'

Mara smiles that nice smile. 'Another time.' If Clair's distress shows in her face, Mara Strait is too polite to mark it. She says in that easy, confidential mother-to-mother tone, 'Look, the kids have a project going and they aren't about to leave until they finish. You might as well come in.'

'You don't have to . . .' What? Be nice to me?

'Really. They're so involved that we could both be on the moon.' The next thing Mara Strait says is so unexpected that it makes Clair jump. 'I really ought to thank you.'

'What?'

'For making everything so much easier here.'

Within the fortress the dark shape stirs.

If Clair feels it, Mara does not; she just goes on. 'Chase and Maddy didn't want to leave Venice, one look at Evarton in winter and they wanted to run away, you can imagine. Then they fell in love with your kids. It's made such a difference to us.'

Us. This is so hard. 'I'm glad.'

Mara holds out her hands. 'Oh, please come in. I could use a little company. Will's out meeting people all the time, students, everybody, he's already got dozens of friends, and I . . . Even with the party, I . . . Women just don't – especially these women. It's . . .' Mara Strait doesn't finish.

Clair nods. 'I know what that's like.' *Peck you to death.*

Mara looks at her with those guileless eyes and holds the door wide. 'I'm dying to have you see what I've done with the house.'

Clair is still rocking in her icy boots, half in, half out. If she comes in, does it make her a collaborator? Is Mara a collaborator? She doesn't know. She doesn't even know if she can be friends with this woman without accepting Strait. That business on the balcony: did she read it wrong? Make it up? If she's so right about the man, why does it make her feel so *wrong*?

'I really missed you at the party, but I'm glad you'll see the house without a hundred people grinding food into the rugs.'

Oh God, Clair thinks because this is another unpleasant piece of business she has to transact – explaining to this *nice lady* why she didn't come to the party when she likes Mara; she does, really, and everybody else in town thinks . . . Oh God. She thinks: why do I keep going Oh God? 'No, really. I'm in kind of a . . .' Hurry. Embarrassed, Clair breaks off. She isn't. It is a lie.

'Oh please come see the house. You should have seen what I had to start with, some of it was pretty, but basically it was a lot of heterogeneous junk. I think Will must have asked every woman in town what to get for furniture. Which rugs. Which lamps.' Unexpectedly, Mara's voice hits a new note. 'Everybody but me.'

It is this shadow of an intimation, then, that brings Clair inside. If Mara comes clean she can come clean. She looks guiltily at the sandy puddles her boots are making. 'Your floor!'

'Forget the floor.'

'I can't stay.'

'I know. I just thought you ought to see what . . . I mean, see how . . . I mean, I want you to see what I've managed to do with all this *junk*.' Mara's expression is complicated, sad. 'Please.'

Not her fault, Clair thinks. *Whatever it is*. 'Just for a minute.' She leans into the mirror that hangs inside the coat closet, pretending to comb her hair. No comb in America can help her now, but she needs time to regroup. She has to clarify things – what she's doing here in the first place, what is her relationship to this attractive woman she likes, would have as a friend except for the one impediment. That she's married to Strait. Finally she arrives at a formula that makes this double vision possible and puts on a smile good enough to meet Mara's smile. Got it. I think. *Not her fault she's stuck with that— Never mind what he is. It's not her fault*. If this is going to work there are parameters.

She can't admit the possibility that Mara has chosen her life.

Mara goes on lightly but there are peculiar overtones. 'Thank God Will let me bring a few of my own things.'

In the pristine hall, Clair sees: on a mahogany side table, a silver card receiver with a monogram. Above the table, an eighteenth-century portrait, looks ancestral. Pottery from Acoma, black and white. Touches that suggest that Mara hasn't always traveled in a world defined by the handsome, savagely ambitious Will Strait.

In the sleek kitchen the kids have put their lunch plates on the counter and set up a Friendly's restaurant on the kitchen table, using components from every Fisher-Price set in the house. They're surrounded by garish hamburgers and hot dogs and horrendous ice cream sundaes made out of Pla Doh. The empty cans sit on the table. The Pla Doh is so new the colors are still pure. Clair notes that Mara gave lunch on ornamented re-usable plastic plates with matching cups and matching paper napkins. All four children's mouths are ringed with grape juice; they turn to her with giddy purple grins. Nell and Davy wave as if this is their place and Clair is only a visitor. In spite of the disparity in their ages, the two big ones are playing nicely with the two little ones. The girls are wearing Mylar crowns. Not fussy little tiaras, fit only for a princess. They have on big, tough, you-can-be-ruler-of-the-kingdom crowns.

'Look, Mom. Look what Mrs Strait made for us.'

'Gee Nelly, that's great.'

Davy says, 'And she had us shovel the walk for you.'

'You must be some kind of mother,' Clair says. Next to this carefully groomed, stylish woman, Clair feels badly put together, a messy, overworked klutz. She'd be a perfect mother and a super housekeeper in some other life but she's too tied up in doing her job and surviving the winter to do it right now.

Mara's smile develops raw edges. 'What else do I have to do?'

'Plenty, I should think. Woman like you.'

She shrugs. 'I manage my family's money.' Mara's self-deprecating manner suggests that this isn't the household budget she's talking about. 'I take care of the kids. And Will.'

There are too many questions Clair can't ask.

She doesn't have to.

'His work. Our life. Will is so vulnerable.' Mara adds without explaining, 'He needs everything I have to give.'

Clair says gently, 'I see.' Then before she can stop herself she says, 'He seemed to be doing all right at the Garsons'.' What is she trying to do here? Drop hints? Warn Strait's wife about her husband or explain why she dodged the party even though she knew Mara would be hurt?

'The Garsons are . . .' Mara's grin is a study. ' I went to school with Gail.'

'So they were your . . .'

She nods. 'Will's the novelty. I introduced them last fall.'

'And the portrait in the front hall?'

'Mine.' As if she's already said too much, Strait's wife pulls herself back. 'Come on. Let me show you the rest of the house.'

And with the dry mouth and itchy palms of a voyeur, Clair follows her. Strait's house. She is inside Strait's house. It's like being ten again and falling into a forbidden book. Dirty, you think. This book is supposed to be dirty. Even though nothing dirty's happening in the part you're reading, something dirty is bound to come up; you feel dirty in anticipation.

'I got here too late to save the living room.'

Clair can almost identify which pieces Strait bought with Jane Stevenson's help and which with Betsy Atkinson's. She knows at once which touches Ginny Arnold added on the special shopping trip that left her with that puffed, possessive look – the ceramic table lamp that will never look right, the floral pillows that are ill at ease in this spare room. With the exception of Mara Strait's few ancestral objects, everything is glossy, new. The room is well arranged but the pieces don't sit well together.

When Strait buys he doesn't go for style, he goes for ostentation. With the exception of Mara's pieces, everything in the room is a shade too bright or a hair too big. The pale leather sectional would be wrong anywhere; the beveled glass in the steel-framed coffee table is too thick. The table crouches like a brute on a silky Bokhara that looks as if it traveled here from a great house where it lived a gentler life. Mara's Queen Anne side table sits apologetically next to a designer model recliner upholstered in pony hide. In a strange way the room gives Clair a sense of their lives together – the big, showy outsider who arranged the Bronte editions in their flashy gold and Morocco bindings on the lozenge-shaped teak shelf by the hideous recliner and the woman whose old money has brought them here from Venice and furnished this room.

Mara is asking a complicated question. 'See what I mean?'

Clair can't stop glancing over her shoulder. At any minute he can walk in. She doesn't know what she expects or what she's afraid of: threat or confrontation or the simple fact that Strait will find her here and in his prodigious, egotistical hunger, assume that because she is here in his house and unarmed, they are actually going to be friends.

'Clair?' with the look of someone who understands exactly what she is thinking, Mara waits.

If he comes in now she can make it out through the dining room before his key clears the lock. She offers, 'You've done a lot.'

'It's uphill. But everything you care about is.' Mara's voice is low but clear, like certain kinds of music. 'Will's learning, but he does better when I'm around to advise. He had more luck with the dining room. Your friend Mrs . . . Kellman?'

'Gellman. Lauren Gellman. They're some of our . . .' Used to be. Some of our oldest and dearest friends. If he comes in now she can always slip through the kitchen door, Clair thinks uneasily. She can grab her kids and go out the back; forget the coat and boots.

'Lauren Gellman took him to an antique shop. I even like the chairs.' Standing with her hand on the simple walnut table, Mara says, 'Will's family were strip miners. Appalachia.'

Big, flashy . . . 'I wouldn't have guessed.'

'He wouldn't want you to. When his grandmother was dying I had to force him to go back.'

'That's . . .'

'Terrible. It's not his fault he grew up hard. He needs nice things.' Strait's wife touches the oversized urn in the corner. 'I suppose it's only logical that he picks the most expensive things. Since he met me he's learned a lot.'

'I see.'

'He's quick,' she says and pulls Clair into the hall.

'I know.' I should go now, Clair thinks. All I have to do is tell her I'm sorry I couldn't come Saturday and go.

But half loyal wife and half conspirator, Mara says, 'Wait till you see the bed he picked out.'

It's like being ten and burrowing through that so-called dirty book and finally coming upon the dirty section – makes you feel dirty even thinking about it. Clair wants to put it down; she doesn't want to put it down.

'He never had much,' Mara says. Then she says what strikes Clair as an extraordinary thing. 'He wants what other people have.'

'I should get the kids.'

'Not yet. Not yet. He worked his way through school.' Mara Strait's tone strikes one more change. 'He won't say what he did.'

Dirty book. She can't put it down. Soiled, she prompts. 'Waited table, probably.'

'I don't know.'

'Or worked in the library.'

Mara's response is so sharp and forceful that it makes Clair jump. '*I don't know.*'

And all the time she's afraid of his coming in. Poised on the stairs, Clair looks over her shoulder. *At any minute.* Her breath trembles. 'He's come a long way.'

'With a little help,' Mara says, running up her heels. 'Some people are proud of coming up from nothing, but not Will. He wants people to believe he's always been here.' As she stampedes Clair into the upstairs hall, Mara puts a hand on her arm.

'What!'

'Don't say anything.'

'What?'

'Promise.'

'Not if you don't want me to.'

The next thing Mara says is disturbing; she could be saying a typical wife thing; she could be laying out a truth; Clair has no way of knowing

131

which. Nor can she find out. 'He'd kill me if he thought I'd told you anything.'

God, this is making her uncomfortable. Is she here for Nick? For Mara or herself? Clair doesn't know. She has the sense that she's dancing at the edges of Will Strait's secrets. *At any minute he can come in.* 'I'd better go.'

But Mara says, as if laying a trail, 'I think his father . . .' and does not go on.

She's at the brink here, they are coming up on the forbidden passage in the book. Clair ought to leave but she can't go now. Oh listen, she tells herself. I need to know this. What? Whatever I can find out. 'You were talking about his father.'

But Mara won't say what she thinks Strait's father did. She keeps her hand on Clair's arm, turning her so that they are facing. 'Understand, he's come up from nothing. And he's worked so hard.'

Face to face with this woman she likes so much that she trusts her with her own children, Clair sees how hard it is for her – whatever it is. Being his wife. This. Because she already feels guilty, because she refused the party, she says, 'You don't have to explain.'

Mara goes on in a voice so light that it seems to float in from somewhere else. 'He wanted me to tell you he's expecting to see his article in the *Alumnus*.'

Clair stiffens. 'I told him he won't.'

'No problem. I promised him I'd mention it to you.' Mara nods; duty discharged. She says with an honesty that bonds them, 'All that ambition. He doesn't know. It's the pressure.'

'I see.'

Mara says pointedly, 'So please be patient with him.' It is no coincidence that the two women have ended in the Straits' narrow bedroom where a worn, handmade wedding-ring quilt is carefully centered on a kingsized bed with an overblown pressed wood arrangement at its head. 'I know it's awful,' Mara says, running her hand over the glossy, gilded travesty of nineteenth-century carving, 'but he's still learning. Understand, you have to allow him a little margin. He's come so far. He'll do anything to get ahead.'

'I'm sorry,' Clair says and covers her mouth. *What am I saying? What are you trying to tell me here?* Clair is distracted by the tortoiseshell comb and brush set on the glass top of the tall, disproportionately skinny dresser.

A smeared mouth print on the surface of the mirror. His hairs snarled in the brush. Only Mara's sweet, expectant look keeps her from running away. It is the vulnerable smile of somebody who is used to being hurt and yet there's not a mark on her. Whatever is going on between them has nothing to do with physical violence; this is not a woman who would tolerate it, much less submit.

'Don't be.' Strait's wife moves her farther into the room. They are in a cul-de-sac. If Strait comes in now he will find her trapped in here where he and Mara sleep, smiling foolishly while Mara takes Strait's tortoiseshell brush and as if she and Clair are old college roommates, absently begins brushing her hair. It is too intimate. Flashing on the ugly scene at the Garsons' party, Clair feels guilty for knowing something this nice lady doesn't, apologetic, confused and soiled.

Mara puts the brush down and smiles a shaky smile. God knows what she and Strait do in here. *Why*, Clair tells herself without knowing why it's so important to convince herself, *they do what most married people do*. This woman is a shade too beautiful, a little too serene, sweetly composed. It is too still in this back room. The windows and the storm windows are locked against the winter cold; the room is close, redolent of the spray cologne Strait uses to mask – or is it to enhance – his own scent. But Clair catches it; when she backs away from the dresser, where the scent is strongest, and bumps the foot of the low bed and accidentally sits down she catches it: pure Strait. There's no ignoring or escaping it.

Strait's wife says, 'He can't help it.' Once she sees Clair is situated, Mara goes back to the smeared mirror. It's as if with her back turned, she can say what she has to say. 'It's so important to him to get everything right that I don't dare tell him when he's got something wrong.'

Oh *God*, Clair thinks and hates her own helpless Oh-Godding. Does she know about the girl from the Inn?

'It shouldn't matter at all but it matters *so much*.'

Does Mara know or doesn't she know?

'He's come so far and done so well and if he doesn't know . . .' Mara shrugs.

Clair's teeth strike like clashing plates. Does she know? What does she know?

Mara Strait goes on as if she has brought Clair here precisely so they can have this conversation. 'But he's quick to learn. Believe me, he's quick to learn.' Then she turns back to the mirror, running her fingertip around her lips as if she's come all the way up here just to fix her makeup. 'And we need to forgive him the things he's learning that he doesn't quite understand. How to *be*.'

Reprise: Clair is filled with pain and confusion of the Garsons' party, her clash with Strait in the tight, frigid space between the velvet curtains and the casements. She feels the night cold. She shrinks from the glassy surface of the remembered ice.

Mara turns. 'Do you see what I'm trying to tell you?'

'Not really.' Oh God this is making her so uncomfortable. So here she is in Mara Strait's house, *in her house* with the delicate job of apologizing for refusing the big party, full of misgivings, diminished and crippled by unreasoning dislike. It isn't fair. She sits on the bed where Mara sleeps with the man, not knowing how to tell her or, in fact, precisely what she has to tell.

But framed in the double-glazed window with the sun at her back, Mara Strait just smiles and goes on. The scent in here is dizzying, the sunshot room is spare and unaccountably beautiful; Mara is beautiful and Clair can't tell whether it's Strait's taste in furniture or her marriage or her own life Mara is talking about, whether, like Clair, deep in her heart Mara knows, and if she does know, whether she can sort the thing out and give it a name. What she says next is astonishing. 'If you love me, try to see.'

Clair's mouth floods with sudden tears. 'What do you want, Mara?'

When Mara smiles, Clair can see sunlight refracted in the big, green-flecked irises of those wide gray eyes. 'I just want to keep having my life.'

In a weakened condition now, both disturbed and moved, Clair blurts, 'I wish!'

Mara sighs. 'I know.'

The sun strikes lights in Mara Strait's hair and makes new lights in those big, pale irises as she finishes in a voice as clear and lovely as water, 'Sometimes you have to let people be what they are.'

Then when she collects the children and comes out to her car she sees Strait's Lexus parked across the street in the shelter of a stand of blasted-looking hemlocks and she thinks, *Oh God*. Has he been here all this time? Has he been waiting for her? But if Strait is half hidden in the shadows on a winter afternoon that's already turned the corner and is heading for night, it is for other reasons. He has a woman with him in the front seat. He is bending over her as if feeding on her.

Clair hates him for making her responsible for the knowledge. At the same time she is thinking: *A womanizer? Is that all you are?*

She doesn't know, any more than she knows why the sight of Strait reaches into her somewhere deep and grips, turning her inside out. Still she imagines she can make it – she can get her kids in the car and slam the doors and scratch off – she thinks she can still make it home in one piece – until Davy smacks Nell and with a heedless screech Clair's little girl goes sprawling on the ice.

Nelly shrieks. In the Lexus, two heads bob up.

Even though she's pretending not to look at the people in the car, Clair can't help but look. Will Strait makes no attempt to hide the woman he's been . . . Oh no, it isn't . . . Poor . . . He makes no attempt to hide from Clair. Instead he bends over his partner for one more kiss and then separates himself from her with a push and in a swift, easy movement as effortless as the spin on power steering he opens the door and gets out, finely machined and grinning. With that unbroken smile Strait steps into the street where by this time Clair is gulping air, scrambling to get Nelly up on her feet.

'Clair, how nice to see you.' Smiling, he starts working her. 'Especially here.' Handsome as before, hearty, tanned, he moves as smoothly as a perfect specimen – no, more frightening, a steely, well-tooled simulaecrum; there is such a thing as being too tall. Strait goes on in that perfectly modulated, artificial actor's voice, 'Captain America to the rescue. Right, Nello?'

Don't touch my . . .

But before Clair can speak the weeping Nelly raises her arms to Strait and begins to smile. 'Right, Uncle Will.'

'Here,' he says. 'Let me put you into the car.'

'Don't!'

'Let go, Mom. He's rescuing me.'

Strait swings Nelly up and holds her high. 'My girl!'

'*Don't!*'

Davy grabs her arm. 'Quit, Mom. He's trying to help.'

After he has Clair's two children buckled into the back seat, Will Strait closes the door on them and once they are shut in and can't hear, he says in a tone that puts her back at the Garsons', 'Remember what I said.' Then he opens the front for Clair, who glares at him with what she now acknowledges as hatred and then looks past his handsome head to his car, where the woman he was with is . . . Oh God, it is. That's silly, voracious Ginny

135

Arnold huddling in Strait's car, sobbing and reassembling herself and trying to hide from Clair all at the same time.

Clair doesn't speak. She just looks. Then with a stiff wave she indicates the house where Strait's beautiful wife and children are in the kitchen, waiting. The car. And looks back at Strait. There ought to be a way to look at a person, she thinks. You ought to be able to look at that person and make that person die.

But Strait is smiling his handsome, false smile. 'Oh, that,' he says, carelessly glancing over his shoulder. 'That's nothing.' And this is how her new friend's husband dismisses the family car parked under the stand of hemlocks and the distressed, furtive woman he has left waiting in the front seat: 'Nothing but trash.'

Strait's hand as he grips her arm and forces Clair into the driver's seat is beautifully articulated, tightening on her bicep and moving her smoothly and releasing her as if generations of engineers have worked on this particular design for just this purpose – slick, inexorable but in no way rough. The big, swift body, the pressure of the hand are perfectly calibrated but as Clair watches, the glossy, high-tech smile goes a millimeter off the mark, synapses misconnected by contempt. Then he says, right before he slams the door on her, 'Don't you imagine for a second that that's anything.'

14

How do you coexist with evil? Daily. People in the outside world can fight and kill each other and have it over with; they may declare eternal hatred and have it over with. Life in the real world is savage. Final. They can declare themselves and walk away from the consequences because the world is big. It's so big they never have to see each other again.

Real people can go to extremes to express their differences, call the cops, take final steps, but antagonists in this enclosed community do not have the liberty. It doesn't matter what's going on between us; the extent of our fear or resentment or open hatred is not the determining factor. Fixed in place by the society and iced in for the winter, these people have to see each other every day.

College society prohibits large gestures. If Mary is safely stashed in an institution, if everybody's secretly glad, it is because she broke the rules. After all, we are intellectuals here, civilized people committed to the life of the mind; no matter what the problem, we pride ourselves on the intellectual's solutions. We find our way through books on child-raising, sessions in getting along together, marriage counseling. It isn't real unless we've read about it in a book.

This is both the delight of life in small colleges and its curse.

Yes the people of Evard are protected inside this feudal city, but we are also trapped here. This icy valley is like a fishbowl, circular, with no hope of escape.

In order to survive, we live not according to absolutes – absolute good, absolute bad – but by the rules of civility. No matter how bad things get between people, civility holds them in place. No matter what hatreds we feel or how badly we want to express ourselves, we live with the consequences of our actions. We live out our lives in the knowledge that we'll have to get up the next morning and face the villain all over again.

Oh, hello. I didn't know you were going to be at this meeting.

Oh yes you did.

How do you coexist with evil? You have no choice.

Clair passes Strait in the hall and meets his finely calibrated, ball-bearing wave with a grimace that passes for a greeting. She waves out the front door when he lets his children out of the Lexus to play at her house. She tries to harden herself to the reproaches of her friends and she tolerates Sam and Fred's little threnodies and grits her teeth. She walks past the auditorium doors and glances in through the glass. Strait is lecturing. This is not like the usual large class, in which students put their feet up on the backs of chairs, eat their breakfast or sleep. Strait's rapt disciples are unnaturally still. He catches Clair watching through the glass and falls silent. In a spontaneous display the group parts like the Red Sea parting; the rapt young men on the right side lean to their right, swaying; the ones on the left fall forward like trampled glass. What point is he making here? It doesn't really matter. Without raising his hand or lifting his voice he has caused this in a swift, effortless demonstration of control. He looks dead at her and smiles.

It is late afternoon. Clair catches Gig Jamison on the walk in front of the Humanities tower. He is scuttling by in an outsized thrift shop tuxedo with a white silk scarf trailing from his neck; his breath shudders and his bones rattle with the cold because he's coming from wherever he's been with no coat and nothing to cover that shaved skull. Clair stops him. 'Gig! Where are you going?'

The only reason he answers is because she's snagged his elbow and won't let go. 'I can't tell you,' he says with a smug little smile. His eyes are rimmed with red; his face looks like a used Kleenex and his teeth jitter, bouncing off each other as if his motor is running too hard. 'Would you let go?'

'I need Sam and Fred.'

He fixes her with those burning eyes. 'They're busy.'

'Have you seen them?'

'I can't talk now, I'm busy. Would you please let go?'

Fire. The kid has caught fire. Clair thinks, I'm glad he's not my child, but she speaks to him as if he is. 'Well I'm busy too! They have work to do for me. It's way overdue. Where are they?'

'I can't tell you.' His look says, *I won't tell you.* This is the shy boy, not nearly a man, who spooked around the publications office all first semester like a grateful elf, nice little Gig from some rural hamlet, who used to blush with pleasure when she or Sally spoke to him because he was too shy to survive in ordinary surroundings, too withdrawn and insecure to fit easily into student life. With his free hand he makes an extra loop of the expensive scarf round his neck and says quietly, 'Now I told you. Let go.'

She's so surprised that she lets him shake her off. She says, 'At least tell me what they're doing that's more important then their jobs.'

'Special projects,' he says over his shoulder. He is like a skater, moving away from her in the early night. He's headed downhill with no indication of where he's going or what he has in mind. His voice comes back to her in someone else's inflections. 'Nothing's more important than this.'

Troubled, she looks after him. He is marked only by the blue gleam of the mercury vapor light on his bald skull and, like a flag of surrender to some alien power, the glimmering white scarf.

Something is smouldering on the floor outside Teddy's office. He's stalking the hall as if his office isn't big enough to contain his anger; Clair sees it in the balled fists and the bunched shoulders, the way he looks at her without seeing. She's disturbed but not surprised. In her present state the dissolution of all things seems not only expected, but logical.

'Teddy, it's me!'

He raises one hand in a half-salute, but he is beyond smiling. 'Bloody fuck!'

'What?' He's so angry that Clair wonders what he's really angry about. 'Teddy, *use words.*'

'Look.' He kicks the institutional trash can on the floor. 'Look in there.'

It smells like an old fire. She looks in at the remains: a heap of charred paper, imperfectly burned. 'What's that?'

'A kid's life up in smoke. It was going to be a pretty good final project until that pompous asshole tore into it.'

Her heart leaps up. 'Somebody I know?'

'Anything to make himself feel big!' The name he comes out with is not the name she expected. 'Fucking Baynard.' Teddy smacks the wall so hard that he leaves a handprint in the soft composition board. 'Fucking Shane Baynard!'

'Baynard.' Clair's so trapped in the airtight world of her own worries that it takes her a minute to relocate herself. Baynard. Oh, right. 'The visiting poet.' Clair's seen him twice: shaggy, bearded, puts on a Byronic slouch, flies in on Wednesdays to teach student writers. Bollingen prize runner-up with three jobs and a magazine to run, comes late and is gone by midnight. In a different season Shane Baynard would be the center of gossip for a week at least, but in the context of Will Strait he's like wallpaper or Muzak, so unobtrusive by contrast that she's forgotten him.

'The great pied piper. Works one six-hour day and collects his check and that is what he does for his money.' The skin around Teddy's eyes has gone white; the narrow line around his mouth is white. 'Doesn't he *know* how easy kids are to hurt? Let go of me!'

'You're yelling.'

'Zack Myer's dropped out,' Teddy shouts. Doors pop open all along the hall. 'One term to go and Zack Myer is an ex-student.'

She picks up the trash can. 'Come on. Let's take this inside.'

Teddy follows, tractable as a child. 'It was a novel.' He faces Clair over the rim of the trash can. 'And you know what? It wasn't bad.'

She puts it down. 'But our famous writer didn't think so.'

'Our fucking famous writer. Of all the stupid, grandstanding, irresponsible . . . Three hundred pages. Three years of somebody's life. I've read it. It's really good.'

'Baynard didn't like it.'

'In a word.'

'But you did.'

'Who cares what I say when the visiting poet tells him otherwise? This guy is his god. A *famous writer.*'

'Right.' The man is a performative act: the shaggy hair and self-important air tell the world that greatness doesn't have to prove itself because great writers get up in the morning knowing more than you. Clair says, 'They're not the same as real writers.'

'What does Zack know? He's only a kid. The great man dumped on him, so he's convinced he'll never be any good.'

'That's terrible.' She wants to say, hey, want to know what else is terrible? She wants to begin but Teddy is somewhere else right now.

'Can't he figure out that these are *kids* he's working with? But no, he comes on like Ernest fucking Hemingway and he's all, THIS IS FOR YOUR OWN GOOD. His own career sucks so he takes it out on our students.'

Preoccupied, Clair considers her own problem. 'Turn him in.'

'Who to? Nick doesn't need this. Not the way he is. Who am I supposed to tell, Ad Bishop between trips to the hospital? George the Great? He doesn't want to hear.'

She tries it on. 'The campus cops.' *What would I say?*

'That's a laugh.' Teddy is at the window now; thin morning sunlight strikes pale lights in his hair. He says in a still, low voice, 'We're in an extraordinary position here.'

'What?' The resonance is arresting. 'What, Teddy? What position are we in?'

But he is on a different track. 'We're fucking *teachers*. Tell a kid he's no good and he believes you. Tell him to jump in the lake and he jumps. Do you know what Baynard did? *Do you know what he did to Zack?* Calls him in about his book. Makes it sound like a very big deal.'

'How do you know?'

'He told me. Zack.' Teddy forgets himself and grins. 'They tell me a lot of things. The great Shane Baynard keeps the manuscript for six weeks without even a note. The kid's strung tight over it, totally wired. Then he summons Zack. He's totally honored, you know, *special conference*, goes in. Baynard is sitting there with two piles of paper on the desk, one thick, one thin, and this great big famous writer smile. Kid is dying and Baynard makes him wait. Then when he can't stand another minute, this guy he *respects* so much picks up the big pile and says, "This." Like, Zack's mind is running eight ways to Sunday, scared, hopeful, can I get it published, will I graduate? Famous writer's got him hanging by his thumbs. Then Baynard says, "This is shit," and knocks three hundred pages in the trash.'

'Why would he do a thing like that?'

'Because he's the teacher and he can do anything he wants. The whole setup is nothing but a power trip,' Teddy barks. 'This sour, broken-down artistic wannabe uses talented kids to set himself up. It's the one place where he can make himself feel big.'

'That's terrible.'

'Doesn't the asshole know how vulnerable they are? Two weeks to thesis deadline and this sanctimonious freeloader who couldn't care less takes the thin pile and waves ten pages with this shit-eating grin and do you know what the bastard says? He says, "And this . . . This I think we can work with." '

'Poor kid!'

'Then he says, "You might as well burn the rest." Fucking poet. Fuck all fucking poets everywhere. It's just like the end of *Miss Lonelyhearts*. He fucking hands the kid a fucking match. So Zack did just what the master said. He did this. Told me where to find it and split.'

'What a waste!'

'First generation in his family to go to college and now look. Thirty thousand a year begged, borrowed and earned, work-study job and all the rest and Zack Myer's through with learning, through with us, through with life, and all because the great writer personally can't get fucking published. I looked him up. The man hasn't had a book in years.'

'You don't think he's going to hurt himself.'

'I don't know.' He stops and turns, facing her with a sober, thoughtful look. Teddy is dead serious now, speaking out of a gravity that he usually tries to hide. 'Do you know how badly this sucks? We struggle out of graduate school and into these places. We're still only people but the book says we're professors. Me. Nick. Responsible. Trusted. And then some torpedo comes in from the outside and throws it all in the toilet.'

Her mind is running in its own groove. 'I know.'

Teddy says, 'Everything we are.' Explaining why he's here and not in banking or publishing, Nick gets that same dedicated, visionary light in his eyes. *If it was money I wanted, I'd be doing something else.*

'They can't tell the difference between us and a guy like Baynard. They think professors are just like doctors. You know, irreproachable. Is that crazy or what?'

It is a rhetorical question.

'We take these jobs and we don't change, but our responsibilities change. People give twenty-five, thirty thousand K a year just to send their treasures to college here. We fucking well owe them something, you know?' He opens empty hands. 'What can we do? We're only people.'

'You're people with PhDs in things they don't know about.'

'We're still only us. And it's our job to be better than just *us*. Professors.' He says again, 'Responsible.' After a pause in which he studies the hillside far below his office window, Teddy turns back to her. 'But what do we have to give them? What are we really selling anyway?'

'Everything you know,' Clair says. 'All those years in school. The books you write. Who you are.'

'No. What we're really giving them is trust. And some outsider comes in and corrupts everything we're trying to do. You want to know the bottom line with kids? You want to know what is the bottom line?'

When she doesn't answer Teddy goes on anyway.

'They're so fucking *young*. When you catch them like that, when you hold them in the palm of your hand, they listen. They listen because you're the professor and they're only students. You can tell them anything you want. And *they believe everything you say*.'

Sally LeFleur has been crying and she won't say why. She's seeing somebody; Clair doesn't know who. Sally's miserable, defensive crouch makes it plain that it won't do any good to ask. It's clear she's too upset to be of any use to Clair here, even though it's time to call all the class secretaries for last-minute addenda to the notes. With a sense of the inevitable, she calls Nick to tell him to send for takeout and put the kids to bed because she has to finish up alone. Then she sends Sally home. 'Sleep. It'll make you feel better,' she says, when Sally's look tells her that right now nothing can.

When she finishes doing her interns' work it's almost 2 a.m. In ordinary time Nick would insist on coming up to get her, but in these extraordinary times he is asleep, poleaxed by exhaustion, before twelve. She's been transfixed by worry for so long that her screen saver has kicked in and the screen's gone blank. It's like staring into the dark. She stores the notes and locks the office. Then instead of heading down in the elevator and out, instead of going downhill to the parking lot, she uses her elevator key to go up. If she just keeps moving she can do this, but without the penthouse key the elevator won't take her to the top floor and the Hickson Lounge. Instead it stops on the last of the office floors. This is Teddy's floor. No matter how many times she stabs the button the doors keep opening on the drab office corridor. At the far end of the hall stairs lead to the penthouse. Stepping out into the gritty institutional hallway, she drags her knuckles along the wall because late as it is she thinks maybe she'll find Teddy in. She can bound into his office like Nancy Drew and pull her best friend along by the hand and take off on a storybook adventure – plenty of excitement, happy ending probable.

Together they can sneak out into the hall and go up the last flight of stairs to the Hickson Lounge. They can catch Strait in the middle of doing something that will get him fired.

Teddy isn't here. Why should he be? Typical Teddy, he tacked a note to his door before he left this afternoon: GON OUT. BACKSON. BISY BACKSON. Oh, Eeyore. In a painful little flip she imagines them both kids again. Beautiful, with everything ahead. Never be kids again, she thinks, going on down the hall alone. Oh, Pooh.

If she opens the last door quietly and goes furtively, she tells herself it's because she doesn't want to deal with Security; the campus cops are literal-minded at best and they would ask questions. It would – right. Thanks, Lauren. It would make her look bad. 'Can't be too careful, Clair.' Not Will Strait, she thinks bitterly. He doesn't have to be careful. I do. She goes along cautiously, not knowing whether she's more intent on catching Strait in something or on not being caught herself.

There's no reason for her to expect to be able to see into the Hickson Lounge. Light comes out from under the heavy paneled door, suggesting that there may be somebody inside, but the glass pane that punctuates it like a speakeasy peephole has been covered from the inside with Mylar contact paper. If there's anything going on in there, it's going on in silence. There are no voices; she can't be sure whether she hears or only imagines that she hears somebody or something stirring in the lavishly furnished private room, settling deeper into a leather sofa or sliding across a silky Oriental rug. At this remove she thinks the scent she catches is more than incense, not just Strait's cologne, but she can't be sure. It smells like dope. If she can only catch him doing blow or smoking dope with his class . . . But unless she can get into the lounge she can't know *what* he's doing, much less prove there's something going on. Never mind what she hoped to do or discover here. Shut out, she's come up empty. As far as Clair can tell there's nobody in the lounge and nothing going on. She wants to try the door; she's afraid to try the door.

Then a hum or a vibration that she took to be the whir of the building's machinery separates itself into human speech. She hears heavy feet hit the floor. Riveted, she whirls and plunges into the staircase before Strait, if it is Strait, comes to the paneled door and opens it and discovers her. By the time Strait, if it is Strait, opens the door there will be no sign of Clair in the empty hallway except for the steel door that's still closing slowly long after she pushes through it and darts down the stairs.

Running through the hall past Teddy's office, Clair fumbles for her elevator key but, unnerved, she sees that the elevator is already engaged: 1, 3, 5, 8, speeding up. Security answering a call from the Hickson Lounge? Somebody coming up to the lounge? She doesn't know. She knows only that she'd better take the stairs and she'd better run.

The flight down the tight staircase is dizzying; in this constricting cement chute her footsteps reverberate, so clamorous that she can't hear anybody pounding down from the top or coming up from the bottom; she hears nothing but the sound of her own flight. By the time she hits the roll bar and pops out the fire door at ground level she's deafened by the sound of her own breath. Then she's arrested – running in midair – black winter sky, black ice! And she flips, breathless and flailing, onto her back.

It takes her a minute to resume breathing so she can get up. For a terrifying second the ice snares her and she struggles in place like a stricken animal. When she does stand everything is so still that she can't know what she's listening for. Oh my God it is so late.

Nothing. She hears nothing but the sounds of heaters and ventilators, the machinery of the college that grinds on in winter, day or night. The people who work Security are cribbed up in their little booth in the foyer of the administration building. Even the last student has gone to earth somewhere, sleeping in a welter of quilts and blankets that smells of unwashed underwear and food eaten hastily in bed and the peculiarly private, sodden aura that accumulates and builds in unaired bedding during a long winter's sleep. Exposed, alone in the night-time shell of this deserted civilization, Clair thinks all the thoughts of a woman caught alone at night.

If she has been followed, there is no way for her to know. The night is so still that it quiets her. She moves slowly, picking her way down the glazed hillside like a refugee finding her way out of a blasted city, skirting land mines with clenched lungs as if one wrong step will blow her apart.

Preoccupied as she is, intent on keeping her feet, she is strung too taut to be aware of the slight movement, the incursion that begins as an imperceptible stir at a point deep in the shadows of the Humanities tower and compounds itself into a glittering, icy rush as frozen spray starts up in front of a needle-nosed sled so low and sleek that it is as one with a rider in black: black sweater, black gloves, black skier's mask. Like a heat-seeking missile the sled with its dark rider zooms into the track left by Clair's footsteps, hurtling down the hill, gathering speed and gaining on her until the *whish* of the approaching projectile makes Clair turn with a gasp. She sees it coming – oh my *God!* – and hurls herself to one side in a crash that brings back the sudden, unlikely terror of Ethan Frome Day and leaves her sobbing in the snow. As she falls in front of the protective trunk of an old copper beech the sled passes – this close! – and disappears into the darkness below.

She gets to her feet. 'Son of a bitch,' she shouts. 'You son of a bitch!' And goes to the call box in the parking lot and pulls the lever.

To Security's credit, there's a campus cop car here within minutes. It's Ray Strang, an overweight retired policeman who tilts his Smokey the Bear hat with a grin. When Clair sees him her heart sinks; why did she imagine Security could help her? 'Why, Clair. Where's the fire, Clair?'

'Hurry, you can catch him!'

'Catch who? Who was it?'

'That's the trouble! I don't know. Some bastard tried to run me down with his sled.' If he'd hit me, she thinks grimly, at least I'd know.

'Probably a student. Kids,' he says easily. 'You know kids. They don't mean half the things they do.'

Her voice is tight with anger. 'This wasn't a kid.'

'You know kids,' Ray repeats, looking up at the darkened buildings on the hill. In this feudal kingdom that makes its own rules the students are to be protected; Evard draws its own lines, which are blurry and poorly defined. When there is a problem, the administration goes to great lengths to keep it inside these walls. *In loco parentis* carried to extremes. This sleepy campus cop has just shown her the bottom line. Much as he'd like to stand here talking, he isn't going to do anything.

Clair repeats grimly, 'It wasn't a kid.'

'Then it's not our jurisdiction, ma'am.' Ray loses interest immediately. He yawns. 'Whoever he is, he's long gone. Probably in bed by now.'

'No. He was headed down. Maybe we can catch him before he gets to . . .' His house? Is it Strait? She doesn't know.

'Sorry, ma'am.' He points to the stone gateposts at the bottom of the main drive. 'Our responsibilities end at those gates.'

'Your car phone. The town police.'

'We keep the town police out of campus matters.'

'This isn't a campus matter.'

'Then I guess if you want to, you can call the police.' He's getting tired of this conversation. 'But I might as well tell you, they'll tell you it's a campus matter and bump it back to us.'

Teddy: *Security. That's a laugh.* 'Dammit. *Dammit.*'

146

'Ma'am.'

She says in a tight voice, 'Look. If you can't do anything about this and the town cops won't, there is one thing you can do, and this is definitely your job. You'd better look into the Hickson Lounge.'

'I couldn't do that.'

'I smelled dope in the hall.'

Damn Ray, he blinks as if he's never heard of dope. 'Ma'am?'

'Pot. Marijuana. Grass. Controlled substances,' she says because he isn't responding. 'Somebody's up there breaking the law. I smelled it in the hall.'

'Oh, ma'am, ma'am. You can smell dope in any hallway in the college and you know it as well as I do. Kids are kids.'

'This is a classroom.'

'Professors are in charge of what goes on in classrooms, ma'am.'

'It's still against the law. The town cops think so.'

'If you want me to, I can drive you home.'

'I'd rather you called the police.'

'Yes, ma'am.' He puts her in the car and closes the door. Then he taps on the window and when she rolls it down he puts his hand on her arm and leans in. He's paternal, almost condescending. 'You know as well as I do, we keep campus matters on the campus, Clair. You know as well as I do, we handle our own problems here.'

What takes her next comes out of nowhere; it is as certain as it is immediate and irrational. In a world with no next steps, what has just happened would be intolerable. It would be insupportable, but Clair makes it home on the strength of what's just come to her.

She has to see Mary Roeg.

15

Ben

At some big corner Ben shrinks from the headlights of an onrushing bus. Dragging his hair down so nobody has to see his face, he ducks into the bus shelter and lines up with the other passengers. When his turn comes he hurtles on, looking so ravaged and dangerous that the driver doesn't insist on his fare. Like an escaped ax murderer, he lurches to the back where he huddles in the corner by the window and rides and rides, sobbing himself dry while the few passengers still out at this hour gather their groceries and their shoulder bags and change seats. Race memory prompts him to pull the cord at a designated spot and as he stumbles off the bus he grabs a handful of transfers, not caring that the driver yells and then, relieved to have him off the bus, lets him go.

The next bus goes direct to the city center; it is as if fate has stepped in to bring Ben what he most wants right now. After all these months of trying to get to this destination, weeks of starting out and not being able to make it out the front door, much less down the steps and to the corner, Ben Messinger is being delivered to the city business district. By the time he gets off he is almost at his destination. He's sore ·all over from the confrontation with his mother, raw and so hungry that all his insides are rubbing against all his other insides, but this small success makes him triumphant. He's made it this far. It's only a matter of time now.

All he has to do is find the insurance tower.

Don't congratulate yourself for doing something you should have done in Venice. *If I'd had the guts I could be dead by now.*

149

Laughing raggedly, he runs from one corner to the next, making forays down side streets, circling uselessly. Is the insurance tower on this street? This one? He doesn't know. He's so wired that he's only now realizing that although he's seen the tower in a hundred TV views of the city skyline, it is not immediately visible from where he is standing. He's too close. Unless he's too far away.

He could ask, but even though he got this far without having anybody faint at the sight of him, Ben is not ready to start conversations. Instead he cross-hatches the financial district, which shut down hours ago. There are few people out in this weather – this weather! He ran away without a coat but is only now noticing. No matter. He won't need a coat much longer. Giddy from the fresh air, stumbling and exhausted, he blunders around the business district for what will seem like hours. It's late. Stone buildings loom on all sides, as massive and foreboding as the effigies of long-dead kings at Abu Cimbal. God, he thinks, if only one of them would fall on me.

But that is not what will be doing the falling. He's going to get to the top of the goddam insurance tower and plummet like a stone angel, smash to bits on the sidewalk. If he can find it. If he can only find the place! What makes him think even if he can find it that he can get inside? It's too dark. He's lost. His hands are so cold he can't feel the tips of his fingers. In his right mind, Ben would probably quit around now, but he hasn't been in his right mind since Venice. Knows it. This, then, is the problem.

It hurts to breathe. Pain snatches his flank; he's been running for too long. Panting, he goes to ground in a doorway and discovers that he's lost. He's under the marquee of an apartment building and, God, it's as far as he can go right now. Panting, he waits in the shelter of the arch. Let anybody go in or out and he'll slip into the revolving door.

Standing still turns out to be worse than running. Everything catches up with Ben. His memory spikes. *San Toma*. It's strange, nothing dramatic, just a little peak like one of those blips on an electrocardiogram. *Me*. Don't worry about what it means, hold your breath long enough and maybe it will go away.

But it doesn't.

He has to spring out of the arch and follow the last tenant inside in spite of this. He slips into the revolving door as if he belongs here. Waving at the indifferent doorman, Ben creeps along behind the tenant, peeling off at the elevator. This place isn't as tall as the insurance tower but he's in such a rotten state right now that he could probably jump off a bungalow and crack like an egg, he thinks, and that would be an end to it. At the bend of the marble hall behind the super's mop bucket, he sees the stairs. The super is off somewhere, answering the house phone or picking up the early edition of the paper to take down to his apartment. He's left his mop to prop the door so he won't have to bother with keys.

It will take Ben a long time to make it to the roof. He climbs for what seems like hours. He has to pee; he wants to die; he needs to eat. Don't bother, pretty soon you won't feel like eating, and pee? You won't ever need to. God, he thinks. Oh, God!

And picks his way across the ribbed copper roof to the ornamental stone parapet with its stone nineteenth-century ornaments: finials, gargoyles, stone lions. Climbs up on the little wall. The air is cold enough to make him a little drunk. It's so clear he gets the idea that a better person just might be able to fly, but Ben is scared of heights, wobbling, exalted and dizzy. *Can't look now.* If he looks he won't have the guts to do the job. Ben doesn't know what he's doing or why he's doing it, he only knows the devils behind him are worse than the plunge ahead so he composes himself with his eyes shut and says a prayer without words, and when he doesn't totter and fall and die by accident, he apologizes to God and spreads his arms. Launches himself.

And then at the last minute screams, 'Oh, my *God*!' and tries to turn himself around in mid-flight and get back to the parapet. Tearing his nails and shredding the tips of his fingers, he makes one last grab for the stone but gravity takes him and he slides down in spite of this, leaving bloody streaks on the uneven stone wall to mark his intention. *At least it's over.*

But. It is. Not. Over.

The landing comes sooner than he thought and it is terrible. It hurts! He is – oh God! – he's smashed flat and breathless on a roof less than ten feet below the spot where he took off, lying on his belly on the yielding tin surface with his heart stopped and his chest compressed and aching.

Not dead. Not even badly hurt. Just dazed, with his knees sprung and all the skin worn off the palms of his hands and his elbows laid open right through the fabric of his sweatshirt.

WHO . . .

He is alive. Before he can stop it from happening, the air has rushed back into his lungs. Ben has begun to breathe again.

WHO DID THIS . . .

'If you say one word . . .'

'OK,' he shouts. It sounds thin but his voice is trembling with excitement. 'OK. OK!'

WHO DID THIS TO YOU?

'I'm not dead.' It rips out of him. 'Hey, everybody, I'm not dead!'

It wasn't me.

He is on fire with it.

And if it wasn't me, then . . .

If he isn't dead, it's for a reason. Survival is to a purpose.

Then there's something else I've got to do.

If only he can get in off this terrible roof before he freezes to death. No. Before the sun comes up and they find him here. Somebody in the next building will pull up the shades and see Ben Messinger staggering around in the morning light and call the cops.

Unlike the insurance tower, the old-fashioned stone building is staged like a wedding cake. This next-to-last tier where Ben has landed is a pretty, useless architect's touch.

Sore in every joint, with every muscle beginning to ache, Ben makes his way across the front of the building, looking for anything, a door, a window, a trap door that will put him back inside. Sliding in pigeon dung, he makes his way along only to discover that the ledge stops at the corner. It only goes across the front of the building.

He can wait to be discovered, but he can't wait. If Ben is still here in the morning the cops will come, along with crisis shrinks and the TV nightly news. *Talk me down, will you . . .* Firemen will come with hooks and harnesses and snake down the side of the building and lock him into a safety vest and when they reach the ground they'll hand him over to Delia, who'll hold him in place and choke the truth out of him. Or else he'll get shipped to the mental hospital. Orderlies will strip him. Everybody will see. *'One word . . .'* He can't even think about what will happen then. Unless he can find a way off this ledge he's going to have to jump after all.

'One word and I'll . . .'

What? What will you do? 'No!' Surprised by rage, Ben hurls himself at the wall, howling like a commando as he claws with his hands and feet, scrambling for the top. He makes it partway up before he loses it and falls.

Anger drives him now. Kicking off his boots, Ben addresses the stone surface with his naked feet and fingers. The building is put together like one of those walls they build in gyms to train rock climbers, carved stone held together by cement. It looks unpromising but it is possible. He thinks. It has to be. Ben may fall a dozen times, he'll be bloody when he reaches the top, digging in with raw fingertips and scraped toes until he heaves himself up and over, but now that he has a reason to live, he'll do whatever he has to do to get back inside. It has become important to survive.

16

'You're looking in the wrong place,' Teddy says as Clair adds a carton of books to her fresh fruit and home-baked burnt offerings and boxes of Godivas and Callard and Bowser's and tins of tea and tokens from the town's jewelry stores and boutiques, silk flowers and wind-up toys, all the objects she has accumulated over the last week, selecting and assembling with the near-mystical concentration of a witch doctor massing fetishes in an attempt to arm the patient against the unspeakable. She is driving north to see Mary Roeg. 'Please don't go.'

'Why?'

'You're making a mistake.'

'Oh Teddy, not you too!' Quick tears make her vision blur. This happens too often now.

'Mary can't help you.' Absorbed, Teddy picks up a book and smooths it regretfully. 'She can't even help herself.'

'Just let me do this, OK?'

'Try and stop you,' Teddy says.

'Right.' She takes a deep breath. 'OK.' Again. 'OK.' She's like a sergeant calling the numbers on a forced march. 'OK.' Let's get this operation on the road. She adds scarves and jewelry and perfumed soap for Mary, drawings from Davy and Nell, letters from Nick and Ad Bishop and fatuous George Atkinson; she's extorted get-well cards from Sam and Fred and Sally and even Gig Jamison at great personal cost, when she knows all the perfumes of Arabia won't help her in this encounter. Never mind. Even when you're not getting anywhere, moving is better than standing still. Clair is taking the long drive upstate to the private psychiatric hospital perched on the Canadian border. Like a secondary character in a heist movie, she's provisioning for this encounter and rehearsing the moves without a clue as to the nature of the caper, blindly trusting that all the necessary objects, all her predetermined steps are really to a point. She gets in the car. She can't leave because Teddy won't let her shut the door. She tugs. 'Don't, Teddy.'

He tugs back. 'Why don't you not go?'

'I have to talk to Mary, OK?'

'What makes you think she can even talk?'

'Oh Teddy please don't. I think she knows Strait. I think she knows him from before.'

'Don't bother poor Mary. She can't tell you anything.'

'You didn't see them dancing,' Clair says. 'Her and Strait, hashing over some old . . . You didn't see her face at the end.'

'I didn't have to see her face. I know what she's like. Too single.' Teddy's expression is sweet, grave. Considering, he amends. 'No. I know what that's like.'

He is trying to tell her something but Clair is on her own track. 'Maybe Strait set her off. Something he said, or did.'

'Everybody's got to get it somewhere.'

'What?'

But Teddy doesn't explain and he doesn't follow up. 'Be cool, Mary's in bad shape right now. When people get like that they don't want you to see them.'

You, with your enviable lives. Grief surprises her. 'I can't just let him steal our lives!'

'Hang in.' Even though they're alone in the street Teddy lowers his voice. 'I've been talking to my kids.'

'Oh, kids,' she says with more anger than she would have anticipated. 'What do they know, they're only kids!' Sam, Fred. Her student *friends*. 'They all love Professor Strait.'

'Not mine.' Teddy means the gay students he counsels. 'They don't like him.'

'They're the only ones.'

'They say he's a homophobe.'

'So are a lot of people.'

She is too pressed to take in what he says as he shuts the door on her. 'Not like this.'

The moment she comes into the uncompromisingly bright day room in the discreetly private facility where George Atkinson has installed Mary, Clair sees that she's in the wrong place. She can't talk to Mary in here. There are no comfortable corners in this room with its Cellotex ceiling and fluorescent strip lights and chrome furniture, no alcoves where people can talk without being monitored. What she can't know until she sees her is whether Mary is also in the wrong place. The metal detector, a double door system constructed like the airlock on a space ship, the turnbuckle that carries objects from the ward into the nurses' station all suggest that Mary is sicker than she thought.

The institutional measures seem extreme.

All Clair's gifts, all Mary's favorite books and the candles and special soaps, all the tokens she collected to arm herself for this encounter have been impounded at the supervisor's desk; for the comfort and safety of visitors and patients alike, nothing unauthorized goes in or out. Locked in the medications room, nurses may already be gobbling Clair's best chocolate chip brownies, smearing Clinique samples on their cheeks and holding the bright silk scarves up to their faces so they can tell each other which of the many colors suit them best.

Clair sits and waits for Mary, who does not come. She checks the clock above the door. Time is intransigent. It refuses to move.

In the open kitchenette in front of the Plexi-shielded double glazed windows in openings as narrow and deep as gun slits in a fortress, patients of radically different shapes and sizes are making chocolate chip cookies. Superintended by an aide, the obese and the unnaturally thin alike are mixing dough ineffectually with plastic spreaders too pliable and unwieldy to be used for anything else. They are trusted to bake, apparently, but not to do it alone. In chairs, on couches and the incongruously festive red plastic banquettes that line the day room, women under heavier medication are plopped like the smily-faced Fisher-Price play people that Nelly moves around at will. Designed to sit where they fall, they wait for nothing with bland, unalterable grins, too zonked to care whether they can see the TV from the spots where the aides parked them after lunch today.

It is daunting, seeing *someone you know* juxtaposed with these exigencies. She can't possibly be this sick. What does sweet, distraught, academic Mary have to do with padded doors and double-shielded windows? If she wants to cook why can't she just use ordinary spoons and knives? Poor Mary is a little depressed, not leveled by some industrial strength psychosis. Her collapse is just that, a logical response to cumulative stress. For a simple nervous breakdown, if women are still permitted nervous breakdowns, this place looks like overkill. She doesn't belong in here, Clair thinks, watching the door to the ward.

Mary will come out and tell me, 'I don't belong in here.'

She doesn't come out at all.

Disproportionately weary, Clair thinks, place like this, who would come out?

Even if the nurse can coax her friend out of her bedroom and down the hall to this terrible room with its bright lights and its chrome yellow walls, Mary can't possibly talk to her here. No civilized person could.

Time creeps.

The corners of the tables are padded. The aide microwaves cookies in flaccid plastic dishes. Even the chairs are bolted down. Clair understands that patients are put to bed in relentlessly lighted rooms with doors left open so attendants will see or hear any unauthorized movement, any untoward act. Forget belts, shoelaces. Oh shit, she thinks. Forget scarves.

What do they think Mary is going to do?

Has she tried to kill herself? Clair doesn't think so. Not sentimental Mary, the overaged but deliberately sexy intellectual with her love for Victorian poets, her Tammy Faye makeup and her gaudy jewelry and touchingly garish silks.

Doubts feed on the details. As Clair waits, her image of Mary flexes and changes. It gets bigger: she sees Mary Roeg altered by her time away from Evard, distorted and grown huge, Mary as mad as Mrs Rochester, lunging out and swarming down on her with sharpened teeth and razor claws, Mary attacking her for being happy when she, Mary, is alone.

OK, she thinks with the guilt of the survivor. Do your worst.

'I'm sorry.' The nurse's voice surprises her. 'I thought this might be a breakthrough day. She won't leave her room.'

Clair can't suppress relief. She's on her feet before she realizes that she is in no respect free to go. In this elaborate mission with no end specified there remain certain necessary steps. She's here until this quest or assignment plays itself out. 'I can't leave without seeing her. I came all this way.'

'All the way from Evarton.' The nurse nods. 'Don't worry, I've arranged for you to see her in the room.'

'I'm so glad.' This, then, is the next step. See Mary in the room. Everything clicks into place or nothing clicks into place.

Is that all we are? Uncertain of the end?

The encounter is nothing Clair expected. Mary is sitting on the last of eight beds at the far end of a ward that is as spare and chaste as a convent or an orphanage. She sits facing Clair with her hair brushed and her face composed and her hands folded on her lap and her feet set together like a little girl's. Mary has gained weight. Without her girdle and bra – my God, are they afraid she'll hang herself on her bra? – without her Power Net underpinnings, she is amorphous. She looks like a big child. It's clear from the careless mismatch of fabrics and colors that somebody else has picked out her clothes and dressed her today. Her hair is clean and freshly brushed, but without benefit of Evelyn's of Evarton it lies flat. The color stops inches short of the scalp, abruptly marking the point in her life when Mary ceased being able to do anything to make herself look better than she really looks.

'Oh, Mary.' Clair advances with her hands out, thinking if they can't find anything to say to each other, at least they can hug.

But Mary doesn't get up and she doesn't raise her arms.

The nurse says, 'She may not want to talk to you.'

Compassion makes her voice soft. 'It's OK. I'll talk to her.'

Except for an apparently comatose patient on the bed nearest the door, except for the nurse who pulls a chair into the doorway so she can observe without being obtrusive, she and Mary are alone. What do I think I'm going to do here? Clair wonders, afraid to begin. Cheer Mary up?

She smiles at Mary.

Without makeup, wearing an expression that makes it clear she is beyond caring about makeup, Mary looks at her out of a bald, naked face.

Clair waits.

Mary waits.

'If you don't have lipstick you can use mine,' Clair says.

Mary bats her hand away.

'That's OK, Mary. If you don't want it, you certainly don't have to put it on for me.'

Standing over the sick woman in her own cool string sweater and leather jeans and Navajo belt, reinforced by full makeup and waiting Mary out

159

with her bright hair crackling and her skin ruddy, Clair Sailor is disgusted by her own good health. She understands that at the moment she's no better than Mary Roeg. She is less.

She can't even control what comes out of her mouth. 'I was hoping,' she says.

She says, 'I just . . .'

Mary says nothing. She doesn't care what Clair *just*.

'I was hoping you'd be well by now.'

In the silence Clair finds herself gauging huge Mary's responsiveness, her potential strength, and for the first time recognizes and acknowledges her real reason for coming today. Greedy and hopeful, Clair hasn't driven all this way and waited all this time to give Mary presents or even to cheer her up. She isn't even here for her stated reason, to ask Mary about Will Strait.

She's here in the locked ward out of the worst of all possible motives. The truth comes out. 'I had to see how you were.'

She's come all this way out of the bare, self-serving need to make an assessment: is this woman ever going to get well enough to come back and do her job?

She is stunned by the discovery. 'Oh, Mary.'

Mary's slumped shoulders and her uninflected stare reproach her. *You don't care about me.* Clair hears this so clearly that she's surprised to discover that Mary has not spoken.

Acknowledging her motives, she feels craven and terrible. Is that all I care about? What happens to Nick and me? Maybe not, but savage in love, she knows it's the first thing she cares about. She says with love, 'Mary, I'm sorry for everything.'

Mary won't speak but she doesn't look away.

'Oh, Mary,' she says stupidly, 'I brought you all these things!' Her voice jiggles. 'Cookies, you know, but they don't want . . . they must not let . . . These nurses. Mary, they impounded everything and they're keeping it at the front desk.' Then because Mary will not stop regarding her, Clair hears herself numbering all the silly gifts and messages that are stalled in the little room behind the nurses' station, dozens of pieces of bright junk that Mary won't want and can't possibly remember and probably will never see, blathering on in a tone of shoddily constructed cheer that cracks in two when Mary says in a clear, uninflected voice: 'You don't have to talk to me like a child.'

160

'Oh Mary,' she cries and then she loses it altogether. She has in all truth forgotten whether she is here for Mary or Mary is here for her. Clair is the child now, pleading. 'If you'd just come home and take your job back he'd go away!'

And Mary – God! In silence, Mary Roeg regards her. The silence goes on for so long that Clair can't know whether somewhere inside her friend a switch has gone off or whether, rather, Mary has gone back inside herself to locate and bring forth a response.

It takes her too long to speak.

When Mary does speak it is in that same cool tone of complete control that comes out of careful assessment of her situation. 'I'd rather be in hell.'

At the door the nurse's head snaps up: noted.

Clair says in a low voice, 'Oh Mary I am so sorry.'

Mary does not say oh, that's all right. She doesn't say anything. It is as if a storm blind has rolled down over her face.

It is an ugly moment. Clair is as naked as Mary now, exposed. She swallows terror but it won't stay down. They are nothing more than two women here, one seated, one not, but she keeps swallowing helplessly because she can't for the life of her say what distinguishes her from Mary at this point or Mary from her, and just as Clair is grappling with this, exhausted and frightened and wildly distracted by the glassy surface of Mary's composure and the basilisk smoothness of Mary's face, Mary begins.

'You don't know what it's like,' she says and then before Clair can stop her Mary goes on, cursing her with a phrase that makes Clair throw up her hands – too late to protect herself – Mary Roeg damning her, 'you with your perfect life.'

'Who . . .' Who have you been talking to?

'You with your nice man and your cute kids and your fuzzy dog with the cute name, how could you possibly know, Clair Sailor. You don't know what it's like to be a nobody. A non person.'

'You're somebody, Mary. You're a professor.'

'Professor. God!'

'You're a . . . good-looking woman.'

'Don't bullshit me. I'm nothing.' Mary's voice is getting big. 'An un-person.' She is shouting. 'Null thing.' Showing her big, square teeth, she names her state in words as frightening as they are absolute. Accurate. They fill the room. 'One woman alone.'

In the doorway the nurse starts up. Clair waves her off. Standing before Mary with her head bowed, she prepares to accept whatever comes.

'You don't know what it's like. Can't possibly know what it's like to go home alone every night to an empty house. Empty bed. Lean Cuisine and too much wine and nobody to drink it with . . .'

If she can get a word in maybe she can stop this. 'I—'

'*Shut up and let me finish.*' Mary glowers. 'You take measures. Desperate measures. Daytime TV. Fucking books on fucking tape – anything to hear another voice, get a cat when you hate cats just to hear something breathing in the house. Weekdays you get by – meetings where you make speeches only you remember, classes you have to teach and, oh baby, those student conferences, lean over your desk and wonder whether the male, man, very young man sitting on the other side hears the noises your parts make rubbing together underneath your clothes but you can't touch him, can't even dream, they're only kids and you leave them alone because it's your responsibility, you leave them alone even when you pretend you could do anything you want with them.

'Fridays are the worst. Put it off as long as you can, try shopping, faculty Happy Hour, go out to eat afterward, you and some book, or you get lucky and go to a party and overstay. It makes no difference. Sooner or later you have to go home alone.' Her voice is ugly, large. 'Do you know what that's like?'

Clair understands there is nothing she can say.

'No way in hell can you possibly know. Do you know a woman can go Friday night to Monday without saying a single word or hearing anybody say her name? Unless you count the 900 numbers you have to call even though you're so sick and ashamed when you get off the phone that you start to cry and swear you'll never do that again.

'You think if you can just get the right clothes and match them up, so you go shopping; you think if you can just change your hair or stop being fat or *smelling bad*, you know . . . So you take another bath and rub more stuff on yourself so you won't smell bad and you rub on other stuff so maybe somebody out there will think you smell good enough to come home to – no, good enough to take home . . .' She breaks off.

Resumes in a conversational tone. 'You probably don't even know how I got this way.'

Across the hall a patient calls and calls in one of those reedy voices that can go on forever; nobody comes. Standing like a student being lectured on bad study habits, Clair waits with her head bowed, guiltily studying her empty hands.

'I was good in school.' She sighs. 'I wasn't cute, so I had to be smart. Got all As, and everybody hated me because they didn't know I'd rather get all Ds if only I could be cute, but smart was the only thing I was good at so I thought, OK, wait till college. Everybody's smart there. Yeah, right. So I thought OK, you'll find him in graduate school. Whole life sitting at a desk.

'So fine. Get your fucking PhD the way Daddy wanted, spend five years rewriting your dissertation, mentor said it was going to be a landmark book and by the time you find out it isn't you're getting old and everybody else has run past you and Evard College is the best you can do.

'So you get spilled out there. Evard. God! You think you know Evard, but you don't, not the Sailors, yoked and going two by two. You don't know the color of lonely. Do you even know what lonely is?'

The patient calls and calls. Clair looks to the nurse in the doorway, who shakes her head. *One of those things*. This place is filled with *one of those things*.

Mary answers her own question. 'Hell, no. How could you possibly know? Come in single, first teaching job, oh *boy*, and wow, you're stuck at the dead end of the world. Terminal nowhere. Nobody comes. Nobody goes.' She groans. 'It's like the officers' club on the night before Pearl Harbor or the Battle of Waterloo. Desperation party with no good end. Smile. Dance, you goddamn fools. In the end all you're going to do is die. Terminal exit. No. No Exit terminal. Walk into Evard and all the usual suspects line up to inspect you – *is she good to eat*? – hanging over you like fucking zombies out of the *Night of the Living Dead*.' Without emotion, Mary smacks her face. 'You're meat.

'Come in single and you're meat. The men, the men, they fuck you and forget you and the wives! They're like dogs looking at you over their paws, scared to death you'll grab their bone when all you want is a little light and beauty, just a little *something* in your life besides your fucking life.'

Clair flinches. There is a red handprint spreading on Mary's face. And she goes on. She just goes on.

'If you're like me you think, not me, no way. You get perky, try a lot of things. Local politics. Line dancing classes. Church choirs! Skiing's another, they see your butt in the Spandex suit and, oh shit. They see your

163

butt in the suit . . .' Agitated, Mary tries to double her full skirt so her heavy thighs will disappear. 'So you put on a big skirt and go to MLA meetings and humanities seminars, run for the college governing board.'

Her voice breaks. 'Concerts. Lectures. Anything that talks. At first you really believe you're going to meet your man at one of these things but after a while you just go so you won't have to be alone, just like the faculty widows marooned up there because he's shuffled off. Go to parties even when you aren't invited and you are charming as hell, good old Mary, you know. You go to bars, but it's been a long time since the guys circled the way they did when you first got here, you know, *mmm, fresh blood.*

'But every fall you cruise the president's reception all the same and for five minutes the new whoever has a fling with you, but they know and you know that it's old. You're old. Hang around anyplace long enough and your blood isn't so fresh any more.

'The town's so small that all the guys that fuck know exactly how old you are. Been there. Done that. Had her. You know.' Instead of waning with despair, Mary's voice is getting stronger.

'They know who's had you and they know who you've had and they know that by this time in spite of the job and all its restrictions, in spite of your charge, the *responsibility*, the students have started looking good to you, oh yum. All those conferences, all those boys in rut with their thick hair and hard muscles and sweet, soft necks and their recovering acne patient sheen. Like you, they're all hard up, stuck alone in this desperate place. After a few weeks even an old bag like you might look good to them. They know you're desperate and you look at them and you think, *oh God*.

'You look at them with their fresh skins and their bright eyes and you know for good and all that where they're going you can't get to, them with their young, sure bodies and the hard knots in their groins. And you can work out and tan yourself. You can get face lifts and tummy tucks. And never ever get back to where they are.

'And the students, those gorgeous kids?' Her face is glazed with tears now; it's taken on the sheen of one of those Russian dolls with doll after doll nested inside, showing exactly the same glossy face. 'You're so old that they don't even look at you.'

'Oh, Mary.'

'Single sucks. Partly it's being a woman.' Mary's expression is uninflected. She isn't angry, she isn't even particularly unhappy. She is, rather, *interested* in the process of laying this out precisely, as if for a class. 'There are other women out there in holding patterns waiting to scoop up single guys. People feel sorry for lonely guys; they have them over, hit on them or fix them up. If you're a woman, it's different. People know it's not their fault you sleep in a cold bed, it's yours. Something you did. Go to sleep lonely and when you wake up, you're old.

'Part of it's being a fucking academic. Guys on the faculty go out to singles bars, but they don't want you along. They're trying to score with younger girls or at least pretend they can, or else they're sky diving or bungee jumping so they can play like they're still young and they have lives, or else they're clumped in some back room at the Evarton Inn playing blackjack or shooting pool, or they're down at Mojo's racing cockroaches and doing dope with townie girls because . . . Because oh shit, twenty-plus years of education and these PhDs would do anything to prove they're not as smart as they are. Nobody wants to be an egghead. You want to know why?

'Because nobody wants an egghead, Clair.

'So the available guys are down at the Evarton Inn or doing tequila or bull shots or boilermakers at Mojo's or getting wasted at John B.'s, or else they're out at the truck stop on Route 28 pretending that they don't teach college and they aren't old. Anything so you won't know how dumb they really are. Pretending that their pickups are tough or their sports cars are glamorous because everybody wants to be sexy and glamorous.

'Instead of fucking academics.

'Which is what they are.'

As Mary falls silent and the silence stretches, the nurse gets up, as if to end the interview.

'Not yet,' Mary shouts at her. 'I'm not finished yet.'

No, you're not finished, Clair thinks, and wishes she was.

'So.' For the first time Mary is looking directly at her. 'Do you want to know what my problem is? I'll tell you what my problem is. Twenty-plus years of education and what do you get?'

What is astonishing is that Mary has delivered all this without rising from the bed.

'At the end all you are is an academic. A fucking PhD.

'PhDs.' She spits it out. 'All that education and they don't know jack. Twenty-plus years of school and they don't know anything. What can you learn in a classroom anyway? What do you learn about life? Read too many books and you get stupid.' Mary's face is taut; she is swelling with anger, filling up with it. 'Too stupid to have a life.'

Her tone brings the nurse.

'You think real life takes place at a fucking desk? How many fucking academics could take out your appendix or fix a parking ticket or jumpstart a car? Half of them don't even know enough to stay married or what to do with kids. *They have to look it up in a fucking book.* Turn a PhD loose in the stock market or a hardware store and they go duh, duh, duh-duh. Twenty-some years in school and we don't know jack shit about the world. PhDs eight ways to Sundays and we can't tell you how to get a family on state aid or run a router or unstick a drain . . .'

She is almost singing now. 'Oh yes we are overqualified,' she cries as the nurse approaches.

'I'm sorry,' Clair says.

But Mary's voice changes; it is light, sweet; words come out like a flight of butterflies. 'And then somebody comes in that *isn't like that* – somebody bigger, handsome, a little bit different, and you see a door opening. He can break you out and take you out into the real world where people do things instead of reading about them. Oh God, the hope. Do you know what that's like?'

Clair snaps forward, riveted.

'No hope and then hope?' Mary is on her feet. She and Clair stand facing. Her fists drop to her sides, heavy, huge. The fingers let go, as if her whole life has slipped from hands that have lost all their strength. She says, 'And then no hope?'

Clair murmurs, 'Will Strait.'

It is a mistake. Mary wheels on her, furious. 'What do you know, Clair Sailor? What could you possibly know?' Outraged, she goes on in a voice that's too big for the room, 'You, with your nice house and your nice kids and your prom date for life.'

'*Koena horra.*' Clair is astounded by the sound of her own voice.

The nurse touches her arm. 'Mrs . . .'

'Sailor.'

'Mrs Sailor, it's time for you to go.'

'How could you possibly know what it's like?'

Mary goes on shouting as the nurse separates them and draws Clair away and out the door and down the hall; they can still hear her as the nurse unpins Clair's visitor's badge because she can no longer see to undo the catch.

As she hands Clair into the first of the double doors that seal the ward from the outside world the nurse says, unaccountably, 'Thank you for coming. You've done her a lot of good.'

'It doesn't look like it.'

'You can never tell how these things are going to go. She's hardly spoken since she got here. This is the most she's ever said.'

17

It is late in the game.

She is a captive. It is not a dream. Clair and beautiful, sad Mara and Mara's extraordinary mother-in-law are hermetically sealed into Strait's car. It is a desperate mission. They are taking Strait's mother to the nearest mall for lunch. In honor of his mother's visit, Strait has given Mara the Lexus for the day. Clair perches in back, directing light patter at Mara's profile even as she studies the monolithic shape that overflows the bucket seat on the passenger's side. It is like riding along with a chunk of granite: Strait's mother is a massive woman with an overhanging brow and cheekbones like slabs, glaring at the world through openings in the flesh and bone like slits in a gleaming Eskimo mask.

It is a revelation. Buried in that face she sees Strait's eyes.

'Erna's here,' Mara said this morning. 'Erna Petrova Stratiewicz. Will's mother.'

It took Clair a minute to assimilate the information that Strait had given himself a name change. 'You don't sound thrilled.'

'It's very hard on Will. She's like a hit and run driver, comes out of nowhere, leaves you smeared all over the pavement and disappears into the night.'

'How long is she staying?'

'Three days.' Mara was like an accident victim, still in shock. 'Three days.' 8 a.m. and she was clearly spent. 'She hunts us down,' she said in a burst of confidence because, mysteriously and in spite of the impediments, she and Clair have become close. 'Try grim reaper, showing up for an accounting. No matter where we come to earth the woman hunts us down and moves in with her *bigos* and her expectations and her incessant harping on what's been done and what remains to be done.'

'What remains to be done on the house?'

'No. On Will. She has an agenda for him. Did you know she has an agenda for him?' Desperate, Mara showed all her cards at once. 'Will's. OK, he's her masterpiece. Drives him crazy and I get stuck coping; five minutes with the woman and Will's reduced to tears.'

'The mother of all . . .' The conversation was so spontaneous, her sympathy so ready that for a second there Clair forgot whose mother Erna Stratiewicz is.

'He's like another person when she's around. Except for meeting her plane and reporting for dinners, he'll disappear. Backs off until she gives up and goes away.'

'Where does he go?' Sly Clair.

'One of his lairs. You know.'

She doesn't know.

While Clair's mind raced ahead, Mara said, 'Naturally it's when I'm at low ebb. The woman *knows*. If I ever needed a friend, I need a friend. I can't do this woman without help.'

'Right,' Clair said. With Jane and Lauren and Ginny Atkinson all begging off invitations and guarding their speech and prejudging everything that comes out of Clair's mouth, she's as needy as Mara right now. 'I'll be there.'

This is so hard! She'd like Mara Strait in any circumstance but in their present circumstances it is incumbent upon her. She loves Mara precisely because she despises Strait. It is a point of honor: Mara's honor, hers. Whatever else may be going on in Mara's life, whatever the exigencies of Clair's, they have to maintain this friendship and maintain it at all cost. It is one of the proofs of the existence of – what? She doesn't know. Decency?

It is as if they share something. What's going on may begin with the women themselves – two handsome, intelligent people just short of middle age who take pleasure in each other's company. Who like watching their children play together – so close! And who are bonded by something they've never talked about. But they are bonded by something more. She and Mara protect and maintain the friendship as if in some way it is their lifeline, a guarantee that when all the other unpredictable elements of their lives have begun to slip, when they've begun to lose even the parts of their lives that until this year they thought of as constants, they will still have this.

They can't name it. The bond. The risk. It's just there. At some cost. As now, when Will Strait's mother fills the horizon.

At least they have escaped the car. She and Clair are sitting at a table in the mall courtyard while under a smokescreen of graciousness, Mara has escaped. *I'm getting lunch,* she said with a desperate social laugh, sticking Clair with this huge, forbidding woman, her responsibility until Mara gets back. *Wait here.*

'You know my boy,' Erna says.

'Oh, yes. Your grandson Chase! He's wonderful.'

'No. *My boy.* You know my boy.' Under the ridge of flesh, those sharp, judgmental eyes are fixed on her. They are unwavering, the color of the bluestone slabs in the college walks. 'Willie. My one and only. So good when he was young. So smart!' She waits.

Clair tries her best. 'My husband says he's invaluable.'

But Erna is not easily satisfied. 'You think he's smart?' Overflowing the chair as she is, she is terrifying and relentless.

'The students say he's wonderful.'

'And you. You think he's smart?'

This is not a conversation, it's a contest. 'Very smart.'

Not enough. Erna's look bores into her. 'And you like him.'

'Everybody likes him.' Defeated by the silence Erna wields like a blunt instrument, Clair jabbers against her will. 'Nick says he's doing a wonderful job. Everybody does.'

'Ah. My son. My only.' She uses the pause like an instrument too, asserting her power over this conversation. Over other things she will not name. 'You know how it is to have an only child?'

'Yes. No. I . . .' Clair is beaten and she knows it. 'No.'

Satisfied, Erna settles back and begins to talk. 'My life after my Gregor die. My son! My only life. I bring him up alone. You know how hard, one woman, no money, but I work in the mine after my Gregor die. I bring him up hard but I bring him up! My one and only. My hope! So I go into the mine, drive the machine into the mountain, the mole, and when is stuck I clear out the rock with my hands. Even with the gloves my knuckles are like balls of soot, my fingers knot like rope. I am ugly from the work but look what I make! He is so beautiful!' Her stony eyes gleam with pride.

'My boy say, I don't want to study and I say, you study. After all he is only a boy. I drive around under mountain in the mole so you can study and you will goddamn study, yes you will. You will get big, will be important. I give everything so you can be an important man. I get old driving in the mountain, coal dust in my nose, in my privates. I can scrub and scrub and never get it out. I work so my boy can be in private school in next big town and I get fat to make me strong enough to earn money so he can have good clothes. I get filthy so his hands stay pink. I buy the best. I get from premium finest store in West Virginia and when it close I buy from J. Press and Company catalog in New York so my Willie can talk good and get rich and make me proud. See. We are doing this for us. Him. Me. So what if sometimes he don't want to do the work?'

She glares. 'I see to it he does the work. What if I come in, find him drunk? I put my head down and run right into him. Butt him hard. Wham. I bowl him over. Hit him with my fists. If I have to, I yell. I sit on his chest so he can't breathe. I pound on him until he promise. I make this man out of a little boy. I make him with my own hands, you understand? You understand what is at stake for me?'

Clair wants to look away and can't. She can't be certain what the old lady is telling her but it is of a piece with her eerie little talk with Mara in the Strait bedroom; she knows and the old lady knows. It makes her afraid. To her shame she hears herself murmuring politely, 'You must be very proud.'

'Proud! I give you proud. You bring up children alone, you know what's good for them. What if I come in, find him drunk? What if I come in, find him another way? I beat him if I have to, push him down and sit on him, if I have to I make him cry for mercy. He promise. No more of that. Plenty of this.' She's breathing hard, as if she's enduring this terrible encounter, not describing it. 'We get up. He get into the state university.'

Wait. Didn't he tell Nick he went to Harvard? 'He told us—'

'Farther than any of us ever go! I work overtime to get him clothes and books. I buy him car. When he lose scholarship I telephone and make him cry and promise to do good. He does good, I can tell you. When he let down on the grades I move to that town. I wait tables. Window where I can see his window? I don't bother him, I just keep track. Where he goes, I am. If he strays, I know. Wrong step and he sees me. So he knows. He is my honor, my God he is my life. I am poor and fat but my Will is handsome and fine. I know I have accent but my boy is gentleman. He does like they do. His children grow up better, you know? It make me better too! You see?'

Clair's insides are trembling. 'I see.'

'Our life will be magnificent. But it take work.'

Clair groans. 'I know.' She would do anything to stop this recital or at least turn it but now that she has begun, this Erna Stratiewicz is like a force of nature. Huge, unstoppable.

'If he slow down, I see it. If he fail, I know. He knows what I do if he fail.'

Then this hard woman drops the words on the tiny round table like chunks of granite. 'You know he will be president.'

He – what?

'Oh Mrs Stratiewicz, I can't . . .' Do this.

'Yes. I know not president yet. Not this year. First big job at this college. Be president here, you see. Then run for senator, I think. Even I know it take time. But then. One day.' She steamrollers on. Her confidence is as terrifying as it is absolute. 'My Willie will be US President.' Then Will Strait's mother Erna Stratiewicz looks into Clair: through the veil of skin and the buffer of flesh, boring into the intricate shield of bone. She penetrates all the clouds of psyche Clair spins to protect herself, parting them so she can glare right into her soul.

Clair taps her clenched fist against her chest as if to protect herself. *God*.

Thank God Mara is coming back with trays loaded with drinks and food packets, bustling into the middle of this terrible encounter so swiftly that Clair can pretend not to hear the mother's last statement. Breathing hard, intent, driven and inexorable, Erna Stratiewicz spells it out. 'And nobody get in his way.'

18

Everything in Clair stops cold. In the shadows that fill the Gothic arch, something denser stirs. At first she perceives it as a blur at the periphery of her vision, down low and to the left, at the point where the stone rib of the arch meets the flagstones. 'Who's there?' Nobody answers.

My imagination, she thinks. Her imagination at work on the rank of forest green plastic garbage bags left in the arch by the college cleaning staff. Bad shape, she thinks. I'm in bad shape, speaking to a bag of—

'Oh!'

Like a living piece of debris, a figure sits among the garbage bags with his back to the cold stone wall. Something about the knot he makes there in the shadows, all tightly curled arms and knees clamped to the chest, makes her advance cautiously. At first she thinks it is a child. No. Older, in spite of the slight frame and fragile neck. This is a student crouched with his head on his knees and his joints locked tight as if he can fold into himself and thus escape his body. She recognizes the buzz cut, the feral angle of the wedge-shaped head where it joins that skinny neck.

'Gig!'

He won't look up and he doesn't answer.

'Are you all right?'

It's clear that he isn't. Much as he wants to disappear, Gig is crouched on the stones, shivering in spite of all his efforts to keep still. Frantic, he shrinks from her with his head bowed and his shoulders heaving under the outsized Navajo blanket coat.

'What's the matter? Gig? It's me. Clair, from the alumni magazine? Sam's friend. You know, Sam and Fred? How about I help you up?' When he still won't answer she leans close. 'Come on. You can't stay here. Let's go find you some coffee.'

He shows an agonized face to her, all yellowish skin and bared teeth.

She makes the mistake of touching him. 'Come on, Gig. You're freezing. Come with me, OK?'

At her touch he snaps into fetal position, toppling without knowing or caring that the side of his face slaps the stone with a smack that Clair will go on hearing no matter how long she lives or how far she travels from this place; she'll hear it every time there is a child at risk. She passes her hand in front of his eyes. It is like passing it in front of a stone.

'Oh God, Gig. Stay there. Don't move, I'll be right back. I'm going for help.'

By the time she comes back with Security, Gig is gone. There's no sign there was ever anybody in the arch, not even a patch of blood in the spot where his bare face hit the pavement.

'Are you sure, Mrs Sailor?' She and Ray have known each other too long for him to condescend but the campus cop tucks a hand under her elbow: *there there.* He thinks I'm sick. Clair recognizes the judgmental tone her friends use. *Strait? It's all in your mind.* 'I don't see anything.' The bastard thinks I'm sick.

Nick is working all the time now, mediating more disputes and processing more pieces of paper. He leaves before breakfast and comes home late, tired and drained; his face has no color. No matter what Nick proposes, a colleague protests. Somebody else mounts a counter-proposal. Relaxed, genial Will Strait sits back, easy in his cashmere jacket and tanned and glowing from the weekend's skiing, while Nick's friends, *Nick's friends* carry the flag for him. Things are going badly in class. Students are beating him to death with opinions taught by the new professor. Pride makes Nick spare her most of this but in the stale, close air of late winter the arguments overflow into the halls and Clair knows; she knows.

Tonight she comes down to find him on the sofa with his elbows on his knees, and his head down. 'There's a plate in the kitchen.'

'I haven't made it that far. It's been a bitch of a day.'

'You're killing yourself.'

He is too spent to deny it.

Clair doesn't mean to reproach him with it, but she does. 'You thought hiring that guy would make things easier, not harder.'

'Nobody can do everything.'

'I thought he was doing everything. I thought that was the problem.'

'He's doing plenty.' He is grave, troubled. 'It's just not what I thought.' This is as close as he's come to admitting that Strait is a mistake. 'It's so damn stupid. I was so sure I had everything under control – classes, the department, Ad's stuff.'

'You never should have taken on Ad's job.' She will not add: not the way you are right now.

'I had to. Now things are getting away from me.' He looks up. 'You might even be relieved. Will's moving into Ad's office.'

'He's *what*?'

'He's going to be acting dean.'

'I thought you were.'

'It was never official.'

'I thought . . .' No. She knows. Everybody in this constricted society knows that the dean's job is the last jump on the springboard to the presidency. 'You mean this guy *that nobody knows* is going to—'

'It was George's idea.'

'I thought George wanted you.'

'Oh, George. George doesn't always know what he wants.' His grin is wry. 'I guess Will convinced him otherwise.'

'Don't.' She hates seeing him like this. In spite of her own feelings about the presidency she says, 'You've given ten years of your life to this place. Everybody knows you're the right person.'

The answer comes too fast. 'Not any more.'

'You're the only person.'

'Not now.' He looks so *tired*. Pain twists his smile. 'My fault, I suppose, for inattention to detail.'

'You've never overlooked a detail in your life.'

'More than one, I think. Ad's job for one.' He's trying to make it sound offhand. 'The Fremont lecture is another.'

'The Fremont lecture!' Trip to Boston, powerful alumni group, five thousand dollar check at a black tie dinner in May; Nick's been working on his text ever since September. 'That's yours!'

'Will is giving it.'

'He can't.'

177

'Is. I guess he did a good show at the trustee meeting.'

'He was invited to the trustee meeting?'

'Turns out he was.' Oh Nick, stop grinning. 'He gets around.'

In spite of the smile he put on for her and can't seem to turn off, Nick looks so drained that Clair says, 'It's OK, Nick. He'll be gone soon enough. All we have to do is hang in until June.'

Nick clears his throat.

'It's a short-term contract, right?'

'Not really.' It's like a kid's grudging admission, dragged out of him. Nick looks like Davy when he's made a mistake. 'He's, ah, on for a little longer.'

'Longer! I thought you only hired him to fill in!'

Another of those things that people in love keep from each other because they are bent on sparing each other. 'We had to make a five-year appointment,' he says.

'But what about Mary?'

'That's another problem.' His eyes are gentle, clear. 'It was the only way we could get him to come.'

'Oh my God. Five years.' Hurtling down on her, beginning on Ethan Frome Day. On the hard drive down from the institution she played this game: it's just till June. You can stand on your head until June. 'You can't! The man is a—' Clair's stopped in mid-speech by a rapid-fire series of unbidden snapshots: tearstained Mary Roeg superimposed on – wait a minute – superimposed on Mara, on Ginny, on the girl at the Garsons' party and – oh this is weird – Gig Jamison. 'He's a . . .' Words desert her.

'What, Clair?' In the silence, something is happening. As she strangles and gropes for words, she sees Nick changing. 'What, Clair? If you know something I don't, why won't you say so?' Intent, he leans in, listening hard even after her voice fails. For the first time since his return from the hospital, Clair has his complete attention. 'What is he, Clair?'

She sees exactly how much this is costing him. If she could name names, give dates, it would be different, but everything that's happened is amorphous in the same way that her misgivings are amorphous: threatening to dissolve under scrutiny. Everything is sliding around. She chokes. I don't even know if that was him on the sled. 'If I knew, I'd tell you. That's the trouble with him!'

'Right.' This is how Nick Sailor, who has defended his choice up to this point and defended it manfully, lets Clair know for the first time that long before she knew it, he had made the difficult transition from his position to hers. Pain drives the words home. 'If we can't say what's wrong, there's no way to deal with it.'

It is late in the day, late in the publications schedule, late in a winter of incessant dismal skies and dirty, frozen slush; even spring break is late this year. Clair has been staring at the screen for so long that she can no longer tell which is display and which is afterimage burned into the space behind her eyes.

Distracted as he is by the special project, worn thin and running on no sleep, Fred Keller has been dutifully entering the last of the class notes, but at some point between the time he came in and now he's drifted over to her desk where he hangs like a reluctant ghost. Now he speaks. 'What is this Professor Strait anyway?'

Her head comes up sharply. 'What do you mean?'

But Fred won't look at her. He says to a spot on the floor, 'I mean, is he an angel or a devil or what?'

She has no answers. 'You never told me what happened to Gig.'

They're friends. There's no reason for him not to tell her everything but he still won't look at her. Or he won't let her look at him. 'Gig's OK.'

'He didn't look OK to me. I called Dr LaMar about it. Did he go to the infirmary?'

'No way. He won't let go and he won't let us go to get him something to help him chill. It's OK,' Fred says. 'Gig's doing OK.'

'Not, I think. What was he doing down there in the arch?'

Confused, Fred blinks. 'It's nothing. Just the new project.'

'New project!'

'Meditation. New level of consciousness thing for Professor Strait. A higher plane. You know. Only Will's special projects people get to . . .' His voice is congested. 'It isn't for everybody, only extraordinary students. The ones he thinks are good enough.'

'Like Gig.'

'And Sam and me, if we work hard. Everything is so very . . .' Confused, he can't finish. Good-natured, usually uncomplicated Fred.

'What are you talking about?'

'It's so amazing. He's not like any professor we ever had.'

Clair echoes his question. 'Angel. Devil. What is all that?'

'Nothing. Forget I said that. I was just wondering. Professor Strait – I mean Will is *so good*, you know, and he knows so much, tells you this, tells you that and then he tells you . . .'

'Tells you what?'

'I can't tell you,' Fred says.

For the first time in the years they've worked together, Clair is at Sally LeFleur's place, a studio apartment above one of the specialty stores on the square. Soot-stained window shades and worn linoleum, cooking smells and the sound of a scuffle upstairs remind her that not everybody in Evarton lives in the privileged world of the college. For Sally, who never had a bed to herself before she got a job and moved away from home, this is a step up. 'Four of us slept together. I never had a dress I could call my own. If I bought something special and I didn't want my sisters to ruin it before I got a chance to wear it, I had to lock it in the trunk of the car,' she told Clair early in their friendship. 'After I got a car.' Unlike the people at Evard, Sally grew up in the hard world.

The contrast makes Clair feel guilty for having what she has, proud for belting Sally into college because she deserves more.

'You were nice to ask me.' Temporarily sprung from Evard, Clair is relieved to be in the one place where she can let down. Of the women she thought of as her friends, Sally's the only one who has never doubted her. Sally won't shut me out the way the others do. 'Listen, there's something I've been meaning to ask you.'

'Something I've been meaning to tell you,' Sally says. 'I wanted to tell you over a meal.'

'No. Something I wanted to tell you.' Clair already knows Sally won't want to hear. 'Sal?'

But Sally doesn't ask; she goes on laying out sandwiches and carrot sticks on plastic plates on TV trays with straw mats and embossed, double-ply dinner napkins in flowered enamel napkin rings, trays set with the Gorham sterling pattern she's collecting, fork by fork. Flushed and excited, she waits until they're both sitting down. 'I wanted you to know first. I may be leaving soon.'

As Sally's guest, Clair is centered on the tweed Castro Convertible Sally has to open every night before she can go to bed, while her friend perches on a low cedar chest with the sadly obsolete look of a Fifties hope chest, every piece of furniture scrupulously chosen and chockablock in this tight little room. Clair sees a door opening. 'Oh Sally, you got into the state university!'

'Yeah, but no.' Color Sally gone. Her tone tells Clair that she's out of this tiny room with its single Queen Anne side chair and hand-hooked Rhya rug; she's walked away from the cracked plaster hung with her Toulouse-Lautrec repros, the Towle tray, all her gallant attempts at decor. 'I'm going a lot farther than that.'

'You got into BU!'

'Not another college, Clair. It's a waste of my time.'

'But your degree. You wanted it so much!'

'Not as much as this.' Sally's lipstick is a shade too dark today, the edges are a touch too sharp; the stripe of eyeliner around her hazel eyes is new, as is the mahogany rinse she's started using to gentrify her crinkly red-orange hair. Underneath the peach blusher, freckles rise on skin so pale, no, skin so thin that Clair is terrified for her – so easily hurt, and in spite of the air of confidence, so young. Sally says as if she actually knows what it means, 'You might as well know, I'm in love.'

Oh God. 'Who is he?'

'I can't tell you. All I can tell you is, we're out of here.'

'You and this man?'

Sally winks. 'What makes you think it's a man?'

Clair yells. 'Because I know you! Come on Sally, who is he?'

'Nobody you know.'

'You're quitting your job so you can go away with somebody and you won't even tell me who?'

'I can't. Don't worry. You'd like him if you knew him.'

'What makes you so sure?'

It is Sally who is yelling now. 'Because you don't know him at all!'

'Like, don't know well, or never met him?'

Sally doesn't exactly answer. Instead she says, 'If you think it's somebody from the college, it's nobody from the college, OK?'

'Then why can't you tell me who it is?'

'I just can't, that's all.'

'Sally, is he married?'

She's pink now, feverish. 'That's none of your business, OK?'

'Oh please. I just don't want you to get hurt.'

'When love comes at you,' Sally says, 'it doesn't come the way you think. So wish me well and wish me out of here, OK?'

Clair discovers that she can't speak. Thumps overhead remind her that she's in a new territory where events march in no predictable order, and, God. See how little Sally has! Clerical job and a twelve-by-twelve room in this claustrophobic town, with no way out and nothing to go back to but a crowded bed on a tenant farm with a widowed mother and too many half-grown kids, no men to love her, just clueless, pimply college kids and the hairy greasers she went to high school with patronizing her, them in their packed jeans with droopy thermal undershirts ringing their thick, hairy necks, heavy-handed yobs intent on keeping local girls in their place. Work an eight-hour day and go to school at night, stay up until two doing class work, who wouldn't want to break out?

Sally is hurt by her silence. 'Aren't you glad?'

'Oh Sally I just wish you—'

Sally says angrily, 'I suppose you think it's Mr Strait.'

'Just tell me it isn't.'

'Don't do this, OK?' Sally's lost weight; insubstantial, newly fragile, she is pleading. 'People aren't always what you think.'

'It can't be him.'

Sally pushes back her tray to demonstrate that the lunch is over. Her voice is harsh. 'Nothing is what you think.'

'It isn't Strait, right? Oh Sally! Is it?'

'I'm not going to tell you,' Sally says.

'It's my gay students,' Teddy says. This is one of the best things about Teddy; he's gone for days at a time but when he drops back into her life he treats it like a continuing conversation. 'You friend Strait treats them like dirt.'

'He's not my friend!' Vindicated, Clair says, 'I tried to tell you there was something wrong with him.'

'There's plenty wrong, I'm just not sure what. My kids think he hates them. Say he plays to the straight guys, makes faggot jokes in class, goes out of his way to say things that make them feel bad. He won't call on them. Not even when he's asked a question and they're the only ones with their hands up because they're the only ones who know.'

'Is that enough to get him fired?'

Teddy's grimace sums it up. 'Who cares what gay kids think?'

'There's something wrong. Even Nick knows there's something wrong, he just can't— won't.' She shakes her head.

'When you sit down with the devil, sometimes you have to sit too close.

I'm going to do some checking. Don't look so down.' He surprises her with a hug. 'Hang in and I'll get back to you.'

'Oh Teddy, be careful.' She means: *I love you.*

'You too.'

'Nick, I've tried not to lay this on you, but there's real trouble with Strait. Teddy thinks the guy is . . .' What? Clair still doesn't know. 'The kids are getting weird. Something's going on.'

'I know. I talk to students too. But all I get is hints. They aren't about to come to us and say.' It's been another long winter day. Nick is trying not to let her see that after all these weeks his hands still shake. 'We'll get through this, Clair. We will.'

He looks so distressed that she goes on quickly, to reassure him. 'Teddy's doing some checking. If he can just find out . . .'

'What?' Nick looks bleak. 'What difference will it make?'

'Maybe you can break his contract.'

'A contract is a contract.'

She hears herself shouting. 'Why do you always have to play by the rules? Teddy's putting himself on the line over this, Nick. Teddy! That's got to mean something.' Teddy, who never puts himself on the line over anything.

'You can't fire a guy on suspicion, Clair.'

'But what if there is something terrible? What if Teddy finds out what it is? What if he can prove it? Name names.'

'You can catch him red-handed at whatever and it still won't factor. He'll only deny it. His word against ours.'

'And he's been around to everybody. One by one.'

Nick surprises her. 'I know.'

All these weeks of not talking about it and now they are talking about it; she turns to him. 'What else do you know?'

'Don't, Clair. I'm only trying to get through this term.' He is still the man she loves but death has been in the ring with them; pull those punches, Clair. Still, he is coming back to her in stages, like an exercise in stop-motion photography. He takes her hands, an idealist who has spent his life in this place and has run his professional life according to its rules. Dear Nick. Nothing has prepared him for this torpedo from the outside world. Now all his instincts are in collision as he struggles with the threat, the imperatives. 'Please.'

183

'What if we can get something on him?'

'It won't make any difference.' This is how he lays it out for her. 'A contract is a contract, Clair. He's not about to back off. The academic job market's so tight that anybody who finally gets a job defends it to the death. Try to fire an academic and he'll sue your brains out.'

Regretfully, she pulls him to the bottom line. 'I think people are getting hurt.'

'Assault?'

'Threats.'

'It's his word against theirs.'

No. Against ours. In this degree she will protect him; she does not speak.

'Do you know how hard it is to get somebody fired? Even if he's an ax murderer the man has an agreement here. Signed and sealed. That guy at Bennington, got bought off, did he really make kiddie porn? Welcome to the Nineties. You can kill your parents and admit it and still get off.' He is hung up on the terrible disparity between the way things are supposed to be in this small, reasonable world, and the way they really are.

'What if it's . . .' Groping, she comes up with a term so old and so accurate that it surprises her: 'Moral turpitude?'

'It's still the Nineties.' Nick is turning into a different person. His voice is hard. 'Moral does not compute.'

'Nick!' It's awful. He's right.

'We are intellectuals here. Everything's up for discussion. Everything,' he says dismally because he has put all his faith in an institution – a way of life – that is betraying him. 'Committees. Boards of appeals. They'd worry it to death, whether the thing was right or wrong. And deadlock over definitions: define right, define wrong.'

'*Wrong* is wrong, goddammit.'

'Try and prove it to a group. We are in an equivocal position here.' Teddy's exact words. With a grunt, Nick takes on the full weight of her suspicions. 'Freedom of inquiry.'

'Oh, Nick!' Don't look so damn defeated.

He shrugs. 'We've lost the right to say a thing is wrong.'

'It's Gig's mom,' Fred says while Sam hands her the phone. They are in the office. Both students are stewing inside layers of winter clothes, sweaty and miserable. 'We tried and tried and she won't listen to us. Will you talk to her?'

Clair covers the mouthpiece. 'What does she want?'

'She wants to know where he is.' Fred's face is a study in helplessness.

'Well, where is he?'

'We've looked and looked. He isn't anywhere.'

19

Ben

Amazing how far you can get once you actually start. Aching and barefoot as he was, half naked and nearly frozen after his ordeal on the ledge where he landed instead of dying, Ben prevailed.

Now he is in Amenia, New Hampshire, hundreds of miles from home. He is standing by the interstate north with frayed Band-Aids on his fingers inside the red mitten and the blue one; he has a multi-colored muffler knit from tag ends of yarn and a black knit hockey hat pulled down over his ears. His feet are cold inside the rubber boots he pulled out of the bottom of the parish goodwill barrel but he's OK. So what if his fuzzy black topcoat does button on the wrong side? What would you expect of a coat that used to belong to a nun?

Even now after some weeks on the road he's giddy with the outdoors. Trees, wow. So much sky after all that stale air and nothing overhead but the ceiling of his old room.

Trying to die and getting snatched back has left him feeling somehow . . . Well. Redeemed. There is no logic to it. Just this phenomenon: at the exact same time Ben Messinger decided not to die, something or someone out there decided he would live. The saving ledge was there precisely because at the last minute Ben twisted in mid-flight and tried to grab the roof. Scrambling back to life.

He's as foul as he ever was; the evidence is written in his body for anyone to see. He doesn't care. Let them see it and recoil; Ben is changed forever, but like it or not he is not dead.

187

He is a different person now. When you don't die, you think of something else to do. WHO DID THIS TO YOU? Never mind. When Ben gets through with the one who unmade him, that person will never hurt anybody again. He doesn't know how he's going to stop what happened to him from happening, only that he is.

It was enough to decide. By the time he hauled himself back up on that roof, he knew. Shivering, he looked down at the ledge that saved his life, at the broken stones and crumbled mortar that marked his desperate struggle back to life. He was so hungry! Death is final, but lives are hung on next steps. His next steps were:

Get down off the roof.

Get shoes. Barefoot and skinned raw, Ben was transfixed, watching the blood freezing on his fingers and toes.

Winter clothes!

Get something to eat.

Find him.

Get some money and go.

Not Ben's fault he could barely manage Step One, or that once he was safely hatched on the sidewalk in front of the building he was quivering with indecision. When you have everything you need and nothing you want, as he did all that time he spent locked in his bedroom, despairing and trapped, you lose the knack.

He knew better than to go back to the house.

After some thought he presented himself at the back door of the convent next to his old grammar school. Whatever Ben Messinger has become, no matter how vile and worthless, he knew the nuns would take him in, no questions and no reproaches. Chapter and verse it was the only place he could think of to go.

They have to help me. It's their job.

He was cold. Barefoot and disheveled. Broke. He walked.

Panic kept him jiggling at the convent door, hyperventilating because somebody was coming and it was too late to hide. What if they scream at the sight of me? What if what happened to me actually shows in my face? What if some nun sees what I really am and falls over dead?

He'd have bolted but his fingers were frozen to the rail.

A nun with the build of a stevedore opened the door: his old teacher Sister Ignatius, the homely, strict woman with Boris Karloff's face – could make you laugh if she liked you, terrifying when you were ten, but still.

She looked right at Ben, saw it all and didn't die. She just blinked. 'Who is it?'

He covered his face.

She pulled his hands down. 'Benjamin!'

Looked right at me. His lips peeled back from his teeth, exposing the naked skull. She didn't even flinch.

'Jesus, Mary and Joseph, what happened to you?'

The last time he saw her he was in fifth grade and the Ig was ten feet tall. Now they were of a height. Her blunt, pink face made him grin, but, God. Could he talk? He hacked.

'Benjamin. Messinger, wasn't it? Speak up. I know it's you.'

He sounded like a cat spitting up a hairball.

'Can you talk?'

The words he finally coughed up came straight off those hastily lettered signs street people carry at intersections, big block letters: 'WILL WORK FOR FOOD.'

'What happened to you?'

WHO DID THIS TO YOU? 'Will work for food.' *Gack*. Odd. In the weeks he spent at the convent, they were the first and last words he would find to say to her.

Won't talk? Never mind. 'I don't know what's got your tongue, Benjamin, but you'd better come in.'

She handed him a tin of Band-Aids. She pillaged the clothes collected for the poor and, abashed, she handed him a pair of her own oversized tennis shoes. She showed him to the shower room in the basement and closed the door on him.

Ben spent two weeks with the sisters in the brick Victorian with iron spikes on the rooftree, shoveling and hauling wood like Igor for Sister Clarice, filing old tests for Sister Dorothy and repairing railings and broken plaster with the Ig, who was a self-taught carpenter. He slept on a rollaway bed in a room off the kitchen where he took the supper plates Sister Margaret made for him and ate like an animal. He left the door cracked to let in their conversation: eight working women in dark street clothes, sitting down to dinner after a hard day. They wore vestigial veils that signified the old-fashioned habit and everything it stood for, but when they sat down like that it was to compare notes on the day. They asked Ben to sit with them but he shook his head.

Shouldn't have to see me close.

Most of the chores he did for them he did while the sisters were next door at the school. He worked fast so he could finish early and get on the phone. 'You can't tell the truth on the telephone.' Old poem. True or not, the only time Ben Messinger could talk the way he did before was on the phone. Before. It made him angry. Why do I have to be the kind of person who has a *before*?

With nobody there to watch him, words came out. It took him several tries to get through to the hotel in Venice where he'd gone with the foreign study program back in September, in his other life. The clerk spoke only Italian and had no idea what had happened to the students or the teacher when the program ended. He couldn't say where they went, any more than he could get it out of his head that Ben wanted to be put in touch with some cosmic Lost and Found.

If he has lost something, it was cosmic. Ben knew this better than anyone, but it was not why he'd called. 'The *signore*,' he said. 'The big *signore*.' Why did he imagine the clerk would understand pidjin English? Or yelling? 'Where is?'

But he did. 'That's what his mama want to know.'

'His mama?'

'Big voice. *Big*. Somewhere USA. I give you number.'

The first few times he tried her she was out. And Ben? Like an autistic child, he lost himself in hard labor, as if through patterning he could relearn life.

'You're not going to tell me, are you?' The Ig had just taken the spirit level from him and was studying the placement of a quarter round in the moulding they were installing in the upstairs hall. It was a Saturday.

By this time Ben had worked with her for so long that he communicated very well without words.

'Don't give me *what*,' she said, irritated. 'You were a nice, ordinary person in fifth grade. A good kid. Open. Now you're wrapped around yourself so tight that it would take the jaws of life to pry you out. What happened to you?'

Ben couldn't answer but by this time he could smile. He could smile and smile and never say.

But the Ig had pulled a hammer out of her carpenter's apron and she was shaking it at him the way she used to shake the pointer in geography class. 'Don't give me *nothing*. What happened to you, Benjamin? Who locked you up in there?'

Put the nail in the spot you've marked and tap it lightly on the head.

'You know damn well you didn't get shut in all by yourself. Something happened to you.'

Place the nail. Hammer it in. If I can do this, what else can I do?

The big nun's voice softened. 'You don't have to tell me but if you're going to save yourself, sooner or later you're going to have to say.'

Put the nail set . . . Not his fault this made his eyes fill up with tears.

Then without even preparing the spot or starting the hole with the nail set, this pragmatic, capable nun put in her strip of moulding with a number four nail. She jammed the hammer back in her denim apron and with the same matter-of-factness she looked up at Ben and said something positively astonishing. 'Let God walk you back through this thing. It's the only way you'll ever walk out.'

God help him, he sobbed.

She said gently, 'You need to rehearse.'

Rehearse? I can't even bear to think about it. Had not. Had managed too well.

'Was it so terrible?'

He shook his head. I don't remember, all right!

It was as if this plain nun with the big hands and the steady eye read him line for line. 'If you want to break its power over you, you're going to have to give it words.'

So he just stopped protesting and let the tears roll down.

So it was Sister Ignatius of the School Sisters of Notre Dame who laid it out for him like a lesson in simple mathematics. One. Two. Three. She did not say 'In the beginning was the word', but it was implied.

She said, 'We have to learn to make sense of our stories, Ben. It's what this . . .' She spread her hands to include her ungainly frame, the convent and all the sisters, the rude streets and the grimy city, the world; his grade school teacher Sister Ignatius, looking at him out of that blunt face with perfect clarity. 'It's what this is all about.'

When he left that place it was with love, but out of fear. How can he rehearse when he's lost all his material? How far will he have to go to retrieve it? He does not know. All he knows is that he has located the source of his grief and out of blind need is moving toward it – by bus, by car or truck, hitching rides with anybody willing to take him, tending north.

Amenia, New Hampshire. Is he near the place? Still far away?

Both. All this way and he has not outrun the Ig, with her imperatives. *You need to rehearse.*

He is frozen, sobbing. I can't.

20

The Sailors have made a mistake. Too diminished by the uses of the winter to guess what escape would cost them, Clair and Nick took the kids out of school and went south for spring break. Nick's parents found them a place. Perhaps guessing all was not well with their son, they even fronted for plane tickets. Fatigue, winter rashes, even Clair's grief began to dissipate in the brilliant Florida glare. Lying on the sand in a place where everything is horizon, you can convince yourself that there is only this. The life you left behind is illusion. Even fears dwindle and lose substance. Is the threat real or were you only imagining things? In this light it's hard to say.

Amnesty, she thought, looking at Nick next to her on the blanket, sleeping as if he could stay forever, fused with the sand. We have won temporary amnesty. When we get home we can go in strong.

Oh lady, *koena horra*. Did you forget?

There are parts of life so precarious that they demand absolute concentration: the encounter with the jungle beast, the rope-walk across the gorge. Let your concentration waver even for a second or see it split between two concerns and that which you most fear will engulf you. The enterprise is lost.

They were only gone a week.

Now, after hours spent waylaid in airports by an early-March blizzard, the Sailors are struggling over the neglected snow that has clogged their front walk in their absence and frozen solid. Clair understands that in the lexicon of checks and balances you can escape if you want to but sooner or later everybody pays.

The winter is taking its revenge.

Things went wrong in the house during their absence: a burst pipe under the back porch, a new clatter in the furnace. Bugs got sick and is at the vet's for as long as it takes to get him straightened out. Clair keeps coming into rooms and looking for a dog to hug. A snowplow crunched over the curb and tore out the small tree they put in last fall. Their sitter forgot to water; most of the house plants are dead.

After vacations Teddy usually presents himself at the dinner table to debrief them, but he's away at another queer studies conference. 'Asking some questions in California,' says the note stuffed in their letter slot. 'Be cool. Hang in.' The empty house is sad. The dead plants are sad. Clair misses Bugs. 'This is the first time I've ever been sorry to get back.'

Nick nods. 'Me too.'

Change waits for that failure of concentration; the Sailors look away for a moment and when they look back their lives are being devoured.

Without asking, Strait has cleared Mary's things out of her office and left them in cartons stacked in the hall. The classic classroom nightmare takes flesh; these days Nick's students sit in his lectures with their heads bent over notebooks or laptops. As their attention flags he begins to pace, which is how he discovers that instead of taking notes they are working on papers for Strait.

Gig Jamison is gone. Nobody knows where or why. Sam and Fred are pale and preoccupied; like a surprising number of others this year they stayed at Evard over break to finish their special project for the charismatic new professor. Something makes them rushed and furtive, quick to pack up their papers and floppies and leave before Clair can see. They look so *young*, so jittery and vulnerable that she wants to hug them: *there there*. She wants to smooth back their hair and study their troubled faces but, like Heathcliff, they shrug her off and slouch away.

Sally comes in to the office scowling and except for business, won't talk to her. Like a crash victim, Sally moves with her shoulders high and elbows tight to her sides. She sits down with a little gasp, as if she's been caught in an unforeseeable accident and her ribs are sprung. Clair suspects that Sally's escape from Evarton has evaporated, along with whatever hopes she'd pinned on the lover she will not name. Every time the phone rings

Sally flinches. Her color is bad. She's angry all the time now. Maybe it's at Clair for guessing who's hurting her or maybe Sally hates her for trying to warn her, or for being right. Unless she hates herself.

Ginny Arnold is gone, and where in better times Pete would have parked himself in Nick's office to talk it out, he's avoiding Nick and Clair. When Clair asks what's going on, Lauren won't tell. The women have closed ranks against her. Standing in front of the college post office where Clair has tracked her down specifically to ask this and other questions, her old friend Jane comes closer than anyone to spelling it out. 'I can't tell you where she is,' she says. She says, 'Where Ginny went is Ginny's secret.' When Clair presses she turns on her. 'How can we trust you after all the terrible things you've said about Will?'

'What!' In the Sailors' absence Will Strait has been busy.

Jane finishes her off. 'After the things you've done to him!'

'What, Jane?' Clair wheels in fury. 'What have I done?'

'If you don't know, I'm certainly not going to tell you.'

'I don't. I don't know!' She is shaking with outrage. 'Who do you think I am? What in God's name do you think I've done?'

Jane is righteous, forbidding. 'You know what you've done, Clair Sailor. You know perfectly well.'

'Jane, what are you trying to make of me? Whatever he says, *I am not that person*. I thought we were . . .' Her voice trails off. *Friends*. Jane has turned and left.

So it is almost with relief that Clair delivers her children to Mara Strait's house. In a terrible irony that defies logic, it is the one place left where she will be taken for who she is. When Mara comes to the door, she will be smiling. So glad to see you. Come in. With Strait away in class, Clair can sit in Mara's kitchen and have coffee and feel a little better, although there's no way in this life that she can sit in Strait's house and unburden herself. Not now. Still if Mara asks she will be tempted, and if Clair asks her a question, nice Mara will answer. Good woman. Like me.

But Mara is dressed for the city. Behind her, the Sailors' babysitter, who is also the Straits' babysitter, waits to take the children to the kitchen for milk and cookies. 'Clair!' Mara's smile is beautiful. 'I'm so glad to see you.'

And conflicted as she is, torn between what she does not know about Mara and what she wants to believe, Clair says in all honesty, 'I am too.'

195

* * *

Something's the matter with Davy. When Wanda, who was originally the Sailors' sitter, brings the children home she's embarrassed and chastened. She stands on the sill with the children behind her and her head bowed as if expecting recriminations. 'For God's sake Wanda, come on in.'

She looks ready to cry. 'Oh, Clair.'

'What happened?'

'It's Davy.' She rolls back the cuff of his anorak. She's knotted a stained handkerchief around his wrist. The dark smears are either blood or ink or both. 'He got cut.' Her breath shakes.

Deep inside Clair, something twists. 'Davy!'

'It isn't *so* bad, Mom.' He isn't crying, but he has been. She can see it in his red eyes, all smudged tears and smeared dirt.

'What happened?'

He grins with his lips locked tight and one hand clamped protectively over the bandaged wrist. She recognizes that look: typical Davy, shaken but proud. 'Nothing.'

'Let me see.' Like a mother bear Clair grabs him, pulling him tight to her side. Now that she has him she's afraid to unwrap the cut. 'Who did this?'

'Nobody, Mrs Sailor. They just got into it, him and Chase.' Like Davy, Wanda has been crying. 'All I was doing was helping the girls make brownies, the boys were *right there* and . . . It's . . . What it is, is, they were doing this on their arms? Like, starting these, like, things?'

Yes, Clair wants to kill her. 'What do you mean, things?'

'At least we got it in time.'

'It's OK Mom, it's no big deal.'

'I washed it out and put stuff on it so it's clean, but not all the black came off.'

'The black!'

'You'll see. Sticky. Smeary. Awful stuff.'

'Wanda, you still haven't told me what happened.'

'Don't worry, it isn't deep.' Hurriedly, she shoves Nell inside. 'You be a good girl, Nelly, OK? 'Bye.' Free at last she flees. Before Clair can call her back she runs for the Lexus where Will Strait leans across the seat to hold the door open with the glow from the dome light outlining his smooth blond head.

'Davy. What did you guys do?'

196

Nelly answers for him, 'They got tattoos.'

'We did not!'

'Oh yes you did.'

'No we didn't. We were going to but you wrecked it.'

'I did not!'

Clair sighs. 'Let's see.'

He unwinds the handkerchief. 'We were only just beginning when Mr Strait came in.' It's like watching an instant replay; with a start Davy turns jerkily and says in a different voice, 'We didn't mean it, really!' Then he starts to cry. 'I said I was sorry but he was too mad to care. I thought he was going to . . .'

'Let me look at that. Oh, Davy!' On the back of his wrist is a short arc. The cut is so thin and shallow that it might have been made with a scalpel. Black. It isn't red with dried blood, it's black, but why black is not the first question she has to ask. Clair says in a low voice, 'Where did you get the knife?'

'His things.' Davy is sobbing now.

'Whose things?'

But he's crying so hard he can't speak.

'Shh, Davy. It's all right, all right? Just tell me what happened, OK?'

'Chase's dad. We were playing in the attic . . .'

'He found you in the attic?'

'No, Mom. We were up there and Chase said, "You want to see something?" So I said sure and he said, "We have to be quiet, it's a secret," and he went under this pile of stuff and brought out this shiny wooden box and he never said we weren't supposed to.' He's running ahead with another wave of sobs. 'So I didn't do it. Chase did it. You know the knife? He found it with his father's things.'

'His *things*?'

'That's what he called them. My father's things.'

She tries to make it sound ordinary. 'What kind of things?'

'I don't know what kind of things,' he says. 'They were just *things*. We hid the box after we took out the stuff we needed and we took it downstairs to Chase's room.' Davy's voice is going out of control again. 'I didn't see the box. I didn't see inside it, I didn't!' He turns on his sister. 'This is all your fault!'

'It is not!'

'You and Maddy were supposed to stand guard! But the dumb girls were off stuffing their faces instead. So Mr Strait came in and caught us. Oh Mom, he was so mad! He screamed and screamed at Wanda for not watching us and then he screamed at Chase and me, you wouldn't believe how loud he was screaming, DON'T YOU EVER TOUCH MY THINGS.' Misery opens Davy's throat; for a moment nothing comes out but pure sound.

'It's OK.' Clair holds him close. 'Davy, Davy, it's OK.' Then she pulls him into the kitchen and sits him at the table and wets a dishtowel and wipes his face and when she finally has him quiet she says as evenly as she can manage, 'Tell me about the knife.'

'It was in this box with a lot of other stuff.'

'What else did he have in the box?'

Pressed, Davy says, 'I already told you I don't know. Other stuff.' In a minute he's going to cry again.

'Like, sharp things?'

'Leave me alone, Mom. I already told you I don't know!'

'The knife you used.' It is getting harder to control her voice. 'What kind of knife was it?'

'It was silver.'

'A scalpel?'

Pressed, he whines, 'I don't know Mom, it was just a knife.'

Something about this gives her the dry swallows. She asks cleverly, 'Why was Mr Strait so mad?'

'He was just mad, Mom, that was all.' Then with the same thoroughness that makes him tell her more than she needs to know about movies he's seen on TV, Davy organizes the memory. 'It was going to be so nice. Chase and me decided we would make pirate signs on our arms so everybody will know we're best friends. Make Xs and mix our blood. You know, blood brothers? First Chase made a cut on me and fixed it with his father's black stuff—'

'What kind of black stuff?'

'It was just *black*. You know.'

She doesn't. 'Davy—'

'So he made a cut on me and then I made a cut on him and we took the black stuff and rubbed it in and then Chase was starting to make another cut but then Mr Strait came in and caught us.' He turns on his sister. 'Dodo. You were supposed to stand watch.' He says to Clair, 'He wasn't very nice.'

Fear thuds into her; it is tremendous. 'DID HE HURT YOU?'
In all ignorance Davy says, 'No Mom, he just got really mad.'
She can't stop shouting. 'DID THAT MAN TOUCH YOU?'
'No, he just spanked Chase.' His eyes are filling again. 'He spanked him really hard. He spanked him with his belt.'
'Oh Davy,' she says. *Oh God.* 'Oh, Chase!'
'He shouldn't have done it. Chase is my best friend!'
'It's OK, Davy.' She pulls him close, locking him to her with strong arms; she is ready to do anything she has to protect him. 'Don't worry, I promise it will never happen again,' rushing on, foolish Clair, 'you never have to go over there again.'
He pulls away. 'No, Mom. No way. I love it over there.' Even though he's too young to know what's going on in his mother's life, the boy's expression tells her that he does know. He is devastated. 'Chase is my best friend!'
'Davy, I can't let you go there . . .' This is a sentence it is beyond her power to complete.
Nelly starts to cry. 'Maddy is my best friend too.'
Struggling, her only son says something Clair never wanted to hear any child say. 'He's the only friend I've got left.'
'Don't say that!' Embattled, Clair is already scurrying ahead, skimming a dozen scenarios and sorting through her options – what to tell Mara, what to do. She hangs onto Davy; she holds him tight, devising a formula that will keep him safe. 'You can play with Chase all you want, OK? I promise. But look. For the time being, I just want you to do it over here.'
'I hate it over here, Mom, we don't have the—'
'I don't care what we don't have.' Clair is looking over Davy's head at Nelly, who has her own agenda. 'You can play with your friends all you want but listen. If you want to play with them at all, you're playing over here.'

It's hard, explaining to Mara without hurting her. She tries to open negotiations by dissembling. 'You've already done too much for them. Now it's my turn.' Clair, you liar, starting gradually. 'Just until we're even.'
'But I love having them.' Mara's tone begins to slide. 'It's the only fun I have.'

199

'I just need to keep an eye on Davy right now.'

'But Davy's fine, he—'

'You know. After what he got into.'

'He didn't get into anything.'

'He's just causing too much trouble at your house.'

'Trouble?' Bemused, Mara says dreamily, 'He's no trouble.'

'Today. He got into trouble in a big way.' Mara sounds so puzzled that Clair says, 'Your, ah, husband didn't tell you?' Nice lady getting ready to be hurt, so keep it light. Clair says clumsily, 'Department of altercations. *The Sound and the Fury*. Times ten. You know. Davy says he was livid.'

'Who was livid?' Odd. Mara's voice is so empty. It's as if the person who lives inside her head has packed up and moved out.

'Your—' Won't – can't – use the name. 'You know.'

'Do you mean Will? Oh no, I don't think so.' Mara just goes on. 'Not Will. Not today. I would have heard.'

'It was probably Davy's fault.' This is so awkward that Clair blunders on without a clue as to whether she's breaking the news or not breaking the news. 'I'm afraid he and Chase got into some of . . .' She chokes on it. 'Ah. Some of your husband's things.'

'Will's things?'

'I'm afraid the kids got hold of some kind of a . . . a . . .' Oh, this is so hard. 'Scalpel?' She trails the word like bait and when Mara does not speak she tries, 'Or a hunting knife?'

'Oh no,' Mara repeats. 'I don't think so. Not in our house. Not today.'

'From a box in the attic.'

'I really don't think so.' Her voice is light enough to float.

'And some . . . what was it, shoe polish? Ink?'

'They must have gotten into my mascara,' Mara says with a little laugh.

'No. They used a knife and some . . . I don't know what it is. Davy says it was silver . . .'

'Oh, my safety razor.'

'If you say so.'

'Oh, you mean that. That was nothing,' Mara says. 'You know how boys are. Pulled the blade out and went to work on themselves. I don't know how they did it, but they did.'

'But Davy said it was a—'

Mara's voice is as clear as rain. 'You know kids.'

'Then your husband doesn't have a—'

'Clair, I can't talk now, can I call you back?'

The next day Gig Jamison's parents present themselves at the publications office, two plain, sturdy, confused country people who look as though they've been bludgeoned by the knacker's mallet and drained of blood. They have come to Evard to pack up his things.

The boy's mother fixes Clair with an intent look. 'Eugene won't be back. He's gone for good.'

'Where is he, is he all right?'

'That's none of your business.'

Sympathy rushes out in words. 'Whatever it is, I'm sorry.'

Now when she least expects it, Gig's mother attacks. 'Sorry isn't enough,' she says so harshly that it flattens Clair.

'I . . .' She flashes on the moment when she found him in the archway. What it was like. What she was like: her failure. 'Oh, I wish!'

'Don't bother.'

'It's too late to bother now.' Behind the angry mother the father shifts from foot to foot. 'We've cleaned out Eugene's room and thrown out his papers and now we're polishing off the rest of his list.' He taps a notebook page filled with his son's painfully tiny handwriting, with addenda like marching chinch bugs cluttering all the available white space.

The mother says, 'He wanted us to come up here and see you.'

'That's the only reason we're here.' They turn away. 'You were on his list.'

Distress makes Clair persist. 'What happened to him?'

'We don't know. Two weeks and we don't know.'

The father says harshly, 'He don't say.'

'Is he—'

With a hand raised like a signal flag, the angular, rawboned father cuts her off. 'No questions. Don't ask us any questions.'

'The only reason we're here at all is you're on Eugene's list.'

'He has a message for you.'

'He says goodbye.'

'I'm so sorry I didn't know him better,' she murmurs – Gig in the archway, Gig in the tux with the foolishly festive white scarf. 'I might have been able to . . .'

It is the father who lays out the accusation. 'You may not know him, but he knew you.'

And the mother who underscores it. 'He counted on you.'

Clair extends her hands.

'He counted on you.' So much for her gesture; the father knocks her hands aside, lamenting, 'We all counted on you.'

This is how Clair discovers that even though he barely spoke to her, she was important to Gig. It comes as a surprise. Guiltily she acknowledges the rest: more important to him than he was to me.

'How could you?' the mother says so bitterly that it diminishes her – no, so bitterly that it diminishes all of them.

In words that will bring Clair to her knees after they've left the office, whether in prayer or in tears of remorse she can't know, the father charges her with the collapse of all their hopes, railing: 'How could you let this happen to him?'

Night. Nick is meeting with George Atkinson and Clair's alone with the kids until nearly midnight. When the phone rings after eleven, she picks up. Hope makes her say, 'Teddy?'

The air gets old before the caller speaks. 'Hello, Clair.'

She won't know what makes her cry, 'Who is this?' when at the sound of the voice all her back hairs stand up and the skin on her flanks begins to crawl. 'Who's calling?'

'It's me, Clair.' The speaker is easy, confident of a welcome, 'Aren't you going to say hello?'

Interesting. For the same reason she avoids him in any gathering, Clair can't bear to have him on the phone. The negative alchemy of enemy souls occupying the same space. 'Nick isn't here.'

'Don't hang up.'

'I'll tell him you called.'

'Don't hang up. I didn't call to talk to Nick.'

'I have to go.'

'Please!' He has the wits not to use her name. In spite of her rude haste, Strait is unnervingly complaisant, murmuring like an actor whose charm is learned, not given, 'I called to talk to you.'

Chemistry: the suaver he is, the madder she gets. 'I suppose you want to apologize.'

'Apologize?' Like Mara, he seems politely baffled. 'Why should I apologize?'

'For yelling at Davy today. For hitting Chase.'

He is doggedly puzzled. 'What are you talking about?'

'You know damn well.'

'I'm sorry, I don't.'

'For saying what you said to them. For leaving those terrible *things* where kids would find them.'

Now the tone congeals. He says carefully, 'What things?'

'You know. Whatever they found.' Clair wants to number them, object, purpose, chapter and verse, but her imagination defies her; she doesn't know what's hidden in this stranger's attic any more than she knows what's inside his head. Her voice is tight with frustration. 'Your things.'

Where he was charming, Strait is cold and deliberate. 'What things, Mrs Sailor?'

'Knives.' The words choke her. 'Whatever else you have!'

Will Strait is not a different person; he is the same person he was when he began this phone call but certain parts of him have been hidden. Now he has decided to let them show. 'There were never any *things*, Mrs Sailor. You're crazy if you think there are any things.'

This makes her shout angrily, 'Then why did you call?'

He will make one more pass at the amenities before everything changes and he attacks – Will Strait, whose charm turns to menace. 'I called because I thought we could still be friends, but now—'

'Look, Mr Strait. This isn't a very good time for this, OK?' She is burbling politely now, anything to get off the phone. 'It's late. I think—'

The air cracks. He has smacked the mouthpiece with his fist. 'That's enough!'

Then before Clair can hang up and thus escape what he is about to tell her, Strait begins in a tone that draws her like a tack to a magnet, fusing her to the receiver, so electrified that separating from it would be like ripping off her ear.

'You want to know why I called? I didn't want to tell you, but you make it clear I have to tell you. This is why I called. I called to tell you that everybody knows about the terrible things you've been doing to me.'

There is no sound except her sharp intake of breath.

'The whole town knows. They all know what you've been doing and they think you ought to be in jail. Do you hear me, Mrs Sailor?'

She hears and cannot speak.

'Yes you hear me and yes you know what I mean. All those things you did to us. That your husband did. Disgusting things. To me. My wife. My innocent children. And we aren't the only ones. Those poor students! Don't deny it, and stop trying to blame us for what's going on, you're just wasting your time.'

She tries to speak.

He overrides her. 'Everybody knows who's to blame. They all know it's you. You and your wonderful, perfect paragon of a husband, father, idol of students, perfect lover, handsome jock with no secrets, big square fool with his store-dummy smile and his two books and eighteen articles, foursquare intellectual without a bad thought in his head or a bad thing in his life, *well that won't wash*!' Aware that his tone is getting out of control, the ruthless, malevolent speaker reins in as Clair stuffs her free hand in her mouth and tries not to sob.

Then he just starts over in that terrible, calm tone. 'So you should thank me for warning you. Understand?'

She doesn't speak but she can't hang up.

He says, 'Are you there? This call is your first warning, Mrs Sailor. You hear? So don't go complaining to your friends because they won't help you now. They all know what you're trying to do to me. The lies. The terrible lies. They know and they won't tolerate it. I won't tolerate it. Understand, you have been put on notice.' His voice is harsh, ugly and contorted. Mad. 'You are on notice as of now. If you do *one more thing* to get in my way here – one more thing, *I am going to hunt you down and find you and when I find you . . .*'

The pause is more terrible than anything he might have found to say to her. Strait seems to know this. He says only, 'You're going to pay.'

Everything stops for too long. He repeats, 'Believe me, you are going to pay.'

Clair won't be able to say exactly when Strait ends his tirade and releases her any more than she knows what his last words are. She will find herself still standing with her mouth wide and the plastic jammed to her ear long after he has finished and hung up, and if she thinks there is one person or one agency in town that she can turn to, man, woman, college administration or campus security, town cops or close friends, she is mistaken; in a prodigy of preparation, he has already foreseen and forestalled it: 'They all know what you're trying to do to me. The lies. The terrible lies.'

And never once in this ugly exchange did he identify himself by name.

21

Ben

What it's about. My God I should have smashed myself flat that night, blood and brains and memory smeared all over the pavement, everything over and done. A dead man doesn't have to think about these things. Doesn't have to, what, Sister?

Rehearse. *Do this,* he said; I believed him so I did. *Do that.*

We were in the Doge's Palace at night, not the whole class just him and me '*not every student*' such an honor, rocking on that marble floor like the master of a magnificent ship with the building slanting and the sounds of Venice reverberating in my mouth: bells, the sound the water makes the *whoom* so mysterious and deep, never heard it anywhere else in my life, I can't stop hearing it. Then we were in the boat – *where did he get the* . . . where were we going anyway? *Going to show you* he said and I asked him where are we going? *Trust me.* And then we went somewhere and I guess . . .

How did we get into the Doge's Palace at night?

How can I rehearse when I don't remember? Feel the Ig boring into me. OK, Sister, I'll admit it. Can't remember. Or won't.

But can bring back the boat ride, two of us and a bottle, other stuff we were doing, joint, OK, maybe coke, such an honor, him and me. Laughing out there on the water, waving goodbye to all the poor souls left behind on the shore while we went riding out, so terribly far out.

We got off in a new, dark place.

Me, him, on the Island of the Dead. So exalted, my voice so hushed. 'Oh! Not supposed to be here.'

And him, who knows *everything* about those places. Explaining, 'The best things happen in places where you're not supposed to be,' my teacher who'd brought me here, brilliant man singled me out, only I was good enough, my leader leaped to the top of a carved stone sarcophagus and stood there with his arms spread, sounding like God.

Then he knelt. Held out his hand. 'Come up.'

'They'll catch us.' I was afraid. A foreigner in this place: police, cemetery guards. 'Not supposed to be here.'

It was his scorn I should have been afraid of, the way he laughed. 'Don't you ever want to amount to anything?'

Like him. Yes I wanted to be like him. 'You know I do.'

'Then come up.'

'I can't.'

'Like me.'

I wanted to *be* him but, 'I'm afraid.'

He gripped my wrist. 'I'll help you.'

Still I hung back. 'You're sure it's all right?'

'Last chance.'

I could see his magnificent life like a train rolling out of the station, only a few seats left on board; this was my last chance to get on it and still I was afraid. 'I can't.'

His voice was terrible. 'Do you want to learn?'

I couldn't answer.

Indifferently, he turned away.

Oh no! I shouted, 'Wait! Yes I want to learn!' *I want to be like you.* My God! I wanted him to be my father. No. Have what he had: beautiful wife, fine children. Be like him, handsome, strong. Know what he knew. He knew everything about life: the best of the best – wine, cities, art; he knew antiques by name and rare books by heart and he knew how to get what he wanted; he was all style and confidence, head and shoulders above the world, and if I was like Lazarus, fine.

'True learning comes at a price.'

Lazarus, who would rather die than starve. I was on the edge of knowing what my teacher knew; I gave him my hand. 'If you say so!'

'Then do what I say or you'll never know anything.'

Before I knew it I was up, slipping on the ancient, ruined stones; I could hear shards breaking off and rattling to the ground like lost fragments of old lives.

'Now don't be afraid. Be honored. You're the only one in the class that I think is worth it.' Yes I was singled out. Special.

Honored. 'Yes sir.' Standing on the crumbling stone sarcophagus where none of the others would ever stand. Learning what they would never know. He chose me.

From where he and I stood we could see all Venice, the life of that beautiful city sprawling on the far shore with its stone angels and winking lights like a toy diorama laid out precisely for us, two equals, two friends regarding it from our crumbling pinnacle in the city of the dead. Standing at the top of the burial city where nobody is found after dark. He lifted his hands. 'See?'

I saw. It was magnificent.

He said, 'Now stamp on the grave.'

'What?' I held back. *Sacrilege.*

'Stamp hard. Where the tenant has gone, we are all going.' So I did: hollow. Inside, the dead stirred. When we were both stamping, exalted, he shouted, 'But not yet!' Put his mouth to the sarcophagus and shouted to the dead of Venice, of the world, 'But not yet!'

'But not yet!' My heart jumped up. Lord, I was high. Pop this, he'd said in the boat. Enhance the experience. Whatever it was, on top of the wine.

Wuow!

'Now dance.'

We danced. And all the time I was ascending. Higher than high and going up. Up. Up. Soon I would be as tall as him.

'Now!' And before I knew or could comprehend it, my avatar, my mentor had grabbed me by the waist in a mad tango and launched us off the edge of the platform, so dark, so many rocks below and us so high, so chemically enhanced that it was supremely logical for me to do exactly what he wanted and not get hurt: 'Now fall.'

I would have done anything for him.

We were so loose by that time that we weren't even bruised.

We got up. He was laughing, triumphant. 'See?'

I saw.

'Make a leader of you.'

A leader!

'A prince. Understand?'

'I do!' It was a big lesson; I was beginning to understand.

This is what he had taught me. You can climb and not be frightened. You can fall and not be hurt. You can do anything you want and never pay.

We got back in the boat and rode and rode and did a couple of lines and laughed and laughed, laughter bubbling up like sobs and our voices split wide open in a never-ending scream, so drunk! And after that.

After that?

Nothing.

His voice, jubilant. 'Next!'

I don't remember after that.

Either won't or can't.

I came to, God, I came to; I was running with my mouth streaming, sound coming out like blood; I was lost, so lost in awful, stony night-time Venice where all the bridges look like all the other bridges and the arches all lead into other arches that feed into paths that lead into other paths and come into squares with churches that look like all the others. You can be lost without knowing it and hurt without knowing how you are hurt; you can be lost and sobbing for help; you can pound on identical doors, all closed against the night, and never find your way back. In that city in that ancient state you can scream and scream and no one will come to the window and nobody will let you in; you can be bleeding, desperate, helpless and cracked in two and nobody will know.

You can be changed forever by what's happened to you.

Whatever happened.

How he taught me, and he did teach me. No, *did that*. No!

What he taught me.

This. Everything he taught me is a lie.

'Son, if you need a doctor I can call the paramedics.'

'No! No doctor!' Screaming, Ben comes back to himself. He can't say what's left him standing at full height on top of a log here in the rest area off the interstate, in Amenia, New Hampshire, windmilling and screaming to wake the city of the dead an ocean and a sea away. 'I'm fine,' he screams so shrilly that it's clear he is not fine. He bares his teeth at the tough old woman in the lumber jacket and the hunting hat, howling until she backs off and he jumps down. 'Just fine!'

'Well you don't look fine.' Except for the hulking shape slouched in the passenger's seat of the pickup she's left running, Ben and the country woman are alone in the rest area, warily skating in place in their heavy boots with the rubber lugs that help not at all on the packed ice. She squints at him with the eyes of an insider in a place where he's the foreigner. 'You hurt?'

'No ma'am.'

'What are you doing here? Son, don't you know?'

The worst part: he doesn't! It's too hard to explain.

'You can't stay here, you'll freeze to death. Come on.'

'No!' He means it; he doesn't mean it. He just doesn't want to get in a truck with an old lady who's seen him this way, rocking on top of a rotting log and howling to death.

'Don't give me a hard time.' Amazing how powerful she is.

'Let go of me!'

'No way.' At her signal the hulking figure in the pickup truck has stepped down and is sliding toward them over the icy ridges made by eighteen-wheelers rolling over the ice. 'You're coming with me.' She and her huge son, who looks retarded, put their hands under Ben's elbows and propel him along. They hoist him over the tailgate and send him sprawling into the back of the truck. Then the old lady lowers the gate and the hulk gives his mother a boost and she lands hard on the truckbed, rolling Ben over so she can look him in the face. 'Where you going, son?'

He's strangling on unspoken words. '*Can't*.' Tell you.

'You going north or what?'

Wheezing. 'North.'

'Where do you want us to let you out?'

At a loss, he shrugs.

'Sure. Fine. Vermont? The border? All you have to do is say.'

I can't. What stalls him, he can't say. Ben knows where he has to go now – all those phone calls – but he knows this too. It isn't enough to locate your enemy. You have to prepare. You don't go on until you are ready to do what needs doing. What? He doesn't know. He blurts. 'Don't know!'

'You don't know where you're going?'

This comes more easily. *Thanks, Ig*. 'I have to rehearse.'

'Son, are you crazy?'

'Yes.' Wham. His arms fly out. 'I mean no!'

'Now you look here.' Somehow the old woman's hands have gotten clamped on his neck; she grips through the muffler and bears down. 'If you won't tell me where you're going, we can just drop you off at state police headquarters.'

'No!'

'Then name me the place.'

Not ready. 'I can't.' But she keeps her hands on his neck. *Don't make me do this.* It comes up like a hairball. Ben is as surprised as anybody. 'Evarton.'

'Evarton!' She sits back on her haunches, disappointed. 'Is that all you are? A dumb college fuck?'

'I can't remember.' Yes, dumb.

'What are you anyway?'

Ben shrugs. He doesn't know. Until he finds out, he can't go in there and locate the one who . . . whatever, much less confront him. *Rehearse.* But what? What terrible force tore him apart and left him like this? Unless he can get strong enough to face the man, he may never find out. The Ig: *Get your story straight.*

'Well you can't stay here. Evarton.' She jumps down and slams the tailgate on him. 'I took you for smarter than that.'

22

Side by side on the bed, Clair and Nick cling like children lost in the woods. Now that she's told him everything, Nick says into her hair, 'Why didn't you tell me?'

They have both been crying. 'First I couldn't. Then . . .' It's too hard to explain: the weeks of strain, the complicated allure of protecting him, the pressure of knowing what she knows that he didn't know. Compounding until she could not bring herself to tell. Odd pride. *I can handle this myself.* 'Then I couldn't,' she says at last.

He can't make himself let go of her long enough to look her in the eyes. 'Why?'

This makes it possible for Clair to say what she does. If good marriages are a legend the partners write for each other and, in love, perpetuate, she has to be very careful what she constructs next. People in love can fight and kill each other on a daily basis because just as surely as the sun comes up, they make it up in love; to do this they need to believe in each other and to believe absolutely. This, then, is the construction she puts on the secret that has fallen between them. 'I was afraid of what you would do.'

'No,' he says quietly. 'You were afraid I couldn't do it.'

Grieving, she begs the question. 'I missed you *so much.*'

'Me too.'

It is too far beyond midnight in the Sailor bedroom, where he and Clair talk with the door latched on the off chance that Davy will wake and hear. On a warmer night they would have retreated to the front porch or gone to the garage to have this out – anything to keep the words from piling up in the house like toxic fumes, drifting through the cracks under closed doors to invade their children's dreams or poison them in their sleep.

Nick says, 'What are we going to do?'

'I'd like to kill him.'

'What, shoot him dead?' He is hurt, bemused. 'People like us don't do things like that.'

She sighs. Nothing in the life of the mind prepares a man like Nick to deal with a man like Strait. 'I know.'

'I've got to do something.' With his jaw squared and his head up, Nick looks like a kid soldier ready to go out to his death: brave and vulnerable.

'Be careful.'

'It's too late for careful. We have to get rid of him.'

Clair wants to undo this, take them back to the point when Strait was nowhere in their lives and she imagined they were safe. 'Let the cops do it.'

'On what grounds? Did you tape the call?'

'Even if I had . . .' She shakes her head. 'He never gave his name.'

'Right.' Nick says.

'You knew about him!'

'I did and I didn't,' he says. 'We don't have enough to go to the cops. You can't even start without witnesses. Proof.'

They aren't just talking about the phone threat. 'Proof of what?'

'That's the trouble. I don't know. They all think we're neurotics up here on the hill.'

'George doesn't.'

'It won't do any good to tell George. George doesn't want to hear. And our friends . . .' Although he began by nibbling at the edges of their lives, the outsider has gnawed deeper than they knew. Strait is at the center now; like a metastatic cancer, he is devouring them from the inside out. 'It won't matter where I go. The bastard's been there first.'

She recites as if it is scripted: ' "What's the matter with the Sailors, that they don't like me when I admire them so much?" '

'Yes.' Nick tries on bitterness and for the first time in their lives together, it fits. 'Nobody ever asks "What's the matter with Strait?" Ten years. You give ten years to a place and when you go to draw on your credit you discover there was never any credit. There was only what they could get from you.'

'I'm sorry.' She is. It doesn't matter about me. I can handle it. But you . . .

'Ten years.' He is not so much defeated as changed by the knowledge that his dogged loyalty means nothing in this altered universe. 'Ten years and when push comes to shove they believe him instead of me.'

The events of the past weeks roar into her head like an express train and telescope, piling up. 'This didn't just happen overnight, Nick. Where were you while he was out on his rounds?'

Then the man she loves most moves his hands down her arms and sets her at a slight distance, squaring off. 'I was right here,' he says evenly. 'I was here the whole time. I had to do my job.'

She hates herself for crying but tears keep getting out and running down all the same. 'You thought he was wonderful.'

'Up to a point.'

'What point, Nick? What point?'

'You don't want to know. I caught him in a major lie.'

'If only you'd told me!'

'I couldn't afford to.' His expression is sweet. Reconciled. 'Winter is a nightmare here. If anything goes wrong, the students get weird; I have to keep it together here. In the interview the guy looked terrific, big hit with his classes and the kids got weird anyway, and you. I brought him home and you started getting weird. First I thought you were paranoid. Then I thought I was getting paranoid. Little things kept happening.'

'What?'

Now it is Nick who is protecting her. 'Just – things. When you're getting through the winter you have to keep your head down – no turnoffs, no time to sit up and look around. Things happened; I had to think it was my imagination. I kept hoping it would go away.' He looks down. 'I'm so sorry, Clair.'

'If only you'd told *them*.'

'What would be the point? Somebody would convene a fucking committee.' He is angrier than she has ever seen him. 'Do you see how impossible this is? Life by committee. Nothing is absolute.'

'This,' she says grimly. 'This is absolute. I wish we could just kill him. Push him off a cliff.'

'No. Whatever he is, you don't want to be that.'

'You don't know *what* I want.' She means: I don't know what I want.

'We have to do it the right way. Step by step.' Moderate Nick. This is how he strikes the difference between them. 'You don't always have to pillage and burn. There are civilized ways of doing these things.'

By this time she is shaking with exhaustion. 'Like what?'

'I don't know yet.' He stands. Stronger than he's been, but not that much stronger, the loving protector who has not yet tested his powers or defined the perimeter. 'I only know we have to try.'

'How can you, when we can't even prove he made this call?'

'I'll get something on him. I will.'

'The students.' She doesn't know why this comes into her mind: Gig. 'There's something going on with the kids.'

'Maybe.' God, he looks miserable. 'I don't know.'

'Teddy thinks so too. He's doing some checking.'

Nick nods. 'I'm going to do some checking of my own.'

'You've already said he covers his tracks. You can't—'

'Please trust me to this. I will.'

'No. Not just you,' she says, and this is how they will restate and consolidate the legend of the good marriage so they can lie down and comfort each other, and if tonight it takes them a long time getting to that good place, it is a function of worry and exhaustion; but because this is something they need in good times and bad, she says now, 'We will.'

Later Nick says to the ceiling, 'When this is done, we're out of here. Can you handle moving?'

'Wherever you go.' This is hard, even in the dark. 'God! He's stolen our life!'

Nick goes on reflectively, 'It's so weird. You think you belong in a place, you think you have friends, and when it comes right down to it you don't have anything.'

'We'll always have Teddy.'

'Oh, Teddy. Teddy is different.' He's right. Teddy is. If she and Nick are the real outsiders in this tight, conventional world that's so rigid and so quick to judge, the fact that Teddy is gay distanced him long before she and Nick even recognized the distance. If Teddy is their friend and will stay their friend no matter what, it is in part because he comprehended his position before they understood that there was an inside or an outside.

Clair loves him because in spite of or perhaps precisely because of this distance, he lives his life with energy and joy. 'I know.'

Like Teddy's, their separation is absolute. It is psychic, not yet physical and not nearly complete, but it is profound. Later she and Nick will need

214

to study the reasons for Teddy's separation and the terrible cost. Grieving, they will consider it at length, but this is in the future. 'Thank God for Teddy,' Nick says.

And although she is too debilitated by the hour and the uses of the night to recognize the nature or the similarity of their positions, Clair adds, 'Thank God for difference.'

By the time they finally sleep it's getting light. Within minutes they are waked by a crash. The resonance is tremendous. It sounds like the earth cracking in two. They sit up with their hearts thudding; paralyzed, they cling. Nick shouts, 'The house!' Barefoot and half-naked, they run outside into the cold dawn.

Their house has been hit by a car.

Somebody must have left the vintage RV in neutral somewhere on the hill. Unless somebody took it out of gear. Somehow the hand brake turned out to be off – was taken off? How did this happen? How? No matter. The hand brake was off and seconds ago somebody or something started the big land yacht rolling. Driverless, the heavy vehicle careered backward, gathering momentum as it skittered over the icy road, jumping the curb and plowing through the bushes, tearing like a juggernaut into the hard stone foundation of the Sailors' house.

'Shit,' Nick shouts to the empty street. 'Shit. Shit!'

Sobbing with the cold, they regard the upended RV, chunks of the brownstone foundation dislodged and lying scattered in the snow. There is a hole in their house. Build your house on rock and discover that no matter how prudent you are, no matter how carefully you plan ahead or try to arm yourself, something big can come along and broach the foundation. Once this happens you are open to the elements. Ice, snow, anything can come in.

It seems appropriate.

There is a hole in their lives.

23

Ben

Like Baron Frankenstein's monster, who holed up in the woods with a friendly blind man, Ben Messinger has found a safe place in exile – the perfect person to tell his story to. He understands now that it isn't what shows in his face that makes him a monster; it's what he has to tell. The story fills him and makes him hideous. He has to let it out if he expects to live. The old lady's huge son isn't exactly deaf but he inclines his mallet head with such a pleasant, unbroken smile that Ben knows that he can talk and talk and never be understood. He can say anything he wants.

The old lady who rescued him from the rest stop has parked Ben and her retarded son in a cluttered rural junk shop to wait out the newest storm. They are sitting in the dust-flocked front window watching the sleet. The blind man didn't care what his grotesque house guest looked like because he couldn't see. He and the monster were a perfect match. As here. No matter what Ben says to him, the old lady's son doesn't register; he only smiles. He's like a huge, misshapen transient from another universe where the dominant life form is more like him than it is like Ben.

Is the enormous child really deaf? It's hard to know. Sitting side by side in recliners in the cluttered display window, he and Ben are pleased with each other's company. Sleet smears the glass on the diagonal, freezing in slashes with such regularity that Ben fixes on the pattern, hypnotized, and where he hasn't said more than a few words in all the months since his world broke apart, the stopper comes loose and he starts to talk. Entire paragraphs, chapters come falling out.

It's hard to explain, your first time in a foreign country, do you know what a foreign country is? Well maybe not, but let me tell you, it isn't like this. It's another world. Things are different; the money is different, what the inhabitants think is pretty different, what their bread is like and how you ask for things and what's written on their signs, even the toilets look different, serving up what you did in this little dish so you have to see; it is so weird!

And you? In a new world where nothing is real, you are different too. If you thought you knew who you were before you got here, you forget.

Nineteen years in your same old house with your same old mother, bus to junior college every day and bus home at night. This is the big escape, they call it, *study abroad*. Get on a plane in New Jersey and when you get off it's all Venice, do you know what Venice is like? I'll tell you what it's like. Pictures can't begin to show it – what the water sounds like underneath the city, going *whoom* against the pilings that hold the whole thing up, what it's like tiptoeing over those stone bridges like the little kid in the fairy tale, or what's going on under them, whether the thing hiding from you down there is funny or dangerous, like the Three Billy-Goats Gruff or the three trolls. Venice. You never know whether there is something lovely or something terrible waiting for you in the night.

You go along for your whole life doing what your mother tells you and then you land here.

Don't be scared, he is at the head of the group, your teacher and your leader, he can speak the language. Follow close, he's the only one who knows the way; it's his job to teach this new world to you, what to look for, how to get around, may be descended from some decaying Italian noble, a born insider in *palazzos* you can only dream about. He holds the power to open all these barred gates and carved doors with their big brass knockers and brass plates and take you inside, and all the time you're freaked and belching from too much travel and you keep hearing the water *whooming* against the underpinnings of this strange new territory and, in counterpoint, the bells. But don't be afraid, he'll take care of you; don't hold back, he knows the way.

You're always at the tail end of the group somehow, end up walking alone behind a bunch of people you're with but are not part of, smartass kids all been to Europe before, been here lots of times, oh yawn; unlike you they live in big cities and come out of private schools and cool places like Yale with their laptops and their perfect jackets and their wraparound shades and the one thing that money can't buy and you don't have and probably will never have, you know, *attitude*. But in the middle of your exclusion and loneliness *he* doubles back, 'Are you OK?' and you know that you may not be a smartass like the paying customers but you are *special* and this alone is worth all the misery. He says you are the only one who's up to the material and you believe; after all, he is a professor, and professors know everything. You are there on scholarship; while the others are bopping in place and giggling you hang on every word, and something else – the light in your eyes, the intelligence? – something makes you special to him.

So you are singled out in this unreal place that is so different from everything you know. You can be different too. Everything is new here – what you want and what you think you want, which more than anything is to find some woman who . . .

Everything. Everything in Venice is either smaller than you're used to or else it is bigger, buildings and churches you only saw in books, big as life and dirtier than you thought. There are all these statues and paintings, great pink women with enormous bellies and incredible breasts spilling out as if they have been hanging up there on the walls touching themselves and waiting just for you. So there's all that *flesh* up there on the wall in the galleries he takes you to study, and the whole time you are studying it, all you can think about is women, heaps and piles of big, pink women rolling over and over and opening themselves up to you and you wonder what Delia would say if she knew about these thoughts you have; she sent you away to get an education and all you can think about is sex. So there you are following, tagging along behind the group in all those dark places, staring at pictures alone because you don't belong in this group, they could care less for you, but as long as you can lose yourself in those big pink bodies, you can forget.

Your mom who kept you tucked under her elbow has finally let you go for once and you are out in the world seeing paintings that are so old and so naked and so beautiful and full of flesh that it pulls you up from the heels and out through your mouth. Body and soul you are being turned inside out and the whole time the professor is lecturing in that voice that would draw even your mother, lecturing in tones that could hypnotize a rock.

'Yours,' he is saying, 'the treasures of the world are all here for the taking and they can be yours.'

Yes he was my idol, he was so *sure*. Then in the late afternoons we would troop back to the Piazza de San Marco to meet his family, his wife and his children waiting for us with big smiles, all three scrubbed and fresh after a nap and a shower at the apartment they'd rented in some palazzo while the rest of us stayed at a student hotel. We'd sit around in a sidewalk cafe with the professor and that beautiful, beautiful woman and his two nice children, drinking *cappuccino* and eating pastries like princes in the world.

I would look at him and think: what you have, I want. What you are, I want to be.

Then he would bend to whisper to his little boy and this *pain* would open in my guts like a spring-driven knife. It stays curled up under my heart most of the time but in unguarded moments when I least expect it, it springs open and stabs. *Oh, Dad. I miss my dad.*

How can you miss somebody you never knew? Why do I miss him so much? The rat left Delia before I was born, I don't even know where he is but at times like that, seeing normal kids with a real father, it hurt like he had been torn out of my side.

I pretended to be looking at something else but all the time I was watching our professor and wondering if he would mind having an extra kid.

So in the cafe I would be watching his great wife and his fantastic kids, I would see this perfect teacher sitting there in the late sunlight and I could not stop thinking, *I wish you were my dad.* And then I would kind of pretend until the waiters cleared the last things away and we had to leave. The group had peeled off in pairs by that time, raunchy guys and stylish, skinny girls who would do anything except with me, leaving me with the professor and his family, and after a while he'd look at me and say, 'Don't you have anyplace to go?'

And I would have to lie. So I'd lope off somewhere and eat standing up and go back to my room alone and go through the postcards I'd bought, you know, the art, pictures in catalogs, and the women I was thinking about were never those rich, stylish, walking eating disorders I was in class with, they were beautiful and huge, like the tremendous women hanging in the galleries, waiting for me. I'd think: if I went out on the Rialto, would I have the guts to stop a hooker? Would I even know which ones the hookers were and how could I explain what I wanted in my no-Italian when I already knew I couldn't afford it, plus I was scared, you know?

So you are away from home in a whole new world where nothing is real and you think, I can do anything I want here, anything, because it isn't real, and then you think, but I'm still me. And until he singles you out and takes you by the hand and shows you, you can't do anything at all.

Then, God. That night he took me out in the boat the world expanded and I saw the universe opening up for me; what a rush, the city of the dead. I was out of my mind on the stuff we had been taking, riding along with my head back and my eyes wide open, pretending I could walk on the ceiling above the world so I didn't see where we were when we dipped into one of the little canals that feeds into the Grand Canal and I couldn't tell you how he did it or which way we went or even what he was doing when he nosed into a dock and we hit the stones with a soft thump and he jumped out.

'Where are we?'

He was already tying up. 'We're home.'

'Home?'

'My palazzo. Not really mine, but, you know, I thought you might want to see where I live.'

Well, I did.

'Something special,' he said and his voice was so blurred that he could have been as drunk as I was. 'Special here.'

'Yes, sir.' I was drunk and stoned blind but in the middle of all the craziness I had this vision of me and the professor sitting at his kitchen table with our heads bent under the lamp light while his beautiful wife made us all better with coffee loaded with sugar and unseparated milk. She could take me up to bed the way my mother used to and tuck me in.

The place was amazing, so beautiful, marble curved staircase with these ancient tapestries hanging down so that in the dark you couldn't tell whether those were shadows like dark lines down the woven pictures or whether they were shredded to tatters with age. Everything was so *rich* and the place so silent, lost centuries locked up in those stones and me and him going up the stairway with him singing a song with words I could not catch and me saying, 'Shouldn't we be quiet so we don't wake up the children?' and him telling me, 'It won't matter, they're in Milan.'

So the kids were in Milan and I guess his wife was in Milan; she wasn't there, the maid wasn't there. There was nobody there but me and my professor, and by then he had promised me a full scholarship at Princeton, which is where he said he taught, and if I got strong enough to make some phone calls after I got wrecked and sent home and found out the truth, if

221

you'd tried to tell me that night that he'd never been near Princeton I would have punched you in the face.

He was all business, he had my Tintoretto paper waiting on the coffee table and he had the paper I'd written about this story by Thomas Mann and he went through them point by point saying how wonderful they were, praising me page by page by page. He said I had an exceptional intelligence and that was why he was giving me this special attention, if I transferred to Princeton we could write a book and make him famous and that would make it worth all the extra time he was giving me and I believed him, wouldn't you?

After all, he was the professor. You might not know it but professors know more than other people and that makes them special, people you can trust. Who was I, a dumb kid from New Jersey, never been to Europe, knocked out by praise, excited and shaky and drunk.

'Oh, Professor Strait,' I said.

I was so honored and then I was even more honored because he said, 'You can call me Will.'

He said he'd brought me here to tell me how good my paper was and teach me what I needed to know to make it perfect. He said his wife was away so it wouldn't matter if we talked late; he said it would be OK if we put on music, some huge, gooshy Italian opera that filled the room and rolled out the long windows and spilled in the canals along with the candlelight because he said – how drunk was I? – the electricity was out. Wouldn't I like to sit down here, where the moonlight fell on the velvet in velvety stripes, and wouldn't I like a snort of that and another drink of this.

'I don't know if I . . .'

'Don't be scared, it's only part of the experience.'

'God I love Venice!' I meant, I love this life!

'You can't be afraid of the experience,' he said in that voice that could convince you of anything. 'You have to be open to experience,' he said.

I didn't know what he was talking about. Open? I thought I was. Listen, he was going to help me transfer to Princeton, he would get me in, and I would have the advantage over the other students because I had already studied the relationship between literature and art in Venice one on one with the best professor on the Princeton faculty. I said that was great when what I meant was, he was great. He said he would mentor me in the program and the lost, hurt part of me that grew up with only half a family processed that and turned it, thinking he meant *father* me. I told him about my dad and he gave me this warm smile that let me know how lucky I was to be there and to have him there.

After all these years of no father I was going to be just like everybody else, and if I believed it, wouldn't you? He was my professor and he was in charge. You believe what your professor says and you do what he tells you because professors are just like *doctors*. Elevated. Irreproachable. After all, they have the power to save your life.

You get that I was out of my mind with everything he and I had been taking and high on bombing around on the Grand Canal, just him and me, circling the city in our private speedboat as if we owned the place. I thought the world was mine. Yes, I was out of it, so far out that when it started happening I didn't even know it was happening, much less what it was.

'Good student,' he said. 'You are such a good student that.' He took his time finishing. 'I think you're ready to learn the rest.'

He said, 'Of all the students I have, you are the one who deserves to know,' he said, and who was I to think anything but oh, wow, and he was moving across the velvety stripes until we were sitting close.

'Come here,' he said. 'Come learn my secrets.' So I did. He had his head bent; I thought he was going to whisper but what he whispered was, 'Do this,' and I was – WHAT! My God, whatever it was, I didn't want to *do this*. He said he was going to teach me to open my mind to the knowledge of the universe, but that wasn't what he meant. I was surprised and scared. I yelled. 'What are you *doing*?'

He grabbed my arm. 'Expanding your consciousness.'

'That's not what you're doing.'

'Yes it is.' He grabbed my other arm. 'Now relax. You're perfectly safe with me. Do what I say. Remember, I am your professor and a married man. Do you think I'd do anything to do you harm?'

But his hands were all . . . Never mind, I screamed, 'Don't, I'm not *like* that!'

Professors don't have to answer questions, they just hit you with another question. 'What do you mean, *like that*?'

'You've got me wrong.' I was so stupid I thought all I had to do was explain and he'd let go.

He did not let go. 'I've got you exactly right.'

'No,' I said. 'No! You don't get it. I'm not gay!'

He slapped my face; he was furious. 'Well, neither am I!'

223

This made me gulp hard because I had to wonder why else the professor would be doing whatever he was doing – looked like hitting on me. I had to wonder what I had said or done to bring this down. I was so ashamed. I was scared I had been sending signals, you know, asking for it without even knowing what it was I was asking for. I was crying by that time, so maybe he didn't understand what I was telling him, words spouting like vomit. 'I was never gay!'

At least I don't think I was.

He hit me again. 'Do you think we'd be here if you were?' He looked at me with such *scorn*. 'Don't you know I hate faggots?'

'Don't—'

'I hate them, understand me? I'm a married man!' His voice was hard and cold, the classroom voice that is built to impress and designed to shame you into obedience. He shook me hard. 'What do you think I'm doing here?'

'I don't know.' He'd clamped down and I was struggling, trying hard to get free and he would not let go and I couldn't stop sobbing. 'I don't know.'

But he had me in an unbreakable grip. He put me at arm's length with this terrible, condescending look. 'Then how do you know what you're like?'

'Let go!'

'Stop that,' he said. 'I'm trying to do something for you.'

'Whatever it is, *I don't want it.*'

His voice was cold. 'Oh yes you do.'

'I don't!' I kept fighting him, I was crazy with doubt and fear. 'I don't want anything. Now let go of me, just let me *out*.'

'Stop it. Quiet. This is nothing to be afraid of, it's part of your education. An important part. Remember, I'm a married man.'

I was bawling like a calf in the slaughter house. 'I don't care!'

We could have been arguing over a late paper. He was relentlessly reasonable. He said, 'This isn't what you think it is. My wife knows all about this and she doesn't mind.' He pushed his big face close to mine: smooth jaw, handsome nose and eyes like uncut blue topaz so perfect how could he be bad. And his look said, I am irreproachable. How can you pull away? 'I have your best interests in mind.'

'Oh don't. Don't *do* this!'

'What do you think I'm doing?'

I was rushed and dizzy; I could hardly breathe. The words came out small. 'I don't know.'

'You don't understand,' he said, bearing down. 'I'm doing this for you.'

'Oh no you're not,' I yelled, my professor, *my own father*, and now he was trying to . . . And at the same time I had this fear, like what if this was a great honor and I was in the wrong because I'd grievously misunderstood him, what if he really knew something cosmic that I didn't know and he was trying to give me this important gift? What if I'd lost it and with it I was losing my one and only chance at the key to the universe? Oh yes I was stoned. I couldn't get it out of my head that this was *Daddy* I was fighting but that didn't stop me howling, I was sobbing with rage at him: 'You're not doing it for me, you're doing it for you!'

'That's your mistake.' He was so reasonable it was awful – all that authority. What if he was right? 'This is the most important part of your education. You'll see.'

'I don't want to see!' I was messed up but not too messed up to throw myself this way and that like a trapped wolverine trying to shake his grip. 'Let go!'

I was struggling, I started screaming, I remember getting one hand free and trying to hit and then I don't remember because he hit me with something sharp and I passed out, maybe just as well because *I could not stop him* and what he did after that – better not to know exactly what he did after that.

The rape was only part of it.

I woke up outside on the stones with shutters closed tight in all the walls around me and doors barred shut and no light showing and nobody on the walks in a part of Venice that it took me hours to find my way back from, wasted and hurting as I was and the whole time I was crawling along I was *so ashamed*. He did this to me and then he threw me out in some strange place; he finished with me and threw me out like the trash. I woke up with every part of my body aching and this terrible, terrible pain, I was bleeding down there on my . . . He cut the . . . I can't tell you what he cut. He forces it; he *marks* you, never mind how, you will never be the same and he marks you forever, marks that change and shames you so you'll never tell anyone. You're too ashamed to look, ashamed to touch except to stop the blood, too ashamed to think about it, much less show yourself to anybody else, not in fear and never in love, so I was changed forever. I am wrecked, forever marked, scarred at the spot to mark what he did to me.

225

You understand I have this missing and *this* left behind on my body, ugly, black, carved and stained so deep that even with a hunting knife I could never get it out.

I found my way back. It was morning again. He was waiting for me in the lobby of our cheap hotel, scrubbed, shaved and with that smooth blond hair as if he'd spent the night sleeping in that lovely palace of his, dreaming clean dreams, and when I saw him I didn't feel anger, all I felt was grief and shame. I never got a chance to speak. His mouth twitched in such disgust that guilt filled me from the ankles on up, like extra blood. *Oh, it's you.*

'You're just in time. The police are here to take you to the plane. Now get out of my sight, you are revolting.' My jaw dropped but no words came out. In the breakfast lounge on the landing above us, traveling families were talking and laughing. I heard kids giggling, like a message from the ordinary world. The others in my group were coming downstairs. He rushed me to the door. 'Hurry. You can't stay here.' He gave me a hard push. 'Not after what you did.'

Outside two guys put me in the car with another guy, no uniforms, who knows who he was or if they were really police; the guy who put me on the plane was just some Italian guy, stocky and handsome with a moustache like barbells and a dark shiny bill on his cap. He spoke no English. It didn't matter. I was done. I couldn't talk anyway. And *this* on me in black ridges: hideous. Didn't want to *be* any more, much less speak.

It had stopped snowing. Ben has either said all this or he has said none of this.

He doesn't know. Either way the memory is back in his head, painful and complete, but, framed in words now, it is, if not tolerable, almost manageable. There is the new possibility that if he rehearses this and keeps rehearsing it he may over the years be able to wear it down so the edges aren't so sharp; he may be able to smooth it like a stone under water and put it away in a place where it hurts, but only in a dull, unbroken kind of way. He may just be able to work on it so it no longer explodes, tearing him apart again and again like a perpetual fragmentation bomb, excruciating, permanently disabling.

Rehearse, the Ig said. *Let God walk you back through this thing. It's the only way you'll ever walk away from it.* Well he has rehearsed, OK?

For what it's worth.

226

Real words escape him. 'What am I going to do?'

The old lady's retarded son regards Ben Messinger with that sweet, unwavering smile. Then with eyes so wide and guileless that it's clear he's never in his life had to see anything ugly or hear anything he doesn't want to hear, the old lady's slope-shouldered, hulking, eternally childlike son lurches to his feet like the escaping monster and turns to Ben, saying with accuracy so stupendous that it will take him hours to assimilate what he is being told, 'Don't be like this.'

24

There is a hole in the Sailors' house where the student RV tore into the foundation. Nobody knows how it happened; the owner swears he set the brake. When the wrecker hauled it out they found that where wood and brownstone join, the mortar had crumbled and several stones caved in. Until the weather breaks there's no way to begin repairs. For the moment the hole is secured with heavy gauge vinyl nailed in place under a fretwork of two-by-fours.

If anything is secure.

When something breaches the fabric of your house it has breached the fabric of your life.

Everything you thought was solid is threatened. If your house can get hit by a car, what else can get hit by a car? You, in your quiet bedroom? Your children playing in the TV room with their friends?

Clair and Nick circle the house as if on a loop. They keep running into each other on the stairs, one or the other going down to the basement one more time to be certain the hole in their lives is at least temporarily closed.

Sally looks up from her desk like the zombie child in *Night of the Living Dead*, caught gnawing on her father's arm – eyes reduced to black dots by the flashlights and her mouth smeared with blood. She waves a cluster of defunct ballpoints as if to prove she'd never take anything of value. 'I'm just clearing out my things.'

It seems to Clair that the whole world is clearing out its things and moving on. 'Your *things*.'

'My car's outside. I was going to call you when I got settled but now I might as well tell you. I'm leaving town.' Clumsy in her haste, poor Sally is trying to fit what's left of her life at Evard in a shoe box already so stuffed with desk toys and coffee mugs that the pens pop out and slither off the pile no matter where she tries to fit them in. Grieving, Sally throws them in the trash.

The more she fumbles the more upset she gets and because they've worked together for so long that in a way it's her life too that Sally is disposing of, Clair cries, 'Oh, *don't*!'

Sally looks up with her hands filled with sweet junk – makeup, wind-up toys, joke presents people have given her over the years. 'I can't stay here.'

'You can't go anywhere, you look terrible.'

'Well thanks.'

'You know what I mean.' Clair wants to hold Sally but she's afraid to touch her; the skin at the opening in her blouse is discolored, the pale margin of a profound bruise somewhere lower down. 'You look like you've been in a wreck.'

She does. Her face has that taut look, as if she's been crying for too long; her skin is slick and charged with blood. 'Leave me alone!' Plastic objects – lipstick cases and beads and Clinique samples – rattle out of her shaking hands, cluttering the desk. 'I have to go.'

'Sally, what are you afraid of?'

'Afraid? I'm not afraid of anything. I'm just sick of winter, is all. There's nothing the matter with me.'

'There's got to be something.'

'Even if I told you, you wouldn't understand.'

'At least let me help you pack.'

Sally is trying to secure the box with a rubber band; one end of the lid pops up. Then the other. The rubber band snaps and flies away. It is too much for her and she shouts at Clair, 'No!'

'You can't just go,' Clair says. 'You can't just walk away from your life.' Distress has tangled her synapses; she can't say what she really means, which is: *my life*.

This is how Sally strikes back. 'I don't have a life.'

'You won't have a life if you turn your back and run out on it.'

'Oh, you. What do you know?' She finishes in a mixture of pity and contempt that cuts to the bone, leveling Clair with a charge she knows; she has it verbatim. 'You with your perfect life.'

It is chilling. I never said it was perfect, I . . .

Koena horra.

Oh my God.

'Who is he, Sally?' Clair cries, devastated because she already knows. 'Who did this to you? You were doing so well here, three promotions, you could work in publishing anywhere. Scholarship to state, and now . . .'

Sally's empty look tears her in two. 'Now it's too late.'

She wants to protest, she wants to hug Sally and say oh no, it isn't too late, but Clair is diverted by the mindless struggle that keeps Sally standing there trying again and again to get a rubber band around the shoe box, as if all she has to do is fit her life in this box and secure it with a rubber band that does not snap and she'll be able to make it out of Evard intact.

What has seized this smart, strong-minded young woman who was so tough and full of promise and reduced her to this? Clair can't believe it's just bad luck in love. Sally is afraid.

Afraid. Strait. Shuddering, Clair comprehends his hatred. *Your perfect life*: the thief of lives. The contempt. It is dizzying, terrible. The waters close over her head.

She is like a diver in black water, striving for the truth of this as she struggles toward the surface: light and air. Of course she knows who took Sally and diminished her, but what exactly has he done to Sally that makes her so afraid of him? What threats did he make to guarantee her silence? To drive her out of town? With an effort, Clair breaks the surface, gasping. 'If you'll just name him, we can get rid of him.'

'There isn't anybody—'

'At least tell me what he's done to you!' Her mind is already running along ahead; if she can convince Sally to press charges, if she can just find Ginny Arnold and make her come forward, then maybe, *oh please* . . . 'All you have to do is say.'

'Nothing!' Sally's words spike like lines on a polygraph. 'He didn't do anything.'

'Don't look at me like that.'

'Don't you tell me what to do.'

'You can't just walk away from this.'

'I can't stay.'

231

'You have to, Sally. Somebody has to! Tell the police!'

Sally's tone is patient, poisonous. 'Tell them what?'

Clair can't answer; she just blunders on. 'It's the only way he can be stopped!'

This is too much for Sally. With a grunt she shoves the overflowing shoe box into the trash and with a wide gesture sweeps Clair out of the way as if she's no more than a swinging door. As she quits the office she lashes out: 'You want him stopped? You're so damn smart, you stop him.' Then she runs away.

When Nick comes to meet his Writers of the Twenties class, his classroom is empty. In the hall outside, twenty-two of his thirty students are lined up, flanking the door. Turned to the wall, they squat with their backs to him. Those who haven't shaved their heads have covered their hair with black hockey hats. He clears his throat. Nobody moves and nobody speaks. They know he is there but not one will turn to face him. He has to hope that this is because whatever they think they're doing, secretly they're ashamed.

He knows better than to speak. Instead he slams the classroom door hard enough to shake the wall and stalks away. He goes to his office and waits. Soon enough one of his seniors comes in.

'What *was* that?'

'I don't know. I didn't want to have anything to do with it. They said they wanted you to get the message.'

'What is the message, exactly?'

'I don't know. But a couple of people are really upset. Gerry Brevard. Brian Dent. I told them to come see you,' his student says, 'but they've gotten so weird I don't know.' Drops this in Nick's lap and then flees before he can ask why.

There is a hole in their lives. Anything could come in.

They are in an extraordinary position of vulnerability.

She and Nick have been downstairs to lock the front and back doors and check the vinyl seal in the cellar one more time. They have each touched the sleeping children and after a struggle are sleeping uneasily, skimming along under a low cloud cover of unpleasant dreams. The thudding that begins in sleep as the footfalls of pursuing monsters follows them into waking life. Somebody is pounding on the front door. Nick tells Clair to stay in bed while he goes downstairs to answer but after one more look into the children's rooms she goes down after him. She can't know whether she follows because she's afraid to be left alone or because she's afraid of leaving Nick alone. She'd like to raise the drawbridge and arm the barricades. She'd like to go places in an armored truck. She'd like to hire a personal security guard for each of them. No. Thirty security guards, just thirty guys with clubs and chains to stand between them and whatever evil awaits them.

Crazy. She doesn't know how she got so crazy. No. She doesn't know how things have gotten this bad.

At the bottom of the stairs Nick is standing with his fists on his hips and his bare feet set wide, as if he's already fought off lions and is waiting to take on whatever comes next. Over his shoulder she can see a distraught young man standing in the front hall. It's nobody she knows.

'I'm sorry to wake you up like this but I had to see you before I go.' He is white-faced, rigid and gibbering. 'I came to tell you goodbye, but that's not all I came to tell you.'

She touches Nick's arm. 'What is it?'

'Nothing.' He keeps his voice light. 'Just a student.'

The night caller's drawn face, the voice shaking with effort make it clear this isn't *nothing*. 'Listen!' He's a nice-looking kid in ordinary times but tonight everything about him speaks of misery and disorder. He won't look at her; he can't control his mouth.

Say it, Clair thinks wildly. Just come out and say it.

Every word costs him. Panic squeezes him so tight it makes him wheeze. 'I came to tell you something else.'

Out of a chronic need to proceed as if things are fine even when they aren't, Nick says as if it isn't three in the morning, 'Clair, this is Brian Dent. He's one of my senior English majors.'

'Not any more. It's over. I'm leaving.'

'Wait. You can't do that. Not so close to the end.' Nick keeps his voice steady, going on in that good old Nick way. 'Whatever it is, it can't be that bad.'

'This is.'

The student is slumped, curved into or around himself, curling as if protecting some grave hurt – like Sally, Clair thinks, and her mouth goes dry.

'I've got something to tell you.' He drags a fingernail down the corner of his mouth, unaware that he's drawing blood. 'Something you need to know. I came because I have something to tell you. It's important.'

They wait.

His breath rasps. Nothing comes out. He falls silent for so long that Clair drums her fists against her thighs and chews the insides of her mouth. She tastes blood; it seems right. The silence goes on until she wants to leap down his throat and grope for the words and drag them out. Nick holds her in place. She knows as well as Nick that when you most want somebody to talk you can't bring them out with words. All you can do is wait.

After ten years of listening to student problems, Nick knows better than anybody how to wait.

Brian stands there for so long that finally the news of the silence reaches even him. When he speaks it is out of sheer embarrassment at the realization of exactly how long he has kept them all standing here. 'I'm only telling you because your name came up.'

Nick starts. 'My name!'

'Otherwise I wouldn't tell anybody.' His voice thickens. 'I'm too ashamed. The only reason I came at all is, I'm out of here.'

There is another silence that Clair is afraid to break.

'It's about Professor Strait.'

Clair's heart makes a savage leap. 'Come with me.'

He pulls away. 'I can't.'

'Come on. Come into the kitchen. You're freezing. You need coffee.' Taking his cold, cold hands she draws him along. 'Let's go in here where the kids can't hear.'

'I can't stay. I just came to tell you . . .' Brian looks over his shoulder at Nick as she draws him along. 'I don't know if I can say it in front of her.'

'You can say anything in front of her.'

'She has to promise not to tell.' He waits until they are in the kitchen and he and Nick are facing. 'You have to promise.'

They are suspended in a little knot under the Sailors' Tiffany shade with the light streaming down on their heads just the way it would on any other night. After a long time in which Nick weighs it – whatever is coming against his responsibilities to the old child or young man standing in front of him, against his responsibilities to the institution – he says, 'I don't know if I can do that.'

'You have to. This is my *life*.' The student is frothing with urgency; in another minute he will fall out and begin to twitch. 'If anybody finds out I'll die!'

Electrified, Clair is already playing out scenarios, weighing possibilities; she is running so far ahead that Nick is surprised by her conclusion. 'Then you're not going to press charges.'

But the student is not surprised. It is a given. 'If anybody finds out about me, my life is over.' He keeps sawing the corner of his mouth with that fingernail. 'It's probably over anyway.'

'Don't talk like that! Sit down. If I have to promise not to tell, then Clair and I . . .' Nick looks to her.

Clair knows how much this is costing him but she knows Nick, too. A promise is a promise, to the grave.

This is how he seals both their mouths, and forever. 'I promise not to tell and she— she will promise not to tell.' He says, 'Clair.' It is an imperative.

She feels like a priest, submitting to the seal of the confessional. 'I promise.'

The next thing has been locked up inside the speaker for so long that it comes out as a wheeze. 'I've been having some troubles this term. I got in too deep.'

Nick leads him gently. 'You mentioned Professor Strait.'

'I did,' he says, so deeply grieved that when he is finished neither Clair nor Nick will have the heart to ask questions. 'I did. Oh God, I'm so ashamed.'

Nick says, 'Nothing can be that bad.'

Clair grabs his arm. *Koena horra.*

It is.

The last thing Brian says to them? When it is done? When they have hugged him and begged him to get help, when Nick has given him money for a ticket to some safe place he says, 'But that isn't what I came to tell you. That's only what I had to tell you so you'd see what I'm going to say.' Brian goes on in a tone of discovery. 'You know, nobody will let you say a word against him.'

'We know.'

'But you need to be forewarned, OK? Professor Strait has been saying some things. About you.' Now he stands in the doorway with the cold dawn behind him; he is drained of words, pale and shaking, and this is what Nick's student says to them; this is the last thing he says and this is what the Sailors will carry out into the coming morning; they will carry it today and they will carry it for the rest of their lives.

'I think he's looking to get you charged with sexual harassment.'

Nick is white with anger. 'My God.'

'When I tried to get away from him? Do you know what he said to me? He said "Hold still, you're only fighting me because of Nick Sailor." He said, "Everybody knows perfect Nick is saving you for himself." '

Nick burns from the inside out: white as ash. He tries and can't speak. There are no words for this.

'But it's a lie.' Clair begs him to come forward. 'Somebody has to tell the truth.'

'I'm sorry, I can't. I can't even tell my family.' Brian Dent stands with his head bowed, the messenger shamed by his message. 'But I thought it might help it you knew.'

The worst thing about a secret is living with it. When he left them last night Brian Dent said goodbye with a shaky, drenched smile as if he had been set free by the simple expedient of shifting the burden of knowledge from his heart to theirs.

Now she has to carry it. She's been carrying it all day, going through the office routine trembling under its weight. It is she who is shamed by the seduction and refusal, the drugs, the violation that is not exactly a . . . The fact that Will Strait is accusing Nick. It is destroying her. Clair is ashamed of knowing as much as she does and ashamed of guessing the rest and she's even more ashamed of being powerless because even without promises to keep quiet she and Nick are muzzled here.

They have lost their place in this terrible, tight world. Until or unless one of his victims is willing to come forward there is nothing either of them can do.

When it came to details of the final encounter, Brian was elusive, vague. He talked in a clotted voice about the unspeakable without being able to bring himself to say exactly what that was.

As he choked on his story, it came to her that what happened to Brian did not quite relate to whatever befell Sally, or Ginny – so odd, the women thought it was love. Love was never an issue in this terrible conflation of flesh; Strait's assault was unwanted and violent, bloody, with – *cutting* involved. Davy: 'His things.'

His things!

She is still at work when the implications come home.

My God, my son Davy, up in that attic with *his things*; it shakes her teeth loose in her head and sends her heart scuttling around her chest. Fear drives her out of the office. Nothing matters now but the urgent need to defend, to protect . . .

She is at her own front door, sobbing over the unyielding lock when Teddy comes up on the porch. 'Don't do that, let me help you.'

'I don't think anybody can help.' She leans into his chest.

Gently he takes the key from her and lets her in. It is with a little shock that Clair looks behind her and realizes that although it's almost five o'clock it is not yet dark. Go into the tunnel of winter with your head down. Look up tomorrow and it may be spring.

A lifetime has elapsed.

Strait came to this place in the dead of winter and it is still winter, but a lifetime has elapsed.

'Oh Teddy, where in hell have you been?'

'Take it easy,' Teddy says. 'I came to meet Nick. I think I've got something on Strait.'

'I'm glad you're here.' She grips his arm and won't let go. 'Something's happened that you need to know about.'

By the time Nick comes in Clair is drained and relieved. Ashamed. In spite of her promises to Brian, in spite of Nick's promises, she's so caught up in the way of the world according to Strait that the lines between right and wrong have blurred.

Everything she does is traduced. Even though she's never before broken a promise, in this new dimension expedience wins over honor. She has told Teddy everything.

'I'm sorry,' she says forlornly.

Nick may or may not understand; a promise is a promise, after all. Like Clair, he may be too far gone in despair to notice when or how he crosses this or any other line. He is brusque with Teddy, grimly efficient. 'OK. OK. What do you know that we don't know?'

'Something that fits.'

Nick says brusquely, 'Clair told you, right?' Nick, who has never before broken a promise. It's as if they have all agreed; deep in this as they are, in deep and bloody to the elbows, they are beyond small points like who has sworn whom to secrecy.

237

'It's worse than I thought.' Controlled as he is, Teddy is systematically shredding a handkerchief, gnawing the hem to start each tear and ripping it into strips. 'Preying on kids!'

Clair prompts. 'You said you were onto something.'

'Right. There was a classics group meeting at the same hotel as my queer studies group. I met this guy at coffee and he asked where I taught. He went to Swarthmore, in Pennsylvania? Get this. He lived across the hall from our man for a year and when he found out Strait had a teaching job he was astounded.'

Clair is waiting. Nick is waiting. Teddy lets them wait a little longer. Then he says, 'Strait was fired from Swarthmore in their third year for beating the crap out of his roommate.'

'He told me he went to Princeton.'

'As far as my source knows he never finished college anywhere. *Voilà*, ergo no PhD.'

Nick says quickly, 'Not according to his résumé. Not according to Jack Nelson, either. Jack says he was at Columbia.'

'Oh, he went to classes at Columbia, he even did some of the work, but he was only auditing. He was never admitted.'

Clair says, 'Then he's a liar.'

'So it would appear.'

'He's one hell of a liar,' Nick says. 'He had Jack convinced.'

'People are very dumb. Turn up in the right places and say all the right things and you can convince people of almost anything.'

'But Jack said . . .'

Teddy shrugs. 'Lean on people hard enough and if you're smooth enough, you can convince them to say almost anything.'

'He's very smooth.'

'He has to be. But that isn't the only thing he's lying about. This is the big news.' Teddy turns to Clair. 'Remember what I said? About how he treats my gay students? This guy from Swarthmore says Strait was a homophobe long before he got to college. Vicious. Violent. The kind of guy who gets into faggot bashing because he's crazy to prove something.'

Nick says, 'His poor roommate.'

'Probably. Then you have to stop and ask yourself why. This guy from Swarthmore? He thinks Strait could be gay.'

Clair says quickly, 'Well so are you.'

'I don't lie about it,' Teddy says.

Nick goes white. 'Then he is a liar. Everything about him is a lie.'

'That's part of it.'

'Why couldn't he just go on and be gay?'

Teddy says, almost offhand, 'Maybe he doesn't want everything that goes with it.'

Clair cuts to the chase. 'What about Mara?'

'That's the next lie he told.'

'That family!'

'It's part of the pattern. Anything to prove he isn't gay.'

Beautiful house, beautiful serene woman. 'Poor Mara.' She is crying. 'Why?'

'Because something backed him into the closet and slammed the door on his fingers. Something—' Baffled, Teddy stops short. 'I don't know.'

'Why did he have to get married?'

'Maybe he just wants the security of the straight life.' Then even though they're best friends, for the first time Teddy shows a part of himself that he has spared her. 'And nobody looking into his face and wondering what he does with which and with whom at night and no friends secretly wondering would he ever hit on their little boys, and nobody scared of hugging him because they just might catch something and while they're at it maybe boil the glasses and his fork because they're trying to be cool about it but they can't stop thinking about AIDS.'

Clair puts her hands out to him. 'Oh, Teddy.'

He grips her hard. 'It's OK. It's OK.' Then with the self-discipline that makes him a brilliant scholar, Teddy pulls himself back to the facts of the moment, going on in those clipped classroom tones. 'Face it, Mara was a Cabot. She has money. Position. All the right things to help a guy that came up from nothing make all the right moves. For all I know she even loves the guy.'

Before Clair can turn this over in her hands and reflect on the implications, Nick says, 'Maybe he's one of those guys who gets married because he thinks if he goes through the motions he can make it go away.'

'That doesn't make you go out and rape people.' Teddy doesn't even notice that he's dropped the cotton shreds and started gnawing his cuticles ragged. He looks up. 'This is about something else. Lies. Something that makes him hate us all.'

Clair is grieving. 'Those poor kids.'

'You mean his kids?'

'No, the ones he's hurt.' This is so hard that she has trouble finding the right words. 'Why does he have to *force* people?'

'That's part of it. Who wants what comes easy? He needs—'

'The violence.' It is Nick who supplies it, Nick who until now has tried to think the best of everyone. 'My student Brian. God knows who else.' He says suddenly, 'Gerry Brevard!'

'Who?'

'Nothing. Just something I've got to find out.'

Clair says, 'We've got to stop him before he hurts somebody else. Blow the whistle on him.'

'Who, you?' In a flash Teddy's all over her, like the defense attorney lighting a fire under his key witness with every hostile question the opposition can hit her with. 'Who's going to believe you? Ms Clair Sailor, who's been chasing the big handsome guy all over Evarton, crazy in love with him since Day One, like half the women in town. Everybody knows you hate him, right, the woman scorned, and he won't give you the time of day. What wouldn't you say about Will Strait just to get even? What lies wouldn't you tell?'

Nick throws the jade ax at the wall so hard that it smashes into green shards. 'I'll do it.'

'You think they're going to blow Clair off and believe you? Nick Sailor, crazy with jealousy from Day One?'

'That isn't true!'

'Or me. Who's going to believe gay old me in the face of this champion of justice, academic paragon and four alarm homophobe who's out there playing on everybody's deepest fears? We're nowhere without a witness.'

'Then we'll find one,' Nick says.

'He makes them run away. What are we going to do?'

Teddy is weighing it. 'Confront him, I guess. Tell him we know what he's doing.'

Nick says, 'Not until we get the goods.'

With a terrible sense of *déjà vu* Clair says, 'He'll deny it.'

'I hired him. It's my problem.'

'Leave it to me. Please. I have to.' Pain surfaces in Teddy's voice. 'It's people like him that give people like me a bad name.'

'Let me talk to Jack Nelson. Go to George. Make some calls.'

'Do what you want, Nick. But leave Strait to me. I need to find out.'

'Find out what drives him?'

'What turned him into – this.'

Clair tries to hold him. 'It may make him do something worse.'

'But it may force him out in the open,' Teddy says.

'It could be dangerous.'

He gives Nick an odd look. 'Most things we care about are.'

Just then the door opens and the kids come in from swim class at the college gym. Wanda delivered them to Evard this afternoon and Wanda has brought them back; this morning Clair was still so caught up in the business of Brian Dent that it never occurred to her to tell the girl not to . . . So of course Davy and Nell have their best friends with them and inevitably they are Strait's daughter Maddy with her sweet, baffled look and his blond, haughty, smooth-haired son Chase standing in her front hall in their beautifully clean down jackets with their clean faces and new snow boots. The discussion is tabled for the moment and while unspoken words pile up, she and Nick and Teddy will sit through a raucous dinner with four giggling kids and they'll keep up the good front until Mara Strait has come and gone, taking the Strait children away with only a slight diffidence because she's been hurt by Clair's decision to keep their meetings confined to this house.

'Creepy.' Teddy goes to the window to watch them leave. 'Seeing his genes in those nice little faces.'

Clair says defensively, 'They look more like her. Poor Mara. It would kill her if she knew.'

But Teddy bores straight to the center, changing everything for her. 'What makes you think she doesn't know?'

They can't talk about it until the children are put to bed.

Then they can't stop talking about it. Nick has brought up the matter of Gerry Brevard, whether he will come in, and if he does, whether for the same reasons Brian Dent did and if he does, whether Nick can convince him to bear witness. There are other questions. How can they expose Strait and still protect Mara and her children? They are contemplating the destruction of a family on the basis of suspicions that, face it, are only suspicions until some victim steps forward and proves that they are right. They are talking on beyond exhaustion when Clair discovers that the ceiling in her pleasant living room is getting lower and the walls are closing in like steel prison walls; it is as if they are frozen in one of those engines of destruction in certain movies, the perpetually contracting box. She can feel the sides getting tighter and tighter, the lid coming down, and the terrible, inevitable absence of light.

25

With a sense of despair, Clair is standing on Ginny Arnold's front porch. She is talking to Pete, but Pete won't let her in. Instead he speaks to her from behind the door, which he has opened just far enough to have this conversation. 'She doesn't want anybody to know where she went. Now leave me alone.'

He sounds so unhappy and disrupted that she wants to go inside and find some way to make him feel better. This is, after all, nice old Pete. 'Aren't you going to ask me in?'

'Why should I?'

'Because we used to be friends.'

'Friends.' Pete opens the door. His hair is all shaggy ends and his jawline is blurred. In the time since she last saw him his shirt collar has gotten too big, which gives him a miserable, untended look. 'Friends, after what you did.'

'What?'

'Sure, friends.' His voice is all rough edges too. 'Some friends.' Behind him she can see the cluttered kitchen; there are newspapers everywhere, food smears on Ginny's formerly gleaming kitchen floor.

Something makes her say, 'Pete, where are your children?'

'Oh shit, if you aren't going to go away you might as well come in.'

The condition of the house makes her heart break. The place looks abandoned, dim and littered with the detritus of a single life, with nobody around to talk the occupant through the ordinary business of the day and nobody interested enough in the life in the house to pick up crumpled office memos or throw out junk mail or wash the dishes or pull up the shades or even bother to turn on a light in the living room. On the coffee table a fork stands upright in a half-eaten can of beans.

'Satisfied?' Pete's tone says, *Look what you did.*

'At least I can help pick up.'

'If you're worried about the kids, Clair, the kids are with Ginny.'

'Is there anything I can do?'

'You? What could you do?'

'I don't know, Pete. Talk to her. Help.'

'What could you possibly do, after everything?' He is all jagged edges. 'They won't be back.'

The place is like an empty heart after the occupant has moved out. Worse, Pete is glowering as if it is somehow her fault. She is working hard to close the distance between them. 'I'm so sorry.'

'Sorry?' The next thing he says will stop her cold. 'You're *sorry* after what you did to us?'

'What?'

'Throwing them together like that.' He is shouting at her. 'Egging her on. Telling her he loved her when it wasn't true. It wasn't his fault, it was yours. He told me what you did.'

'Pete, you're not making sense.'

'You and your lies.' Now that she's looked into his marriage and seen the torn stuffing, Pete Arnold maneuvers her into the door and opens it. He gives her a push. 'He told me all about it. It's not his fault she hurt herself.'

'Oh my God what happened to her?'

Rushing her across the porch and down the steps he says, 'I think you'd better go.'

Nick is in George Atkinson's office. George asked him to sit down and he's refused. It has been a hard interview, with Nick the reluctant messenger, presenting the only charge that he can prove. Applying for the job here, Strait faked his résumé. Not the worst offense, but the one he can prove. George is less than pleased. Nick says, 'I'm sorry.' *Why should I have to apologize?* 'I thought you ought to know.'

'I know all I need to know.'

'The man falsified his résumé.'

'Will and I had a full and frank conversation about his qualifications,' George says.

'Then you knew.'

He smiles that political smile. 'I knew all I need to know.'

Nick can't afford to let his anger show. 'I thought the PhD was one of the requirements for any job here.' He can't afford to add, *up to and including the presidency.*

'You know, Will warned me. He said you'd say something like that.'

Nick hears, but he doesn't register; he's too intent on the truth. 'If a man is going to lie about a thing like his degrees—'

'Spare me your snap judgments. A college is a complex instrument with many moving parts, Nick.' Still seated, the suave elder statesman, George smiles a smile so slick that it may have been taught. 'We're more concerned with what the candidate *projects.*'

'What if . . . if . . . Ah, I don't know how to say this.' Nick is so intent on being fair that he sounds compromised by his material, guilty. He is trying to do this cleanly and without reference to the ugliest truth. 'What if the candidate isn't what he says?'

'We can't hold up every little thing for scrutiny.' But now George is studying Nick. 'Sailor, if there's anything you have to tell me that's going to change things, now's the time.'

It just escapes him. 'OK, George. There is something.'

George leans forward in his chair. 'What?'

Now Nick struggles to bring it out without bringing it out, talking in that veiled way people do when they are disgraced by carrying ugly truths. He is protecting Mara, yes. And discredited as he is, preceded in any encounter by Will Strait's lies, he is doing his best to protect himself. 'Something's wrong. I have some information that . . .'

'What?'

'I can't tell you. Trust me when I say Strait is bad for this place. The wrong person for our students.' The effort leaves him drained. *There.*

And George is going on as if he has said nothing. 'And?'

'I can't tell you any more.'

'You haven't told me anything.'

There is an intense, desperate silence in which Nick weighs it: the terrible responsibility of honor, his duty to the unsuspecting wife and the children who must never know. 'I'm asking you to trust me on this.' Nick chokes on it: punctilio. Promises. More. The fact that there is no honorable way of telling. It would hurt too many people.

'Can you prove it?'

'No.'

George shrugs. 'Then you can't expect me to do anything.'

'Then you don't believe me.' It's over. Nick is through here.

But George is not. 'This is exactly what he told me to expect.' Now the college president whom Nick has worked with all these years, who he thought knew him, gets to his feet. Resting his fists on the big mahogany desk, he attacks. 'I know you're jealous of him. He told me you weren't exactly friends but I'm sorry to see this pettiness, especially in you.'

'All I'm doing is asking you to trust me.'

'After the things I've heard, I'm finding that difficult to do.'

'What are you talking about?'

'Until we have a chance to formulate the charges, I'm not at liberty to say.'

'The charges!'

'I'm sorry, Sailor. I think you'd better stop wasting time on ugly insinuations and clean your own house.'

Nick is rigid, trembling. He struggles with his worst instincts and wins. Until he can prove what he knows, he can't do anything. He does not speak.

'He's the best man, that's perfectly clear.' George sits to indicate that the interview is over. The family photos are gone from his desk; his new briefcase is initialed in gold. He is halfway to Washington. He walks Nick to the door. 'Look how much he's already accomplished here.'

It's late. Even though it's a short walk from her house, Clair pulls her car up in front of the Stevensons' house on Jane's aerobics night because these days she's increasingly reluctant to go anywhere on foot after dark. She needs to talk to Gabe alone.

When he comes to the door he looks surprised. For a minute he forgets who he thinks she is, and smiles the old smile. 'Clair!' Then he remembers and says hurriedly, 'Jane isn't here.'

'I know. I wanted to talk to you.'

'Sorry. I'm neck deep in student papers. This is not a good time.'

'Gabe, I know you and Nick are at odds right now, but I need your help with something.'

Her friend Gabe says without conviction, 'Another time.'

And pressed by approaching night, by the proliferation of secrets and the sense she cannot shake that she has been followed here, Clair says, 'There won't be another time.' She is trying to move past him, to get inside the house she knows as well as her own, and because they were friends for such a long time Gabe stands back and lets her in. It's worse than if he had not let her in. He stands in the doorway to the living room, waiting for her to precede him, just the way he would for any stranger in the house. It's only been a few weeks since she and Jane stopped seeing each other but everything has changed – carpets, the arrangement of small objects, the color of the cushions on the sofa. This is not Jane's taste; it's someone else's taste. Under a pin light on the mantel she sees one of the Straits' Acoma pots with its black and white markings displayed like a little jewel. It's like coming home to find your country has been occupied by a foreign power.

'Oh Gabe, I miss you guys so much!'

He gives her the grace of a rumpled smile. 'You said you had something to tell me.'

'God. This is so hard! We've got trouble. Nick and I. I don't think we can do this alone. We need your help.'

'What do you want me to do?'

It's so obvious she hardly needs to say, 'It's Will Strait.'

All Gabe needs to do is wait for her to sort it out, but he won't. Instead her old friend says with great grief, 'Oh, Clair.'

'What's the matter? Why are you looking at me that way?'

Gabe says sadly, 'I heard you were acting a little crazy.'

'*Crazy!*'

He is so patronizing, so ready with his sympathy, that his next words drive her out of the house forever. Good old Gabe whom she will never forgive says generously, 'But if it will make you feel better to sit down and talk, by all means sit down and talk.'

'Who, me?' Fred Geller says too fast. 'I'm fine.' Clair knows that no matter what falls between them, Fred is her friend and they'll stay friends, but right now more than he wants to stay friends, he needs to get out of here. He just doesn't want to be in this conversation. Her student intern addresses her fondly but with regret, as if he's at the Departures check-in with carry-on luggage and a first-class ticket, heading out. 'I'm fine, Clair.

Just fine. Sam's fine. Everything is fine. You want to hear it from Sam, you ask Sam.' He is already in transit. 'Really, I promise. Everything is fine.'

But when she catches Sam Jones alone in the office and begins the delicate business of asking how he is, her favorite student turns on her so quickly that she has to wonder whether they were ever really friends. 'What are you doing here, Clair? What exactly are you trying to do?'

'I just wanted to know.' *Oh, God.* 'I just wanted to know if everything was OK with you.'

'What do you mean, is everything OK? Why wouldn't everything be OK?'

'I mean, in class?'

'Class? What class?' His pupils are huge; his skin is so pale that it comes up blue under the spattered freckles. 'You mean Professor Strait's class? What is it with you, Clair, with your questions and your, like, insinuations? Why have you got it in for poor Professor Strait?'

And after school in a stab at apparent normalcy in a slanted world where nothing is normal, Clair's sitter Wanda brings the Strait children over to play at the Sailor children's house until six when, without coming in, their mother comes to the door to take them home.

The suicide changes everything. Checking the carrels before the college library closes at ten, the night librarian finds a window open, and cut into the table with a sharp instrument a diagram and a cross, X marks the spot.

I WILL LAND – HERE.

But as it turns out the student in question is not smashed in the courtyard with all the blood draining out of him, spreadeagled on the ice. Campus security investigates but nothing untoward has happened on the grounds of Evard College, at least nothing that they can find. For a time it looks as if nobody has been hurt. Because he's still covering the last few of Ad Bishop's responsibilities as dean, Nick has been called to stand vigil during the search. Without knowing why she has to wake the children and come out with him, Clair waits in his office in the Humanities tower, putting their children to sleep on sofas so they will not have to know what happens next.

Then near midnight police in cruisers with revolving dome lights come up the hill, rolling so slowly over the ice that their progress makes almost no sound; there are no horns, no sirens. Nobody has phoned ahead to break the news. They come in V formation in complete silence, a grim cortege.

There has indeed been a death.

The victim is Nick's student Gerry Brevard. The police say he threw himself in front of a train, a clear suicide. When he met the engine head on he was naked. It's as if he wanted all evidence – every mark on his body – destroyed. It looks as though the deceased hid near the viaduct as the train started across, waiting for the last possible moment. Then, too suddenly for the engineer to respond, much less pull the emergency brake, he just – *showed up* in the cone of light the engine headlight cast, flew into the white blaze like a human pinwheel with his arms thrown out and his legs spread wide, and if Clair wonders whether it is a suicide or murder, Nick and Teddy are the only people she can tell.

The stunned engineer reports, 'He was like, I don't know, wide open like a starfish, spinning out there in the light.'

There isn't enough left for an inquest. There is only enough left to scrape into a body bag and send to the Evarton funeral home where, within hours, the grieving parents will be summoned not by George Atkinson, who left for Washington on short notice, but by the newly anointed acting president, Will Strait.

Teddy helps the Sailors carry their sleeping children out of the Humanities tower and to the car. He goes with them as they take the children home to bed. He follows Nick to the basement to inspect the imperfectly sealed gap in the foundation and then he lingers in the living room until Clair understands that tired as they all are, none of them feels safe enough to be alone. She doesn't much want Teddy out of her sight either. She's afraid of what happens to people she lets out of her sight.

'If you want to, you can sleep here.'

'Who's going to sleep?' Teddy is grave. Without spelling it out he says, 'It's getting too big. He is.'

'Then you think it was Strait.'

'I think he would do anything.' Teddy corrects himself. 'Will do anything. And then he'll do anything to cover it up.'

'Throw a kid in front of a train?' Nick shakes his head. 'It's too overt. He would never show himself like that. He's too smart to show himself.'

'You think he was smart, hurting people and swearing them to secrecy when he knew sooner or later somebody always talks? Whatever it is that drives him, it's driving him harder now.' Teddy says, 'It's in the air.

He started by not wanting anybody to know what he was doing, and he got away with it. Now he thinks he can do anything and get away with it.'

'Murder?'

'Maybe. If you're as crazy as he is, you'll do anything to cover your lie. I think . . . it just . . .' Teddy's hands sweep wide. 'Got too big.' The gesture takes in the room, the frozen world outside.

In that second the air stops moving. In the next, something new comes into the space between them and Clair goes cold. It is as if there is a ghost in the room. 'What are we going to do?'

'Be careful. Be very careful. He's over the top,' Teddy says. 'I think he's out of control.'

It is Nick who puts the question this time, the former Boy Scout who is by oath learned by rote. 'Physically strong, mentally alert and morally straight,' and who puts his faith in clean fights and logical solutions. 'What are we going to do?'

'Something,' Teddy says. 'We have to do something soon.'

It is a hasty funeral. The parents can't bear to think about their son's ruined body being shipped home like so much freight or lying above ground unprotected, open to the slashing sleet. Leveled by grief, they are desperate to see him safe in the earth.

At the graveside, acting president Will Strait gives the eulogy. After all, wasn't he the dead boy's favorite professor? Gerry Brevard is being buried on the far side of Administration Hill. The family has petitioned and as the first grand gesture of his new office the acting president has agreed that the student can be buried in the college burial ground because he loved Evard and was so happy here. He is being put in the earth with a small cluster of ex-presidents and key trustees dating back to the nineteenth century and, improbably, two Chinese who died at eighteen far away from home, killed by the Spanish influenza some ninety years ago. In an amazing concession to their grief, Strait has agreed to let the dead student be planted between the forlorn Chinese, in a grave prepared in September for an ancient and ailing trustee. As they did every fall, Evarton gravediggers prepared several sites before the ground froze and covered them with battens and canvas, in case.

Now the mourners assemble around the undertakers' Astroturf, spread to conceal the marks their acetylene torches have left in the newly de-iced earth. The Astroturf is off key in this setting and disturbingly festive, a Kelly green swatch in grimy snow.

Clair and Nick stand on one side of the grave with townies and reporters, nobody they know, while the parents line up with the college community on the far side. They make a solemn little phalanx behind Will Strait, who regards Clair with a cold smile. *It's you.* Before she can figure out what to do with her face he turns that same smile on Nick with teeth bared in such vicious triumph that she is astounded to discover that no one else marks it.

Then at the last minute Teddy Hart slips into the group on the far side of the grave, back from wherever, looking rushed and concentrated. She can't help it; she's so glad to see him that one hand flies up in an involuntary wave. He sees her and grins; then, with his hand raised like a priest giving the benediction, he ducks his head and disappears behind the massed bodies of Gabe and Jane Stevenson and poor Pete Arnold so swiftly that she is afraid for him. Teetering on the edge of the undertaker's pathetic, garish artificial grass she cranes, trying to see over the crowd or through it; she tries desperately to locate him, speed-reading faces through the ranks to the back. Is Teddy still there? Is he not there? What did he say to her this afternoon? *Wish me luck.*

She said, 'You can't go alone.'

'If you come I'm never going to be able to bring him out into the open.'

'You can't go alone. Promise.'

'I promise,' Teddy said, with that gallant, irresponsible grin. 'But you know me.'

She wants to vault the grave and rummage through the crowd until she finds Teddy. She wants to make him promise if he won't let her come along then he'll at least let Nick ride post for him. She wants to run after her only friend and beg him not to do this; as soon as the ceremony breaks she darts around the grave and tries to find Teddy, but Teddy is already gone.

26

Clair is waked in the night by coughing; hers, Nick's. The house is filled with fumes so vile that she rolls out of bed in a panic and starts running. Nick is running. The kids! Clair hears the children gasping in their beds. What is it? The boiler? Hell opening? Is the whole house going to blow? Got to get out of here, no time, no time even to wonder what . . .

She rushes into Davy's room and finds him choking like a drowning swimmer. Covering her face as if she can filter the poison, she yanks him out of bed. She is aware of Nick pushing past with Nell in his arms; he sets his daughter down and wraps his pajama top around her face as if that will keep her from taking in too much of whatever it is they are breathing. Then he takes a chair and smashes the window. Within seconds the Sailors are on the back porch roof with night air like knives scoring their lungs, terrified and scrabbling for a perch on ice so slick that there is some question as to how long they can hang on. Nelly is crying. Davy is trying not to cry.

It is enough for Clair that they can breathe.

From here it is a long drop to the glittering ice. Try it? Sure. And break both legs. They cling like shipwreck survivors, shouting for help.

Later she will wonder how long they would have spent out there if their neighbors on both sides had been Evard faculty, safe behind their expensive combination storm windows, convinced that whatever happens to the Sailors is imagined, nothing but a product of their paranoia. Gabe. Pete. Even Josh Gellman, who is usually kind: *Remember the boy who cried*

'Wolf'. I think you'd better cool it, Clair. After a while even your friends don't hear.

As it is, the old man who lives on the downhill side is a retired custodian who didn't get around to putting in his heavy frame storm windows this year because of his bad leg. In other years Nick has gotten up on the ladder to help the old man do the job, but this year, things happened. Like so many of the old whose waking lives aren't active enough to put them to sleep for long, the man next door is a light sleeper. Like so many of the old who must live vicariously if they are going to live at all, he is naturally curious. Waked by the crash, their rickety neighbor does not discount it, *oh it's only* and dive back into sleep. Curiosity overcomes a natural reluctance to step onto the cold floor. He has snapped on the bedside lamp and come to his bedroom window. He is curious, but not curious enough to open it and let in the night.

Nick shouts and waves but the light confuses the old man and he does not immediately see them. Clair shouts. The children shout. Bemused, their next door neighbor blinks into the darkness; he sees only his own reflection in the glass. They see him scratching his head. In another minute he's going to shrug and go back to bed, leaving them here on the roof until they freeze to it. Morning will find the four of them still exposed, sheathed in ice like figures in some war memorial.

'Wait!'

Clair cries, 'What are you *doing*?'

Defying gravity like a prize skater, Nick stands. He is snapping an icicle off the overhang. Then, leaning out so precipitately that Clair is afraid he's going to slip and fall into the dark below, he throws the chunk of ice at his neighbor's window.

The crash makes the old man jump. 'Bingo,' Nick yells, grabbing the drainpipe so he can lean out farther. 'Mr Petrund!'

With an effort the old man lifts his window. They can see him tugging at the heavy frame. He sticks his head out. 'Who's there?'

'It's us, Mr Petrund.'

'Where are you?'

'Over here!'

'Why, Mrs Sailor. What's happened to you?'

'We're stuck.'

'Looks like it! Aren't you cold?'

Nelly yells, 'I'm cold.'

Davy yells, 'I'm freezing!'

'Is that you, Davy? What are you doing out there?'

'We're stuck!'

'Mr Petrund, can you help us?'

'It's almost zero, Sailor. You shouldn't have the kids out there.'

'Can you call somebody to get us down?'

'You shouldn't have been out there in the first place.'

'It was an emergency.'

'What?'

'There's something the matter with the boiler!'

'What?'

'I *said*, there's something the matter with the boiler!'

'Are we talking explosion here?'

'I don't know!'

'You'll have to wait a minute,' he calls. 'I'm going to have to go down cellar and see can I find my ladder.'

'No, Mr Petrund. Wait!'

'It may take a while.'

Together, Clair and Nick yell, '*Don't!*'

'I thought you wanted to get down.'

'Please,' Clair calls. 'Dial 911 for us.'

'And even if you don't want to get down, it's bad for the children.'

'Please. Just dial 911 for us, OK?'

'What are you doing here?'

'Just ask me.' Teddy stands just inside the door with his chin jutting. They are in Mary's office – no, this is Strait's office now, along with the ailing dean's office in the administration building and the Hickson Lounge. Add George's office, unless the man is stopped. Spread yourself in enough places, Teddy thinks, and nobody can keep track of you. Although Strait sits behind Mary's desk, there is nothing of him in this room. Their plump colleague's plants and her Pre-Raphaelite repros have been removed; Mary has been completely effaced but even though Strait's books occupy Mary's shelves, there is nothing personal about the space he's taken over: no small objects on the desk, no pictures on the walls.

Strait does not speak.

Whatever he does to them, Teddy thinks, he doesn't do it here. The room is as bleak as the surface of the moon.

255

'Ask me.' He's bigger than I am, but I can still fight him. 'Go ahead.'

'I did ask you.' Strait sits with his chair tilted and his feet on the desk as if there is nothing to be discussed here.

Teddy keeps his voice low. 'I know what you are and I know what you've done.'

'Who, me? I haven't done anything.' Strait's smile is as bland and empty as the office walls.

'There are people who say you have.'

'Then why aren't they here?'

God damn you, Teddy thinks. 'I know what you're doing. What I don't know is why.'

'Always a pleasure to see you.' Strait's feet thump to the floor and Teddy turns quickly, ready to fight if he has to, but the big man only swivels the chair so he is facing the deep night that fills the window. Strait's tone is dismissive. 'Now if that's all.'

'You know that isn't all.'

'I said, *if that's all.*'

Teddy swallows his anger; what he says comes out wrapped as tightly as a series of little packages. 'Gig Jamison. Brian Dent. I'll be in my office if you want to talk.' In the door he turns so that he is watching when he says the next thing and Strait goes rigid. What he delivers last, which will draw the destroyer out of Mary's office and into Teddy's, is another name. 'Gerry Brevard.'

Teddy goes down the grim, night-time hallway to his own office. It's so late even the campus cops have gone somewhere to sleep. Too late to be out, he thinks. Too late to be doing this. With a sense of inevitability, he sits at his desk without any clear idea of the form the confrontation will take when it comes. Can he threaten the man out of town? Shame him? Trap him into some kind of confession? He doesn't know. This is just something he has to do. Like Strait, he will turn his chair to face the black emptiness outside the window. Some things are easier said to a listener whose back is turned. He sits facing the window long after the door opens and the still air in the room begins to stir as someone large comes into the room.

Strait doesn't say anything.

Teddy doesn't say anything.

The silence is long. There is no sound in the room except for the hiss of the hot air system. No, except for the tap of Strait's knuckles on the corner of Teddy's desk and the rasp of the big man's breath. The silence is terrible.

It is Strait who finally speaks. 'You don't know anything.'

Now it is Teddy who makes the intruder wait. 'It's people like you who give people like me a bad name,' he says at last.

'We have names for you,' Strait says. 'You and your kind.'

Teddy's fists clench. He is trembling with the effort to stay still. He keeps his chair turned to the window. He has to let this play until he knows what he needs to know. He begins quietly. 'Why is it always the weakest ones?'

'You're fishing in the dark,' Strait says. 'Pack it in.'

'Why the women? What were you doing with those women?'

'Women!' Strait hawks in disgust; something wet hits the rug.

Still Teddy doesn't turn around. 'Right. The lie. You despise them because of the lie. Who started it, anyway? What did they do to you?'

'I have nothing to say to you.'

'But you're here.' Teddy's throat is tight with anger.

Strait's voice is unaccountably sweet, complaisant. 'I thought we could be friends.'

'Well you were wrong.'

'I thought you of all people would understand.'

'Understand! Force? Whatever you did with the knife? What could we possibly have in common?'

'You know.'

'I hate guys like you. Think the closet is an armored car that you can ride out in and waste everybody. What started it, Strait? Ambition? Fear? What bent you out of shape and made you lie? *What made you hurt all those poor kids?*'

Strait manufactures polite laughter. 'Who are you to speak to me like that? Faggot.' He spits again.

'Or is it who?'

'Shut up.' The phrase he pulls out to assail Teddy is an old one – musty, antiquated. Weak. 'Shut up, pansy boy.'

'Our students! People who trust us. Do you know what this does to trust?'

'I said, shut up.'

'They're only kids! All that, and then anything to keep your secret. Murder? Right. Well, get this. I know what you did, OK? I know what you

257

did and I can prove it.' This is not exactly true but Teddy is pressing hard. 'You might as well tell me why.' The words come out rapid fire, clipped and sharp. 'Was it the lie that bent you out of shape like this? Is it the pressure that got to you?'

'Fucking queer.'

'What made you like this? Or is it who?'

Strait says, 'We have names for people like you.'

'Names. You even lie about your fucking name.'

'No!'

'Stratiewicz, right?'

'I was never Polish, please! Old Boston family. Brattle Street.'

'What's the matter with being Polish?' Teddy is rocked by a wave of something he does not quite recognize. 'What's the matter with being what you are?'

'Harvard, OK? Princeton is good enough for you?' This is so strange; Strait's speech is newly inflected, as if translated from a foreign language; his accent is sliding around. 'Pride and joy. How could you know? Queer like you, how could a queer know?' He seems as cool as Teddy is trying to be but strain alters his voice. 'People like you couldn't possibly understand people like me.'

'What did you expect to get from lying?' Teddy asks. 'Money? World-class power?'

'I get what I want,' Strait says.

'Take no prisoners, bury your corpses, anything to hide the truth. What is it, Strait? What makes you what you are?' Teddy's chest is tight with frustration; he wants to turn around and hit the guy but he still thinks he can wait him out. It is getting harder. All this abuse and so far he has learned nothing. At least nothing he can use. 'And why do you have to hide?'

'No hide!'

'What is it, the sex police? What are you afraid of?'

Strait's voice goes up an octave. The effect is astounding. 'No hide, I just . . . See? Make Erna proud.'

Gotcha. Teddy swivels so they are facing. 'Erna? Who's Erna?'

Strait is standing closer than he thought. Teddy gets up. Strait is taller. Heavier. Smoothly raising both hands with a controlled force that will make itself manifest even as Teddy gropes behind him on the desk for something to use as a weapon. He pushes Teddy hard.

Teddy pushes back, making an ugly thud on the big man's chest. It does not budge him. He rasps, 'I'm not the only one who knows.'

'Lies. Nobody listens. The Sailors are nothing now. And you. You're not stable.' Strait pushes again. 'Everybody knows.'

For a second they stand, suspended. Teddy grits his teeth. Strait considers. The closeness, the silence compound to fill the air between them in an interminable moment with no logic and no apparent end. There is nothing but hatred and silence like twin snakes eating each other's tails. It is intolerable.

'You didn't think I would let you leave here,' Strait says.

In another circumstance they would have been at home in the morning to get the terrible news. In the old, lost life a dozen people would have called. As it is, nobody knows where to find them. In ordinary times they would have walked the children to the school bus and gone up Administration Hill to their respective offices. The Sailors would have been on the scene along with everybody else. Part of it. As it is, they are sadly distanced. They will find out late. Like everything else that's happened to them in this dreadful winter, this will leave them feeling negated, remote from the world as they thought they knew it.

For a moment they don't know, and it is a blessing.

Clair and Nick and their children are ensconced in adjoining rooms in the Evarton Inn, just waking up to a hot breakfast brought by Room Service. The Fire Department can't tell them what went wrong with the boiler but last night the fire marshal did say that until they can determine the source of the fumes, the heat is off, and the boiler can't be repaired until the house is completely cleared of pollution, which he estimated would take at least twenty-four hours. With a sense of being let out of school, Nick called the emergency night number for the oil company and put the problem into their hands. Then he slipped into the strange hotel bed next to Clair and they set the alarm for nothing.

Once she finds out what's happened on the hill at Evard, Clair will be too grieved to know whether she could have prevented it, any more than she knows whether it would have been better or worse to find out first hand.

At the moment she and Nick and Davy and Nell are sitting down to a splendid meal none of them had to make. It's more breakfast than she has seen in one place in the last twenty years – what happens when you let the children order. They have juice and grapefruit halves and coffee in the Sheffield pot with the hotel emblem, yes, but in addition they are humming and mumbling over pancakes with Vermont maple syrup and drawn butter, plates of Evarton sausage and Canadian bacon, hot cereal; they have cherry Danish and croissants the hotel has flown in from Boston, along with today's *Globe*, a special treat for news-starved readers ordinarily stuck with the local tabloid and stale news as reported by city papers days before but delivered when and as the local postmaster chooses.

Rested and feeling safe for once, Nick and Clair and the children tumble in the oversized bed, snug under a blanket of morning papers. They make a warm, tight family unit. With its tall ceilings and its tatty elegance, their hotel room could almost be in London, Paris, anywhere, and for the moment Clair wants to pretend that they are far away from their problems. It is like a holiday. Nick has only afternoon classes today and Clair has already decided to blow off work. Sprung from school because they woke up late and can't possibly go in their pajamas, the children are treating it like a party. Later Nick will put on the night clerk's overcoat over his pajamas and drive barefooted to the Sears at the mall and bring back clothes and shoes for them. New clothes. It is like a party with presents.

Then Nick calls the oil company for a diagnosis. He is on the phone for too long. His staccato questions bring Clair back to real life in a hurry.

'What,' she says as he hangs up. 'What was it?'

'Nothing. They drained the pipes before they could freeze.'

'Don't, Nick. That isn't an answer.'

'OK.' He makes sure the children are deep in TV cartoons before he says, 'It was a toxic element introduced into the system.'

'How did it get there?'

'They don't know.'

'For God's sake!'

'Somehow.' Troubled, he shakes his head. 'Something.'

'Or was it somebody?'

He doesn't answer. 'Yesterday. It happened some time yesterday.' Nick is trying so hard to keep it light that the strain shows. 'Davy, I need you.'

Davy tunnels up from the foot of the bed. 'What is it, Dad?'

'Did anybody come in the house yesterday?'

'Just us and Wanda.'

'Anybody else?'

'What do you mean?'

'Did anybody else come inside?'

Clair adds, 'Like, into the basement.'

'Did you see anybody?'

'I don't think so.'

Nelly says, 'I did.'

Nick is intent on Davy. He grips his shoulders. 'You're sure?'

'Daddy, I did.'

'Yes I'm sure. Dad, don't squeeze so tight!'

'Daddy!' Nelly jumps on the bed so hard they have to look at her. When she has them both listening she says proudly, 'I did. See,' she says to Davy, 'you don't know everything.'

'Shut up.'

'Nelly, *who*?'

'Who was it?'

'Him,' Nell says, so full of importance that Clair doesn't know whether to hug her or hit her. 'Mr Strait,' she says. As her parents' expressions begin to slip she adds, 'It was only for a minute.'

'My God, Nelly, we told you never to—'

Davy punches her. 'Creep!'

'Ow! It's OK, Mom, he said you told him to come in. He said he had to take care of something in the basement.'

'Oh, *Nell*!'

'He said it was important.'

'Nelly, I thought we told you never to—'

'I didn't,' Nelly says, suddenly aware that they are not pleased by this news. 'I didn't let him in! Wanda did.'

Later they may question her more closely but suddenly who came in or exactly what he did there ceases to be an issue. The phone goes off like an alarm clock.

Clair picks up. 'Hello?'

'He kissed her and she let him in,' Nelly mutters, too late for her parents to hear or mark what she is telling them.

A voice Clair knows is saying politely, 'Is this room three oh three?'

'Yes, this is room three oh three. Who is this?'

A woman's voice. 'Clair? I'm calling for Clair Sailor.'

'This is Clair Sailor.'

'Oh, Clair. I thought that was you but I had to be sure.' It is Jane Stevenson. 'It's Jane,' Jane says in tones so neatly modulated that it is frightening. She could be an old-fashioned club woman making a call to someone she doesn't know: remote, tentative, polite, going on in that genteel, apologetic voice. 'Jane Stevenson. I know we aren't exactly close, but I didn't want you to find out about this from some absolute stranger. It's . . .'

Her material seems to be too much for her and she breaks off.

In ordinary time Clair would say, 'Come on, Jane. Cut to the chase.' But she is cold and still, afraid of what's coming.

In the background Davy and Nell are mumbling in chorus, telling Nick how they never meant to, always do what Mom says but Davy was upstairs with Chase, and Nelly, well, Wanda wanted Mr Strait to come in and play but Nelly knew she wasn't supposed to let anybody in with Mom away but listen this wasn't just anybody, this was Maddy's father and you couldn't just make him stay outside like that when you're playing with Maddy, after all he is her daddy, especially since he is so nice, he asked for Nelly's *special permission*, Daddy, he got down on his knees just like the Prince in *Snow White* and besides, it was only for a minute . . .

But Clair stops hearing. She stops caring. There is something awful in the air. She knows without being told, but she can't get off the phone until she has heard it spoken.

'Something I've got to tell you,' Jane says, willing Clair to ask her what. *Take your medicine.*

She waits.

'Something terrible. I don't know how to say this.'

Then for God's sake say it.

'Something's happened to Teddy.'

Nick is at her side now with his head pressed close to hers, sandwiching the receiver so they can both hear what Jane is saying, so they speak as one although they will find different words to express their rage and grief.

Clair says, 'Oh shit!'

'Oh my God,' Nick says.

'I'm afraid he's dead. They found him this morning on the ground outside the Humanities tower. He fell eleven stories. It looks like he jumped out of his office window.'

They are bereft of words. The silence is thunderous.

'I feel terrible. Gabe feels terrible. Everybody feels terrible. I know you and Teddy were close so even though we aren't exactly friends any more, I wanted you to hear it from somebody you knew, you know? And if it makes you feel any better, you might as well know everybody says he probably did it because he had AIDS . . .'

Clair knows better; instead of showing her grief and so saying something that will let Jane feel big because she's called; instead of giving Jane the single scrap of information, she says in a still, cold voice, 'Who says so?'

'Oh you know, everybody.'

'Strait?'

'I know you don't like him, Clair. Everybody knows you don't like him.'

'I said, was it Strait?'

'Oh, probably. I suppose so, but listen, it doesn't matter now. It's terrible he had to die but at least it was quick.' Jane's voice is rich, full. Sorrow over Teddy makes her gushy. 'I suppose we should be grateful. You know, glad for Teddy instead of sorry. Of course we'll all miss him but everybody knows anything is better than AIDS. At least he was spared the torture.'

'Goodbye, Jane.'

But Jane won't quit; she finishes in tones that Teddy Hart would have recognized and dissected for Clair alone because in ordinary life he avoided confrontations and instead processed affronts as he did innuendo, by making a joke of them. In life before Will Strait it was Teddy's choice to turn the ill will of others aside with laughter. He would have mimicked Jane's last words before she gives up on the conversation entirely and leaves off trying to make Clair respond as if she has not been grievously injured; Jane finishes in an unforgivably bright little voice that goes up and down in the involuntary hahaha that she hopes will smooth over this and every other situation, 'And we were spared watching him suffer.'

27

Ben

Now that he has brought it back Ben feels both better and worse. Venice, entire. Knowing should be a relief but it is not. He is brought up sharply against the fact of Ben Messinger, who will never be completely whole again.

Remembering leaves him . . . objectified. It is as if the important part of Ben stands apart. At a safe distance, where it can see clearly without being hurt.

It is like looking at an object.

This part of Ben that notes and judges is remote from the self who went to Venice and trusted someone and was changed forever. For the first time he can see that person from the outside. But at this distance what he sees is surprising.

That person is not a monster. He is a victim. That poor bastard, he thinks. What did he know? What did he know anyway?

Chilled, he steps back inside and feels it all over again, the destruction, but as he grimaces in pain the old lady's retarded son repeats; it may be the only sentence he knows. It is like a blessing.

'Don't be like this.'

Right. If he's ever going to do anything about this he has to quit thinking and start doing. He can't afford to nurse his misery any more. Therefore when the storm ends and the old lady comes up from the back of the store to collect her son from the plaid Barcalounger in the shop window, when she offers Ben a ride to the next place he says, 'Not yet.'

She is small inside the plaid blanket coat but tough, standing on the splintered wooden floor with her feet lost in old-fashioned black galoshes; her son rises, smiling. If he did in fact construct those astonishing last words, 'Don't be like this,' it is nowhere written in his expression.

The old lady looks frustrated, as if tired of studying a map to noplace. 'Where you going instead?'

'Nowhere. Yet, at least.'

'You can't stay here.'

Bemused by the frozen patterns on the glass, he sinks back into the used Barcalounger. In the shadows somewhere behind the old lady, the proprietor stirs; Ben says, 'I'd like to.'

'Nigel ain't running a shelter here.'

'WILL WORK FOR FOOD,' Ben says with that old indigent grin of his and the proprietor reads him better than the old lady does.

She says, 'No way.'

'Way,' Nigel says. He's short, slight, easy inside his skin.

'What's he gonna do that you can't do for yourself?'

'Talk to me,' the black man says.

Oh thank you. Words, Ben thinks. Hundreds of thousands of words. But the only one he can think of is, 'Cool.'

Nigel says, 'But you're going to have to bust ass for me.'

Oh thank you.

So instead of leaving in the old lady's pickup Ben holes up in the junk store, taking a cot in the back room in exchange for hauling cartons and sweeping up for the owner, who's lived in these parts for so long that the locals have forgotten that they used to think his color made him different. If this Nigel likes Ben it may be because Ben is different, doesn't belong here, doesn't belong in the state much less the town, doesn't much look like he belongs anywhere. At noon every day Ben slip-slides down to the diner for Nigel and brings back coffee and two subs loaded with salami and peppers and a poker hand of processed American cheese slices that still hold the shape of their wrappers. While they eat, Ben and his boss sit around jawing about the weather, the day's news, whether it's better to put the assorted table lamps Nigel has for sale on the tables he also has for sale or keep them clumped in the back with the stand lamps, like flocking with like.

They talk at such length and about such ordinary things that it would put even a TV soap fan to sleep: the weather, the stock and ways to make it move faster in a time of year when nothing is moving because of the thing they talk most about, which is the weather. It is as if Nigel knows Ben's soul is rubbed raw and this is the only kind of talk he can tolerate. They talk about the weather and the stock and the stock and the weather and what may be coming up tonight on the only TV channel that comes in clear in this isolated town. It is so boring that it is wonderful. Ben is boring. Nigel is not boring but he puts up with Ben out of some tacit understanding that Ben wants more than anything to be boring. Ordinary. Great! It's like being in a convalescent ward with no emotions to get in the way of your recovery, which hangs on these regular, banal conversations that fulfill some of the same functions as white dinners on hospital mess trays, just what you ordered and on schedule, healing precisely because they are so bland and regular. Schedule itself is bland and reassuring. Nothing untoward, nothing unexpected.

He won't know it but it is the contact that is bringing him around. This is Nigel's gift to him, the unaccustomed creature comfort – being able to sit here talking about nothing to somebody who treats him like an ordinary person.

All day Ben and his boss talk and at night he sleeps like a stone, but there is more. He feels useful. For the first time since he left the Ig with her kindness and her routine specially manufactured for him, he has work to do.

With a surprising sense of pleasure Ben organizes the store, putting tables with matching chairs, rockers with rockers, beds with matching dressers. He even cleans the dingy insides of the front windows with ammonia and newspapers he tears in strips, noting how many events have come up and gone down since he stopped reading the papers. Then he goes into the display cases. He won't linger over the used jewelry because it makes him sad. Instead he takes oil and wipes new guns and guns so old that they're all seized up, arranging them in the cabinet by size and type.

It is interesting, working with the guns. Pistols. Revolvers. Shotguns. Rifles. A month ago, before he stepped outside himself and had a good look, he would have loaded one and put it in his mouth. He might even have had the guts to pull the trigger. If he'd killed himself, cool, if he'd only maimed himself that would have been OK too because whatever happened to him, at the time he still believed he'd brought this misery on himself and he honestly thought that no matter how bad it was, he deserved it. Now he's not so sure. He's lost the urge to die. He's even outgrown the desire to kill the man who tore his life open and left him this way.

Sure he is gathering strength for a confrontation, but Ben knows now that it won't be murder or even attempted murder. It's not in his makeup. He also knows that he has to lay back. He has to wait until he figures out what to do.

After Nigel goes home Ben eats the other half of his lunchtime sub. He has it with the extra Coke he brought at noon. Then he watches TV for a while on the old mahogany console set with the round picture tube; he feels like a sailor seeing life in black and white through a porthole low in his ship's belly. Near midnight he retreats to the office in the back and makes third-number phone calls that won't show up on his employer's bill. Instead they will show up on Delia's. He feels bad about ripping her off like this, but in its own way this is as good as sending her a note. When she gets her bill she'll know not to worry.

The charges won't amount to much and if she wants to, Delia can check the area code on the number he is calling from; she may even dial the number and if she does, she'll get Nigel. By the time Delia gets her phone bill Ben will be out of here. But she'll know where he has been. It's his way of letting her know he's OK. She'll know he was still all right as of whatever day he places the last phone call which, he estimates, will be shortly before he thanks Nigel and clears out of here.

He places his third-number call and waits while the chime chords sound and the computer generated operator thanks him for using AT&T and connects him.

All this time Ben Messinger has been more or less struck dumb by what happened to him. For a long time he couldn't say a word, but no more. Thanks to the Ig and to a retarded man whose name he never even learned and thanks to this guy Nigel who offers kindness in exchange for company, he can talk just fine.

When the big professor picks up the phone it is Ben who will do the talking. He has written a dozen speeches for this occasion but, strangely, even though he's called several times there is one speech and one only that comes to him once he has made the connection. It's the only one he feels like delivering.

This is interesting. He does all the talking in these encounters. It is his listener who is mute. After the professor *you call yourself a professor* says 'Hello' in that automatically superior and irritated voice of his, he falls silent. What is he waiting for, Ben to identify himself? He doesn't think so. Maybe it's the only possible response to the news Ben is bringing, that you can swear a person to secrecy, 'our secret', but if it's ugly enough, sooner or later what you have done will come back on you.

It is the same every time.

As the phone rings in the sleeping household, Ben starts to count. *Ring*, the man stirs; his sleep is broken. *Ring*, he rolls over and pretends it isn't happening. *Ring*, somebody has to answer or it will wake the children. *Ring*, he has to catch the phone or his wife will answer and he can't afford to have that, not now that he is awake and understands who's calling. Three more rings and he's crossed the bedroom and is in the hall; he may even have begun to close the bedroom door. On the fourth he has the door shut because he can't afford to wake his wife and have her ask who's calling. This is not a question he wants to be forced to answer.

This happens too regularly now for him to be able to convince that pretty woman that it's another wrong number.

The phone rings eight times.

On the ninth he picks up. The professor speaks in the cold voice of the naturally superior. 'Who is this?'

Ben always says, 'You know who this is.'

If he does know, the professor won't acknowledge it. He won't speak again. He may not be listening. But he doesn't hang up, either.

'You know who this is,' Ben says again, toying with the idea of giving a different speech this time.

There is no response. It is as if he has said nothing.

Ben will give it time before he speaks because the professor does not hang up. Whatever happens, he never hangs up. 'I know what you did,' Ben says.

There is no sound at the other end, not even the starched and ironed cuff of the listener's pajamas brushing the receiver. If Ben is lucky he may hear the clock strike somewhere far away in the house but tonight he does not. It is well after midnight.

He has no choice but to finish saying what he called to say. 'I know what you did,' he says and then he says what he really called to say. It's all he has to say right now. 'And I know where you are.'

To nothing. It is as if he has said it to nothing.

The silence stretches like an Arctic plain.

In the end it is always Ben who breaks the connection.

But one of these nights, if not tonight then one of these nights, Ben will say what he really called to say, what he's been girding for and preparing for and collecting himself and saving money for and, OK, praying for the strength to do even as he tries to formulate a plan; what he will not say tonight then tomorrow, or the day after tomorrow: *And I'm coming*. Watch out for me.

28

Typical Teddy, just when you need him most he's gone.

Clair is too devastated to reason. It's been a day. Teddy's been dead for a day and she hasn't begun to absorb what's happened.

She is not running away from her thoughts, exactly, but she *is* running. She is running up the stairs in the Humanities tower even though the elevator is in perfect working order, cursing and smacking the rail because she *will not* cry. Instead, Goddammit, she replaces grief with rage. Damn Teddy for being gone like this. It is insupportable.

He is gone as completely as if somebody had contrived to lift him off the face of the earth.

He's . . .

He's already been cremated. When the police finished yesterday, Teddy was picked up by the local funeral home according to a standing order he must have placed and paid for some time when his friends weren't looking. Unless somebody else saw to it on Teddy's behalf when Teddy wasn't looking.

What else did that person order for him?

Never mind that this is exactly what Teddy would have wanted. ('I'm looking at a no frills non-funeral. When you're dead, what do you care what happens to the rest of you?' he said when they used to talk about last things. 'You can cut me up and put me down the Dispos-al. It's only leftovers.' At the time it was a joke. 'Fine,' said Clair, 'and you can put me in the trash masher. Bury me in the back yard, or stick me in the deep freeze until the ground thaws.')

271

The ashes are being shipped to Utah, where his aging parents live a life so alien to his that everything about the Teddy she loves is beyond their comprehension. They won't come to Evard, there will be no bereft, bewildered mom and dad at the graveside, angry because Teddy didn't have to die, and never in their worst dreams do old people with an only son imagine that they will outlive him. Nobody will confront her over Teddy's open grave and blame her.

If Teddy is dead it is Clair's fault for letting her concentration waver.

She should have followed her friend away from that sad funeral, dogged his footsteps, shadowed every move. She should have handcuffed herself to Teddy and hung on, ready to fight to the death for him. She should have been there with him that night, his soul's fierce bodyguard, instead of clinging to her icy roof, preoccupied by her own survival. Failing all that she should have been there when he plunged, standing at the bottom to catch him. Instead she was deep in escape at the Evarton Inn. She overslept and woke up in a tumbled bed, lulling her heart with hotel food while Teddy lay on the ice twenty floors below his office, dying. If she'd only kept track he'd be alive. *If only I could have been in two places.*

Now she is climbing the twenty flights as if she's in training for a major event as yet to be identified.

Nick is still in class. Nell and Davy are in the charge of two cute teenagers who work in the dining room at the Evarton Inn; Wanda doesn't know it, but she's been fired.

It's almost six. In ordinary time she'd be heading home but the repair guys aren't through and even when they've finished the job it won't make any difference.

Clair will never feel at home there.

She ought to be in the office, picking up hard copy to work on; she ought to be back at the house quizzing the repairmen about the heating system; she ought to be chivvying masons, contractors, pressing them to mend the breach in the foundation and install dead bolt locks and window stops, securing the house against intruders.

Instead she is climbing the stairs of the Humanities tower as if exercise will make her strong enough to make it up the last flight to the Hickson Lounge. Fear clogs her throat. It won't come up and it won't go down. It is as thick and pervasive as blood.

Teddy didn't just die, she thinks, too wired to know what comes next. Her imagination stops at the doors to the Hickson Lounge. There is only white sound where Strait's name should be. *Teddy didn't just die.* Never mind that Security and the police call it a suicide. Sad, but no scandal. There are no scandals up here on the hill, she thinks, soured by resentment; enclosed here, we are protected. The college is, after all, a sealed environment.

('Besides, he had a case of You Know. AIDS,' the chief of detectives said to Nick. 'Excuse me, Ma'am.'

She slammed the door so hard the frosted glass rattled. 'You're wrong!'

'Lady, you shouldn't be here.'

Don't you give me that little-woman look. 'He was my best friend. We're family.'

'Well you still shouldn't be here.' Grimly pleased because there are some problems even a college can't keep hidden, the detective chief was interviewing everybody in the adjoining offices. He dropped his voice. 'It's one reason we rushed the cremation. All those blood products. He was sick all right. Count on it.'

Rage gave her voice a ripsaw edge. 'What makes you think so?'

The chief turned to Nick with a blunt, hick look that meant: *control your wife.* He said with careless cruelty, 'Well look at the way he lived. Some of the stuff we found in the guy's apartment. You can imagine.' Then he said to Nick in that offhand, confidential way that made Clair want to murder him, 'Being as he was, you know. Light in his shoes like that. He could have *flown* out that window like a goddam butterfly. Listen. Maybe that's what he thought he was doing.')

She is nearly there, going down the bleak, grimy hall past the yellow plastic tape that seals Teddy's office: POLICE LINE, DO NOT CROSS. In spite of the grim legend spelled out on the tape, the effect is colorful, almost festive. The window inside has been sealed too, although at dawn yesterday police found it standing open, office in perfect order, no signs of an intruder, no indication of a struggle, everything as the occupant left it when he – face it, lady – when he jumped. Clair might almost be OK with Teddy's death, she just might be able to handle it if the investigator hadn't added with that same cruel indifference, 'My condolences to you and to the family. You can decide if you want the parents to know he changed his mind at the last minute. My men found streaks where he'd tried to grab on to the windowsill.'

If Clair ran the stairs to get here it may be because she needs the momentum to make it up the last flight to the penthouse.

She doesn't know whether she hates Will Strait more than she is afraid of him, much less whether she expects to search an empty lounge or find him there and force a confrontation. This stops her at the top. It takes her a long time to collect herself. All she can hear is her own breath hissing. She pushes through the metal door that gives on the penthouse floor.

At the far end of the hall the mahogany doors to the Hickson Lounge stand like paired monoliths. She had forgotten how big they are, how heavy. Richly carved as tables of the law, they stand closed to the outsider, bearing inscrutable messages. What makes her think they won't be locked against her? Oh my God, this is so dumb, coming up here alone and without a plan beyond the blind need to be here. What is she trying to do anyway, go where Teddy went? She can't think; the air is rushing. Uncertainty leaves her brittle as an anatomy teacher's skeleton, badly propped and about to topple. Putting out a hand she steadies herself and, running her fingertips along the moulding, picks her way down the endless hall to the lavishly furnished lounge the outsider Will Strait has claimed and colonized under the rhetoric of Victorian Studies.

As before, light from under the closed doors throws a gold stripe on the hall carpet. As before, the beveled glass diamonds in the doors are covered, so no one can see in. There is no way to stand outside here in the hall and know what has transpired. This time she is going in. To her astonishment, she knocks.

There is no sound inside. Nothing stirs. Nobody answers.

She knocks again.

Nobody comes.

She calls. 'I know you're in there.'

Apparently he is not.

She won't use his name; she shouts. 'You!'

Nobody answers.

This makes her both more afraid to go in and less afraid to go in. What's happened to her that has left her so confused and indecisive? Tough Clair Sailor, who always has a plan. She hangs in air outside the closed lounge for so long that her knees lock and her throat is frozen. Then she tries the door.

It is unlocked.

He has left the place wide open.

No fool, she waits. She has no idea how long she stands there or what she is waiting for. Then the heating system kicks in with a ping that makes her jump and she pushes the door open just wide enough to let herself in and quickly pulls it shut behind her.

This is nothing like Evard.

It is like coming into the palace of a sybaritic prince, lush and secret and suggestive of forbidden rooms hidden beyond the one she enters. She is not quite ready to move forward. Aware of shapes at her back, she whirls. They look so real she almost speaks to the two figures that flank the entrance. A pair of dummies stand guard on either side of the double doors, sweet-faced plaster boys who used to model children's polyester Sunday suits in the front window of the town's defunct drygoods store. The dummy on the left is draped in silks with his head wrapped and studded with a brooch, proud as a little pasha. The one on the right stands with his pink plaster belly naked and his forlorn pink plastic bulge that signifies a lack of private parts exposed and only his head covered, with a pair of Jockey briefs carelessly draped as if the owner had taken them off in a hurry. Around the naked boy dummy's neck is a camcorder. The effect is innocent, obscene.

Clair scratches herself without effect; just underneath the skin, something she can't reach has come to life and begun crawling. The Persian prayer rug in the doorway where she is standing is sticky. Spilled wine, she tells herself. At least she thinks it's spilled wine. On the carpet by the deep sofas, overturned wineglasses lie glued to the nap while abandoned ashtrays tip their contents into the mixture – cigarette butts, roaches, glassine envelopes and Polaroids cut to confetti.

She feels unclean just being here.

The long room is opulent and as densely furnished as a Victorian Turkish corner, rich with brass and strewn with mirrorwork pillows and intricately patterned rugs. Except for the circles of light cast by the brass table lamps with their brass shades, the room is dark. The floor-to-ceiling windows are smothered in fringed velvet draperies that must have come from the Garsons' house; the day has died and the early winter night has marched on the town without reference to anything that goes on in this room. Where the draperies in the Garsons' ballroom are green these are the color of old port. They hang heavily, weighing down the rods. Yellow light strikes a sheen in the nap of geometric carpets from Turkey, Afghanistan, India and, in the midst of these rich, restrained patterns, a bright pink silk floral rug spreads like an obscenity. Golden highlights gleam in rubbed wood table tops and the highly polished surfaces of carved teakwood and rosewood and walnut and mahogany, carefully chosen antique wooden furniture artfully placed among the heavy leather chairs and squashy leather couches, deep enough to drown in. It is like walking into a rich man's library.

Then she kicks over a pile of magazines and a flood of pages filled with body parts cascades across her foot, slithering out like living things exposing themselves in three colors – cocks, vaginas, breasts and balls, closeups of every possible protrusion and orifice in every conceivable conjunction. She marks as well the displays flickering on the computer screens ranked on a long table at the far end of the room and amends her previous thought. It is like walking into the library of a rich pornographer.

God, she thinks. The camcorder. There must be a VCR. What else; her intestines twist, what else? And turns to the details.

She thinks she hears small living things rustling among the slick pages of the discarded magazines, skittering around the Moroccan water pipes and hiding behind erotic miniatures, seething among the illustrations ripped out of volumes sprung from the library's forbidden Zeta Collection, night creatures running just underneath the surface like so many rodents feeding on the remains of whatever prey Will Strait chooses to bring here.

'Oh my God,' she says aloud.

'What did you expect?'

He is here. Clair grunts. Surprise kicks her in the belly.

She springs away, trying to feel her way backward to the door with fingers that have lost all sensation. As she does so, the tall outsider gets to his feet in a rush of shadows at the periphery of the room, so deep in the far corner that she cannot immediately separate his outline from the surrounding darkness. She would turn and run but she can't. She is afraid to turn her back on him.

Squinting, she sorts and identifies the shapes and kinds of darkness in the corner: the shrouded window, the leather chair with its back to the room. Strait has been hidden there, slouched in front of the draped window with nothing to mark his presence but his silent breathing. He has been sitting there in front of the sealed window, looking at nothing. As she watches he emerges from the darkness and stalks toward her, no more than a big, moving shadow in a space that is all shadow. In this unreal circumstance his voice is resonant, compelling, a high priest's voice, challenging her at the gates to a forbidden temple. 'What do you want?'

'Nothing.'

'What did you come for?'

I'm not sure. 'I'm not going to tell you.'

'It's all right,' he says in that low voice, contrived to command, to lull, to seduce into compliance. 'I don't mind your being here. You'll want to see what I've done with the place.'

'Don't come any closer.'

'Oh don't mind me,' Strait says. He is moving with slow grace, quiet, so clever that in this light it's hard to make sure he *is* moving. He keeps his tone calm and even, as if she is a wild animal he can control by talking. 'After all, we're all friends here,' he says easily. 'Especially now. Good friends.' It is an obscenity.

'We were never friends.'

'But it's not too late.'

'Oh yes it is.'

'I hope not. We can still be friends if we try, Clair. You, me, Nick and Mara. You'll see. We'll be good together. Just give it a little time, Clair.'

She pushes against air as if that will stop him. 'Don't!'

'Don't what, Clair?'

Don't use my name. 'You can't keep me here!'

'What makes you think I want to keep you here?'

Clair, dissemble! She can't. 'I know what you did to Teddy.'

He does not address this. He may not even hear. Somehow, without her noticing, Strait has managed to close the distance between them, advancing not like an enemy but like a lover, uncertain of his welcome but certain of his attraction, broadcasting mixed desire and good will like a spray of pheromones. Now he comes into the light and she is struck as she has never been struck before by exactly how handsome Will Strait is. The classic head is a logical refinement of the stolid mother's heavy skull and slabbed flesh but when her grandly constructed son lifts his head the planes are transformed; his face is her face, but with a difference. This flesh of his mother's heavy flesh comes from the same two-room shack in the same mining town but it has been somehow refined and made beautiful. He comes out of Erna's poverty but he moves with the ease of a rich man who has spent his life saying all the right things in all the best schools. It is as if Strait has taken the genetic components handed him and through sheer force of intellect and will turned them into gold, and if he advances on Clair Sailor now it is because he has worked hard for this position and he will do anything to protect it.

Yet the fringed eyes are wide, the expression uncomplicated and so guileless that even she is halted.

This is how he works on people. In a momentary, irrational flash of doubt Clair feels guilty for intruding, for believing in evil. Doubt makes her gasp.

'It's all right.' Strait is smooth, inexorable. 'You're perfectly safe with me.'

'No!' She shrinks; the vibration of his voice sets a nerve in her back to jangling – a little twinge in the soft spot just below the ribs that makes the skin twitch. It is a calculated resonance.

'I just wondered what you came here to do, Clair.'

She is stopped by something bulky. He's backed her into a sofa. 'Nothing.' This is the end, she thinks. He is going to hurt me now.

Strait just says in a kind of sweet regret, 'You're too smart to come up here for no reason. What are you really doing here?'

This surprises her into truth. 'I don't know.'

'Did you come to see me?'

'No!'

'Then what did you expect to do?' He is so close that she can feel his clean breath on her face. If she can't stand fast he will tip her off balance and level her. He moves with the confidence of a long-awaited lover; in another minute he'll be close enough to take her in his arms. 'What did you expect to find?'

Her disgust takes in the room. 'This.'

His arms drop. 'I see.'

'So you might as well let me go.'

'Why, Clair? I'm not keeping you.' Strait sighs as if she has disappointed him in love. 'So you got what you came for. Evidence, if that's it. You have what you want.'

'No.'

'Then what do you want?'

Now, oh God, the rational part of her says, Careful, Clair, do you want to end up like Teddy? And the part that is in control rushes ahead, saying, *I don't care*. 'I want you out of here.'

He only smiles that lover's smile. 'I'm afraid that's out of the question. It's too bad we can't forget it and be friends.'

'You can't pretend this isn't happening.'

'Poor Clair,' he says. He is monstrous in his condescension. 'Oh, poor Clair. You guess this, suspect that, but you don't know. You don't know anything. You don't know anything and here you are, ready to run out and make all kinds of accusations. Well just try it. You go on out there, go crying about something you don't know and can't prove and you'll see what happens. You're crying about nothing to a bunch of people who've already stopped believing you.

'They don't believe anything you say, Clair.'

Intolerable. True.

'It won't matter what you think you know or what you say. You'll find out that all your friends have turned against you. They all think you're crazy, Clair.'

With his curved hand he reaches out and gently brushes her face, pulling his fingers down her clenched jaw as if his touch will relax it.

'Poor Clair.'

And even as she recoils Clair understands how his victims are drawn; repulsed, she says, 'I know what you're doing.' Take *that*, she thinks, panting hard.

Startled, he gives her a hard look. 'Is someone calling you?'

But she is intent on her warning. 'It can't go on.'

'Someone phoning in the night?'

'Phoning? No.'

In one of those lightning changes he shrugs it off. 'Never mind. It's not important. What do you think you know, dear?'

'You know what I know.' She thinks of Gig, who is too far gone to tell anyone what happened to him. She thinks of Brian Dent, who swears he will never tell and she thinks of dead Gerry Brevard who can't tell; she thinks of her student friends who imply but never *say*, exactly; she lies. 'And I know how to prove it.'

Her split second's advantage, whatever it was, has vanished. Strait is all facade again, glossy, impervious. 'And?'

'There's this.' She kicks the pile of magazines.

'Don't count on it.'

'All I have to do is tell someone.'

'Go ahead, try it. Say anything you want. You already know what people think of you,' he says. 'And Nick,' he says. 'They're formulating charges.' He says, 'They know you'll say anything to protect your stupid husband.

279

Nobody believes you, Clair.' In all this he has not broken rhythm; he says so smoothly that it almost goes right by her, 'The only person who believes you is dead.'

'Then I'll bring them up here and show them. All this!'

'Oh, this,' he says indifferently. 'Tomorrow none of this will be here.'

She is shaking. 'This isn't all.' Out of desperation or folly she arrives at the bottom line. 'I know about Gerry Brevard.'

'Funny,' he says, 'that's what your friend Teddy said.'

'Teddy!' So Clair understands what Will Strait is telling her, that he will never tell her outright. More. He's letting her know that he doesn't care whether she knows he killed Teddy because she is nothing to him. Powerless. She simply doesn't figure.

'Say what you want. You know they think you're crazy,' he says, and smiles because he has cut her off from her life as effectively as he has Teddy from his.

These last two days she's tried to replace grief with rage, but until this instant her two driving forces have been at war, tearing her this way, then that. She has tried hard and not quite managed it. Until now. Rage grips her and rage brings her home. She leaps away from him, shouting: 'I don't care what they think. I know!' Clair is standing in the clear, trembling and breathless.

'And I won't stop until everybody knows.'

He does not try to keep her. Instead he spreads his hands as if to show her that nothing is going to happen to her, at least not here in a college building where there has already been one death this week. He is calm, assured. Smiling. He is the insider now. Then Strait says in that even, actor's voice that he uses to threaten as skillfully as he does to charm. 'And what makes you think you can do this before I destroy you?'

She turns in the doorway. 'Nick,' she adds. 'Nick knows.'

His aspect changes. 'Then you don't care what happens to him.' He weights the pause. 'Or those nice children of yours.'

'I'll kill you before I let you . . .'

'Sure,' he says bitterly. 'Sure you will. Pretty you, with your perfect life where nobody ever kills anything. Nice house, two cars, the dog, two cute little kids.' Then his tone changes abruptly; he is meditative, almost mournful, 'Too bad about our children, you know? They're such good friends, I thought our little girls and boys were going to make the difference between us, four nice children playing together side by side, so pretty, of course their parents will be best friends. I thought if they could just play together for long enough, then sooner or later it would bring us together. Me, you. Nick, Mara, all four of us laughing and going places together, so nice. It's just . . . I need what Nick has, all right! *Man's* kind of man, Nick is. You have it all, you two, nice jobs at a perfect college, nice sex in your perfect marriage in the middle of a perfect, perfect life. Nice. So comfortable! So free of secrets and ugly ambiguities.'

He is almost home now. Harsh. Full of hatred. 'So very full of nothing to hide.'

And this is how Will Strait tries to finish her. He makes her wait and then he says, 'Even you would have to admit it's not so perfect any more.'

Her hands fly. 'Shut up.'

But he has stopped hearing her. 'Oh, you'll be fine,' he says. He says, 'You may even walk free.'

Then his voice drops. 'But you'll never be the same.' He says, 'You already know this.'

He is right. It's true. Clair murmurs, 'Oh my God.'

'God!' Will Strait is laughing now, and it is the laughter she will remember long after she's fled him down the hall and hurled herself through the metal door and hurtled down the stairs to the twentieth floor; she'll remember it after she's run the length of the hall past dead Teddy's office sealed with yellow tape and hit the next roll bar and headed down the stairs she climbed such a short time ago; she will remember it tonight and tomorrow and every day of her life – Will Strait's boast, unless it is a curse.

'Oh,' he says, still laughing. 'God. God is only God. You are only you and I am the one with the power to say what is and is not straight. Nothing is straight. Or everything is. You'll never know, any more than I know, but I am the one with the power.

'I can change lives forever.'

And even after she has forgotten everything but the laughter she will remember this: what he says next. It is ugly. Undeniable. True.

'I already have.'

29

Ben

Now that he's here Ben is so intent on what he's doing that he almost bumps into the lady hurtling out of the tall college building. When she dodges him with a wild little cry he thinks: What if she's running from the same thing I'm looking for? Don't get crazy. Spend all your time in your own head and you get paranoid, that's one thing Nigel's taught him. Go brooding over who wrecked the world and pretty soon that person is the only one left in it. The shape of what happened to you fills the horizon, obscuring your vision.

This lady probably had a bad day at the works, bad love affair, bad hair day. Whatever. If he tried to stop her to ask she'd jerk away with that look that Ben is getting used to: What are you, crazy? He doesn't know. Not really. Still, when she hits the top step running, when she slips on that patch of ice that thawed during the day and has just refrozen, it is Ben Messinger who grabs her sleeve and keeps her from falling.

She thanks him nicely even though she looks ready to do murder. Ben really does want to ask her, do you know something I need to know? But she thanks him once more and hurries away, sliding downhill in the darkness.

He can't say why the encounter stalls him.

He is stopped dead outside the Humanities tower.

It may be the overwhelming sense that he doesn't belong here. In another dimension Ben might have come to this nice college town as a freshman, the whole deal, bright pre-law with his Patagonia sweaters. Land's End anorak, with his hair rough and his shoelaces untied, smiling the smile of the entitled. That might be him crunching over the hill at the center of that bunch of jocks with their bare heads and their jackets open, backpacks and hockey skates slung over their shoulders, but that would have been in a life without Venice. Down in the town a church bell has just rung six and here on the hill the college bell ringer is bonking out 'Yellow Submarine', and not too well, on the Evard carillon, slurring chords so light-heartedly that Ben understands that other people don't live the way he does.

Listen, nobody needs to live the way he does.

He sits down on the steps. The day is over. Everything that thawed to mush this morning has refrozen. Where it looked like spring when he set out from Nigel's place, frozen snow slipping off the trees in bright sunlight, it is turning back into winter. It may be winter forever.

Riding over in the delivery truck with Nigel, he had been struck by how beautiful the college town was, how Christmas card pretty, postcard nice, nothing bad could happen in this New England landscape with its granite town hall and its white frame churches, and nothing could go wrong in that little toy college up there on the hilltop. Then he remembered that the mint-perfect professor had hopped over here from Venice and slipped into this ideal setting. They took him in without question, he can do anything he wants here. *After all I am your professor* just walked out of Venice and moved on this place without a thought for Ben Messinger or anything he did to him back there. Nobody even guesses how ugly the man really is, like shit in milk, or a toad in your navel.

Well he is here to show them.

Nigel let him off at the town green. They looked at each other and didn't speak. There was too much to say. If Nigel guessed what drives Ben he had the grace not to judge his new friend and not to comment and not to tell him it was OK for guys to cry if they needed to. In the handful of days Ben worked in the store, Nigel was content to let him rattle on about the weather and the stock, the stock and the weather, returning coin in kind. Nigel didn't even ask why Ben thought he wanted a gun, nor did he wonder why he wanted a gun when he was scared to touch one, much less clean it, until Nigel made sure it would never fire. He just took the clip out of a little .45 and turned it over to Ben with a nod that let him know that this was appropriate. When Ben said he had to go, Nigel contrived an errand in Evarton so he could bring him in the truck. Parked opposite the local diner, he made Ben wait while he brought out his wallet.

Deliberately, Nigel moved bills from pile to pile on the seat, muttering over them until he built a stack he liked the looks of, forcing it on Ben as payment for services rendered. They still hadn't managed to say much. Each reached into his heart and brought out the best words he could find to sum it up.

'Have a good day,' Nigel said.

'Be cool,' Ben said. *Oh thank you.*

Nigel smiled. Ben smiled. They parted company, satisfied.

In the Evarton diner he ordered a steamed cheeseburger, no problem. He even exchanged a few words with the counter man before he moved to a corner table. He waited until a bunch of students came in, kicking ice out of the rubber lugs on their boots and complaining so heedlessly that it made Ben homesick for something he's never had. No. For somebody he can never be. Birds fall on a weak bird and pull it apart but people are dumber; nobody in that diner could see that Ben Messinger is a wrecked person; as far as they knew he was as good as they were. More or less. They just let him slide his chair over to their table and ask questions; he could have been any other student. 'Oh, him,' one said. 'We don't know him, we're pre-meds. But the English majors say he's got this, like, special office. Up at the top of the Humanities tower.'

'Where's that?'

'What are you, from Mars? Tallest building. Top of the hill.'

'Cool.' Like Lazarus at the feast, he was starved for more, could not keep himself from leaning in politely, like, could they please just let him listen? Let him hang in long enough and he might even blend in and turn into just another person. But hey, they knew Ben didn't belong here, won't ever belong, dressed all wrong, goes around with this weird look, like, intent, like a dog listening to one of those whistles that are pitched too high for people, stupid Ben to even imagine he could change this. Those shiny pre-meds in the diner were all, like, do we know you? Still Ben hung in with a desperate grin until they turned on him: what is your *problem*? Nobody said anything, they just sat there not talking, looking at him until he got up and went away.

Now he is here, freezing his butt on the top step in front of the Humanities tower.

In another minute he will go in.

In another minute.

Ben Messinger, who has come back from some kind of gross death of the soul and is still feeling his way here.

Hard to explain, he supposes, why coming to this dinky college in this icebound Monopoly board maple-syrup-and-apple-cider town has left him feeling so forlorn, no. Bereft, when he could never in his life come to Evard because Delia can't afford it. Even if he got some kind of scholarship he wouldn't fit in, not with these cool yuppies' sons from two-profession homes who go around in the family's castoff Volvos and Beemers with their parents' arrogance stamped into their faces. Princeton, he thinks with a sense of loss, and is surprised by the sour taste this leaves. You bastard. Well, here is a little Princeton just my size. And you're here, too.

It gives him a grim pleasure to know the son of a bitch has already tainted the place, spreading himself like ink in water, staining and spoiling.

Two students waddle over the ice like ducks in galoshes, laughing. One gives the other a shove that almost knocks him off the sidewalk. The first shoves back and as they grapple and slip on the glazed surface, Ben's heart breaks a little. His hands twitch; for a minute he imagines he can get up and lope after them, they'll bash him on the shoulder and he can be one of them. No way. They see him and veer off, slip-sliding past the theater and the chapel.

At the far end of the walk light spills out of open doors in a Gothic entry. The last building on Administration Row sits in the snow like a little cathedral but there are so many people going in and out that Ben knows it's not church but the dining hall that draws them, even as he knows there is hot food waiting on steam tables for people who've never had to think about how it got there or who's going to pay for it – so much of life taken as a given when for Ben, who never had much, everything has been taken away.

With a shrug he gets up and pushes inside the Humanities building. The student at the desk gives him a look. It is a mark of progress that Ben is able to say without choking, 'I'm a special student of Professor Strait's?' Stronger for having something no one else knows he has, he touches the gun in his pocket.

'Oh, you want the Hickson Lounge.' The student's eyebrows do a trick that tells Ben what he thinks of Strait's special students.

When he reaches the penthouse he is stopped by a placard taped outside the Hickson Lounge. CLOSED. The place is locked. Inside, someone is moving. He can hear him. He puts his face to the glass diamonds in the doors, trying to see in. They are covered from the inside. He supposes he could take this excuse to go away, but he won't. He isn't leaving. Putting his back to the wall just outside the doors, Ben slides down, folding into a squat that is just uncomfortable enough to keep him alert, no matter how long he has to wait here. He supposes that's Strait inside, moving heavy objects; he hears the sound of furniture sliding across the floor and the decisive *chunk* of books hitting an institutional trash can, but what if it's just the janitor?

It's taking too long. Strait. He's sure of it. So what if it takes all night. He'll wait. What else has he got to do but wait for this encounter?

He has to come out some time.

Ben's legs cramp. Groaning, he changes his position. It's taking too long. It's taking so long that he's scared of forgetting his lines. Whatever thoughts he had when he got out of the elevator, whatever speeches he had come prepared to deliver have fled him. He matches his fingertips, rehearsing.

It's been an hour.

He has to come out some time.

Behind the locked doors the phone rings. Strait's voice – yes, he recognizes Strait's voice, that false cheer he manufactures specially to lull you – Strait's voice goes on for a minute or two. The tone is so false that Ben doesn't bother to put his ear to the door. He already knows Strait won't say anything that figures. He's talking about nothing to somebody who doesn't matter. Finally he hangs up. Then Ben hears drawers slamming and the activity inside accelerates, the professor winding up what he is doing.

He has to come out some time.

Now.

Will Strait, erstwhile director of the nebulous arts program in Venice, so suave, so voracious, spat out and reborn as Professor of English at Evard College, Will Strait comes out of the Hickson Lounge in a rush, intent on what he is doing. He's moving too fast to see that there is a someone waiting out in the hall at the top of a building that is essentially shut down for the night. He walks right past Ben with his plastic garbage bag, which he tips into the incinerator chute at the far end of the hall. The good professor in his blue tweed jacket with the suede elbow patches, finishing up after a long day of teaching looking as fresh as he did when he walked out of the house this morning. Keeps an electric razor in his desk, oh yes he does. But his overloaded garbage bag sticks in the narrow chute. He gives it an extra push in an attempt to get it moving. He pulls the door wide, leans in.

I could grab his heels now, Ben thinks madly. I could tilt him and shove him right down after his garbage.

No he can't. Even if he could the chute is too narrow. Strait has his whole arm inside, fretting and poking until with a sucking sound the bag lets go and plummets to the basement.

When he smooths his hair and turns, Ben is standing directly behind him.

Strait looks right at him. He is without expression.

Face to face with the man like this, confronting the destroyer who's filled his thoughts to the point where he can't function, Ben is beggared. He can't think of anything to say. Not a word. Instead he holds his position: close. He is waiting for Strait to freak at the sight of him. It won't do the job but it will be a beginning.

The professor only tilts his head slightly, squinting as if Ben's standing so close that he can't make out who he's looking at.

Ben waits. He's been waiting for so long for this encounter that his breath backs up. He's overfilled, like a tire. What did he expect? Did he expect him to take one look, curse God and die?

At least he could see him. Say it. *Oh, it's you.*

Instead Strait blinks politely. 'Do I know you?'

'No,' Ben says heavily. All his breath comes out at once. 'You don't know me.'

The professor shrugs. He makes as if to excuse himself. 'If it's about your grade, I never change grades.'

'This isn't about a grade.'

'Then you'll have to excuse me, I was just closing up here.'

'Not yet.'

'Sorry, I was just leaving.'

'No.'

Strait gives him a push. 'I *said*, I'm leaving.'

'I said no.' He pulls out Nigel's gun. 'I don't think that's a good idea.'

Will Strait's eyes flick up and down, sliding back and forth between Ben's face and the little automatic. He runs his tongue around his mouth.

It is a measure of the man's madness that Ben can't know whether he is afraid or titillated. He says in a low voice, 'I think you'd better come inside.'

You bet.

Nice place, Ben thinks, big chairs, lots of light, low moon rising outside the long windows where the winter night looks clean and fathomless. Nice place once, but it is Strait's place now. I wonder if this is where he does it.

'Sit down.'

Probably: the pervasive aura of stale cigarettes and good dope. Ben says, 'I don't think so.'

'Sit down. You're perfectly safe. After all, you're the one with the gun.'

Ben nudges the air with the barrel. 'Aren't you supposed to be afraid?'

'Why should I be afraid? If you'll just sit down, we can talk like gentlemen.'

Because he can't think past this second, he does as the professor says. Strait has made a half-turn. Ben barks, 'Don't move.'

'Don't worry,' his enemy says smoothly. 'Relax. I'm just getting us a drink.'

'I didn't come here for a drink.'

'But you won't mind if I have one.' It is uncanny. Here is the predator of Venice, the polished monster of all his worst memories, moving around the Hickson Lounge as if none of the above had ever happened, as if nothing had happened and Ben's problems are all in his mind, OK? Here they are occupying the same space, here's Ben, holding a gun on Will Strait, and his quarry, if that's what he is, the hated object of his search, is calmly segueing into the cocktail hour as if nothing untoward is going on here. The man could be sitting down with any student at the end of a long day with the contents of the coming night known only to him. The perfect host. God! Strait opens the front of a mahogany cabinet and comes back with a decanter and two glasses. 'Port?'

'No thank you.'

He pours him a glass anyway and thrusts it on him, watching all the time to see whether Ben will have to put down the gun so he can handle the stemmed crystal. When he manages both, Strait fills his own glass and, still standing, studies him. 'Do I know you?'

'No.'

'I keep thinking I know you.' Then the professor says with the practiced ease of a con artist who will use any old line of dialog, no matter how trite, in the interest of expediency, 'I'm terrible about names but I never forget a face.'

'You never knew me,' Ben says.

'You're sure?'

'But I know you.'

'That's what I was afraid of.' Strait sighs. 'Oberlin, was it?'

'No.'

'The French program, at Arles?'

'Venice.'

'Oh,' he says. 'Oh, Venice.' For the first time he looks at Ben as if he really sees him. His voice brightens. 'You've come back!'

'Yes I've come back.'

'And you were . . .'

'Ben Messinger.'

'Ben. Of course. Little Ben, who was so gifted. Now I know why you're here.' Under cover of this flurry of conversation, the professor does the improbable. In spite of Ben's warning glare, in spite of his short, ugly gesture with the gun, Strait sits down right next to Ben on the deep leather sofa without any sense that this might be personal space he is intruding on. He smells of sweat from his efforts, sweat imperfectly masked by the spicy deodorant in a musky combination that makes Ben sick with memory. 'I'm so glad you've come.'

Ben raps his knee with the gun. 'You're what?'

'Don't do that.'

'I said, you're *what*?'

'Glad,' Strait says and for the first time since he's known the man, Ben sees that like all his expressions, this one is put on crooked. 'I'm glad you've come.'

'I wouldn't be.'

'But of course.' It is a strange, sickening fugue that wavers between threat and seduction. Call-me-Will Strait with his breath smelling of port is pouring more port into Ben's unaccountably empty glass, sitting too close for comfort but never overstepping the circle of space Ben has carved out for himself and drawn a ring around, urbane, condescending call-me-Will just going on as if Ben isn't dying in his dirty socks and he, Strait, has nothing to be afraid of, saying in those superior tones he is so good at, 'Of course I'm glad. You're one of the best . . .' He breaks the sentence for too long before he says so significantly that Ben can't miss what he is really saying, ' . . . students I've ever had.'

Ben says, 'That's why I'm here.'

That smile! 'For more.'

This is said with such mad confidence and such contempt that Ben has a hard time holding still so he can do this. He's ready to fly into a million pieces and kill the man with shrapnel; he wants to break the port glass and grind it in his face; he wants to beat Strait to death with the butt of the gun and jump up and down on his shattered skull. When he can speak he says, 'Not really.'

'You want me to hurt you again.'

The words boil out. 'I want you never to hurt anybody again.'

'You know you don't mean that.'

'You don't know what I mean. Yet,' Ben says.

'You were the best, you know. Are the best. So gifted, so much promise. You know I've missed you,' Strait says.

'Don't.'

'We can start over.'

'I could shoot you right now.'

'No you couldn't.' With each affront Strait has slipped closer. Now he is inside the circle Ben drew to protect himself. He'll have the gun in another minute, he'll drop Ben Messinger and put one foot on his chest while he calls the police – unless he really is crazy and thinks he can start Venice all over again.

Abruptly, Ben pokes the gun into his chest. 'Get back.'

'Don't do that,' Strait says. 'Not when we're—'

There is a knock at the door. Somebody – a student? – calls, 'Professor Strait.'

'We're not anything,' Ben says.

'Come back later,' Strait calls to whoever is at the door. He turns back to Ben, all charm. 'Now.'

'No!' Pushing hard, Ben leaps up.

Strait is so baffled that Ben has to wonder whether while they were sitting here something snapped and the man has gone over the top. He says in that hurt, cajoling tone that Ben remembers from Venice, 'But you came all this way.'

Ben's voice is louder than he remembers it, and now that he has it back he says what he's come all this way to say. 'You have two choices,' he says, looking down at the man on the couch who does not look smaller but rather so large and so threatening that Ben has to make his voice bigger, just to get through to him. 'You can quit your job and go. More. Quit teaching forever, or . . .'

Strait is on his feet now.

Ben finishes. 'Or you can watch me turn you in.'

'You're crazy.'

'Yes!'

'You!' Strait begins to laugh. 'Who's going to believe you?'

The student outside knocks louder. 'Professor Strait.'

'They'll believe me.'

'Sure. Sure they will.'

'Professor Strait!'

'I said go away!' Strait turns back to Ben, veering crazily between apprehension and the contempt that runs along underneath everything he does. 'Sure they'll believe you, unstable college dropout like you, mental patient probably, tried suicide, running around with an empty gun.' There's something the matter with his laugh. 'Who's going to believe anything you say?'

'Oh, they'll believe me all right.'

The student calls, 'I'm not going away, Professor Strait.'

'Who's even going to listen?'

What Ben says next has been coming for so long from so deep and at such speed that even he is surprised. He is stunned by fresh knowledge: how strong he is. How far he's come. What exactly is the nature of his power. The guilt of the victim gives way to the force of the avenger. His voice is low, steely. Sure. 'They'll believe when I take off my clothes and show them what you did to me.'

'Then I'll have to kill you,' Strait says.

But by this time Ben is at the door. In another second he has it open. Strait lunges after him, too late. The hall outside the Hickson Lounge is by no means empty. Ben and his pursuer have hurtled into the puzzled student who stands waiting at the door with his mouth fixed in greeting. This arrests Strait with his fist clenched and threats congealing in his throat, as terrible and confused as the Wolfman in the middle of the change – half professor, half destroyer. Both, but which? He can't hurt Ben. Not now. He won't hurt anybody else tonight, at least not here; Ben will see to it. The waiting student yips in alarm because as he runs past, Ben seizes his arm with demon force and hauls him into the stairway, muttering and grappling. He won't let go until they are both safe in the main elevator, plummeting to the lobby. Ben, who has made a mortal enemy, and a nameless student who is nothing in this game.

30

Now when she is at the bottom, shaken by her encounter with Strait and most in need of Nick, he's gone. She can't reach him even by phone. It is both terrible and inevitable. If she had worried about all the right things, maybe none of this would have happened. Teddy would not be dead. She would not be a stateless person, standing in the lobby of the Evarton Inn with no friends left and nobody to turn to, reading the note the desk clerk has just handed her.

Strait's calculated destruction is nearly complete.

Nick won't be back until late. He had to drive Ad Bishop to the Emergency Room. Chest pains, looks bad. He and Carrie Bishop have to wait while the doctors decide whether to admit Ad or release him and send him home. It may take a while. Kids are safe in the dining room. Don't wait up. Right, as if she'll ever sleep again. She needs to disgorge this material and process it – her discovery, the threats; she needs Nick. Now everything has to wait.

She finds Nell and Davy at the corner table, surrounded by the rubble of half-finished hamburgers and fried chicken, French fries and onion rings, with every possibly condiment bottle open on their table, grinning with full mouths as their favorite waitress recites the dessert menu one more time. Strait has destroyed everything but this. It makes her feel rich, this closed corporation she and Nick have created, their own support group, still young enough to love without judging and believe without question – her children. Theirs. Davy and Nell turn with joyful grins. 'Hi, Mom.'

In a time when she has nothing, she still has this. She tries to give them everything she has, holding love in her two hands and offering it to them as best she can: 'Hi guys.'

After dinner Clair pulls her children into the big bed with her for too much TV. Then she marches them through the rituals of bath and tooth brushing and bedtime prayers to prove that home is wherever the family is, but no matter how she strings it out, sooner or later she has to say good night. Then she gets on the phone, calling the night man at the heating company, badgering the contractor at his home number because she already knows what nobody will come right out and tell her, that the Sailors are stuck in this hotel for the weekend and out there somewhere Will Strait is pacing, calculating his next step in what she takes to be a battle for her life.

Alone with her fears, she scrambles like a rat in a squirrel cage, gnawing at the wires with a bleeding mouth. In all the scenarios she runs – tracking down Gig, finding Sally or Brian Dent, forcing someone to bear witness, going back to Pete Arnold, even confronting Mara – she can't come up with a tactic that works. Chill, she tells herself and can't stop replaying Strait's words: *What makes you think you can do this before I destroy you?*

Something, she thinks with her belly convulsing. I can handle it, she tells herself. As soon as I tell Nick.

Then Nick calls from the hospital; the racket suggests he is at a pay phone in the corridor. 'It's heart,' he says. 'Worse than they thought.'

'Nick, I need to—'

'What? I can't hear you.' He is shouting over background noises.

'I can't do this over the phone.'

'Carrie made me promise to stay.'

'I'm afraid to leave the kids.'

He responds to her weighted pause. 'She doesn't have anybody.'

'I know.'

'Are you OK?'

'Oh God, Nick. I . . .' She tells him what she knows he's waiting to hear. 'Sure, I'm OK.'

'Are you sure you're OK?' he asks, willing her to be OK.

She wants to jump out of the phone and tell him, anything to get him here, but clinging to the hotel phone, she is struck by an unexpected stillness. The air has stopped moving. Without seeing, she sees Nick: the eyes, set deep in green bruises; she sees the white ring round the mouth, the sum of his own brush with death and his struggle with Strait compounded by the cost of keeping it together for her. So in the end all she can say is, 'You've got to do what you've got to do.'

'And you'll hang in tomorrow.'

She makes a quick decision. 'For as long as it takes.' If close marriages survive on the legend the partners write, she has to keep it together for him precisely because he is keeping it together for her. 'I love you, Nick.'

'Me too. Look, one good thing has come out of this. Ad and I had a lot of time while we were waiting for them to take him in, and look . . .' Now it is his turn to weight the pause before he goes on in a brighter voice. 'He believes us. Everything.'

'Ad! What can Ad do about it when we can't do anything?'

'We're going to the police. Until then, stay out of his way.'

Clair's waited for hours to talk to him; the residue of the night's encounter lines her throat like scum so that she has to cough before she can say, 'Nick, it may be too late for the—'

'Really,' he says urgently. Nick, who knows none of this. 'Stay out of his way.' The noise rises behind him: mingled voices and footsteps, the sound of heavy equipment moving. 'We're headed for the ICU. I love you but I've got to go.'

She doesn't know what can be done, only that she is going to have to do it herself.

Once the children are safe at school, Clair goes by the house. Displaced, she's like a mother fox trying to hurry its young back into the proper nest, even though it is spoiled for her. There's only one truck parked outside – not a good sign. Nothing has been done to the hole in the foundation. The same vinyl still covers the spot. In the cellar, the stove pipes connecting the boiler to the chimney are down and the motor has been taken off, probably to the shop for repairs. Unless it needs replacing, the plumbers offer, but they don't know. None of the heating people are around. In the far corner, plumbers have been at work in sooty water. Careful as they were when they drained the pipes, they overlooked the separate system under the back porch. One of the radiator pipes has burst. It will be late afternoon before they get the damage repaired and probably Monday before the boiler is back in commission and the Sailors can move back in.

Yes she is disenfranchised. Moved out of her life. She doesn't know what she will have to do to get it back.

Because she needs some outward and physical proof of the existence of Clair, she goes upstairs to pick up a few things.

It is like marching on a conquered city or coming into the galley of the *Marie Celeste*. The house has lost its soul. After only two days even their most precious objects are filmed over like the eyes of a beloved animal dying from neglect. Everything is in place but slightly off kilter, as if misarranged by the hands of a careless invader – magazines left open at the right page but crumpled, toys strewn, clothes still on the floor where she and the people she loves best dropped them at bedtime the other night, everything abandoned as if marauders had swooped down on this civilization without warning and seized them and carried them off so quickly that nobody had time to cry out.

'Oh, Teddy!' she says aloud but *will not cry*.

She digs under the bed and pulls out the suitcases they brought back from Florida, sobbing for breath as she throws in the family's belongings, anguishing over how little she can make fit. It seems important to retrieve everything that matters – clothes to tide them over until Monday, her notebook, novels she won't have time to start, jewelry she doesn't need, a green stone whale Teddy gave them and the little Kandinsky from over the mantelpiece – perhaps imagining that she can arrange their things in the room at the Evarton Inn and turn it into home. She moves through the abandoned rooms collecting blindly, as if she can shore up these possessions against her ruin and somehow ensure the safety of the family, and if someone else is in the house, if somebody has been here before her, going through her things for reasons even that person would not be able to identify, if that person is here in the house at this moment, hiding in the guest closet with his fists clenched and his chest tight, she will be too distressed to know.

And if he begins to stir, to ease the closet door open . . .

She jumps. 'What!'

'Ma'am?' The plumber is in the bedroom. He's come up from the basement to ask whether she wants the new pipes wrapped or whether she wants to take a chance on their freezing again, bad winter, you can't play it too safe. With a sigh for the sooty wet tracks his rubber boots are making on the Chinese rug, Clair closes the suitcases and lets the plumber help her carry them out of the house.

As she goes down the steps, something in the house rushes out like a tremendous sigh.

Once she has everything unpacked and installed in their hotel rooms, a pathetic shrine to lost pasts, she goes to the police.

By the time the chief of detectives is through with his last appointment and ready to talk to her, it is late morning. She won't know that he's already spoken to Ray in campus security, who has her number, sure he does. He's talked to Ray and he's told the desk sergeant, 'Let her wait. She needs time to cool down.' It won't help that he knows her from the suicide – the scene of Teddy's death – nor will it help that he's formed his own opinion of this pushy Sailor woman who claims she has something to report. 'You know those people at the college,' he says right before he goes into the waiting room. 'Neurotic, all of them.'

He greets her with that tired *oh, lady* look that she will learn to hate. Has righteous, convincing, deceitful Will Strait been here before her? She can't know, any more than she can know what lies he would have spread like poison seed.

But she has the detective chief's attention, at least for now.

'You came to report something?'

The hell of it is, she doesn't know how to begin.

He says politely, 'Is it about that suicide?'

'It wasn't a suicide. Teddy didn't . . .' She stops. Yes, Strait has been here before her; she can see it in the detective's eyes, in the impatient set to his mouth. She already knows what he'll say. Case closed. She starts over. 'Sexual harassment. For one.'

He sighs. 'Oh, ma'am. Somebody hitting on you?'

'Hardly,' she says. 'There's something terrible going on.'

'Up there on the hill.'

'At the college. Yes. People in danger.'

'Have you reported this to campus security?'

'Why would I want to report to campus security? There are lives involved. It's . . .' It's murder, I think. No. I know. She groans. She already knows what he will say. Lady, it isn't murder. It's all in your mind.

'Well, ma'am, you know they like to solve their own problems up there on the hill.'

'But this is a police matter.' Strait as much as told her he killed Teddy and it won't make any difference. What can she say to convince him? 'Students are getting hurt.'

299

'Sexual harassment, right?' He almost yawns.

'Worse. I think . . .'

'Sounds like an administrative thing.'

'The college isn't touching it.' It's clear the detective has already discounted her. He's sitting at his desk but the part that pays attention has already put on its hat and gone across the street and is ordering lunch. 'Drugs. Threats. What do I have to do to get the town involved, get killed?'

Weary, polite, he lays it out for her. 'Come in with somebody who has the grounds for a criminal complaint. We can't even go up there and investigate unless somebody files a criminal complaint.'

'Can I get him for assault?'

'Yes, ma'am, if you can prove he assaulted you.'

'Aren't you going to take notes?'

'In time, ma'am. In time. Now. This man. It is a man, right? This man hit you or shot at you?'

'Not exactly,' she says, despairing. 'It was more like a threat.'

'How do I know he threatened you?'

'You have my word.'

'Unless you can prove it, there's not much we can do.'

She snaps, 'How am I supposed to prove something only I know? Look. God! How can I? Please. There are lives at stake.'

Right, lady. She knows that look. 'Ma'am, until somebody walks in here with a bona fide complaint and evidence to back it up we can't even go up there and investigate.' He is on his feet and he stares until she gets to her feet. 'We need names. Dates. Witnesses. Who did what. How, when and where. So unless you've got something more on this, I think we'd better call it a—'

'I'm going,' she says.

As she comes out of the police station, a young man is lingering at the top of the stone steps, apparently trying to make up his mind whether to go inside, and in a flash of wishful thinking she imagines it is one of Strait's victims coming forward. She already knows that like the few hopes she started out with this morning, this is an empty hope.

The stranger sees her and hesitates. Nice face, Clair thinks, sensitive mouth, rough hair, capable hands sticking out of a coat that's too small for him, nice kid, and he is looking at her with such intensity that she thinks, I wish! This is so hard! If only you could speak. This is how bad Clair is today; she's so starved for kind words that she's stalled here on the steps of the police station, unaccountably drawn to this young stranger with the nice face. Careful, don't let him catch you staring.

But he is staring at her.

She inclines her head like a traveler trying to make out a street sign in a foreign language.

He says, 'Do I know you?'

It takes her a minute. 'No.' She sighs, 'I'm sorry, you don't.'

Still they remain fixed, oddly suspended.

'Excuse me.' She makes as if to go on past. His look holds her in place – shimmering, as if he's at the edge of saying something she needs to hear. She asks, 'Is there some way I can help you?'

'I don't know.' He breaks open in a smile. 'The police here. Are they any good?'

'They don't listen.' She makes a face that says it all. 'Why, are you in trouble?'

'Yes. No. Not really,' he says.

'Well, good luck.' With regret, she starts down the steps.

'Whatever,' Ben says, and runs down past her, heading for the town green and the bandstand where, although Clair doesn't know it, he spent most of last night alert and terrified, shivering under a quintuple layer of newspapers and a tarp ripped off from a construction site, listening for Strait. Once in the night he heard footsteps. Him calling. Or thought he did. He has to do something. He has to do it soon.

But the lady says you can forget the police.

So it is Clair who turns Ben away from the police station, for now, at least. What's the point of telling the cops if the cops in this town are just going to blow him off?

He won't come back until much later, after the counter man in the diner tells him a guy is looking for him, big, handsome, cashmere jacket. Asked for him by name. Right, he is in danger.

Fear will drive him back to the police. He will come back to the station at the point in the afternoon when the light changes, sending the day over the hill. Too soon it will be night. He will tell as much of his story as he has to, to get action. No. As much as he can bear to tell.

After the chief of detectives hears Ben out he will ask the hardest question. 'Are you willing to submit to examination to a police surgeon?'

Ben has not done all this and come this far to back out at the last minute.

'If you say so,' he'll say with his jaws tight and his breath shuddering. 'Yes.' And with lives at stake the detective will try to reach the police surgeon and come back from the phone with a piece of paper Ben is to present at the hospital.

'Tomorrow,' the chief will say.

'Too late!' Ben will cry, banging on the desk. Tomorrow is too late. He needs better, and so he will begin the treacherous business of hounding his persecutor, going where he goes whatever way he can – walk up to the college, run to find out where he's gone or where he may be expected later in the day, hitch a ride on a delivery truck if he has to, anything to keep track of Strait while every force within him converges, rushing toward a confrontation.

The chief calls after him, 'Tomorrow first thing.' And if the chief of detectives begins to put the pieces together – complaints from that Sailor woman, now this, from this young stranger – well.

But that is nothing to Clair, not now, not really, as she hurries away from the police station with no plan and none in prospect beyond surviving until she can talk to Nick.

The high school girls who usually wait tables at dinner are there when she goes in for lunch. 'Hey,' she says to her favorite. 'Why aren't you in school?'

'Oh,' the girl says as carelessly as if this is of no more importance to Clair than it is to her, 'didn't you know, the governor died. We got a half day. Aren't you going to order?'

She's already running for her car. Calm, she thinks. I am completely calm. Not really. When she opens the car door she leaps back with a guttural roar of disgust. There is a cellophane-wrapped sheaf of white roses laid on the driver's seat like a coiled snake.

Driving too fast, she parks on the wrong side of the street in front of her house and leaves the motor running. She slips and falls twice going up the walk. No, the plumbers say, the school bus did not drop Nell and Davy at the house. It takes her ten minutes to reach the school, a rambling one-story brick affair on the outskirts of town. There are no children waiting for her at the flagpole and she has to knock several times before she can bring anybody to the door. The principal is surprised. 'Why Mrs Sailor.'

'Where are my children?'

'We tried to reach you but you were out. We couldn't just send them home alone to an empty house so we called your backup number and the parents said they'd be happy to take care of them.'

'My God.'

'Mrs Sailor, don't look so upset! They're perfectly fine. They're with their best friends. Mr Strait picked up all four children and took them to his house.'

'Where are they?'

'Why Clair.' Mara's expression sweetens at the sight of her. 'I'm so glad.'

'Mara, my children.' Clair keeps herself from losing it altogether by holding onto the fact that they're playing upstairs just the way they used to. She calls, 'Davy, Nell!'

'Oh Clair, don't stand out there waiting in the cold. Come in. Come on in.' Strait's wife is pale, tremulous but disproportionately pleased to have Clair here in her orderly front hall again, so pleased that she seems not to catch her urgency. 'Let me give you some coffee. It was terrible about your house, I wish—'

But Clair is murderous. 'I said, *where are they*?'

'Oh, the children.' Mara looks at Clair with those beautiful pale eyes of hers, eyes that are empty of everything, even guile. Without guile she says, 'Sit down. They're coming right back.'

'You mean they aren't here?'

'Not yet. They'll be here in about five minutes,' she says.

Clair can't say anything. She is completely and irremediably stopped. *My God. Oh, my God.*

'Are you all right? It's so nice to *see* you,' Mara says. Mara is packing. Behind her, the living room is in perfect order but at the same time it is in disorder, cartons, tape, bubble wrap, as if certain precious objects are being packed for an unexpected move, and Clair is so fixed on this, so riveted that she hardly hears Mara saying, 'I suppose you wonder what the mess is about. I'm going away for a little while. Another reason I'm so *glad* to see you,' she goes on with that light, unreal sweetness. 'I want us to part friends—'

'Stop it, Mara. Strait. Where has he gone with the kids?'

But elegant Mara is intent on her own trail of wishful thinking and she goes on as if she and Clair are friends all over again. 'When Will told me you wanted us to keep the children for the afternoon I was so glad. I thought we could still be . . .'

Oh my God Clair is angry. No. Terrified. She takes the neck of Mara's sweater in her fist and gives her a little push. 'Did you ever think that Will tells lies?'

Wounded, she sighs. 'I hoped we could begin again. Oh, Clair!'

'What has he done with them?'

'For God's sake, Clair, they're perfectly fine!' All hurt feelings, Mara disentangles Clair's fingers and lowers her hand for her. 'They've gone to the movies with Will.'

'Which theater?'

'They'll be back any minute.'

'I said, *which theater*?'

'They're at the Showcase out on Route 304, the new Disney cartoon, they begged and begged. For God's sake, Clair, the movie's almost over. They should be back here in ten minutes.'

'Are you sure?'

'Look. Here's the paper. Look it up in the time clock. Friday matinee, it started at one. I don't know what . . .' Mara's voice constricts; she's ready to cry. 'Oh look.' There are footsteps on the porch. She brightens. 'For heavens sake will you relax now? Here they are. Chase. Maddy. Come on in. Where's Daddy?'

'He dropped us off.'

'Where are Davy and Nell?'

'Oh my God, where is he taking them?'

But the children are ignoring Clair. 'It isn't fair.'

'What, Chase?' Clair goes on her knees so she can take the boy by the shoulders and look directly into his eyes which are unnervingly like his father's. She looks straight into him and says, 'What isn't fair?'

'He took Nell and Davy sledding.'

Maddy says, 'He took them sledding and he wouldn't take us.'

'Maddy had hysterics.'

'I did not.'

'Maddy begged and begged but Daddy said not this time, this is going to be special.'

'Where did he take them?'

'Up. You know, up on the hill.'

'Which hill?'

Maddy says, 'He told us to tell you, but I forgot.'

'No he didn't,' Chase says.

Now Mara too goes on her knees to question her son; she is just as anxious to know but she is doing a better job of keeping her tone under control. 'Which hill, Chase?'

'The big one.'

'Oh my God, Kingman's Gorge? Frontz Peak?'

'I don't know.'

Mara tries. 'The hill at Uncle Vance and Aunt Gail's house?'

And Davy's best friend Chase Strait, Chase Strait who is only eight years old, speaks to his mother in his father's tones: convincing, smooth, but with a hint of impatience. 'How am I supposed to know? Daddy said it was special. Daddy said if he didn't say I wouldn't know, and you wouldn't get mad at me when I said I couldn't tell you.'

Clair takes too long reaching the base of Frontz Peak. The road is decaying and twice she almost slides into the ditch that runs along the verge before she pulls into the turnaround marked by the Parks Commission sign. The way to the top is closed. It's been closed ever since the old accident and her mouth floods and her loins flood with weakness when she sees that many snows have fallen since it was last used. An hour. It's taken her an hour to reach this point and even in this light she can see that there are no fresh tracks. My God, they must be at Kingman's Gorge, her children being pushed downhill by the man who has threatened to destroy her.

If he's trying to destroy her, it's clear he knows how to start. Her children are at risk and she's already wasted an hour.

The lip of Kingman's Gorge is littered with the frozen-over remains of Ethan Frome Day – red and black banners deep in the ice, and like a surreal memorial to a war fought on a distant planet, an ice-glazed snowman fused by ice to the top of an abandoned keg. There are no cars here. There haven't been any cars. As far as she can tell there are no new footprints, no children and no traces of children, nothing but herself and the cold and the void.

Still she traverses the lip of Kingman's Gorge from the gentle grade near the parking lot to the far end where the cliff drops off into craggy nothing and rises from nothing on the far side. She doesn't think Strait has brought her children here but she can't leave until she's made certain. Sobbing for breath, she reaches the far point. It is from here that she can see across Kingman's Gorge to the hillside where the Garsons' brownstone dominates the hill. The massive, massively ugly house spreads double wings like an ambitious tombstone, marking the death of the mill owner whose struggles created Evarton in the dim nineteenth century and whose ambitions made the tiny college.

Nell. Davy. Over there. He has them.

On the far hill the Garson house is lighted up. Cars are coming and going; delivery trucks stand in the glassy drive and if that is Strait's Lexus in the turnaround, if Strait and her children are laboring up the hill to the stark peak behind the house, she will not be able to see them from here, which means that Clair has to run all the way back to the car, sobbing, slipping this way and that on the ice and falling many times, desperate because she has to go around by the long way to reach the Garsons' house where, it he was telling the truth – if he ever tells the truth – Will Strait has taken her children with she knows not what in mind.

She drives headlong, as if there is no ice. For her there is only this. This is worse than Frontz Peak. It is worse than Kingman's Gorge. Go up the Garsons' hill, climb on past the house, take a pick and haul yourself up the glassy hill to the top and you can dominate this little world. Throw yourself on a sled and start down that hill and nothing can stop you, unless you are as strong and densely muscled as a fit man and as agile as a strong woman and big enough to pull the sled around and roll out before you hit something and shatter into bits. You can hurtle into the house and smash yourself to a bloody spray or you can skirt the house and as surely as a rabbit on a ski jump roar down to the bottom of the hill and hurtle on, suspended in midair for a single soul-shattering instant before you plummet to the rocky bottom of Kingman's Gorge.

When she's taken the car as far as she can she abandons it in the clogged driveway and runs the rest of the way uphill to the Garsons' house. Gail comes to the door. She's dressed for a party. 'Why Clair, how nice! Will said you might come.'

'I'm looking for my children.'

'Oh, don't worry,' Gail says. 'They're adorable.'

'Where are they?'

'They're around here somewhere,' she says. 'I just saw them, cute little things, I just saw them and they're perfectly fine. Now for grief's sake come on in,' she says in that oblivious hostess tone that will not be stopped and can't be interrupted. 'You're just in time for the party. We know how you and Nick feel about Will, so we weren't sure whether to invite you, but we're really glad you came.'

'You don't hear me. Gail. I'm here for my children.'

'And we hope Nick is coming too.'

'Gail, where are my children?'

'Don't worry, Will has them. They're perfectly safe.'

'Where?'

'Outside,' she says absently. 'I think he took them outside. Don't worry, they'll be back any minute,' chic Gail Garson says in her gracious hostess tones, perpetually out of it, so anxious to please. Behind her in the marble atrium there is a bar set up and people are stalking each other in stiff little groups, trying to disassemble and reassemble in some formation that looks more like it's having fun; Clair is in pain now, aching like a dying runner, but the good old cocktail party murmur runs along just the same. Gail says as if nothing is wrong here, 'Meanwhile come in and have a drink. We're expecting Mara, and a lot of your friends are already here.'

'Where did he take them?'

'I know they're dying to see you.'

'What's he going to do to them?'

'Take them sledding, I think. Clair, what's the matter? What's the matter with you?'

'Where?' She's about to grab Gail and shake her when she sees a pale face hanging in the air at her back. Familiar? Who? It is a young guy lugging a case of wine, must have come in on one of the delivery trucks, drifting close as if he's trying to overhear – not one of Gail's usual helpers, and the look he gives her is not usual; the young man is intent, watching Clair with an urgency that makes her clutch her throat as if starved for breath.

Then he disappears. Just sets down the carton and hurries away. Gail has just said, 'I don't know. I think he was taking them sledding behind the house.'

Clair says, 'Wait!' I ought to . . . But he's gone. I need to . . . The kids! No time, my God, I'm out of time.

It is a hard climb to the top of the hill and Clair is so intent on what she is doing that she won't hear the kitchen door open in the back of the house. Ben Messinger crashes out running but slows down as soon as he spots her. He's scared for this lady but he has to follow deliberately, not let her see until he knows what they are heading into and what he's expected to do: Ben, who climbs with an increasing sense of mission. He has no idea what that mission is; he may not know until they arrive at the moment. He doesn't even know what the moment is.

Still he can by God keep track of her and by God he's going to help this time, Ben Messinger, who fell into terrible danger because he was too young and ignorant to help himself. Therefore he moves slowly, letting the running woman outstrip him by several yards so that somebody standing on the summit might see Clair lurching upward next to the glassy tracks the Garsons' bobsleds have made, but that person might not see that Clair is being shadowed by a second party who is going to change the equation here.

Strait is indeed standing at the top of the hill. There is something dark at his feet: a sled. He could be an ice sculpture of a Greek athlete poised on the little pedestal the peak makes, but he is an athlete who has taken prisoners. He has Davy and Nell, clamped tightly to his sides. Wriggling, Davy sees her. 'Mom!'

So much for sneaking up. It's clear that what started as fun has stopped being fun for them. Nelly is weeping. Both children are struggling against him, crying, 'Mom!'

'Why Mrs Sailor.' So smooth! They could be at a faculty tea.

'You,' she says to Strait and can not find the word for him. There are too many. None. She shouts, 'Let them go.'

'Is it all right if I call you Clair?'

'I said, let them go.'

Strait says with a dazzling smile, 'I'm so glad you've come.'

'I have a gun.'

'No you don't,' he says. 'People like you don't have guns and if you do, they're never loaded.'

'What do you want?' she cries.

'If they're loaded, they can't use them.' He shrugs. 'Kids.'

'What do you want from me?'

'Good answer.'

'It isn't an answer.'

'It's an A-student question,' he says. 'I was counting on it. You little people. I can always count on you.' He gives the children a squeeze; they growl in pain. 'I so hoped we could be friends and now . . . Now we're going to be friends. I don't want your children,' he says, pushing Davy down on the sled. He holds him in place with his foot, moving the sled forward and backward with his toe. 'I only did this to get you here.'

'This was to get – me?' Forward and backward. He could let the sled go at any time.

'It's the only way I could make sure you would come.' He sees Clair bunching her shoulders – what does she think she's going to do? Does she imagine she can rush him? 'Don't come any closer or I'll kick this child downhill so fast he won't stop until he reaches the next planet.'

Her teeth have locked in terror; she hisses, 'What are you going to do?'

'Why,' he says, 'what do you think we're going to do?' His voice spreads, seeping into her pores like sludge. 'We're going down that hill. One way or another,' he says. When he goes on it is in that same voice, reasonable and mad. 'Come up here where I can take your hand.'

'No.'

'Come up here with me and I'll let go of your children.'

'Let Davy go.'

He releases Nelly instead. She comes running down to Clair who puts the child behind her. 'Davy. Please. Please let him go.'

'Not until you come up here with me. Leave the little girl.'

Trembling, Clair sits her down on the ice. 'Mommy, don't!'

'Stay here.'

'That's it. Now, slowly. Don't think you can fight me, because you can't. Don't think you can outsmart me because nobody does. That's better. Now.' Like Michelangelo's God reaching for Adam, he takes her hand and when he has it, yanks her to him so quickly that he jerks her off her feet.

'Don't!'

'Shh. We have to talk.' He maneuvers until he has his arm round her throat, clamping her tight to his chest. Then he gives Davy's sled a little push designed to send him skimming out of reach but as Clair shrieks her son throws himself off the sled, sliding with one hand knotted round the front runner until, gasping, he skews it and veers into the snow a few feet away.

Strait holds her still and does not speak.

She does not speak.

Where shadows are creeping up from the bottom of the hill, the late winter sky is filled with light. It is as if they are at the top of a roller coaster, poised with all of frozen nature halted, a panoramic background for this tableau, everything suspended in the moment before the plunge.

Then she looks at the ground Strait has chosen and goes cold. It is level for a few feet behind him. Then it just drops off.

What looked like the top of a steep hill is rather a promontory; she sees that the hill is a shell, with the earth behind it sheared off by a glacier some millennia ago. She and Strait are locked together at the top of a cliff so extreme that she can only guess at the shape of what lies at the bottom, although she knows its name.

Its name is death.

She and Strait stand like lovers, locked in a last embrace.

I hate what you have made of me.

'I can kill you right now if I want to,' he says.

This is how far she has come. 'Go ahead.'

'I may want to,' he says. Then he says coolly, 'But that's not what I need right now.'

'What do you want?'

'I told you.' Strait's voice is dry as old firewood, evenly inflected, mad. 'This isn't a matter of what I want. What I want doesn't matter. It never did. I learned to hide what I want because I want what Mother wants, you understand?

'And you have met Mother, so you know.

'But there have been mistakes. There have been too many mistakes and when I look back at what went wrong all I can see is you, Mrs Sailor. You and your perfect husband perfect Nick, standing in my way. So I don't want you but I need you,' he says.

'I don't understand.'

'I need your cooperation. Nick's. I need you both, but, as I have you here . . .' He tightens his forearm on her throat, making her aware of his power, 'you'll have to do. I need you to come down the hill with me and walk into the Garsons' beautiful party with me and I need you to have a goddamn good time. I need you to show everybody that there's nothing wrong between us, we are even friends.'

This, then, is the full measure of his madness. She takes it and despairs. Anything can happen here.

Yet he says in that same even, civilized tone, 'Don't ask me what I'll do if you refuse. You already know what I'll do.'

If Clair is aware of someone approaching – Ben Messinger on light feet

310

– Strait is too fixed on his plan to note the change. She temporizes. 'What makes me think you won't kill me anyway?'

'Kill you? Why should I want to kill you now, when we're all friends? It's time to celebrate.'

'Celebrate?' She is watching Ben. A shadow. There. Not there.

'The party.' He tightens his forearm; she can't breathe. 'All that down there. Vance is holding George Atkinson's telegram direct from Washington. He's going to read it to the group when you and I go back down and get our drinks so you can be the first to make a toast. So I've done it, it's official. Perfect Nick wasn't good enough for the perfect job. I'm the new college president, not you. You, with your . . .' It is an obscenity. 'Perfect life.'

She is strangling; no sound comes. No matter. She doesn't need to tell him he is mad. There is an ugly silence in which she hears nothing but her own struggle for breath.

'Well everybody can see who's perfect now.' When Strait goes on it is in a strange new voice, as light as a boy's. 'Perfect, Mother.'

As uncertain. 'Is this enough? I am a married man now, I have two big children. Look, I even had a boy! I gave you a boy to shape, Mother, and now I give you the rest, so we can quit and call it even, yes? All those years in that tomb of a mine, eating the mountain, and all for me, all that work and nothing to show for it. Well, now you have me. A college president. How much more do you want? What else do I have to be to pay you back? Look, Mother, president; president for good and all, aren't you excited? Aren't you even pleased?'

If he sees Davy approaching on his belly, aiming the sled at his ankles, he takes no notice. 'There!' Davy gives it a shove.

Oh my God, Clair thinks, teetering.

But Strait dodges as neatly as a matador doing a Veronica, holding Clair so close to the edge that everything stops. The sled whips past and goes clattering in its long progress over the cliff and down the sheer wall of frozen rocks. Somebody screams.

Strait jerks her back, saying in a child's reedy voice, 'Did I do something wrong? Shit no, Mother. I did everything right! Everything you wanted, right? I've got it all, perfect family, perfect life and now I don't have to do it any more.' He yanks Clair off her feet. Will Strait is far beyond his original scheme, beyond whatever damage he hoped to do to Clair; he's beyond reason now, beyond everything. She can feel his wet breath in her hair.

'I don't care what happens any more. It won't matter what I do or who I do it with, it won't matter what happens to me now.'

This is true. There's something going on at the bottom of the hill. Like villagers with torches streaming out of the castle in pursuit of the monster, people with flashlights are surging into the snow, raising their voices like barking dogs.

She won't know what Ben Messinger shouted as he rushed through the Garsons' kitchen or whether or not he showed himself; she won't know whether it was someone there or if it was Mara who called the police or whether they came on the detective's orders, but she sees all the doors to the great house lie open and she sees a convoy of lights fanning out from the doors, forming and re-forming as people make their way upward, advancing on the hill; she becomes aware of distant sirens hooting, voices rising above the noise. She sees blue and red lights playing on the frozen snow – police cars turning off the main road onto the serpentine drive up to the big house. Nearby Nelly is crying miserably and Davy, where is Davy?

Strait's mouth is close to her ear. 'Do you hear me?'

She is in crisis; Strait has not given her enough breath to answer; in fact he seems to have forgotten her, clamping her neck in his locked arm and rising to a point somewhere beyond his full height, standing so tall that he leaves her gasping with her feet kicking helplessly several inches above the ground.

'Yes she hears you,' Ben Messinger says.

Strait whirls, astounded. 'You!'

'And I hear you too.'

'I thought I got rid of you!'

'You can never get rid of me. I know what you did,' Ben says. He is harsh, firm. 'And now they know too.'

Strait puts Clair down but does not let her go.

Dizzy, she staggers as the air rushes back into her chest. The first people from the party are approaching. Someone – Mara, she thinks – cries, 'Will!' Is that Sally LeFleur? Another voice cuts through all the others, oh my God it sounds like Nick – her Nick struggling up the hill shouting, 'Clair!'

Down by the big house a man's voice is magnified, amplified. It splits the air. Everything splinters. It's like driving a wedge into a piece of ice. 'Will Strait. Police!'

Now Strait sees what he has been too obsessed to see. He hears. 'Police?'

312

'I told you,' Ben says. His voice is hard and strong. 'I told you I'd show them what you did to me. And I did.'

'Police, Strait. Come down with your hands up.'

'Proof.' Blood rushes behind Clair's eyes and warms her loins. Everything rushes out of her. 'Proof.'

While the desperate Will Strait looks over their heads as if he really is king of the world, surveying the situation with the eyes of an expert surgeon performing triage, for it is he who brought them here and he who will determine who will live and who will die. Below them on the hill the climbers are converging. It is as if everything in Strait's life has for the first time been brought together here – elements of love, hate, clandestine violence and deceit. Witnesses and survivors, the wronged and those he hasn't had a chance to wrong. He draws himself up to confront a new audience and almost without thinking he lets Clair go.

Clair is free but so close to Strait that for a ruinous second she thinks of pushing him off the cliff. *I hate what you've made of me.* Poisoned by rage, smirched and changed forever, sick with grief for the life she has lost, she shakes her head and backs away to join Ben Messinger, who has collected Davy and Nell.

The young man stands with his head up, confronting Strait with a grace and assurance that are new to him. 'I showed them what you did to me, you understand?' So it will be Ben who finishes him. 'So they know.' He is savage, joyful. 'Everybody knows.'

First nothing happens.

Then . . .

Then everything does.

Something leaves Strait. Clair can see it. It is dark, palpable; it is like watching demons desert a corpse. When it is gone, the man is emptied out. With the hounds of hell climbing the hill to take possession, Will Strait stands before her looking open, untroubled. He is regarding them with the clear eyes of a child. He stands with empty hands hanging loosely at his sides, strangely relaxed.

'I see,' he says. 'I see.'

He sounds relieved.

Then Strait raises his voice like a star at an awards ceremony, speaking to Clair, to Ben, to the seen and the unseen, spectators and victims, those he has wronged and those he will never have a chance to wrong and those he has deceived and could go on deceiving if he wanted to because he is what he has always been, handsome, convincing, smooth and sure. 'Thank you,' he says. 'Thank you all. I want to thank you all for coming here.'

And then with a smile of astonishing sweetness, as if all things have been reconciled by this convergence at the crest, he steps off the cliff as happily as a dancer at a summer party stepping off the diving board.

Like so much about Strait, the worst remains hidden. They will not know for weeks that the body will never be found.

The Sailors will wait at the Garsons' house until the police have taken statements. Clair will look for Ben and discover he is gone. When everything is done the faculty and townspeople, guests and the help alike turn their backs on the Garsons' beautiful surroundings and their well-stocked bars and their filled chafing dishes and silver trays of hot *hors d'oeuvres* and begin straggling back to their cars. The Sailors make a solid phalanx, hanging together as if they will never let anybody tear them apart.

As they leave people make a point of patting Nick on the shoulder, murmuring, making awkward gestures, clumsy speeches, anything to tell him this, that is not true and will never be true, that they can resume as if nothing had ever fallen between them, they can be friends as if none of the above had ever taken place.

Jane Stevenson runs to catch up. 'Oh, Clair!' When Clair sees her and then whips her head round and walks on, Jane runs to stand in front of her, saying in that sweet, full voice of hers, 'Oh, Clair, we have to . . .' Jane lets it hang for long enough for them both to sum up everything that has been lost between them, and then she tries to give it all back to Clair saying, 'We have to talk.'

'No,' Clair says because this part of her life has ended. 'I don't think so Jane.'